I0714852

RETRIBUTION GAMES

COLLECTION 2

ELLA MILES

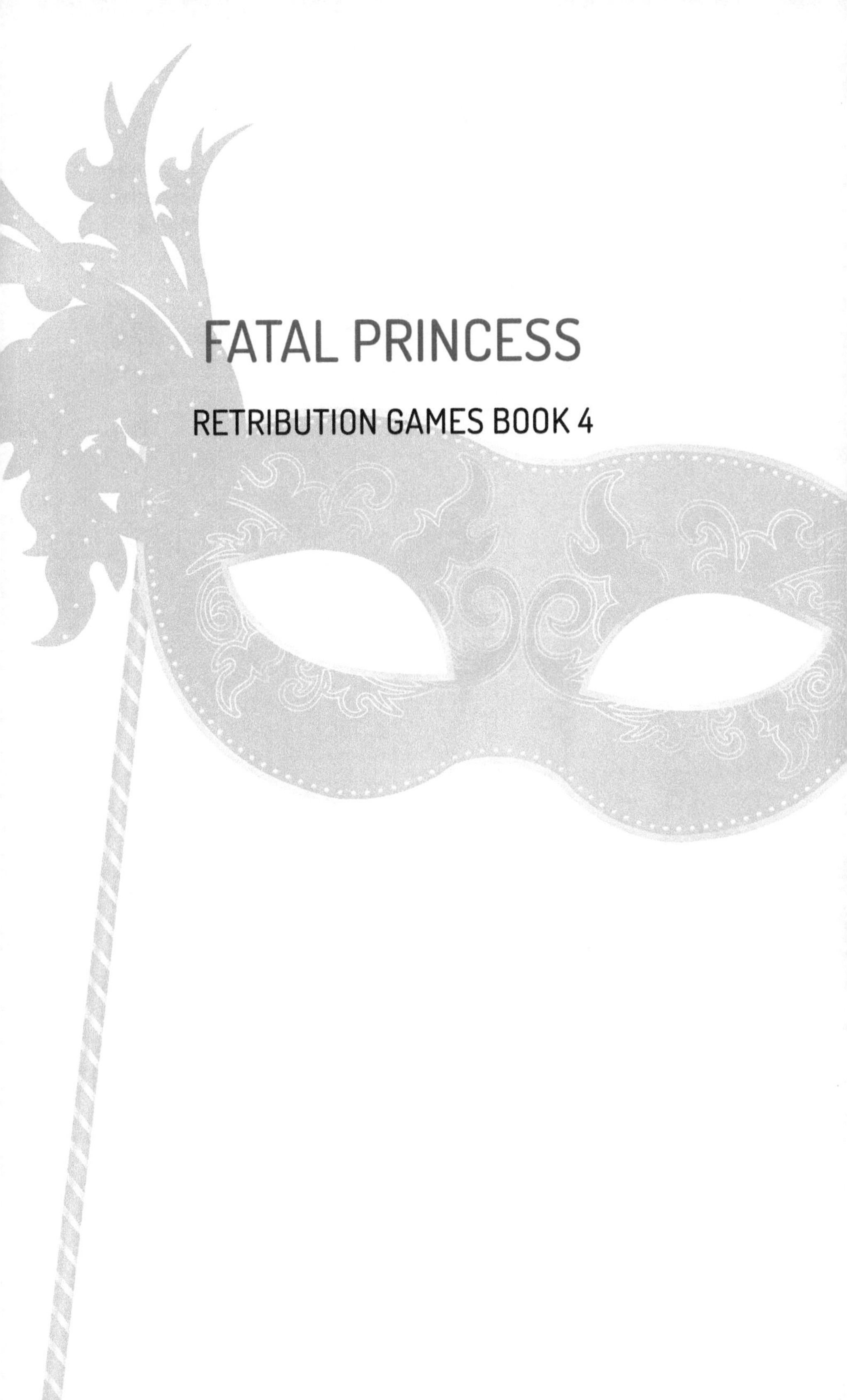

FATAL PRINCESS

RETRIBUTION GAMES BOOK 4

1

RI

ODETTE'S ALIVE.

I barely remember or understand what part I played in it all, even after Odette told me the truth.

I didn't kill Odette despite what everyone in this room thought. I didn't harm her. I helped her, although Beckett might see that as just as much of a betrayal.

It's not a betrayal I deserve to die for, and yet he was going to kill me for killing his wife. He didn't give me a chance to explain myself. He didn't even try to figure out why I would have done such a thing.

Nothing.

He just dragged me here in front of everyone and was about to shoot me dead tied to a pole, even after I saved his life.

It didn't matter.

It didn't matter that I loved him or that I thought he loved me.

None of it mattered—for Beckett, it was always *her*. He loved her more than anything, even when he found out she was lying to him. I wasn't allowed such luxuries.

Because of *her*.

Odette is currently gripping his hand like she never left. Like she's loved him the entire time she's been lying to him.

Beckett doesn't bat her hand away. He holds hers right back. He still loves her. He'd die for her.

She just left him.

She's not worthy of his love, but I'm not going to be the one to explain that to him. If he's too big of an idiot to see how she's playing him, then that's on him. They deserve each other.

The only problem is my heart—my stupid fucking heart. It fell in love with a man who loved another woman. A man who would never love me no matter what. A man who used me to find her. A man who would have killed me to get what he wanted.

I stare at their joined hands—thump, thump, thump—and my heart still beats for him. Still yearns for him. Still has a sliver of hope that I'm missing something. He couldn't have possibly planned on killing me, right?

My brain reminds me—I'm still tied to this pole, and she has him.

I don't know what happens next. One minute I'm tied to the post, stupidly yearning for a man I can never have—the wrong man —and the next, chaos erupts all around us.

I can't understand what the crowd is shouting or why they're all rushing the stage.

I don't look at Beckett. I can't look at him, but I do look at the rest of the guys. Hayes, Lennox, and Gage all have their weapons drawn. Caius's jaw is on the floor as he stares at his sister—alive.

A bullet flies past my cheek.

Fuck.

I have no time to sit here and wallow in self-pity. I have to get free of these chains, or I'm going to end up dead.

I tug on the metal clasps, but they're solid. I'm not strong enough to break them.

I push my hands up the pole until I can reach my head. Digging around in my nest of hair, I desperately search for a bobby pin—the most useful of hair accessories. I almost always have a pin stuck in my hair for these very situations. Luckily, I find one quickly.

I push the bobby pin into the lock, twisting it around until I feel the chains drop away. I'm free, although I don't have much chance of getting out of here alive.

I don't have any weapons. Even though Odette is alive, I don't trust that no one here still wants to kill me. With the fighting all around me, a rift in the organization has clearly exploded with lots of battling opinions and goals.

My only hope is to slip out of here undetected.

I'm about to jump off the stage when I hear Gage say, "This way, Princess."

Is he talking to me?

I flip my head over my shoulder as I crouch on the edge of the stage, about to run in the opposite direction. I don't trust Gage. I don't trust any of them. They brought me here. They tied me to the pole. They were going to watch while Beckett killed me.

Gage frowns when he sees my expression. Hayes looks heartbroken. Even Lennox looks disgusted with himself as he watches me.

"I don't trust you—any of you!" I scream at them.

Gage tosses me a gun, and I catch it in midair. I cock my head and stare at him.

He doesn't say anything. He doesn't beg me to trust him. He offers me a choice completely my own—jump off the stage and fight my own way out or take the help he and the others are offering.

Another bullet flies by. I don't have time to think through my decision, so I go with my gut and follow Gage.

Gage holds out his hand to help me off the stage, but I don't take it. I jump down behind him, landing hard on my feet.

Hayes and Lennox follow after, each with their gun out and flanking me like they will shoot anyone who comes close to us.

I'm not sure I believe them. This is their family, after all. Most of the people here belong to the Retribution Kings. The guys grew up with these people, vowed to protect them. They wouldn't shoot their family to protect me.

Gage pushes through the crowd, and I follow tightly after, hoping no one will notice us making our escape. I'm also praying I wasn't a fool, and Gage isn't just leading me somewhere for Beckett to finish me off after the fighting is over.

A man's eyes widen instantly as we pass.

He notices me.

I hold my breath. I don't have a great angle to shoot him, but I lift my gun anyway, hoping to kill him before he shoots me.

A shot from behind me beats us both, and I watch the man fall to the ground. I turn my head in time to see Lennox lowering his gun. Lennox shot him—a Retribution King—to save me.

I gape at Lennox, stumbling to a stop.

"Keep moving, Princess," Lennox says with a smirk. His eyes twinkle with amusement, enjoying proving me wrong.

"This doesn't mean I trust you—any of you," I say.

"We know, but that's just because we kept you in the dark of our real plan," Hayes says.

Real plan?

I glare as I search Hayes's eyes for an answer. "What do you mean?"

"Enough," Gage says sternly. "We have to keep moving. We aren't safe yet."

He's right.

There will be a time for questions later.

Now we have to get somewhere safe.

Our pulses race as we move through the crowd as quietly and discreetly as possible. Thankfully, there is enough fighting and gunfire that no one else seems to notice us as we weave through the mass of people.

Hayes suddenly hisses from behind us.

I stop, turning toward him to find a red gash appear on his cheek.

"Keep moving! Don't stop," Hayes says.

We move faster, trying to avoid any more stray bullets as we run through the auditorium.

"This way!" Gage shouts back at us.

He ducks into a corridor, and we all follow. The sound of gunfire immediately softens as we enter a tunnel.

There's a door at the end of the tunnel that leads outside, but Gage doesn't lead us that way. Instead, he runs his hand along the wall as we walk. He stops suddenly, popping a door in the wall open.

"Where does that lead?" I ask, stopping suddenly.

"To your safety," Gage answers vaguely.

I frown at him as I stare down the dark tunnel. *Do I go down this hidden tunnel or out the main exit?*

I hear the crowd getting louder, and I know they are headed this way. I need to decide.

I take a step toward the tunnel, but none of the guys move to follow. "Are you guys not coming with me?"

Gage shakes his head. "You'll pop out in an abandoned house. There's a car there that can take you anywhere you want, but we have to stay here. We can't be seen with you." He rubs the back of his head. "Not right now, at least."

I nod slowly, understanding.

"Thank you for getting me this far."

"It was the least we could do," Lennox says.

I look to Hayes, his cheek now covered in blood. "Get that looked at."

He smiles brightly. "Of course, Princess. Now get the hell out of here. We'll see you soon enough."

I smile back and am about to step into the tunnel when a voice rings down the hallway.

"Fighter, wait!"

Beckett is running down the corridor toward us. I don't see Odette, but I assume she's right behind him. His eyes are big with concern, and he's clearly out of breath. There's blood on his shirt, but I don't care.

At least, that's what I tell myself—I. Don't. Care. About. Beckett.

He keeps running down the corridor. "Wait!"

My heart skips a beat.

I want to wait.

I want to hear him out.

I want to know what the hell happened back there.

I want to give him the benefit of the doubt.

But I can't.

I just can't.

I can't go there with him again.

He fucked up.

I'm done.

I'm in this for myself from now on.

I look to Gage, trying to figure out if he's going to let me pass when his boss is running toward us, yelling for me to wait.

He gives the slightest of nods, and I know he won't let Beckett come after me. I don't know why, though. I don't understand any of their loyalties, not anymore, but I don't hesitate.

I run through the secret door and into the hidden tunnel. I hear the door snap behind me as I run, descending into darkness.

With each step, I wait to hear sounds of the door opening, of footsteps following, of Beckett catching up to me.

The sounds never come.

I'm free, at least for the moment. I should take the opportunity to run, to escape this world and completely disappear. But I don't want to spend my life running.

I'll stay and fight. But for now, I need one night away from all of this, and I know exactly where I'm going.

I TREK through the tunnel for close to an hour before finally reaching the end, where a ladder leads upward. The tunnel has been completely empty except for me, so I've had plenty of time with my thoughts—not necessarily a good thing.

I've alternated between going back to find out what Beckett was going to say and going back to kill him.

Somehow, I manage to do neither of those things and keep walking. I climb up the ladder and press against the door above me. Carefully, I raise the wooden board and push the end of my gun out before popping my head out.

I scan the small bedroom surrounding me. I've come up just beside a bed, so I can't see much. Slowly and silently, I hoist myself up and look around the edge of the bed. The room's empty.

I stand and move to the door of the bedroom. I press my ear against it and listen once again.

Nothing.

I need to keep moving. I can't stay in this house. *Who knows how many of the Retribution Kings know about this escape hatch and will come looking for me here?*

I move silently through the house, finding a set of keys hanging by the back door. I grab the keys and head into the garage, where I find an old car.

It will do.

I climb in and start driving, knowing exactly where I'm going. I'm not going to run, not really, but I need a break. I need one night to relax. Tomorrow, I go to war again.

I drive quickly, assuming the car is traceable, but it doesn't matter. Soon everyone will know where I've gone. It will just be a matter of which of my enemies decides to come for me first.

When I arrive at my apartment, I'm exhausted. So much has happened since I was last here, but all I want is to see Lucy. I need to see my friend, the one little part of my life that's normal. I need to warn her to get away. She's not safe being my friend, not anymore.

I knock on the door, so I don't scare Lucy by barging in. It takes her a minute to come to the door, but as soon as she sees that it's me, I'm tackled inside the room by both her and Loki.

I laugh, knowing I made the right decision to come here. I'm sure Vincent, the Retribution Kings, and every other gang is monitoring my apartment, but I don't care.

"What are you doing here? And you look—"

"Like a mess?"

She nods.

I sigh. "It's a long story, but I thought I'd spend as much time as I have with you." I don't mention her leaving, not yet. Vincent has used her to control me my entire life. Every man in the competition could use her to control me.

I need her somewhere safe or at least safer. She'll resist. She always does. But I'm hoping this time she might listen to me.

"Go shower, get cleaned up. I'll get the ice cream ready, and then you can tell me all about it."

I nod without smiling. "Don't answer the door if anyone comes. Just come get me."

"I won't answer the door," she says slowly, realizing I'm not out of danger.

When I'm satisfied she won't open the door, and no one is coming in the next five minutes, I head to my bathroom to shower.

I take far too short of a shower, but I don't want to leave Lucy alone and unprotected. And I want to maximize what little time I have left with her.

I throw on some comfy sweats and an oversized T-shirt before throwing my hair up in a messy bun. Then I head back to the living room, where I find Loki snuggled up next to Lucy on the couch. She holds up a pint of chocolate chip cookie dough ice cream to me.

I take the pint and spoon from her with a smile.

She takes a bite of her own Cherry Garcia ice cream. "So, want to tell me what happened?"

I shake my head. "The usual crap. But it's different this time, Luce. I think you should consider leaving. Go to Australia, or Switzerland, or Thailand, anywhere you want. Just somewhere far away where it will be harder to get you."

Lucy frowns. "I'm not going anywhere, and neither are you."

"Why not?"

She moves the ice cream around in her pint but doesn't answer right away. "Because I'm not in danger."

"You are."

"I'm not. Trust me, Vincent won't let anything happen to me."

I frown. "He's threatened you my entire life."

She shakes her head. "There is so much you don't know, Ri. So much."

"What are you talking about? What aren't you telling me?"

She bites her lip and tucks her long blonde hair behind her ear as she considers her next words. "I'm sorry, but I can't tell you—my safety depends on it. But I'm not in danger. And you can't run. You have to stay. You have to find the best guy to marry."

"I'm not going to marry any of them. They all suck."

Lucy's quiet, too quiet.

"Luce, talk to me. You're scaring me."

She shakes her head and shoves more ice cream into her mouth, staring blankly at the wall across from us.

I set my own ice cream container down on the end table, and then I grab her shoulders, forcing her to look at me. "What do you know?"

She swallows hard, and her bottom lip trembles. I tuck her hair behind her ear, trying to comfort her.

"Who threatened you?"

"No one. I'm fine. Just listen to me—stay in the game, marry the best man, and after it's all over, you can find a way to get out."

My eyes cut back and forth over hers as I read between the lines of her words, searching for what she's not telling me. The only way Lucy stays alive is if I finish the game. If I don't, Vincent will kill her.

I pull her into a hug.

"I will. I'm not running."

Lucy hugs me tighter. "I'm not running either."

"Fine. Let's eat our ice cream and watch an action movie to take our minds off things."

Lucy scrunches her face in disgust.

I laugh, falling back onto the couch. "Horror movie?"

"No way."

I frown. "Comedy?"

"Romantic comedy."

I sigh. The last thing I want is any movie that reminds me of Beckett or love, but I settle into the couch as Lucy picks out a sappy movie.

I eat my ice cream slowly, savoring every bite and barely paying attention to the movie on the screen. Being back in this apartment reminds me of other things, of the last time I was here with Beckett, of fucking him for the first time.

I don't regret it, I realize. I don't regret any of it—any of the kisses, the touches, the fucking, none of it.

I should regret it—my heart now feels like it's been stabbed by a million tiny little knives that will never heal—but I don't. For a moment, he made me feel alive. He made me believe there were good men out there and that it was worth fighting to be the one to choose the man I spend the rest of my life with.

The sounds of footsteps in the hallway rush to my ears, despite the blare of the television. Someone's here.

Beckett?

The other guys?

Vincent?

Someone else from the game?

Who?

The footsteps fade, though—someone who lives in the apartment building. No one is coming for me.

That's a lie. Everyone is coming for me. It's just a matter of who comes first and when.

Every footstep, every sound, every door slam from the hallway has me on edge. Lucy obliviously watches the movie, unaware of any of the danger.

Whoever comes, they won't come for her. I'll make sure of it. She'll be safe. That's the only thing I can get right, keeping her safe. She's been my friend for so long that I'll do anything for her.

There's a knock on the door.

A knock.

"Lucy, take Loki and go to your bedroom."

She doesn't ask questions, calmly doing as I said.

I walk toward the door with my gun, ready to shoot whoever is behind the door. If it's Beckett, I'll shoot him in the groin, and then he can explain to me why he almost killed me for a crime I didn't commit.

I chuckle inwardly at that thought.

My guess is it's Beckett or Gage and the rest of the guys. No one else would knock. The assholes in my life would barge in and try to take me as their captive.

I open the door, expecting Beckett.

Instead, I find Ryker leaning against my doorframe with a soft smile on his face.

3

BECKETT

THE LOOK on Ri's face as I run to her will haunt me for all of my days. Her gaunt face, tear-streaked eyes, and stern frown broke my heart. I can see how I'd broken hers. Not just broken, but I shattered her heart beyond repair. The damage I did—I won't be able to fix it, not as long as I live.

The thought shatters what's left of my own heart as I watch her disappear into the tunnel.

It's clear what Ri thought—I was going to kill her. She didn't see the truth. For that, I can never be forgiven.

Gage snaps the door shut behind her as I reach the guys.

"Where is she going?" I ask.

The guys all look to Gage. He's the one who appears to be making the decisions at the moment.

"Somewhere safe," he answers.

I take a deep breath. I want to know where. I want to go to her immediately, but we have bigger problems at the moment.

"Promise she'll be safe," I ask, my voice cracking, my body screaming to run after her as I stare at the space in the wall where she disappeared.

"Ri will be safe. No one knows about this tunnel except us,

Caius, and his father. This was an emergency escape for the leader. She'll be safe," Gage says.

I nod.

"Who was attacking?" Lennox asks.

"The Retribution Kings. They were mad with what I did."

"Our own people were attacking? Are you sure?" Hayes asks.

I nod.

"Jesus Christ. We need to get out of here then," Hayes says.

I agree.

"Beckett!" her voice sends chills down my spine. It's a voice I've longed to hear again. I've wanted to hear her voice for so fucking long, but now it sounds like nails on a chalkboard.

I turn in time to see Odette and Caius running toward us. They're out of breath when they finally reach us.

"How the hell are you alive?" Lennox asks, staring at Odette with anger in his eyes.

I look around the group, and it seems everyone except for Caius has a stern glare on their face as they stare at Odette.

"We need to get somewhere safe first, then Odette can explain what happened. We can go back to my place," Caius says, placing a comforting hand on her back.

"No," I say.

All eyes are on me.

"We go to the cabin. It's further away and safer. Your condo will be the first place they look," I say.

Caius opens his mouth to argue, but he sees the look on my face and doesn't say anything.

We all start jogging out toward our cars when I feel a hand brush against mine. I glance down to see Odette's fingers threading through mine.

My hand goes cold at the sight, and I harshly pull my hand away.

She frowns at me.

I don't want to think about the truth—we are still legally

married. And yet she's tricked me and lied to me—god knows what the truth is.

We make it to the SUV, and all pile in. Lennox takes the driver's seat, and I take the front passenger seat. I don't want to sit for an hour next to Odette while we drive.

Gage and Hayes climb in the back, and Caius sits next to Odette in the middle row, comforting her like she just survived extreme torture. Although from the looks of her, she looks pretty damn healthy to me. Not a mark, scar, or bruise is visible on her skin.

I turn on the radio as soon as Lennox starts driving, making it clear to everyone there will be no talking until we get to the cabin. I should be thinking about the repercussions of my actions. About the men that will be coming after us or about how Odette is alive, but all I can think about is Ri. I hope like hell she's run far, far away from here.

Because if I have to watch her forced to marry another man when the games are over, I'm not sure I can handle it. I'm not sure I can handle watching her go through any more pain.

Lennox pulls up to the cabin far too soon.

"It's safe," Gage says from the backseat.

We all climb out and head inside, going straight for the liquor. I pour myself a drink, not bothering to ask anyone else if they want one before walking out onto the back deck.

I need plenty of fresh air and a lot of fucking alcohol in my system before I have this conversation.

Odette is the first to find me outside.

She walks toward me with her arms outstretched, expecting me to welcome her home. She expects me to hug her, to love her again. But the truth is I'm not sure if I ever loved her in the first place.

Instead of holding her, I lift my drink to my mouth as I stare at her. She gets the hint and stops.

"I—" she starts.

"Wait until everyone else is out here. That way, you only have to tell your story once."

She frowns. "You don't want privacy?"

"No."

I pace on the deck while she quietly takes a seat on one of the wicker chairs. Everyone else files out quickly and sits on the various chairs and benches. I'm the only one who remains standing, leaning against a post.

"Start talking, Odette, and don't leave anything out," I snap, more fury spewing out of my lips than I realized I had.

She looks to Caius and then back to me, taking a deep breath. "Before our wedding, there was a death threat against me, a plot to kill me. My father's condition was poor, and we knew he wouldn't survive much longer, so we couldn't postpone the wedding."

"Who is we?" I ask, interrupting.

Her eyes flutter to Caius. "My father, Caius, and me."

I frown. Caius knew more than he was telling me—the bastard.

I take a long sip of my whiskey.

Odette fidgets with the ends of the strands of her hair, but she continues. "We knew you and I needed to get married and initiate you in as the leader as soon as possible. But we also had to protect me, so we also changed the date of the wedding—to throw everyone off. And as soon as the wedding was over, I needed to disappear."

"Disappear maybe, but die?" I growl.

"Disappearing wouldn't have helped. They would have still come after me. I had to die in order to stay alive. And you had to think I was dead—everyone did—in order for our plan to work. If you weren't devastated, no one would have believed I was dead."

I have so many questions, but I start with, "Who are they? Who wanted you dead and why?"

"Vincent Corsi. He's been trying to destroy the Retribution Kings for years. We cause the most conflict with the various gangs when we take retribution into our own hands. My father almost started an all-out war between the gangs, and Corsi wasn't happy about it. He wanted to teach my father a lesson in retribution to show that he had all the power in this city. He wants the Retribution Kings under his control, so he called for my death."

"You knew Odette was alive?" I ask Caius.

"No, I didn't. I knew that her life was at risk and that she was going to try and disappear, but after I saw those horrible photos, I thought she was dead—same as you," Caius says.

I don't know if I believe him, but I want to hear more of what Odette has to say.

"How did you fake your death? And how did Ri come into this?" I ask.

Odette sighs.

"I hated leaving on our wedding night, but I knew that's when it had to be done. I needed blood—a lot of blood. So I drew my own blood and spread it around the room to make it look like I'd been dangerously close to death when I was taken. But I needed an attacker, someone Caius and my father wouldn't recognize. I couldn't just use anyone."

"How did you rope Ri into this?" I ask, losing patience with her.

"After she interrupted our wedding, I knew she was exactly who I was looking for. I didn't realize she was a Corsi; that was just a bonus. I just thought she was a scared girl in need of some money. Once I told her my story, she agreed to help me without payment."

She takes a deep breath and then continues. "I knew you'd go downstairs to get my medicine, so that's when I had Rialta come to my room. She pretended to fight me, to threaten me. She did cut my skin and make me bleed, but I was willing to endure that in order to survive."

"So then you spent your time on some private island living the good life while everyone here thought you were dead? The fake photos of your bloody body were a nice touch. Whose body did we bury? Did you kill someone to pretend they were you?" I rage.

I'm pissed, beyond pissed. I can't believe she would do this to me. I can't believe I ever loved this woman. I can't fucking believe I fell in love with a monster.

"The body was a woman who died of cancer, similar age and build."

I shake my head as I pace. "Where have you been all this time?"

"My plan was to run, to always be running. I'd wait tables, bartend, clean houses, pick up any job I could to survive. I thought I'd be giving you a better life. You could take over as leader—I knew you'd be amazing at it, Beckett. You deserved to be the leader, needed to be the leader of the Retribution Kings.

"But I also knew that you deserved to find someone who didn't lie to you, someone you chose to love, not a fake like me. I did love you, and I still do, but I didn't think I was enough. So I thought the best plan was to fake my death—save myself and let you live your life." Her voice is practically shaking now.

Caius goes to her and puts his arms around her shoulders, tucking her into his side. He stares at me like he can't believe I'm not the one holding her right now.

Everyone else stays in their seats, though, watching her closely. I can't read any of their faces. I don't know if they trust her or not, but I know what I believe.

"Stop your tears. You chose to leave. You chose to keep me in the dark when I could have easily protected you and kept you safe. You ran. You chose to go it alone. You didn't give me a chance to decide if I really loved you despite the lies."

Odette pushes Caius off her shoulders as she stomps toward me with fire in her eyes. I don't cower. I don't back down, even though I'm pretty sure she's about to slap me.

"You have no idea what I've been through these past few weeks!" she yells.

"And you have no idea the pain I've been through!"

She frowns and pulls up her sleeves, revealing a plethora of scars and bruises on her arms. "I was free a grand total of one week before I was taken. I was tortured and raped and abused. My life was threatened every night, and I wasn't sure if I was going to wake up the next morning or die in my sleep. I've spent every day regretting my decision. Every day realizing the mistake I made in not trusting you. It's made me realize how much I love you. I'd do anything for you."

I narrow my eyes as I study her bruises—they're real enough, but that doesn't mean I believe her story.

"How did you escape?" I ask. She grew up in this world. She could have had as much training and skill as Ri, but I doubt that.

"I was released with a warning to you. You have to step down as leader of the Retribution Kings. Otherwise, they will kidnap me again and actually kill me."

Her story is a mess, full of reasons not to believe her. Not to mention she has never told me the truth in her life, so I don't trust a word she says without undeniable proof. Even then, I'm not sure I'll believe her, not when I saw a video of Ri killing her, and it turned out to be a lie.

But I have one question left. There's only one question that could give me some answers.

"Who took you?"

Her nostrils flare as she thinks of the evil who took her. "Enzo Black."

4

RI

"WHAT ARE YOU DOING HERE?" I ask Ryker as we both stand in the doorway of my apartment.

Looking at his black, mid-length hair and devilish grin, he's the last person I expected here. Ryker has a reputation as one of the cruelest leaders, but after he offered up two of his men to help me, I'm not sure if his reputation is warranted. It doesn't mean I trust him either, though.

"I won the game."

Oh, shit. He's here to collect his prize—me.

"You can go to hell. I'm not going to let you kidnap me, treat me as your possession, and then let you rape me. I'll kill you first. Ask Leighton what happened to his men when he tried it." I slam the door in his face, but he catches it with his hand.

I aim my gun at him, expecting him to do the same, followed by a dozen men filing into my apartment. Instead, Ryker puts his hands up in the air.

"I'm not here to kidnap you. And I would never think of raping or hurting a woman."

I frown. "Your reputation says differently."

"And your reputation is that of a damsel in distress, nothing

23

more than a princess who can't take care of herself. Neither of our reputations tells the whole truth."

I don't drop my aim as he slowly enters our apartment, his hands still up.

"I'm here to protect you," he says.

"Why?"

"You're my responsibility for the week. If anything happens to you, Corsi will have my head, and my men will be without a leader once again. So my loyalty is to you for the week. I will do everything in my power to keep you safe."

He seems genuine, but I don't trust him. I don't trust anyone—not after Beckett betrayed me, the only man I thought I could love.

He puts his hands down, but I don't drop my gun.

"I'll take you and Lucy wherever you want, but you can't stay in this apartment. It's not safe. Too many people know about it, and too many people will come looking for you."

"How do you know about Lucy?"

"I did my due diligence."

I was right. Everyone knows about Lucy, and she's not safe.

"You'll take us anywhere?"

"Anywhere." He nods.

"Even if I wanted to go to a rival gang? You'd take me there? Make sure we were safe?"

"I promise to take you wherever you want to go. You will not be a prisoner with me. If you want to go back to Beckett, I'll take you."

I don't ask how he knows that's where I would want to go.

"If you betray us if you fail to keep us safe, if you trap us or hurt either of us in any way, I will kill you. My father and I will ruin your entire gang and everyone you love, do you understand?"

Ryker smiles. "Of course, why else do you think I'm here? The goodness of my heart? I may like you, but I wouldn't be risking my life to protect you if it didn't serve my own self-interest."

His smile is what gets me. It's so genuine and sweet, not to mention the light behind his eyes. He plays the villain well. I've seen his monster act firsthand, but his men respected him and wanted to work for him.

This could be an epic mistake, but then again, I'm used to making epic mistakes. I wish I could rely entirely on myself, but I don't have a choice. There are too many people that want me and will have no problem hurting Lucy to control me.

I'll go with him for now, but that doesn't mean I'll trust him.

"Take us to a private house rental. Pay in cash. Only you are allowed to know the location, no one else." It's a lot to ask. He'd be lying to his men, hiding the truth from them. I don't expect him to agree.

"Your wish is my command, Princess."

I frown, lowering the gun for the first time. "Don't call me Princess."

He chuckles low and deep. "Okay, Rialta."

I wince. "Don't call me Rialta either."

He raises his eyebrows. "What would you like me to call you?"

"Ri, just Ri."

"Well, Ri, give me five minutes to figure out a house we can go to and something to tell my men as to why they won't be seeing much of me this week." He pulls out his phone.

I'm still not sure I should trust him, but I accept that he won't try to shoot or kidnap me in the next five minutes, so I leave him in the living room and head to Lucy's room.

She opens the door with a frown. "No."

"No, what?"

"No, I'm not going. I have school, a job, a life. I'm not going to live in some random house with a guy I don't know. This place is impenetrable. No one will hurt me here!" She crosses her arms and sticks out her hips with a deep pout on her face.

"Luce, please," I say softly.

"No."

"Luce, how many times have I been kidnapped over the years?"

"That's not fair. I haven't—"

"Lucy," I plead with my eyes. Loki trudges over to Lucy's side and licks her hand encouragingly.

"Fine, but you're going to explain to Frank why I don't show up for work. I don't have any tests this week, so it shouldn't be that big of a deal if I miss class. And I get the best room."

I smile. "Done."

She rolls her eyes and then stomps back into her room to start packing. I start to head to my room to pack as well but stop in my doorway.

"Only one bag!"

"You're no fun!" Lucy yells back, making me laugh.

I gather a backpack worth of clothes and toiletries quickly, not really caring which clothes I pack before moving on to the more important things—weapons. I pack several knives and guns before heading back out to see if Ryker has found a place.

He looks up from his phone when he sees me. "You pack light. I like that."

The next moment, Lucy rolls out an oversized cheetah-print suitcase with Loki's dog bed and a bag of his supplies sitting on top.

Ryker frowns, rubbing the back of his head as he stares at her. "We're going to be gone less than a week. Is all that shit really necessary?"

"Yes," Lucy spits back.

Well, there isn't going to be any love lost between the two of them.

Loki decides to take a moment to inspect the new person in our apartment. I expect him to bark or jump on him. Instead, he wags his tail as he licks Ryker's hand.

"Huh," Lucy says, looking at Loki's reaction and then to me.

Maybe I was right to trust Ryker, but it's still too soon to let my guard down. I won't let the fact that Loki seems to like him mean I give him my full trust. Loki also liked Beckett, and he almost killed me.

"Found a place?" I ask Ryker.

"I did." He holds out his phone to me.

I take it and see a house listing that says sold. I scrunch my nose. "You bought a house? How did you make this happen so quickly?"

"I'm always looking for new safe houses. I bought this one last week. No one knows about it but me. It's fully furnished and safe. But if you'd prefer me to find another place, just say the word."

His eyes are sincere. I still don't understand why he's helping me, not really. Why would he even enter the game if he doesn't have some ulterior motive?

I hand him back his phone. "This will work."

He nods, tucking his phone back in his pocket. He looks down at Lucy's bag. "You able to carry that thing? I need to be focused on our safety, not worried about your bag."

Lucy crosses her arms over her chest and huffs. "I can roll my bag just fine."

"Good. Ready, Ri?"

I nod, reaching for my gun at the same time Ryker grabs his own.

"Shoot to kill, Ri."

"I will."

"Let's go." Ryker leads the way out of my apartment, followed by Lucy rolling her bag with Loki right beside her, and I take up the rear, hoping Lucy won't get caught in any crossfire.

I don't know what awaits us. Vincent or Beckett or others might be waiting to attack us, so our only shot is to get out of here as fast as possible.

The hallway is clear, as is the garage when we make it down the elevator. We make it all the way to Ryker's car without being attacked.

Lucy and Loki climb in the back seat while Ryker and I quickly hop in front. Ryker and I are both still gripping our guns as he pulls out of the space.

"That was strange," I say.

"How was that strange? You two overreact," Lucy says from the backseat.

"No, it was strange. There are too many people after you. We should have been attacked," Ryker says.

There's an unease that circles through the car. Even Loki stills as we all stare out various windows, just waiting to be ambushed. None of the following uneventful miles we drive ease our anxieties.

And then it happens.

The car is bumped from behind. We surge forward, Ryker barely hangs onto control.

I move to point my gun out the window, but Ryker grabs my arm. "Don't put yourself in danger."

"Someone has to try and stop them."

"Then that someone is going to be me. Take the wheel."

He slides up in his seat, motioning for me to take his place. For a second, I look at him like's fucking crazy. But then the car rams into us from behind again, and I realize now isn't the time to argue his judgment.

I hop across the center console and into the seat, taking the wheel just as he pops open the driver's door and hangs from the car like a badass, and shoots at the car behind us.

I look in the rearview mirror and see the car spinning to a stop as Ryker swings back in. He rolls over my lap until he reaches the passenger's seat.

"Do you see anyone else?" I ask, gripping the wheel hard, ready for almost everything.

"There's no one behind you—"

A popping sound interrupts him, and I feel the car jerk as I drive.

"Someone hit the tires," I say, feeling the tug of the car, knowing it's not going to be drivable much longer.

Ryker turns to Lucy. "When Ri stops the car, run in the opposite direction of us. They will be focused on Ri. Run and take cover the second you can. We'll find you as soon as it's safe."

Lucy looks to me, and I nod, agreeing.

I turn the car toward an alleyway before it becomes completely undrivable. The second I stop, Lucy and Loki jump out and start running down the alley.

I reach for my door, but Ryker stops me. "Let me take the lead."

"I don't take orders, and I don't let others put their lives before mine," I say with a frown and open my door before Ryker can stop me.

Immediately, bullets fly around us as I duck behind the door and fire back.

"Do you know who they are?" I ask Ryker, who has climbed down next to me and is shooting at them.

He narrows his eyes. "They are the Lolitos."

He hesitates a moment as he looks at the men shooting at us.

I stop firing and look at him.

"You know them?"

"Some of them used to be my friends."

I frown. "Then why are they..."

"They think I'll turn on you, that I'll help them. They aren't participating in the game. They just want you dead, and Corsi's legacy destroyed."

"So why aren't you giving me to them?"

"Because I keep my promises."

He jumps out in front of our car door with a new vengeance before I can stop him. One after one, I see him take down our attackers without hesitation.

I'm frozen.

These men were his friends, and yet he's killing them all.

My mouth is agape as I watch him murder friend after friend until there is only one man left.

Ryker stares him down, aiming the gun at him, but doesn't fire.

The man facing him doesn't lower his gun, though. Instead, I see his eyes cut to me. He's about to shoot me. Despite all of his friends being killed, he doesn't think Ryker will shoot him.

Ryker's hand trembles. Whoever this person is, he means more to him than all the rest.

"Drop your gun, Hector." Ryker's voice is strong and determined, meant to show Hector how serious he is.

"She has to die, Ryker. You know that. She can't live. Corsi can't continue on. You joined the game to have their power, but we decided to destroy it, so there is no power to be gained."

"You can't shoot her. Drop. Your. Gun."

"You won't shoot me. And you definitely won't kill me. We grew up together."

"Please," Ryker says, his arm shaking so much I'm afraid even if he fires his gun, he'll miss.

I should shoot this man. I shouldn't make Ryker decide. But somehow, I can't do it. I can't be the one to end this man's life—Ryker's friend.

Maybe he'll shoot me and put me out of my misery. I've only had a broken heart for a few hours, but I can already tell it's something I can't endure for a lifetime.

I close my eyes, willing him to shoot me, to end it all right here.

I hear the pop of the gun.

I don't feel any sharp shock of pain, but then again, I'm so numb at this point I doubt a bullet would make an impact. Nothing can be as painful as a broken heart caused by broken love.

I open my eyes, looking for the wound on my body to see how long it will take for me to bleed out and die. But as I open my eyes, I can't find an obvious wound anywhere.

My heart sinks as I look out and find Ryker standing over his friend's limp body. Ryker's breathing is slow and steady, while his eyes are locked on his friend.

Ryker shot his childhood friend to protect me.

I don't understand why.

I don't understand if he's really afraid for his own life if I die or if he thinks keeping me alive is the best for his own gang. *Or maybe there's some other reason he's not telling me?*

All I know is he's going to be as broken as me now. He'll never forget this single kill as long as he lives.

Slowly, I walk over to him and place my hand gently on his shoulder.

He jumps at my touch.

I open my mouth to apologize, but I slam it shut. Nothing I say can take his pain away.

"Let's find Lucy and get out of here," Ryker says, shaking my touch off as he walks away.

I stare down at the man who wanted to kill me, the man Ryker killed to protect me. So many men have died trying to kill me, so many more will, and all for a chance to steal everything my father has worked for.

I don't know how to stop it—the unending bleeding—but I'm going to find a way. The pain and suffering have to stop, and I'm the only one who can.

5

BECKETT

WHEN ODETTE SAYS that Enzo Black, my half-brother and full brother in every way that matters, was the one who took her, my blood boils. It takes everything inside me not to strangle her to death right now.

She's a fucking liar.

I know she's lying. My brother would never do that. And if he did, he would tell me. It would serve some purpose. He wouldn't hurt me like this. He wouldn't make me think she was dead for weeks. Even if he was trying to help her, he would have told me the truth by now.

Or Kai would. Or Siren, Zeke, Langston, Liesel. Someone would have told me.

No, she's a liar.

I don't believe one word of her story. Not. One. Fucking. Word.

I don't know what to do next, but I do know I'm not thinking clearly. I want to kill her for what she's done, for putting Ri's life in danger.

The problem is I don't think killing Odette will solve much. It will mean I'm no longer married to her, but also every Retribution King will be after me. And I can't help Ri if I'm being chased.

"Say something," Odette pleads, reaching her hand out to touch my chest.

I take a big step back rather than letting our bodies touch. If I did, she'd be dead.

"You don't want to hear what I have to say," I growl so deeply the entire forest shakes.

"Beckett, you're my husband. Of course, I want to hear what you say. I've done everything I could to get back to you. I—"

"Enough," I command.

She closes her mouth.

Caius stands behind her like he wants to kill me. I still suspect he knew more than he's letting on. I trust him about as much as I do his sister right now. I don't trust any of the Retribution Kings either.

I look around at the other guys. I do trust Gage, Lennox, and Hayes. They helped get Ri out when I couldn't. They protected her when I couldn't. And they are looking at Odette, a woman they've known all their lives, with disdain in their eyes. For now, I'll trust them.

"The Kings are here," Gage says, pulling out his phone and reviewing the perimeter of the property.

Fuck.

I knew they'd come; I just wanted enough time to hear Odette's story. I've heard it, and it's bullshit. I don't need to hear more.

"Gage, take Odette to one of the rooms and keep her there until I say otherwise."

"Baby, tell me you believe me. Tell me you still love me because I still love you," Odette tries again.

I don't say anything. Gage grabs her arm and guides her inside the cabin. She doesn't put up much of a fight—big, fat tears stream down her cheeks and wobbly bottom lip.

It won't work on me, though. I'm heartless where she's concerned.

No, you gave your heart to another woman, a worthy woman. It's true, even if she now hates me because she thinks I betrayed her. That's really why Odette will never have my heart again.

"Lennox and Hayes, strip Caius of his weapons and lock him up in another room."

Caius moves to grab his weapons, to fight back, but they grab him before he has a chance. They've been friends a long time, so I wasn't sure if they would follow my orders or his.

Hayes grabs Caius's gun, Lennox Caius's knife. Quickly, they have his hands behind his back.

"I didn't know anything! And I believe every word of Odette's story. She was kidnapped, raped, and abused by people you call family," he yells and thrashes.

"I know, and it's why I don't trust you. I don't blame you for believing your sister," I reply.

"She's your wife!" Caius spits out as Lennox and Hayes start walking him to the door.

A roll of rage washes through me when he says 'wife.' Technically, it might be true, but she doesn't have my heart. I thought I loved her, and I was wrong. There is only one woman I love—one woman I've ever loved. And I fucked it all up by thinking I loved Odette instead.

Lennox and Hayes drag Caius away.

I follow after, heading to the front of the house to meet my fate. I check my weapons, ensuring I know where they are, but the sounds of cars and men tell me that it doesn't matter how many guns I have on me, I won't be able to fight my way out.

I walk out the front porch as I see more than a dozen men getting out of their cars.

Stan steps forward. He's one of the elders, the one who helps when I'm not around.

If they'd let me leave, I'd give him my position in a heartbeat, but I have a feeling they won't accept that. I know too much.

"Stan," I say in the way of a greeting.

"Beckett." He nods back at me. "We have a lot to discuss."

I raise an eyebrow at the men behind him. "It seems like you came here to kill me, not to talk."

"No, of course not. We came here to clear up the misunderstandings."

"Of course," I say sarcastically.

"Are you going to invite us in?"

I look out at the number of men that keep driving up. I think they're up to over twenty.

"I don't think we'll fit, and I'd rather not get blood on the upholstery. It will be a bitch to clean."

Stan laughs. "Oh, Beckett. We won't be getting any blood anywhere. We just want to talk."

"Then we can talk out here."

He sighs but doesn't fight me on it.

"What happened?"

"I don't have to defend myself. I'm the leader of the Retribution Kings. You all have to listen to me."

"That's not entirely true. We picked you as our leader, but only if you finished the final task of getting retribution. You didn't kill Rialta Corsi."

"And good thing, too, since she didn't actually kill Odette and isn't responsible for her death. Good thing I didn't start a war because you told me to. I would have doomed us all."

Stan frowns. "So you knew Odette was alive?"

"No, I didn't, but I did my own homework. I wasn't going to kill someone without hard evidence."

"Well, we'll ignore your indiscretion because it ended up being the right thing."

"Oh, you'll ignore it, will you?" I grit out, my voice full of anger. "You wanted me as your leader; this is what you get. You have to trust that I make the right decisions for everyone."

"We do, of course, we do."

"Then why are you here?"

"To see Odette. We are overjoyed that our princess is still alive."

"She's resting. You can see her later. As you can imagine, she's had a long day."

"Sure, sure."

"Why are you here?" I growl.

"We need to finish your initiation."

"I think killing Rialta is moot now, don't you?"

"You have to complete your retribution task. We all did. We can't trust you fully until you complete it."

"What task? And if I complete it, that's it? You'll trust me fully, and there will be no more meetings like this?"

"You will have everyone in the Retribution Kings' full loyalty."

"Odette is alive. There is no need to get retribution for her. What do you want me to do?"

Stan smiles deviously.

Chills race over my arm and all over my body. I don't trust his smile.

He pulls out his phone and hands it to me.

It's a video. I'm reluctant to press play, sure of what the "evidence" is he's about to show me, but I need to see it.

I press play.

There's a grainy video of one of Enzo's yachts with Odette standing on the top deck. Enzo and Kai are on the deck too. Odette is yelling, but there is no sound. I have no idea what she's saying or where they are.

I'm sure Stan is going to make it out like Odette was kidnapped and being held against her will. This was either photoshopped, or she climbed aboard the ship just to get this footage.

I hand the phone back to him. "It's going to take more evidence than this to convince me that my brother took my wife and held her captive all this time. The last time I was shown a video like this, it wasn't the whole story. I'm not going to go after my own family until I have much more evidence."

Stan frowns.

"Enzo Black isn't your family anymore. You took a vow when you became our leader. You became a Monroe. Your loyalty should be to us, not them."

"I can be loyal to the Retribution Kings and still not kill my own brother with barely any evidence."

"Half brother—Enzo is your half brother you didn't even know about most of your life."

I want to punch the foul smirk off his face, but I don't think it would help the situation.

"I want more evidence," I grit out, trying to keep my temper at bay.

"Has Odette told you what happened?" he asks like he wasn't listening the entire time and knows exactly what Odette said to me.

I take my time answering, studying him closely. I don't know how he could have been listening, but I decide to go with the truth. "Yes, Odette told me her story."

"And what did she say?"

"That Enzo kidnapped her."

"Your own wife told you what happened. That's all the evidence you need. She told you the truth, and now you must get retribution for her."

I close my eyes, keeping my rage in, instead of letting it explode out of me. My brows pinch together, and I swear I'm getting a full-on migraine from this conversation.

"Odette just went through a very traumatic experience. I'm not sure her memories are to be relied on. We don't know if Enzo kidnapped her to hurt her or save her."

He shakes his head in disgust. "I understand that your feelings are a bit complicated, which is why we have taken it upon ourselves to study the evidence. Odette was kidnapped by Enzo Black. Your final initiation task is simple—kill Enzo Black, put an end to his empire, and then you'll be king of the Retribution Kings."

His words show how little they know. The way to end the Black

Empire is not to kill Enzo; his wife, Kai, is far more in charge of things than he is.

"And if I don't?"

"You have one month to complete your new task, same as before. And if you don't, we'll kill you."

My jaw ticks, and everything clicks into place.

This is why they picked me. They've wanted Enzo dead this whole time. They wanted someone from his inner circle to have the knowledge and motivation to kill him. They didn't count on me falling out of love with Odette, though.

"Where are your men?" he asks.

"Inside resting."

"I'd like to chat with them and add some new soldiers to your ranks to help you complete your initiation task."

He tries to brush past me, but I step into his path. "I'm happy with my current team, thank you."

"You don't have a choice. Right now, I'm your second. And as a fully initiated member, I have more power than you do, especially now that you are on thin ice."

I stare at him and then out at his men. I have two choices.

One—go along with everything he says. Let him keep some of his men here as spies and basically jailers. Then I'll figure out how to get rid of them later.

Two—fight now.

The first option might be smarter, but the second option gives me a faster chance to go after Ri.

I have no idea where she is or if she's safe. What I do know is that she's pissed. She cared about me, possibly even loved me, but after what I did, she'll hate me forever. She'll never forgive me. Every second I let her keep thinking that I have less and less chance of her forgiving me, of her loving me ever again.

I look at Stan and make my choice; the only route I'm willing to take—I fight.

WE HOTWIRED a car and found Lucy and Loki about a block away before we drove the rest of the way to Ryker's new safe house in complete silence. Not even Loki made a sound, sensing Ryker's agony and not wanting to add to it.

I drove following the in-car directions with Ryker in the passenger seat, his eyes open. Clearly, though, his mind was still on the last man—a man who was obviously a close friend. He shot and killed that friend to protect me.

I stop the car in front of a large Tudor-style mansion. None of us immediately get out as we stare up at the old home, full of character and vast rooms. There look to be so many rooms I'm afraid none of us are going to feel safe in the house.

"It has the top-of-the-line security system installed. I just finished installing it myself last week. I'll make sure it's hooked up to both of your phones too. It's a fortress, and no one knows we are here. You won't be found."

I think of the tracker I swallowed so Beckett could always find me. I consider telling Ryker but decide against it. The only man who can find me here is Beckett.

Whether I admit it or not, I want Beckett to find me, if only so I can rip out his heart for what he did to mine.

Ryker gets out, followed by Lucy and Loki, and then me.

We all get our bags. Lucy drags her large roller behind her, while Ryker and I each carry small backpacks into the large mansion.

When we enter, the vastness of the house is overwhelming. The ceiling stretches three stories up. The stairs curve up to a long sideways hallway leading each wing of the rectangular-shaped house. On the first floor, I can see rooms as far as I look in all directions.

Lucy releases Loki, who runs full speed down the first-floor hallway. She looks at Ryker. "I hope you aren't attached to any of the furniture. Loki loves to chew up new furniture."

Ryker just smiles at her. "The furniture came with the house. It was one reason I bought it. I'll sell it as soon as we leave. So no, I don't really give a damn if a couple of pieces have a few holes, dog stains, or loose threads."

Lucy laughs. "Some? More like all." She follows Loki to explore the house, leaving Ryker and me standing in the entryway.

"This house had to cost you a small fortune. Why get something so big and expensive?"

"We have a couple of small safe houses, but many of my men know where they are. This house was meant to be a safe house for as many of my men as possible. I feel it's my job to protect them, and a house like this could have done that."

"I'm sorry you wasted it on us then."

He turns to me. His body is weary, like he's just weathered a terrible storm, but he pulls strength into his eyes as he looks at me. "Don't be sorry—about anything."

And then he walks away.

I shouldn't push him, so I don't follow him. I give him space to deal with his emotions.

Lucy is loudly making food in the kitchen, and I consider spending time with her, but I'm far too exhausted for her company.

Instead, I head upstairs and choose one of the first bedrooms with an attached bathroom. I sit in the tub for a solid hour before climbing into the oversized bed, hoping sleep washes away my exhaustion.

Beckett plays in my head the second I close my eyes. His cocky smile, his sharp eyes, his rippling muscles, his arm protecting me. And him holding a gun to my head.

He was going to kill me.

He was going to kill me.

He was going to kill me.

I repeat the words over and over. To remind me of the pain of what he did. To remind me that I can't love him. To deepen the knife in my heart.

Tears spill onto the silk pillowcase, escaping my closed eyes.

It hurts, it fucking hurts. And I don't know how to make it stop.

I lie in bed for hours, willing myself to sleep. I try to convince myself I'll feel better in the morning if I can just get some sleep.

But sleep never comes.

Agitated and uncomfortable, I decide to head downstairs to get some food. If I'm lucky, I'll find some alcohol to soothe the ache in my chest and hopefully knock me out to sleep.

I walk into the kitchen and stop when I see a shadow standing in the kitchen. I reach for my gun before realizing I didn't bring one down.

Stupid, stupid.

"Forgot your gun?" Ryker says.

A whoosh of a breath eases out of me when I realize it's Ryker and not an intruder come to kill me.

"You scared the crap out of me." I walk over to where he's standing with a cabinet open over the fridge.

"Sorry. You should always carry a gun with you, Ri. You can never be too careful."

I nod. "I know. Today has just been..." I sigh. "The worst day. I'm not myself. And I'm not thinking straight."

Ryker pulls a bottle down from the cabinet.

"The house came stocked with liquor too?"

"The last owners must have left this bottle of whiskey, but it'll do the trick," he says.

I nod.

I find two glasses, and he pours the amber liquid. We each end up with more than three shots worth in our glass, but I'm still not sure it's going to be enough.

Ryker takes his glass and walks out onto the back deck. I follow him, not sure if he wants to be alone tonight or not. But there's something about being under the dark sky, the bright moon, and chill air that puts everything in perspective in moments like this.

I lean against the railing of the deck as I sip my drink. Ryker does the same.

For a moment, there is just comfortable silence between us as we drink and look up at the sky. All of our answers will be given if we just stand here long enough.

"Today was one of my worst days, but I don't understand why it was one of your worst days, Ri."

I sigh, not sure I want to discuss this with him. "Because today I learned how foolish I had been to give my heart to a man who oblit-erated it the first chance he got."

"This is Beckett, I assume?"

I nod, almost ashamed.

"Tell me what happened."

I chew on my bottom lip, not sure I want to open my heart to more heartbreak of having to relive it all. But I need to talk to some-one, and after what Ryker did today, I trust him a lot more than before.

"Short story is I fell in love with him. I thought he fell in love with me. But in reality, he was just playing me. He thought I was the one responsible for killing his wife. Instead of talking to me about it, he decided to kill me as retribution in front of his people."

My hand shakes as I speak, and I find I'm rattled to my core as I speak the truth of what happened.

Ryker places his hand gently on top of mine, gently calming me with his touch.

"He'll come for me. Tonight. Tomorrow. The next day."

"To finish what he failed to complete?" Ryker asks.

"No. It turns out his wife is alive, so obviously, I didn't kill her. But he'll still come, though."

"What makes you so sure?"

I look at Ryker. "Because he always does."

I lift the glass to my lips and finish the rest of the liquor. It burns going down, making me feel something other than my broken heart for a split second. I wish it would last, but it won't.

I only hope the mixture of exhaustion and alcohol now warming my system will be enough to get me to sleep soon. Sleep is the only way to numb the pain. Although, I suspect my heartbreak will even seep into my dreams.

Suddenly Ryker speaks. "I'm going to play devil's advocate for a second."

I narrow my eyes. "What do you mean?"

"I think there's a reason Beckett always comes back to you."

I shake my head. "I don't understand. Because he hates me and wants to ruin me?"

Ryker laughs. "Maybe. You know him better than I do, but I'm going to call it something that is very much like hate. As rich and deep as hate, but it isn't."

I glare at him with a deep frown as I pull my hand back from his touch. "Love. You mean love."

He nods slowly, eyeing me skeptically like he thinks I might punch him for even suggesting it.

"It's not love. No one would try to kill someone they loved."

Ryker goes silent, and I realize what I just said.

"I'm sorry—I didn't mean—"

"You did," Ryker cuts me off. "That's okay, but you're wrong. I killed Hector. He was a friend. It wasn't romantic love, but you could say I loved him. Before today I would have said I would give my life to protect him. But then today happened, and I had to make a choice.

"I had to put you and my men above him. He wouldn't have stopped; he would have come after us. I knew his skill; he would have eventually succeeded if I didn't stop him. So I killed someone that I loved."

His words hit me hard. I know the kind of pressure Beckett was under as the new leader of the Retribution Kings. *Did he have to make a similar choice to Ryker? Did he have to choose between two people he loved? Between revenge for Odette and me?*

It doesn't heal my broken heart, but it does put his actions more into perspective.

"What do I do now? How do I get out of this?" I ask Ryker, not really expecting an answer but just needing to say that out loud.

He sighs.

"There isn't any hope that I survive these games and get to choose my own fate, is there? I'm doomed to be married to a horrible man who will rape me and use me as an incubator for his sperm. I'll be disposable as soon as I produce a male heir. That's my future."

"It doesn't have to be."

"No? I don't see a way out of this. Not anymore."

"Yes, you do." Ryker uses a finger to turn my head in his direction, tilting my head up so that our eyes are level with each other. Our lips, our entire bodies, are so close that our breaths are hot on the other's skin.

"You win."

I chuckle. "Not likely. Vincent will never let me win. He'll manipulate the last games to make sure I lose."

"Maybe. Or maybe you find a way to beat him at his own game. You find a way to manipulate him into giving you the advantage, and then you kick all of our asses."

I frown. "Don't you want to win?"

"I want to ensure my men stay alive, that's all."

"But if you lose, that means you've most likely been killed."

"As long as my men are protected, I don't care."

"You're a better man than I realized."

He smiles gently.

"But even if I win, I still have to marry someone. I still have to produce an heir to take over my father's kingdom. I still—"

"Then you pick the best fucking man. A man you want. A man who will treat you with respect. A man who will love you like you deserve to be loved."

"And you think you're that man?" I exhale, barely able to breathe.

His lips brush mine. It's a soft, sweet, tender kiss. His touch steals my breath and soothes my aching soul—two broken people sharing a healing kiss. The problem is the holes in our hearts are too big to be healed, even by a kiss like this.

He pulls back. "No, I'm not that man. You already know who that man is."

Then Ryker walks back inside, leaving me alone on the deck under the stars with the tingle of his kiss on his lips.

I know exactly who Ryker thinks I should be with, *but why couldn't I have fallen for a man like Ryker?* He's kinder and more self-sacrificing than I realized. He deserves to be a leader in Corsi's kingdom.

Instead, I fell for a man as fucked up as I am. A man who will never admit his feelings for me. A man who threatened to kill me. A man who has saved me more times than I can count. A man who fucking loves me but will put his pride first. A man who chose another woman.

Beckett Monroe.

I look out into the darkness. He won't come tonight. But when he does come, I'm going to be ready to punish him for every transgression he's ever committed against me.

BECKETT

I KNOW my odds aren't great. It's me against a couple dozen men unless Gage, Lennox, and Hayes realize what's happening and decide to fight. But I'm done living my life for others. I'm done living afraid. I'm done hiding my feelings and letting others dictate my future.

For the first time in forever, I know what I want. I realize my mistakes, and I won't be repeating them. And I'd rather go down fighting for what I want than living a lie for another second.

I draw my gun and fire into Stan's leg before anyone realizes what's happening.

Stan curses but doesn't reach for his weapon immediately. He may have been chosen as the number two, but he isn't a skilled fighter. He's young and inexperienced.

It gives me a slight advantage for a second before he starts barking orders. I'm not sure the men even realize what happened at first.

I need to make a run for it. My choices are to dart into the woods or jump in a car and hope I can outdrive them.

Neither are great options, but I have to try. I won't die with Ri not knowing the truth.

I dart into the house, deciding that it gives me some cover until I decide which way to make my exit. Or it becomes my gravesite when they decide to just blow the house up rather than deal with me.

No, they won't do that. Odette is inside; they won't hurt her.

I slam the door shut and close the half dozen locks shut on the door. It will help to keep them out for at least a few minutes.

I consider asking the guys for help, but I won't ask them to betray their own families for me. I'm on my own.

I run out the back, deciding my best bet is to disappear into the woods. Suddenly, Hayes pokes his head out.

"I heard a gunshot," he says.

"I shot Stan."

"Oh." Hayes grabs his gun, and then Lennox is right beside him.

There's a loud bang against the front door.

"Let me go out the back. I'll disappear into the woods. You stay. I won't ask you to betray the oath you took to your families. All I ask is you help me escape the house."

"No," Lennox says, stepping forward.

Gage pops out of the other bedroom and is now looking at me as well.

Fuck, I made a mistake. They are going to turn me over to Stan. I shouldn't have come back into the house.

"We are on your side, not the Retribution Kings. You are our leader. We trust you, not Stan," Lennox says.

"Even if that means you're betraying your people? Betraying everyone you've ever loved? I'm done being a Retribution King. I'm going to be living my life on the run. I refuse to do what they ask of me."

Hayes grins, almost excited by words. "I never liked being a King. I always wanted to be a rebel."

"I'm tired of being lied to. I trust you, not Caius, and not the other Kings," Lennox says with a vengeance in his eyes.

Gage finally chimes in too. "You already know I'm on your side."

I suck in a breath, feeling a heavy weight on my shoulders. It was easier to fight and possibly die when it was just my life on the line. Now it's these three men too, and I'm not sure I made the right decision.

"How do we escape? There are over twenty men outside at Stan's command ready to kill me if I don't finish my initiation task."

"They still want you to kill Ri even after it's obvious she didn't kill Odette?" Hayes asks.

"No, they want me to kill my brother for taking Odette, even though I know that's not what happened."

"Lying bitch," Lennox says.

All eyes turn to him. "I didn't believe one word she said. She's playing us all. She's a Retribution King through and through. She and Caius have set this whole thing up to cause a war."

I nod my agreement. "They chose me as the leader and made me fall in love with Odette, so they could set up my brother in hopes that I would start a war with him. I don't know why they want Enzo dead, but they think since I've worked for him for so long that I know how to defeat him."

Gage curses under his breath.

"We need to get out of here. Should we run into the woods? Find an abandoned house to wait them out or hotwire a car?" I ask, spitballing ideas.

"No, the house is a fortress. Completely bulletproof and bombproof. And they already have the house completely surrounded," Gage says.

"Then what?" I ask.

Hayes grins sadistically. "We pick them off one by one."

Everyone pulls out their guns and nod in agreement. I suspect there is more to each of these guys' stories about why they don't like the Retribution Kings. They so easily believe their former family would betray me.

"Where are Odette and Caius?" I ask.

"Tied up in separate rooms," Lennox answers.

"Then let's do this."

"The glass and walls are bulletproof, so it shouldn't easily shatter, but it will eventually," Gage says.

"What's the plan, then?" Hayes and everyone else look at me.

"Each of us takes a different direction. I'll call everyone on a group call. Keep the line of communication open. If you're wounded or need help, say so. No one plays the hero," I say.

"That includes you," Gage says, narrowing his eyes at me.

I nod.

"I'll take the front," I say.

"I'll take the back," Gage says.

"West," Lennox says at the same time Hayes says, "East."

I pull out my phone and dial them all at the same time. I put my phone on speaker and slide it into my back pocket.

"Can everyone hear me?" I ask.

"Loud and clear," Hayes answers back.

"Yep," Lennox and Gage answer.

I raise my gun as I lean against the frame of the front window and peer outside from the corner of my eye.

I don't see Stan anywhere, but I do see at least five men trying to break down the front door.

One of my guys starts shooting. There is no going back now.

I slip the window open wide enough for me to shoot through the space, and then I fire as well.

I hit the first attacker easily enough, and he drops to the ground. The others return fire, but I don't back down. Gage said the glass is bulletproof; it's time to find out.

I keep shooting but refuse to duck as the bullets fly at me. I can't help but flinch as they hit the window next to me that shatters slightly but doesn't break.

I exhale a deep breath.

"Everyone good?" I ask.

Three *goods* ring back at me.

I grin, believing for the first time that we are going to win this fight and win big. Then it will only be a matter of finding Ri and figuring out a way to not have a dozen gangs after us.

It takes about five minutes for me to kill the rest on my side of the house.

I still hear gunfire ringing out.

"The front is clear. Who needs help?"

But before I can move, I get all clears from everyone else.

"Meet in the living room," I say.

When I see everyone walk in unscathed, I relax.

"They were idiots for attacking the house when they knew how protected it was," Hayes says as he falls into a chair.

Lennox and Gage sit on the couch while I stand in front of the fireplace.

"Did anyone kill Stan?" I ask.

Everyone shakes their heads no.

I run my hand through my hair. "Fuck, he must have escaped. The slick bastard wouldn't even stay and fight."

"But he will bring more men. He'll come after you and threaten everything you care about unless you do as they want. You'll never be safe again," Lennox says.

"We'll never be safe again. Are you sure you guys are ready for that life?" I ask.

"We're with you," Gage says as the others nod.

"What do we do now?" Hayes asks.

"We find Ri, and then we find a way to win the game and end the Retribution Kings."

Silence stretches around the room as the guys exchange glances.

"What?" I ask.

Hayes scratches his head and then finally speaks. "Ri hates your guts."

I chuckle as the guys stare at me like I've lost my mind.

"I know she hates me."

"If you go see her now, she's going to kick your ass. And she's way better skilled than those guys we just fought."

"I know. She hates me, and it's well deserved, but I have to go see her. I have to fix things," I say.

Hayes smirks. "I'm going to enjoy watching her beat you up."

The others chuckle.

"If she beats me up, that means she'll see me. I'll accept whatever punishment she needs to inflict; I just need to see her."

"This is going to end badly. She really hates you right now," Hayes says.

"She also loves me," I say.

No one argues with that.

TWO DAYS PASS.

No one attacks us.

No one comes looking for us.

I'm almost impressed by Ryker's ability to find a safe house that no one has actually found.

Lucy has been going stir crazy in the house. She's an extrovert who likes to be busy. She likes school, work, and being around people. Unfortunately for her, Ryker and I haven't been the best company these days.

Ryker and I have been enjoying the peace and quiet. Neither of us is used to getting a quiet moment to think. And every night, we have met out on the back deck and talked when we couldn't sleep.

He told me about past loves. About what taking on a leadership position meant. About what he wants for the future.

I tried everything to not talk about Beckett, but in reality, it was all I talked about. It's all I've thought about. *Why hasn't he come?*

I thought he would at least come to finish what he started. I'm definitely not expecting an apology.

He's forgotten all about me now that Odette is back. He's probably fucking her brains out and hasn't given me a thought.

He loves her, not me.

I'm so stupid, so foolish.

"Stop it," Ryker says as we once again stand under the moonlight.

"Stop what?" I ask as I drink my midnight whiskey.

"Stop beating yourself up. It's not your fault you fell in love with him. It's his fault he hurt and betrayed you. You did nothing wrong. Loving someone is never foolish, even if they didn't deserve it. Falling in love with him shows how big of a heart you have. You're incredible to love someone with so many faults. You saw the best in him, and there is nothing wrong with finding the best in others."

I sigh. "But is it foolish to keep loving him?"

Ryker sighs as he tucks a strand of my hair behind my ear. His touch sends chills through my body.

I lean into him, and then our arms are wrapped around each other. We comfort each other the only way we know how, but it's not enough. Hugging each other is nice, but we would both rather be hugging other people. This is all we've got, though.

A throat clears, and Ryker pushes my body behind his. We both drop our glasses and draw our guns, aiming into the darkness of the forest beyond the deck. I try to move out from behind Ryker, but he holds me steadily behind him.

"Who's there?" I ask.

There is no answer, but a chill creeps over me. I instinctively know who it is.

"It's okay," I whisper in Ryker's ear.

He leans his head in my direction, and I can see the yearning in his eyes. He wishes I wasn't fine. He wishes he could protect me. He wishes I wouldn't say it's okay for Beckett to come back into my life.

I'm not saying any of those things, though. I'm not letting Beckett back into my life. I'm just saying I won't let him hurt me again. He can't hurt me again. I won't let him. But I plan on hurting him plenty for what he did to me.

Slowly I move out from behind Ryker. He tenses, the muscles in his back rippling to hold me back, but I gently shake my head and step around him. I'm not going to face Beckett again while ducking behind another man. I'm going to face him face to face.

"You going to show yourself? Or hide in the shadows like a coward?" I ask, my voice full of sass.

Chuckles ring out, but they don't belong to Beckett.

I smirk as I see Hayes, Gage, and Lennox step into the light from the deck.

"You might want to put the gun down, Princess, if you expect Beckett to show his face. We all know your motto of shooting first and asking questions later. We all know you'll shoot his balls off," Hayes teases, walking up the deck like he's my best friend.

He comes in for a hug, and I let him wrap around me. I relish his touch. I've forgotten how much I consider them friends.

"And he would deserve it," I say.

Hayes shrugs. "Yea, but then you'd be sad because you still secretly want his cock."

I growl.

Hayes laughs and then lounges on one of the chairs on the deck like he's ready to watch a good show.

Lennox greets me next. "Give him hell, Princess," he whispers into my ear when he hugs me.

I nod.

Lastly, Gage embraces me. "But not too much hell, Princess. He has a story to tell, as I suspect you do too. That story might change your heart quite a bit."

I frown.

"Why do you let them call you Princess, but I can't?" Ryker asks.

"There's no controlling these dogs," I say with a huff.

"That, and we have an intimate relationship with Princess," Hayes says.

I roll my eyes. He's just trying to get Beckett riled up.

Ryker tilts his head and raises his dark eyebrows at me.

I shrug. "I've fucked them. Actually, I fucked them all at the same time." I grin brightly, not ashamed of it in the least. It was still one of the most erotic moments of my life if you exclude my experiences with Beckett. And I do—I want to forget all my times with Beckett.

"We'd be happy to repeat the performance, Princess," Hayes says.

I glance over to see Lennox and Gage looking at me with heat in their eyes. My core heats at the thought. It's probably exactly what I need to get over Beckett.

Instead, I turn and look out into the darkness. "Still a coward, I see."

After a beat, I see his shadow move.

My throat tightens up, and every emotion possible overtakes me when I see him. I avoid his eyes, not wanting to see how he feels when he looks at me. Instead, I examine the rest of him.

His jeans hug his thick muscular legs. His black shirt is tight against his body, but I can't tell if there is any blood or dirt on it. I suspect that's why he is almost always wearing dark shirts. There is no gun or weapon in his hand. He stands like an easy target in front of me. Oh, how easy it would be to shoot him in the balls as Hayes said.

I smile at that thought, even though I won't.

Actually, I might.

But then I look at his face. The hardness, the sadness, the emptiness. The look of longing, and want, and desire. It's all there in his brown pupils. He doesn't have to say a word for me to see his pain. He doesn't have to move a muscle. I know.

Then why?

Why?

Why?

Why?

Why did you try to kill me?

Why did you go back to her?

Why did you choose her over me?

And why come back to hurt me all over again?

I tear my eyes from him and look at the others.

"Where are Caius and Odette?"

Lennox snickers. "We left them tied up in the cabin by the lake."

My eyes widen. "What? Why?"

"That's what happens when you lie to everyone," Gage responds.

I frown, completely confused.

I look over to Beckett to see if his face will confirm or deny the facts. His expression doesn't change. He just stares at me like I'm breath itself.

It doesn't change anything, even if it's true. I don't understand what Caius and Odette did to piss them off, but I suspect they are safe. Beckett might be pissed with his wife for running all this time, but she had her reasons—reasons I can understand better than anyone.

Ryker is still gripping his gun, but it's now aimed down at his side. He's ready to step in if I need him.

My gun, on the other hand, is aimed at Beckett. He doesn't flinch when I move the gun. In fact, I'd say his sad eyes are begging me to shoot him to put him out of his misery. That would be too easy, though.

"What are you doing here, Beckett?" I ask, lowering my gun and putting it into the back of my joggers.

If I spill any of his blood, it will be with my bare hands, not a gun.

He doesn't answer me. He just looks at me, and I swear he's holding his breath. There is no smart comment. No 'I'm here to beg for forgiveness.' No 'can we talk in private away from all of these guys.' Nothing.

I bite my bottom lip down so hard in frustration I swear I draw blood.

"Did you lose your vocal cords in a fight, or are you just not going to talk to me?"

Beckett is silent.

I don't know what game he's playing, but it appears he isn't going to talk to me.

Fine.

If he wants to act childish, then fucking fine.

I don't know what he's doing here if he won't talk to me.

I turn toward the guys, hoping they have answers.

Gage is frowning at Beckett.

Lennox rolls his eyes with a soft smile.

Hayes has a shit-eating grin on his face.

And Ryker looks as lost as I am.

I have no idea what to do.

But I have so much pent-up anger inside, so much rage. And my chest—every pump of my heart fills it with pain, and it's all because of him.

"You were going to kill me," I say, my voice shaky and my palms sweaty. "You were going to shoot me in the head in front of every-one." My voice is stronger this time.

I turn back and look full on at Beckett. His hand is in his pocket, and he doesn't flinch at my words. His lips don't part to argue back, so I continue.

"You manipulated me, played me because you thought you could pull a confession out of me. You thought I was responsible for your *wife's* death."

I take a deep breath. "All you had to do to find out the truth was ask. You could have shown me the fucking evidence and seen if I could have explained what the hell happened."

I feel a tear in the corner of my eye, but I don't let it out. I refuse to show him how much he hurt me.

"Odette is alive. I didn't kill her. In fact, I helped her. I'm sorry that by helping her, I hurt you. But if you truly love her, you can't blame her for doing what was best for her. And you can't blame me for helping the woman you love," my voice cracks.

I can see the guys out of the corner of my eye stare at me in confusion. But this speech isn't for them; it's for Beckett.

"And yet, you come here and don't apologize. You don't even have the balls to speak to me. I hate you! I fucking hate you." My tear slips out, dammit.

I'm out of breath.

I'm exhausted from not sleeping well.

And I hate myself as much as I hate him.

Because I still love the bastard.

He's not mine, he's hers, but I still love him. I want the best for him. I couldn't shoot him even if I wanted to.

I have to stop loving him.

He's not mine.

He never will be.

It's not going to be easy, but I have to start the process of healing. There is only one way to stop the bleeding.

I turn to Ryker, who is looking at me with sad puppy dog eyes. I grab the back of his neck and jerk his lips to mine. It's a harsh, messy kiss. Our lips barely meet. I'm kissing his cheek as much as I am his lips, but I don't care.

Beckett probably thinks I'm doing this as revenge or punishment for what he did to me. But this is all for me.

I need to move on from Beckett.

I need to stop thinking about him every second of every day. Stop pining for him. Stop believing in the fairytale that one of us will win the games, and we will live happily ever after together.

We are nothing but toxic destruction to each other. He may not have a heart that he ever gave me, but mine is demolished, broken beyond repair. It may never work properly again, but I have to try. I deserve to try. I deserve to be happy. I deserve so much more.

This kiss is the start of that recovery.

I need a night to forget about Beckett. A night to feel alive again. A night to hope.

I expect Ryker to pull away. He's already kissed me and told me he isn't the man for me.

He doesn't pull away, though.

Beckett doesn't attack us or say anything.

The other guys just watch intently like they wish they were the ones being kissed.

Ryker grabs the back of my neck and tilts me back as his tongue slips roughly inside mine. It's hot and thick in my mouth and not a bit gentle.

Thank heavens for that. I don't need gentle. I need rough animal sex to make me forget. I need to forget the man standing not twenty feet from me that I thought was the one I've been looking for my entire life.

Ryker's other hand moves to my hip as he pulls me roughly against him. My breath catches in my throat as he begins moving his hand up from my waist to underneath the hem of my shirt.

His thumb strokes my bare stomach, and I shiver. I move to pull away, thoughts of why I shouldn't do this starting to sneak in, but he sucks on my bottom lip, sending an unending wave of pleasure through my body, and I no longer want to disengage.

As great as Ryker is, though, he's not enough. Not nearly enough.

Not when Beckett is right there.

Not when I want to run to him and tear his clothes off and attack him. I don't care that he's married. I don't care that he loves another woman. I don't—

Fuck, I have to stop.

I grab the neck of Ryker's shirt as I start guiding us backward.

I will not look at Beckett.

I will pretend he doesn't exist.

I will think of all the other hot guys on this deck.

I will think of all the other incredible guys in the world.

That's my mantra as Ryker and I walk to the center of the three other guys who have been watching us kiss wordlessly.

I pull my lips off Ryker. He protests, trying to pull my lips back against his, but I hold up one finger to his lips. Then I turn a heated gaze on the three guys sitting on the deck.

I don't say a word, but they all know what I'm asking—the same thing I asked of them before.

The reasoning this time is different. Last time it was about defying my father and giving myself control. This time it's about moving on, but both times are about saving myself.

I turn my attention back to Ryker as I kiss him once again. I'm not sure if any of the guys are going to answer my request. They have their boss to consider this time. I gave them all an open invitation, but it's up to them.

Hayes is the first to accept my invitation. He gets up from his seat and comes up behind me, sweeping my hair off the back of my neck and kissing me in the nook at the base of my neck.

I gasp as shockwaves burst through me.

I see Ryker eye Hayes, and for a moment, I think Ryker might protest sharing me. If he does, he can leave. This is about me and my needs. If he isn't up for sharing, then he can suffer alone.

Ryker doesn't say anything or seem upset as he nibbles back on my bottom lip. Suddenly he spins me around until I'm facing Hayes.

Hayes grins down at me. "I always knew someday you'd ask for seconds." Quickly his lips crash down on mine. He tastes like bubblegum and smells like citrus. He kisses lazily like he knows he doesn't have to try hard to get my panties wet. And he doesn't. His kisses are fantastic—just enough tongue, just enough pressure, just about enough.

Ryker takes Hayes's former spot behind me until I'm trapped

between two hard bodies. Ryker nibbles on my earlobe, and I buck as his teeth scrape.

Jesus, they're going to kill me. What did I get myself into?

I want to glance over at Beckett to see what he's doing. I'm about to break away and do just that when Lennox stands, blocking any view I would have had.

His eyes glaze with need as he walks toward me with a serious expression. Before he even gets to me, Hayes has spun me towards Lennox. Lennox catches me and dips me back as his lips take a turn with my mouth. His might be the most aggressive kiss of any of them so far. It takes my breath away, and I barely have a chance to breathe in his scent. It's musky and manly, and just how I knew he'd smell.

Lennox lifts me back up and spins me back around. His hand palms my breast as I arch into him.

"Take it back. Take it all back. Your pride. Your strength. Your heart. Take it all back, Princess," he demands into my ear.

I purse my lips, barely able to breathe, before Gage steps in front of me and demands his turn. His kiss is the softest and most tender. His kiss gives me time to breathe, but not enough to think.

Then Gage takes my hand and leads me forward. I look down and see the others have pulled a coffee table from inside out onto the deck. They've laid a thick blanket and pillow on top.

I bite on my bottom lip as I stare at the scene in front of me. Thoughts of the last time I let four men have their way with me rush through my head.

Gage releases my hand and puts his hands in his pockets as he watches me make my decision. They all do. Hayes is the only one who raises an eyebrow in challenge.

I smirk at him, knowing this is how I take my heart back. I fuck them—all of them.

They are all great guys, but I probably won't fall in love with any of them. I'm not sure any of them would want me to anyway.

Next time I fall in love, I won't fall easily. But this isn't about falling in love. This is about taking back my heart.

I take a step toward the coffee table and then lie down on my back on top of the blanket and pillow. My heart is beating a million miles a minute, my breath is too fast, and I'm sure they all think I'll back out at any second. But I won't, I need this.

Then I make a conscious decision—one for my benefit, not his. I look at Beckett and take back my heart.

9

BECKETT

I DON'T SPEAK when I see Ri.

I thought I'd have an endless stream of words to say. I thought I'd apologize, be down on my knees begging for forgiveness. I thought I'd try explaining the truth of what happened. I would explain, show her the video, beg, and plead.

I'd tell her how I feel about her.

I'd tell her that I love her, not Odette. Not any other woman—her. It's always been her. I've never loved like I love her. She's my equal in every way.

And then I saw Ri. I saw her standing next to Ryker. I saw her, and I knew that I had no right to speak. No right to beg for forgiveness. No right to plead down on my knees.

Ri had every right to her anger.

Every right to want to murder me for what she thinks I've done.

And any words I said wouldn't matter. Not until she got out what she needed to say, so I gave her the floor. I let her speak. If I had even said one word, I wouldn't have been able to stop myself from crumbling to the ground in apology. So I kept silent.

Listening to her words was torture. I could feel her pain with every syllable.

I stood still, knowing if I moved I'd break. My heart was just as broken as hers, but I'm not as strong, not nearly as strong as her.

She doesn't realize it—that she holds my heart in her hands, but she will. She'll stab it the first chance she gets, but I don't care. As long as she realizes it's hers, and it will always be hers.

So I keep silent.

I just watch and endure.

And endure I do because Ri doesn't stop at just yelling at me. No, she has to punish me even further by kissing Ryker. And Hayes, and Lennox, and Gage...

Every kiss is a bullet through my heart. I have no idea how I'm still standing, still breathing, still fucking alive. Probably because Ri deserves to torture me until my very last breath.

But then she does something I know I won't survive. She lies down on the coffee table in the middle of four horny assholes, laying her body out for them to do what they want with it.

Fucking hell.

Someone just shot me now. My fist twitches wanting to go punch every single man surrounding her. Most are supposed to be my friends, only one my enemy. But some friends they are if they are willingly kissing and touching what's mine.

They know how I feel, and they are still going to do this. If I somehow survive this, I'm going to kill them all for this.

And then Ri looks at me, the first time since she started kissing Ryker. There's a change in her eyes. This isn't about me. This isn't about punishing me. This is about her.

About her needs.

Her taking back control.

Her finding her strength.

Her becoming whole again.

My chest tightens at the sight—how fucking incredible a sight it is. My eyes widen in wonder as I look at her. Ri isn't one to back down in defeat. She always rises back up—always.

I will too.

If I'm her equal, I have to become stronger. I have to stop putting my feelings above hers. I have to become more.

I wish I could give her an encouraging word, a smile, something that shows that I'm not only okay with her doing this, but I encourage it. All I can muster is a solemn nod.

I'm not as strong as you, Fighter, but I will be. I'll have to be.

Then she looks back at Hayes, who is standing between her legs. Ryker is on one side, Lennox on the other, and Gage is by her head.

I can do this. I can do this. I can do this.

Gage kisses her upside down as Ryker and Lennox each palm a breast. Hayes kisses over her pants between her legs.

Fuck, I can't do this.

I'm sweating and jittery and want to disappear into a puddle on the floor rather than watch this.

But then Ri lets out a throaty moan. For some reason, that single syllable calms me. It also stirs my dick, but it washes through me like a warm drink.

Ri needs this to reclaim herself.

I can't give her what she needs right now, but they can.

Ryker lifts her shirt up, exposing her tight abs. He kneels next to her and kisses each rippling muscle, worshipping her body like she deserves. Now I realize my role—ensure they treat her right. Treat her better than I ever have. If they hurt her, I'll step in. Otherwise, I'll watch from the darkness.

Gage lifts her shirt all the way off.

Silence stretches as all the men admire her bare torso. She's not wearing a bra; all that remains is her pajama pants.

I can barely see her body from my angle, but it's enough for me to vow I'll never hurt her ever fucking again. I'd say she looks like an angel, but I know she's anything but an angel. She's a skilled warrior capable of defending herself against anything.

Lennox and Ryker take no time devouring her nipples with their mouths. Her back arches into them, and soft moans are pulled from her lips. Gage lets a few escape before he plants his lips over her mouth, muffling the sound a little.

Hayes continues to kiss gently over her pants but doesn't move to take them off.

I focus on her eyes. They come alive with each kiss and touch of one of the men. She doesn't look at me, and I don't expect her to. This is about her, not me, but damn do I want her to look at me. Selfishly, I want to see the full pleasure she's feeling reflected in her eyes.

She hasn't had much pleasure in her life, so I'm grateful for every drop of it she'll experience, even if it's not me giving it to her.

"Please," I hear her beg. "Please, I need more."

Her eyes are locked on Hayes, who chuckles back at her.

"So needy, Princess," he responds, hooking his fingers under the waistband of her pants and then pulling, yanking them off her body in one fluid motion. And then she's completely bare to them.

Her skin glows under the moonlight, and I'm thankful for how private this backyard is. I can barely stand that these four men get to see her body.

She's not yours. She can do what she likes with her body.

I just hope someday I'm worthy of her again. Even if I hadn't royally fucked everything up, I'm still not sure I would be worthy, but I'm going to try every day.

Hayes kneels between her legs, and every other man's movement slows, letting her focus all of her attention on him. Their eyes lock, and they both lick their lips at the same time. Her chest rises and falls, and I swear his does too at the same time. They are perfectly in sync. He knows exactly what she needs.

He lowers his head between her legs, never losing eye contact with her. He's giving her complete control. Just before his tongue reaches that apex between her legs, she nods slightly, giving him all the permission he needs.

He licks up her slit, so slowly I think it's going to take all night. At that moment, there's a connection that beams off of Ri. It's like she's connected to all of us at that moment. We'd all do anything for her. She has that effect on men. It could be why so many of us want her, will fight to the death for her.

But I'm the only one willing to give my soul up to her. I'm not touching her, not kissing her like the others, but I know the moment she feels my vow hit her through the darkness in a delicious shiver up her spine.

I vow to love you forever.

I vow to be worthy.

I vow to give you my heart and soul.

Even if you don't choose me, I'm yours.

She doesn't have to look at me to know she feels it. She closes her eyes as the guys devour her, just enjoying the moment.

She reaches out to them, trying to touch them, to undo their pants, to give them a little of the pleasure they are giving to her.

Each of them slowly swats her hand away, kissing her palms, stopping her from touching them. This isn't about them—this is all her. That or they think I'll murder them if they sink their dicks into her.

Hayes slips two fingers inside her, his tongue flicking over her clit.

Come, baby, come for them. Take back your heart, your strength, your everything. Take my heart, my soul, my very existence along with it.

She bites her lip as she writhes between their touches. Her body shakes slightly, but she doesn't come yet. They all intensify their actions. They stroke her faster, suck her harder. She's close but not there yet.

With one word, I could make her come at this moment, but she has to find it herself. She has to let go of all the pain I and every other man in her life have caused her and take herself back.

She needs to recapture every bit of control and every bit of who she is.

She inches closer but still doesn't come.

The guys try harder, but it's not about what they are doing—it's about her. She's the only one who can control if she can come or not.

Come, Fighter.

Then, almost as if she'd been holding back to spite them all, she glances my way, and I see sharp daggers in her eyes a second before she looks up at the sky. Like the goddess she is, she explodes like a shooting star across the sky.

The sound she makes vibrates through the night air and shoots through my chest. It breaks me and heals me at the same time. Her sound is pure hell and heaven. It's every emotion she's ever felt wrapped up in one sound.

The guys step back from her as she comes. None of them can take their eyes off of her. They all just watch incredulously at the woman they just worshipped. A woman who should be broke and battered just reclaimed her power.

Everyone is silent, not sure what to do next. Ri stands, not the least bit concerned with her nakedness. She struts inside the house with all of us drooling after her.

We all stare for a moment, and then Ryker breaks the silence. "Damn man, how were you ever foolish enough to hurt that woman?"

I sigh. "Because I'm a fucking idiot."

I FELT like a goddess coming under the moonlight and stars. It felt freeing to be touched by four guys at once without them wanting anything in return from me. If I'm not careful, I'm not going to be able to come without multiple men worshipping me.

I chuckle.

I've only made it just inside the house. The lights are off inside, so they can't see me. I touch my bottom lip as I think about what I just did.

Again.

This is the second time I've had multiple guys fuck me at once.

And yet, all I want is one.

I take a deep breath, my lungs rising and slamming down in my ribcage. I feel better than I have in days. From the orgasm, from making Beckett watch, from making him suffer. He may not love me, but he definitely didn't like me shoving that in his face.

I'm not healed. I'm not magically fixed, but damn do I feel better—stronger and in more control.

I watch the guys for a second longer before I head up the stairs. I fall into bed, not bothering to shower or wipe their scent off of me. I just collapse and sleep for the first time in days.

———

I wake up to see it's still pitch-black outside—so much for a long, refreshing sleep.

I sigh and pad to the bathroom to pee, hoping I'll be able to fall back asleep afterward. The second my feet hit the ground, though, I realize my waking has nothing to do with a full bladder. I have unfinished business with a certain someone, and it needs finishing —now.

I wrap a robe from the closet around me, put my gun in the pocket, and then head downstairs. It's early in the morning, but I might as well make myself a cup of coffee to wait for him to wake up.

I make it down the stairs, and the hairs on my arms stiffen— Beckett's awake.

I consider running back upstairs and pretending to sleep, but I won't cower. I need to face him. I got my strength back; now I have to deal with reality. I'm sure he came here for answers, needing them as badly as I do.

He wants to know why I helped Odette, why I lied to him. I need to know why he was going to kill me, but not after taking my heart and soul and everything I am. He could have just killed me without making me fall for him.

I walk to the kitchen and see him sitting with his back to me at the circular table, staring out the back window. His back straightens when he hears my footsteps and feels that it's me.

He doesn't say anything.

Neither do I.

I walk to the kitchen to make a pot of coffee, not because I really want the caffeine, but just to have something to fidget with before talking to him. Once I hear him say he loves Odette, his wife, I'll crumple—not fully, not all the way again, but it will be hard to hear that he'll forever be out of my life.

I get to the coffee maker and see a pot already made.

I sigh—so much for that plan. I pour myself a cup and turn to face the man I will probably always love.

He doesn't turn around. He lets me come to him.

I take a seat opposite him, staring down at my coffee. After a few breaths, I finally look up.

He looks broken but not as shattered as I'd hoped. His eyes are puffy; his entire face looks swollen like he hasn't slept in weeks. His hair is disheveled, and his clothes are wrinkly, like he hasn't changed in days. Somehow, he's still the best-looking guy I've ever seen.

Earlier, he didn't talk, but I have no doubt he will now. He was letting me get everything off my chest before, and he knew there was no use talking to me until I had gotten out every emotion I was harboring.

Now that I did, and we're alone, he'll talk. Somehow that makes me more nervous. My hands begin trembling around the coffee mug.

"Why are you here?" I finally get out. I need to hear him talk. I need to hear that he loves her, that it has always been her.

The croak that initially leaves his throat is my first clue that he's as anxious as me. "I'm not sure you're ready to hear the answer to that question yet."

I frown. "I wouldn't have asked if I wasn't ready to hear it," I snap.

"Well, I guess I'm not ready to answer it yet."

I shake my head; maybe we aren't going to be civil. "You made me fall in love with you. You took my heart, my soul, fucking everything. And then you dragged me in front of the Retribution Kings, tied me to a pole, and were about to shoot me for a crime I didn't commit. You didn't once ask me about what you found. Didn't give me a chance to explain myself. Didn't give me a chance to tell you that I was helping Odette, that I saved her. Your plan was always to kill me in front of everyone, regardless of what I did or said." I catch my breath and glare at him. "You could have just killed me; you didn't have to be so cruel as to make me love you first."

"You love me?"

I roll my eyes. "Not really the point." I'm not about to tell him flat out that I love him to his face, not after what he did.

He rubs his head, the muscles in his bicep flexing.

"Tell me," he says.

"What?"

"Tell me what I didn't give you the chance to say before. Tell me what you did for Odette."

He doesn't deserve an explanation, but I want to get everything off my chest and be done with him after this conversation.

"I was running from a man named Kek."

Beckett doesn't react. I assume he'll yell at me for not telling him who my stalker was earlier when I knew his name, but he doesn't. His face remains neutral and impassive, so I clarify. "Kek is the man who has been stalking me."

He nods slowly but doesn't say anything. No veins bulge on his head; his cheeks don't turn red; he just waits patiently for me to continue.

Huh?

"Vincent hired Kek to be my bodyguard and companion. He wasn't much older than me, so Vincent thought we would get along."

Beckett doesn't ask any questions. He's completely patient, giving me the floor. It feels strange, almost like I'm telling the story to myself.

"At first, Kek did his job. He helped Vincent train me on how to defend myself, how to wield a gun. He and Vincent taught me everything I know." I swallow down the part of me that feels grateful to two men who helped give me the skills to protect myself while also offering me up as a complete sacrifice.

"Kek came up with this idea one day to help protect me. He thought that if I could self-hypnotize, then even if the worst happened and I was kidnapped and tortured, at least I could be ordered to forget the pain."

Beckett's eyes widen, and his nostrils flare at that, but he still doesn't speak.

"So for years, he worked on that with me. He helped me learn how to hypnotize myself, to help me forget things in case I needed to for my own sanity. It worked. In order for my mind to forget, all I need is a single phrase whispered in my ear."

Beckett leans in.

"No, I'm not going to tell you that phrase."

He smirks and shakes his head.

"But somewhere along the line, Kek no longer became my friend or protector. Maybe he never was. I was too young to do much about him at first. But eventually, Vincent realized Kek's intentions had changed and fired him. He would have killed him, but he vanished, and that was good enough for Vincent."

Beckett's throat bobs up and down, and I can see the question in his eyes.

"Ask me," I say, knowing what he wants to ask.

"Did he—did he rape you? Abuse you?"

"Not in that way, no. But he did hurt me."

The veins in Beckett's arms pop as his hand fists. I can feel rage rippling off him.

"I was running from Kek the day of your wedding. He's the one man who scares me. He's the one man who knows the phrase that can control my mind, make me forget. He knows my physical skills—my strengths and weaknesses. As much as I want to face him, I can't. So I ran and ended up crashing your wedding." I wince. "Sorry about that."

He shakes his head. "Don't be."

"That night, I was hiding in the hotel when I ran into Odette during the reception. I saw terror and fear in her eyes. I didn't know who she was running from, but I knew it was the same fear I was harboring. I told her I'd help her, so I did."

I meet Beckett's gaze, unsure of how he's going to react. He looks heartbroken. I may have helped Odette, but I also caused him so much pain while he endured her being gone, thinking she would never come back.

My own chest tightens, thinking about the suffering he went through. It's the same heartbreak I feel now. He must have felt so betrayed.

He deserves to hear the rest.

"I hid in your hotel suite, hoping to god I wouldn't have to hear any newlywed sex." I wince, remembering them coming into the room. The sounds of their laughs, their kisses—they sounded so fucking happy. My heart swelled listening while also feeling like I was invading a very private moment.

"And then you left to go get her bag. We had limited time before we knew you'd return. We knew there was a video camera, so we had to make it look real while also not seriously hurting Odette so she could run."

I close my eyes, remembering it all clearly now.

"I used a knife. I sliced her skin. Her screams were real. I hated hurting her, but it was the only way. She had a bag of her blood I burst against her chest. That's where most of the blood came from, not from any real wound I inflicted.

"I tied her up, and then she had me call a number for her. I don't know who the men were that helped her escape, but my job was done. Before I left, I knew I could offer her one last thing. I wasn't sure what my future held. I knew that the same dangerous people that were after me could have been after her. If they caught me, I might tell them the truth about Odette—that she wasn't dead."

My throat closes up, thinking about how desperate Odette was at that moment. "So I told Odette my greatest secret."

Beckett leans so far forward in his chair over the table that he might as well be sitting directly in front of me with no table in front of us. He holds his breath as he waits.

"I told her the phrase that would make me forget. She used it. I forgot. Then I ran into Kek in the hallway. His knife cut into my skin, mixing Odette's blood with my own. Helping her almost got me caught, but my adrenaline must have been high because I fought him off and got to the elevator before he could follow me. That's when I ran into you."

We stare at each other across the empty table, lost in each others' eyes, knowing this might be the last time we sit like this. I don't know if his feelings were ever real toward me, but mine certainly were.

This is the last time I'll let myself feel any glimmer of love for him. After today, I'll lock it all away. When I hear about him and Odette living happily ever after, I won't secretly be pining for him from a distance.

I beg Beckett to speak first. I'm not sure I can say another word. I'm not sure I can bear my heart for much longer. He needs to say his peace. He needs to finish breaking my heart. And then he needs to leave me, forever.

"Please," I whisper so quietly I'm not sure he can hear me. There's a tear at the corner of my eye, but I refuse to release it until he's gone.

Beckett takes a long time to respond, his face looking like he's about to shatter right along with me. He opens his mouth and closes it so many times that he begins to look like a fish to me. It slightly lifts my mood.

Finally, he says, "I don't love Odette."

LISTENING to Ri's truth broke me. She's so selfless, so strong, so determined. I don't know how it was possible for me not to fall in love with her for so long. I don't know how I could have ever loved anyone else.

It's why there's a damn competition to win her. Men want her not just because they get her father's kingdom but because they get her—a strong, fearless fighter. A woman that looks like a princess and fights like a warrior. She's everything I've wanted and everything I never knew I wanted.

I hate myself for making her feel like I didn't love her, like I'd ever choose another.

"I think I just had a hallucination. Can you repeat what you said?" Ri asks.

I sigh.

She's not going to believe me, just like I don't believe Odette. Ri's story matches Odette's, but I know I'm still missing a piece of the puzzle. I need to talk to my brother. I need to figure out the truth, but I need Ri more.

"I don't love Odette," I repeat firmly, so there is no mistaking my words.

Ri blinks, her only reaction.

"I don't know if my marriage to Odette is still legal, but if it is, I'm filing for divorce today."

Another blink.

"I don't believe Odette's story, not fully. I can fill you in later on the rest of the details she shared with me, but I don't believe her."

Double blink.

"I believe you, Ri, every word."

Her mouth falls open, but then she snaps it shut. Two more times, she repeats the action until she's starting to look like a shocked fish.

I smile at her.

"Ask me again."

Color seems to return to her face, and her eyes water.

"Ask me again," I repeat.

She clears her throat. "Why are you here?"

"I'm here to win you back."

"You tried to kill me. I'm not sure you can win me back."

"Except I didn't. I didn't try to kill you."

She crosses her arms across her chest, and her face turns defensive. "You most certainly did. You dragged me into that arena. You tied me to a pole, showed the evidence on the big screen, and then you aimed a gun at my head."

"I didn't." I rub the back of my neck, knowing she won't believe me, but I have to try. I'll keep trying every day until she does finally believe me.

She racks her memory, trying to remember that night. I'm sure most of her memories are foggy after whatever that bastard Kek did to her mind, so I explain as simply as I can.

"In order to become the leader of the Retribution Kings, I was given a final task—get retribution for Odette. Everyone has to get retribution in order to join. It's the final act of initiation."

I bite my tongue, not wanting to say the next part. This is going to get worse before I can make it better.

"The task wasn't a problem at first. I assumed it was your father; everyone did. That is until I found the video of you."

"The video that didn't show the whole truth and that you never once showed to me or asked me about?"

I nod slowly at her anger. "Yes, at first, I thought it was true. I was angry. I wanted to end your life then and there for what you did, but then I studied the video more. If you had wanted Odette dead, you would have ended her life swiftly. She was no match for you. The fight was long and drawn out, and all of her wounds were superficial, not enough to cause the amount of blood we found."

She frowns, her eyes narrowing at me, not understanding what I'm saying.

"So I had Gage dig deeper. He found the truth, but by then, it was too late. I was out of time."

"How were you out of time?"

"If I didn't complete my final initiation task, they would kill me."

She gasps. She cares about me far more than I deserve.

"The problem was I didn't have much proof other than my gut. What Gage found wasn't enough to prove to the room full of people that you didn't hurt Odette, not when Caius was filling their heads with lies."

"I'm confused. You tied me to that pole. You were going to kill me even knowing that I didn't kill Odette?"

"No," I say firmly.

"No?"

"No, I had a plan. Gage, Hayes, and Lennox. I brought you there, knowing Odette would show herself. Gage tracked her to town. The plan was to play on Odette's emotions. I figured Odette would still have feelings for me, and she wouldn't let me die."

Ri frowns, still not understanding.

"When it came time, I turned the gun on myself since they were going to kill me anyway. I was never going to shoot you, though. And I figured if I threatened my own life, Odette would show herself. I was right."

Ri's eyes are big, and her breath is finally calm. "And if you were wrong?" she whispers.

"Then I would have shot myself. The guys knew their job was to get you out of there and take you wherever you wanted to go. They were to help you run, to get free."

"But..." She bites her lip and tucks the robe tighter around her body. "But you'd be dead?"

I nod. "Better than you being dead."

She blinks rapidly, trying to process everything I just said. I didn't try to kill her; I saved her. I don't love Odette.

"This can't be the truth," Ri whispers.

"It is." I want to say more—how much I love her, how much it's her that I want, that I would die for—only her.

I'm not sure she's ready to hear that yet. I'm not even sure she believes me or even can.

Then she looks up, and I see tears spilling down her cheeks.

I frown, not understanding why she's crying. I can't stand the distance anymore, though, so I jump out of my seat and run around the table to her. I yank her chair back and kneel between her legs. Looking up at her, I watch tears roll off her chin and drip down onto me.

"Fighter, why are you crying?"

She shakes her head, the tears falling faster now. "You're a bastard."

I frown. "I mean, I am, but I thought you would at least appreciate the 'me saving your life' part." I try to smile, try to make her stop crying.

"Not for that, although you should have told me the truth."

"That my dead wife that I suspected you of killing was, in fact, alive, although I couldn't figure out why you didn't just tell me or why my wife was on the run, and I couldn't make sense of my feelings or yours? Which part should I have told you?"

She hiccups. "I'm mad at you for not spilling your guts the second you showed up tonight. For letting me—" she gulps. "Letting me fuck four guys in front of you. That had to have been torture for you."

I grin. "It was torture, but mostly because I wanted to join them. It didn't hurt me that you were doing that. We've made no commitment toward each other—no vows, no promises. And in this world, I'm not sure we will ever be able to make promises, but that doesn't stop us from having feelings."

"I still don't understand why you let me fuck them."

"Technically, you didn't fuck them. They pleasured you, and I knew you needed it. You needed to get your anger out. You needed to heal your broken heart. You needed to know that you were strong enough without me or any other man. That way, if I'm lucky enough to have you choose me someday, it will be because you want me, not because you need me."

She touches my face, her hand caressing my cheek. I close my eyes and lean into the soft touch.

"I wasn't sure if you were ever going to touch me like this again," I whisper.

"I wasn't sure either."

Then she grabs my chin roughly to force our visions to meet, her eyes like fire. "Don't ever hide shit from me again. And don't ever push me to fuck other guys so I can get over you. I love you, you bastard. But I'm going to be pissed at you for a long, long time."

I grin like the fool I am—a fool completely and entirely in love with this woman.

"I love you too, my fighter." We still have a lot of truth left to tell each other, so much history that needs to be shared and blood that needs to be spilled. A wife and Retribution Kings need dealing with. A game is still lingering, and we need to figure out how to win or escape to be together.

All that matters right now is this moment. We love each other. When I kiss her, that's the only thought on my mind.

I LOVE YOU—THOSE words ring in my head over and over. Lucy has said she loved me a few times, but I don't recall Vincent ever saying those words to me—or any other man for that matter.

I never knew how good it could feel.

"Say it again," I beg.

"I love you, Ri." He kisses the corner of my mouth.

"I love you, Princess." He kisses down my neck.

"I love you, Fighter." He kisses open my robe.

I gasp, my head falling back as he pushes the robe open.

"Your turn," he says, licking his tongue over the top swell of my breast.

"I hate you, Beckett," I say as his tongue halts to a stop.

"I hate you for letting another man touch me when you knew I was yours." I kiss the corner of his mouth.

"I hate you, Bastard, for letting me take my heart back when I gave it to you freely." I kiss down his neck.

"I hate you, Hero, for being willing to kill yourself in order to save me." I kiss over his heart.

I can hear his heart thumping slowly in his chest; each painful beat is only for me.

I kiss him hard on the lips. "I love you, Beckett, even when I shouldn't. Even when you're a married man and I'm nothing more than a prize in a game I can't win myself. I can't promise you anything. I can't promise you marriage, kids, or a life in the suburbs any more than you can promise me those things. But I can promise that no matter what happens, I'll always love you. You have my heart, and I'll protect the piece of yours that's mine with my life."

He captures my lips with his, and I melt against him. I forget everything I was thinking. I forget about how much it will hurt when I eventually lose him, either when one of us dies, when he has to return to Odette just to stay alive, or when I have to marry another man to keep him alive. Our future is going to be riddled with heartbreak and pain no matter how much we love each other.

But when he kisses me, I forget about all the pain my future holds, and I just feel him—the wetness of his tongue, the expert way he moves through my mouth, the moans he pulls from me, and the growls he makes in return.

"I'm not going to give you up. Not ever. Not for any reason. I don't know how we are going to win the game, but if I were to bet, I'd bet on us," Beckett says. "Love always wins."

I smile even though I don't believe his words.

"Kiss me," I whisper.

"I'm going to do a lot more than kiss you. You thought what the guys did to you earlier was erotic; just wait until I get through with you. You won't even consider what they did to be an orgasm," he growls.

I grin wider. There's my jealous man.

Then he lifts me up and spins me around until my ass is on the kitchen table. His eyes roam up and down my body, only covered with my robe.

"I like this—easy access," he says, flicking open the tie that's holding my robe together.

I shrug my shoulders, and the robe falls to my waist. His eyes heat at the sight of my naked body, and he bites his bottom lip, just staring at me.

I'm pretty sure I could come from that look alone. It's so fucking hot, making wetness spill between my legs.

"You're going to kill me if you don't fuck me soon," I moan.

"Then I guess we are both going to die tonight. I need to take my time with you. I need to show every part of your body how much I love it until you believe me."

"I do believe you."

He shakes his head. "You do, but it's tentative. You still think Odette is going to walk into the house, and I'm going to go run to her side."

"I don't."

"A tiny part of you does, and I don't blame you. But I'm going to change that with how I make love to you."

Chills race over my body. "No one has ever made love to me."

He cocks his head with a grin as he pushes his pants down. My eyes get hung up on my favorite appendage of his straining in my direction. "I've made love to you every time I've fucked you, and this time there will be no denying it."

Then his body covers mine as he kisses me. His lips are hot against mine as our naked bodies push against each other. My breath catches in my throat, and I know I'm losing oxygen, but I don't care. I wouldn't stop this kiss even if it meant my death.

His hand slowly works its way down my face, over my neck, along the swell of my breast, and down to the curve of my hips. Finally, his hand lands on my thigh.

"I love every part of you—every curve, every muscle, every softness, every hardness," he says.

He kisses over my throat, pulling sharp moans from me. "I love the sounds you make when I kiss you."

His mouth tenderly kisses my nipple, and then he bites down suddenly, eliciting a yelp from me and a dirty look in my eyes.

He grins playfully. "I love your feistiness."

His hand dips between my legs, feeling the wetness there. "But most of all, I love how you make me a better man. I'm not worthy of you, but I'm going to spend my life trying to become the best man I can for you."

I don't know if I should believe him. Every other time we've made promises, we end up hurting and betraying each other. Each time I've ended up hurt, but this time feels different.

When he kisses me, he's saying he won't let anything come between us ever again. I may be foolish to let him back into my heart so easily, but for a moment, we can be happy again.

"Beckett, I need...," I moan as the ache between my legs grows. I need him inside me. I need him a dozen different ways. I need him to erase every other man's touch. I need...exactly what he's fucking doing.

His fingers push inside me, filling me as his mouth teases over my breasts. My hands run over his rippling back, pressing him hard against my body, but it's not enough.

I reach between his legs, finding his hard length. At my touch, he gasps. I almost come at the sound of his emotional cry.

We lock eyes, and we know we can't wait.

I pull him toward my entrance, and he grabs my hips as he sinks inside me one inch at a time. Every inch is like he's reclaiming my heart and soul. Each inch is a surrender of his own heart and soul. He pushes in so slowly until finally, he's sheathed himself as far inside me as he can get.

My chest rises and falls quickly against his as our fingers intertwine, mirroring our bodies.

"Is this real?" I ask as his lips lower to mine.

"As real as it gets."

Then we devour each other as his hips begin to rock. My hips angle up, meeting each of his thrusts.

He said he was making love to me every other time we've fucked, but this just feels so different. It feels like a promise of forever.

We don't say the words. We don't make the vows. We don't even voice our love to the other. We just move together, our bodies doing all the talking.

Our soft moans turn louder and more carnal.

Our movements quicken uncontrollably.

Our kisses become hungry, devouring, and painful, drawing as much blood as saliva.

We're going to wake the whole house, but maybe that's the point. Beckett looks deeply into my eyes like he's opening up his soul to me. Making sure the others hear is clearly the last thing on his mind.

My mouth parts and the sounds that escape my body are unlike anything I've heard. The softest whimpers, the loudest cries, the most desperate pleas of this happiness to never end fill the kitchen.

"I don't want this to end, Fighter, but I can't hold back much longer. I'm about to fucking explode, and I need you to go with me." The veins on his forehead fill, and I can see how much he's holding back.

I don't know how he was able to put together so many words, but I can't get anything out except a whimper.

The sound must be enough for Beckett to know that I'm close. He grins, pushing his torso harder against my clit and I come undone. I don't know the exact sound I make—a combo between a wild cat and a siren—but it explodes out of me.

I take several deep breaths, trying to come down from the high of my orgasm, when I notice Beckett on top of me, just staring at me with a shit-eating grin.

"What?" I finally pant out.

He shakes his head, smiling brighter. "You're fucking incredible."

I blush. "You are too."

He kisses me tenderly, and I feel tears welling again. Beckett notices immediately. His grin turns into a stern grimace."Babe, what's wrong?"

I brush the tears off my face. "I'm just scared to lose this again."

He nods as I see similar tears in his own eyes. He doesn't promise we won't lose it again because he can't.

"I need you again," he whispers into my hair, still with his hard cock in me.

I feel my own need growing again as well. If I can't have him forever, then I want him as many times as possible today.

BECKETT

I WANT to promise her forever. I want to promise her that nothing will tear us apart, and we'll never again experience pain and loss. I want to promise her the world.

But I can't even promise her that I'll still be breathing tomorrow. The Retribution Kings may even come attack and kill me tonight. If not them, then Corsi, Ryker's men, or dozens of other groups.

She's in just as much peril. I'll do everything I can to keep her alive, but there are too many people that want to end the Corsi mafia empire. With her death, there would be no heirs, no one to inherit. The group would descend into chaos and lose all its power.

All I can promise her is now—fucking right now.

She still has doubts about my feelings toward Odette.

She is still upset about letting the others touch her when she thought the worst of me.

If I can wipe away any amount of pain or frustration, I will.

"A bed this time?" Ri asks.

I shake my head with a sly grin.

Her eyebrows raise, and she licks her lips in anticipation.

"Do you trust me?" I ask.

"I gave you my heart. Even when I pretended to take it back, it was always yours. Of course, I trust you."

I stand up, off her body still pressed against the table, pulling my cock from her. I pause for a second, enjoying the view of her spread naked in front of me—our sweat and fluids glimmer off her smooth skin.

She blushes when I slowly peruse her body. It's adorable.

I hold out my hand to her.

She takes it with a playful glint in her eyes.

As soon as she's up, I spin her back flush against my front.

She groans as I stroke down her back.

Then I kick her legs wide and press her front against the table. I grab my phone from my pants on the floor.

She yelps in surprise just like I knew she would as I press my cock between her spread legs and thrust inside her in one stroke.

"Jesus, I love you inside me," she croaks out.

I grin as I send a one-word text and then toss my phone back on the pile of our clothes. I return my gaze to her ass, focusing all my energy on her.

Thirty seconds later, the first pair of footsteps hit the kitchen floor.

The man pauses, unsure of what to do.

I grab onto Ri's hair, fisting it in a ponytail and pulling her head up. "Look up, baby."

She does and finds Ryker standing at the entrance to the hallway. His eyes are wide as he stares from her to me, his mouth agape.

He clears his throat. "I'll just go—"

"Princess, do you want him to go?" I ask, knowing she needs to decide. She felt guilty for letting them touch her, but she shouldn't. If she needs to show them how much she's mine and not theirs, then here's her chance.

The others join us a second later before she even says a word.

Gage frowns at me, unsure I should be putting on a show.

Hayes grins and crosses his arms as he leans against a door-frame. He knows exactly what this is, and he approves.

Lennox snickers and shakes his head.

"Stay," Ri gasps.

I wasn't sure if she was going to want this or not. If I talked to her about it ahead of time, she would have said no. But just like last night, when she needed them to touch her, she needs them to see she's not theirs today.

She's not mine either, though. She's Rialta Corsi—mafia princess and fierce fighter. She doesn't need any of us, but she chooses us. And right now, she's choosing me.

I need to make this quick before she loses her nerve, so I thrust hard and fast. Between my quick strokes and the added eyes on her, she'll come quick. My girl is a bit of an exhibitionist.

I'm a little overprotective, too, though. The only way I could do this is if they could see very little of her best body parts.

I grip her hair harder, knowing she likes it. I sink between her ass cheeks further and further, fucking her so hard that the table shakes.

The guys don't move. Their eyes are locked on Ri. They're all better men than me.

Her panting picks up, and I feel her tightening around my cock. She's so fucking close, and I know exactly what I want the climax to be.

"I love you, Rialta," I cry out just as she finally releases her orgasm, and I shoot my load inside her.

I may not be able to offer her a marriage, but I can at least offer her a public declaration of my love every chance I get.

"About fucking time," Hayes says with a slow clap.

I roll my eyes as I pull out of her.

I grab her robe and drape it over her before quickly yanking my pants up.

Ri takes her time pushing off the table and wrapping the robe around her. She's completely spent.

"Breakfast? Coffee?" I ask her.

Ri walks past me, straight to the kitchen.

I frown, and the others ease closer, unsure of what's next. *Did I piss her off with my little stunt? Is something else wrong?*

She can have doubts about my love for her, but I have no doubts about her love for me.

"Ri?" I ask.

Suddenly she spins and runs toward me, a kitchen knife in her hand. I'm so shocked; I don't even defend myself. The knife comes dangerously close to my heart.

"No more pretending you know what's best for me," she says, shaking the knife against my chest.

"I won't."

"No more making plans without talking to me first."

"I promise, except in life or death situations where I don't have a chance to talk to you."

She growls.

I laugh, my hand raised in front of me.

She smiles with a shake of her head. She tosses the knife into the sink before kissing me.

I drop my arm as the guys fill the kitchen.

"I don't know whether to start planning a wedding or a funeral," Lennox says.

Ri sighs. "Neither. We can't get married, not when Beckett is technically married to someone else. And Vincent would kill me if I married without his permission. And we're both too stubborn to die."

Lennox laughs at that.

Ri hops up on the corner of the counter and grabs a banana. Her robe falls open as she peels it open, revealing her glistening curves.

All eyes go to her naked body and her mouth as she starts slowly eating her banana.

The controlling, protective alpha male in me wants to rip her off the counter, carry her upstairs, and teach her about flaunting her body in front of the others. But I know that's not going to win me any points with her.

"What?" she asks, acting completely oblivious.

I raise my eyebrow, and my eyes sink into her naked flesh.

She looks down and rolls her eyes at us. "It's nothing you all haven't seen before." And then she goes back to eating her banana without a care in the world.

I half chuckle, half curse under my breath.

Ryker makes another pot of coffee while Hayes pulls out ingredients for pancakes.

Gage opens his laptop at the kitchen table, and Lennox pretends to help Hayes, although he's useless as a cook.

I walk over to Ri, about to tell her how much I miss her body already. I want us to sneak into the backyard while Hayes finishes up breakfast, but suddenly a large Great Dane comes barreling through the kitchen.

Hayes has a stack of pancakes going, and the beast goes straight for them.

"Loki, no!" Ri yells, but it's too late.

The beast has snatched the pile and taken off through the house.

Ri winces when all eyes look at her. "That's Loki. He's Lucy's guard dog."

Lucy walks into the kitchen at that exact moment. "Oh, is that what he's supposed to be? He's more like an untrainable snuggle bug."

Ri rolls her eyes as she pats my shoulder, telling me to move so she can hop off the counter.

"He lets you know if he likes someone or not. For example, we would have never trusted Ryker if it wasn't for Loki."

"Oh, so it was Loki who convinced you? And here I thought it was my charm," Ryker says.

Ri retrieves Loki, and then we are all crowded around the

animal, giving him belly rubs. Somehow the beast gets more pieces of pancake for being a 'good boy.'

"So, who are all of you?" Lucy asks.

"You've already met Beckett and Hayes. But this is Lennox and Gage," Ri says, introducing them to her.

"And you all work for?" Lucy asks suspiciously. She doesn't trust people easily, it seems, probably a smart trait.

"Me," I say, putting my arm around Ri's shoulders.

Lucy's eyes bug out. "Oh my god!" she squeals. "Are you two?" She looks back and forth between us.

"Did you not hear the racket they were making this morning? Ri's a screamer. She woke the whole damn house up," Hayes says.

Ri shoots him a scowl, which just lights him up more.

"No, I'm a deep sleeper, and this house is huge. But really? You're together? Are you getting married, because I've always wanted to be a maid of honor and I love planning weddings and—"

"Luce," Ri cuts her off with one stern word. Then Ri looks at me with a sadness I wish I could erase.

"Oh, yea, the whole game thing," Lucy says.

"Among other things," Ri says with a pause. "We are just happy to admit our love out loud. For now, that's all we can promise each other."

I take her hand and give it a squeeze.

Lucy grabs Ri's other hand. "I want to hear all the yummy details, though. Hay-boy, bring us pancakes when they are finished."

Ri flashes Hayes an apologetic look as her friend drags her outside to discuss how good I am at fucking her.

"You better hope you are as good of a fucker as you think. It would be pretty pathetic if Ri says she enjoyed us fucking her better," Hayes says.

I growl. "If you weren't in charge of food, I'd pummel your ass."

He laughs and goes back to making pancakes.

"She's a treat," Ryker says, staring at Lucy.

"Yea, she's a pain in the ass, but she's been Ri's only friend for a long time. I don't think we're getting rid of her," I say as Loki rubs up against me, begging for ear scratches. I lazily comply.

Ryker looks at me. "I know you love her, and she loves you and all of that, but she's still my responsibility to keep safe this week."

"I'll keep her safe."

"I know you will, but it sounds like you have a bigger army after you than she does. It might be best to stay apart until you've dealt with that."

I frown, not liking the idea, but it may be true. I look to Gage behind me, the one I trust the most, silently asking him for his thoughts. He just shrugs back at me.

"You can stay around and help protect her, but I'm not going anywhere. Together we can all keep her safe," I say.

Ryker nods.

"Are you really going to stay in the game, knowing that even if you win, she'll never want you?" I ask.

"I stay in the game to protect my men. As long as I show interest in Corsi's daughter and it looks like I still have a chance, he won't attack them. He'll think that my plan to take his empire involves the game and nothing more."

"Do you have a bigger plan?"

"If I do, I won't be sharing it with you."

I grin. "Fair enough. But you're willing to die for your cause?"

Ryker nods. "I am, just like you."

"Unfortunately, the men I have left to protect are very few. Most of the Retribution Kings want to see me dead."

"They'll come around. You're new blood and will do things differently. Plus, if Odette Monroe is alive—"

"She is," I confirm.

Ryker's eyes widen. "Princess was telling the truth. I thought she was hallucinating after a broken heart."

"Nope."

"Well, then I take it back. They'll never forgive you for

throwing their princess away, only to fall in love with someone else. Relationships in this world are political. They are about the joining of gangs and organizations—making power moves. They chose you because they wanted something from the Black Empire."

"They want me to destroy them."

"Ah," Ryker says.

"Any reason you can think of that the Retribution Kings would want to end the Black Empire? Kai and Enzo rarely start fights anymore, and they just stick to themselves."

Ryker thinks for a moment. "Not sure, but my guess is an old grudge. The Retribution Kings don't let any crime go unpunished no matter how long it's been. I suspect the only way for you to get back into their good graces is to pay the price for the crime committed against them."

"That would be with my death."

"Ouch, they aren't a forgiving bunch."

Lennox glares at Ryker.

"No offense, but it's true," Ryker says.

Lennox shrugs.

"Then I would suggest you find something they want more than killing you or your family. If you win and marry Ri, you get the Corsi mafia empire. That's far more valuable than anything your brother and sister-in-law have."

I nod. "But the only way to do that is to divorce Odette, for which they'll kill me. And then convince Corsi I'm worthy of it, which will be an uphill battle. Vincent doesn't think I have anything to offer."

Ryker laughs. "You're the leader of the Retribution Kings and have strong connections to the Black Empire. And you just made an alliance with me. I'd say you have plenty to offer."

"I need to make a phone call," I say, offering no other explanation as I walk out of the kitchen. I roam through the hallways until I find a private room to make my phone call.

I have my brother's number memorized. You don't leave important numbers lying around in your contacts. And you never know when you are going to need to call for help and only have access to someone else's phone.

I dial and wait and wait and wait.

It goes to voicemail.

Strange, but not completely out of the norm.

I try Kai's number.

Siren's.

Zeke's.

Liesel's.

Langston's.

No one picks up.

I send a text to Enzo saying it's urgent.

Nothing.

I frown.

Are they in the middle of a war? Is that why no one is answering? They are all locked up in a battle and can't be bothered to answer a text or call?

I run back through the house to find Gage.

"I need eyes on my brother, on his family," I say.

Gage just nods and goes to work on his computer.

I run my hand through my hair as I pace around the kitchen. My brother and his family are in trouble, and I've done nothing to help. In fact, I've made things worse by trying to stay away from my destiny. I should be there supporting them, not here, pretending I can be a leader, pretending that I'm enough to be Ri's partner.

I'm not.

I'm not a good guy.

I've fucked up more times than I can count. I've hurt my family. I've made poor judgments. And they will think Ri is just another mistake.

Ri makes eye contact with me from where she sits outside, listening to Lucy ramble. Ri nods her head every once in a while and smiles at her friend, but her eyes never leave mine. They notice the way my shoulders tense. They notice the veins struggling in my forehead. They notice my pacing.

Ri says something to Lucy, and then Ri is walking toward me. I stop moving, waiting for her to get to me. Only when her arms are wrapped around my body, do I breathe again.

"What's wrong?" she asks.

"I think my brother and his family are in trouble."

"Then we have to go help them," she doesn't hesitate.

I nod, my head resting on top of hers. I have my own problems, so does she. But it means the world to me that she'd drop everything to help my family.

Gage scowls at his screen.

"What is it?" I ask, still holding Ri tightly in my arm.

"They're fine, currently on Langston's private island."

"What do you mean they're fine? Are you sure they aren't being held captive? Are any of them missing?" I run over to stand behind the computer screen.

Gage tapped into their security system. He won't be able to stay long until Langston or the system kicks him out. I'm surprised he got anything.

But there they are—my entire family. They're sitting outside, around a fire pit. The adults are all drinking wine. The kids are mostly asleep in their parents' arms.

I do a quick count. Everyone is accounted for and safe. They don't look distressed.

And then Enzo looks right at the camera like he knows I'm watching. Like they let me get a glimpse in order to prove a point.

A second later, the feed dies.

I slump back.

Ri catches me.

She's the only thing keeping me on my feet.

They all knew I was calling, and they didn't answer.

Was Odette telling the truth? Did they hurt her? Take her?

I swallow hard against the lump in my throat, but it stays lodged.

I'm suffocating; I can't breathe.

Voices are saying words to me, but I can't register them.

I fucked up in the past. My mistake almost cost the family everything, but they said they forgave me. They said there was nothing to forgive. But I couldn't stay. I found Odette. I found a way out. But...

I blink rapidly.

What if they didn't forgive me?

I'm only Enzo's half-brother. We've only known about each other for a few years. Maybe what I did was unforgivable.

A slap stings across my cheek, and I look down at the feisty woman who inflicted the blow.

"There you are. Talk to me, Beckett. What are you thinking?" she asks, gripping my cheeks and keeping my attention firmly on her.

"I'm thinking that my brother hates me. I have no family," I say, completely defeated.

I look past her at the other guys watching me.

"Do you think Odette was telling the truth? Her crazy ass story didn't make a lick of sense," Lennox says.

I shrug. "Maybe. I don't know who or what to believe anymore."

Ryker licks his lips, deep in thought.

"What are you thinking?" I ask him.

His brow furrows. "It's just...once you become a leader, that becomes the most important thing. It comes before family, before spouses, even children. It definitely comes before half-brothers. It has to. That's how our world works.

"Enzo has to put his men, his empire, before you. You're the leader of the Retribution Kings now. It wouldn't shock me if he sent a letter to them declaring war. If I was him, I wouldn't take your call. I wouldn't talk to you unless it was in formal war negotiations."

"Actually, it's his wife Kai who is in charge," I mumble back.

"Then she made the decision. She didn't have a choice. You picked your side the second you took the crown. Now you're on opposite sides."

Fuck, I'm pretty sure Ryker is right.

I won't be getting any explanations or evidence to prove that Odette's story is false.

I look at Ri. We are completely fucked.

BECKETT FOLLOWS me to my bedroom, but I doubt there will be much sleeping tonight. It's not because we're going to have crazy animalistic sex all night, but because Beckett is a mess.

Every blood vessel in his eyes is shot, his clothes are disheveled, he hasn't taken a shower, and he's barely eaten anything all day. And he's barely talked.

I assumed it was because he doesn't trust anyone, but I'm beginning to think it's because he's hiding a sin that cuts deep.

I gently close my bedroom door and lock it as Beckett continues his pacing into my bedroom. I consider my words carefully, knowing he's close to a mental breakdown.

"Tell me why you left the Black Empire," I say.

Beckett sits on the edge of the bed, burying his face in his hand. His shoulders rise and fall violently, and I'm not sure if he's crying or just trying to catch his breath. I want to hold him, but he needs his space, too. I sit next to him on the bed and gently put my hand on his shoulder, letting him know I'm here for him.

"I can't," he eventually says.

"Why not? You can trust me."

"It's not that." He stands abruptly, pacing once again while I stay seated on the edge of the bed.

I wait for him to explain more.

"It's—I—I just can't share yet. You would think differently of me, less of me. And I just—I can't." His eyes look like he's about to spill enough tears to fill Lake Michigan. The pain he carries is overwhelming. It's more than what happened to his arm, more than what I felt when he betrayed me. He hurt someone he truly loved, possibly even killed them.

My heart breaks for him. I want to take away his pain. I want to carry some of it myself, at the very least.

"There is nothing you could say that would make me think less of you."

Beckett turns and looks at me sternly, his eyes a deep-sea of brown and agony. "This would."

"Tell me; it will make you feel better."

"I don't deserve to feel better."

I frown. "That's not true. Of course, you deserve to feel better, to not carry the pain yourself."

Beckett shakes his head. "This time, I do. It wasn't like what happened with us, Ri. I didn't protect someone I should have. They died because of me. The only reason I can even be with you is because you don't need me to protect you. I never lied when I said I can't be your hero. I'm nobody's hero."

"You're my hero, and I'm yours. Whatever happened, whatever we are going to face, we face together. But we can't do that if you don't tell me."

"It's my burden to bear."

I sigh. We are going around in circles. It's clear at the moment he won't tell me what happened. We've shared a lot of truths with each other today; maybe it's not fair to ask for more so soon.

Instead of asking again, I just sit and watch Beckett pace until he eventually talks again. "My brother wouldn't hurt me, though. None of them would."

I nod, encouraging him to say more.

"Odette has lied to me so many times. I don't believe a word she says, but I saw the video."

"Just like you saw a video of me killing Odette. You can't always believe what you see."

"Yes, but that combined with how they're reacting now… I don't know what to think." Beckett sits on the edge of the bed and then falls back in despair.

I lie down next to him as I stare at him. "Maybe your family realized that Odette was bad news, saw she was still alive, and they questioned her with the intent to return her to you. Maybe they rescued her and were about to return her to you. Maybe there's an explanation that makes sense."

"Maybe, but whatever the reason is, they should have told me, or they should have answered my call to explain to me now."

I rest my hand on his chest; he's right. So much pain could be avoided if we were all just a little more open and trusting with each other.

"What do we do now?" I ask.

"We win the game. We find a way to destroy the Retribution Kings from within. And then I talk to my brother and find out the truth."

I nod. It's all we can do, but even though our future seems bleak, it still hurts that he didn't mention us. There was no mention of us together. I don't care if we get married. I don't care if we have to be kings and queens of a criminal organization and rule together or if we run away and hide out at the end of the earth. It makes no difference to me; I just want my life to be mine. I want the choice to be mine. And I choose him—I want him in my life.

He's not mentioning it because it's a promise that neither of us can keep, not because he doesn't love me. But I need hope, to know there is a one percent chance of being together in our future. That's all I need—one percent. Just the possibility will keep me fighting.

Beckett rolls over to look at me, and I see what he can't say in his eyes. I have to remember—baby steps. We shared a lot today. We said we love each other for the first time. We shared a lot of history and pain. That's a good start; the rest will follow. That is if we live long enough to survive it.

His lips brush mine. At first, I'm hesitant—I want words, not kisses. I want truths spoken out loud; not promises only whispered with our bodies. But as his lips brush mine, I melt against him.

I can't deny myself a chance to have him. Not when life is too short. Not when there is no promise of tomorrow or even an hour from now, not in our world.

Our lips are the only thing physically connecting us as we kiss. We don't reach out to claim more. We take our time, like two teenagers kissing for the first time and not wanting to take things too far.

His tongue parts my lips and sinks into my mouth. Mine battles back in a swirl of endorphins releasing in my body. One lick, and I need more—so much fucking more that my body literally aches for this man from my lips all the way to my toes.

"Why do I want you so much that it hurts?" I ask.

"Why can't I stay away when I'm just going to end up hurting you in the end?" he says.

Neither of us gets an answer to our question.

Our lips lock, and we don't stop again.

Our hands reach out and run up and down each other's bodies.

I never changed out of my robe, so he has easy access to my body. My struggle to reach his skin is harder, but I manage to push his shirt up enough to touch the ridges of his abs and the soft tufts of hair that disappear into his pants.

What starts off as soft and loving quickly turns rough and frantic. As much as we love each other, we are also pissed the fuck off that we love each other. Our lives would be so much easier if we didn't.

I should be focused on getting my freedom back.

He should be focused on becoming the leader he was always meant to be.

Instead, we are tangled up in each other. We're destined to be the death of the other.

"I'm not going to be gentle," he growls as he yanks on my hair to access the sensitive skin behind my ear.

"I won't either." I dig my nails into his chest until I draw blood.

Our eyes turn to fire. We are too perfect of a match for each other. Too fiery. Too independent. Too stubborn to surrender to the other.

It makes for fucking good sex, but it doesn't lead to the best decisions outside of the bedroom.

I jump on top of him and ditch my robe, straddling him and pinning his arm above his head with both of my arms. His strength far outweighs mine, even with all of my strength pushed into his one arm. He won't let me pin him for long. I need to use better techniques if I'm going to win this battle—and this is definitely a battle.

A battle for us to keep our hearts. To stay sane. To not let our love overtake everything else. It's a battle to prove we won't let our love overwhelm us.

It's a battle we will both lose.

My teeth scrape down his chest, over his scars and the Retribution Kings' tattoo on the center of his chest.

He growls deeply; I smirk.

His hips buck, and suddenly, I'm pinned beneath him. He rips his shirt off over his head.

I grin—one step closer to him getting completely naked. I'll take that as a win. I'm naked beneath him, and his hungry eyes look over every slick spot of my skin like he owns it.

"I'm no one's property."

"I didn't say you were," he replies.

"Your eyes did."

"I'm not responsible for what you make up in your head."

I knee him in the balls, wounding him enough to grab the knife tucked in the back pocket of his jeans. We haven't brought much violence to the bedroom before, but neither of us is the lovey-dovey type. We can both only handle so much lovemaking. We need it rough and controlling and feisty.

He grins, cocking his head when he sees the knife.

"You're not going to win," he smirks.

"I'm better with a knife than you are, old man. You rely too much on your gun."

"Is that true?" he chuckles.

I nod my head slowly, my eyes peering into his completely in lust.

"You make me want to fuck you and cut you at the same time. No one else drives me so crazy like you do," I say.

He moves to pin my hands again, but I slice through the air, nicking his palm.

The deepest growl I've ever heard from him vibrates through the room.

I grab his palm with my other hand and bring it to my lips, kissing the shallow wound that I know hurts like a deep paper cut. But when my tongue brushes over it, his eyes roll back in his head, and his cock pushes between my legs. It's pure ecstasy instead.

My other hand lets the knife trace down his chest, over his tattoo that says his heart and loyalty belongs to a group that has done nothing but betray him time and time again.

He gives me a warning glare.

I smile deviously and strike through the crown with the knife, defacing the tattoo in one quick sweep.

"You're mine, not theirs."

He knocks the knife out of my hand and flips me over in one swoop. My ass is in the air pressed against his front as his hand massages it.

"And you are one wild woman who needs to be punished for cutting me not once but twice."

His hand comes down on my bare ass.

I yelp at the sudden sting and am shocked by how wet I get from having my ass slapped.

"I need to be punished more. That cut on your chest was deep; it's going to leave a mark."

He complies, slapping my ass again, pulling a deep whimper from me.

I feel sticky, warm blood from his hand as he hits my ass. It hurts him as much as it hurts me, but we both welcome the pain. It means we are alive. It means that as long as we keep feeling, we get a chance—a tiny, infinitesimal chance, but it's a chance of happiness.

"You drive me fucking crazy, Princess."

"You make me want to be saved by the handsome prince, Hero."

He growls as he almost always does when I call him Hero, but I won't stop saying it. He's my hero. I didn't need someone to physically save me, just someone to love me. That's all I've ever wanted—to be loved.

I feel him rubbing his wet and swollen cock at my ass, not my vagina.

Fuck, what did I get myself into?

I cut him, egged him on, made him bleed—of course, he's going to retaliate. He's the leader of the Retribution Kings. It's their specialty.

"Why so quiet, Princess?" Beckett asks as he rubs his swollen dick against my asshole.

"How do you always seem to win our battles?" I groan when his cock rubs from my slit all the way to my ass, spreading my wetness along the length of me.

He leans forward until his breath is hot on my back. "Pretty sure we're both going to win tonight."

Next thing I know, his cock is pushing at the entrance of my ass. I'm sweating and tense as my muscles refuse to let him in. I've been fucked in the ass before, but every time it takes some convincing.

He doesn't tell me to relax. Instead, he runs his nails down my spine, and I feel my body loosening, letting him further in. I'm reminded who's behind me. A man who loves me in every way possible. A man who wants everything from me just like I want everything from him.

It's then that I let him all the way in, that I want everything from him. I want him inside me as deep as he can go. I want him. All of him.

"Jesus, you're incredible," he mumbles almost incoherently as he thrusts inside me.

I flick my hair over my shoulder and shoot him a fiery look. He better give me the best orgasm of my life if he doesn't want me to make him bleed again.

I feel his blood on my ass as he slaps me again, sending tingles radiating through my body like tiny firecrackers going off.

"Who fucked you in the ass, Princess? Lennox? Gage? Who?"

"I—I, uh, don't know." Beckett is thrusting into me so hard and fast I can barely keep up.

"Good. When you think of men fucking your ass, you think of me."

I grin. "Jealous prick."

"When it comes to you, always. Do you understand?"

His palm comes down on my ass again when he doesn't get the answer he wants from me. I almost refuse to say anything just to feel that sweet sting again vibrating through my body and making me pant even more for him.

"When I think of fucking men, all I think about is you, Hero."

"Stop calling me Hero."

"I can't. You're mine, and I'm yours."

The next thrust pushes us to a new place, one where neither of us can talk. He pumps in and out, his hand finds my clit, intensifying my pleasure until I'm shaking, barely able to keep myself on all fours on the bed.

And then we come together. It's messy and explosive. It's everything that we are.

We collapse together on the bed. We're covered in sweat, cum, and blood. Neither of us gets up to clean off. It's the mark of each other, and there is no rush to remove that.

Beckett pulls me tightly to him, and I let him, even though I'm not sure how either of us is going to be able to sleep.

"I love you, Ri," he says into my hair. They're words neither of us were able to say when we were fucking.

I grin. "I love you too, Beckett."

HE CAME IN THE NIGHT, and she's gone.

I don't know how he does it. But the night is his friend. More than his friend, it helps him lull us to sleep; it hides his footsteps; it covers his tracks.

None of us wake.

None of the security cameras catch him.

But we know who was here.

Kek.

The only man Ri is truly afraid of. The man who has the keys to controlling Ri if he wants to with one phrase. Her former friend and protector turned stalker, kidnapper.

And now he has her.

I failed.

I woke up in a sweat-induced nightmare. I reached across the bed for comfort, but she was nowhere. Not in the bathroom. Not in the kitchen. Not in the backyard.

Now, it's five in the morning, and I'm standing in the kitchen with everyone, including Lucy, trying to figure out how the hell this could have happened and how we get her back.

Gage and Lennox are on their computers, going through all the security footage to see if we can find them, but the man knows how to evade cameras. And if he used the phrase to control Ri's mind, she knows how to avoid them too. They aren't going to show up on any of the footage.

Hayes is staring out the back window like she's somehow going to show up there—not really helpful.

Lucy at least made some coffee for everyone. She hands a cup to Ryker, who takes it and slings the cup against the wall across from him. Coffee and shards of ceramic go everywhere.

No one chastises him, though. It's how we all feel.

He growls loud like a wounded animal. "How did I let this happen! I shouldn't have let her sleep in her room. I should have been with her. I should have at least had shift changes where someone was always awake. Stupid, so fucking stupid! I—"

"Ryker," I stop him.

He looks at me like he wants to kill me. I know the feeling. I want to kill myself if I let anything happen to Ri.

"This isn't your fault. It's mine. I was with her. I failed to protect her."

"Yes, but Corsi will blame me, not you if anything happens to her. And my men, my family, will suffer because I failed."

I nod slowly. "We'll get her back, and she'll be safe."

"We only have three days! And we have no clue where she is."

He's right. We don't.

I look around the room as everyone's eyes are locked on me, waiting for me to say something.

I don't have a good answer.

Just like I couldn't promise Ri that I'd marry her, that I'd spend my life with her. I can't promise them that I'll get her back before it's too late. It could already be too late. But my heart—oh, my fucking breaking heart…it needs hope. We all do.

"Rialta Corsi is the strongest person any of us know. She's a fighter. She'll survive until we find her. Or she'll escape long before we get to her because Rialta Corsi doesn't need a hero; she can save her damn self," I smirk, thinking of the times she's said similar words to me.

The security footage comes up empty.

All the places Lucy can come up with that Ri might be lead to dead ends.

Loki is useless as a scent dog.

All of Ryker's and my contacts don't have a clue where Kek is or even who he is. He's like a real-life ghost. Everyone has heard the name whispered about like a fairytale, but no one has ever met the man in real life.

It's early afternoon. We've wasted almost a full day before I start to get desperate. I call Enzo, Kai, Siren, Zeke, Liesel, Langston. I call them all. I beg for their help, not for my sake, but for hers.

No one answers.

No one calls me back.

I'm dead to them.

I'm a traitor.

I storm back into the dining room, our makeshift headquarters in the search for Ri. Everyone is out of leads. It's hard to find much when we are basically stuck in this house. If we leave, we'll have the Retribution Kings on our ass.

The Retribution Kings.

A thought hits me hard and fast. It shocks my heart that I would even consider it—a choice that will end in unending heartbreak for me. But it could save Ri, and right now, that's all I care about.

I walk over to Lennox.

"I need you to contact Caius for me," I say.

Lennox frowns from his seat behind his computer. "Are you sure?"

He doesn't ask why.

I nod. "Call him. Let me know when you have him."

All eyes are on me once again, but no one speaks. No one asks for more info on my plan. We all just want to protect Ri. Not even Ryker asks what I'm up to.

I stare down at the fresh wound Ri caused on my palm. It hasn't scabbed over yet, probably because I keep picking at it with my teeth.

"You should really let that heal," Lucy says, staring at my hand.

"I can't."

"You'll be no use to her if you have an injured hand. Follow me," Lucy says as she walks into the closest bathroom.

She opens the cabinets and quickly pulls out some ointment and bandages. She demands my hand. It's the first time I can see why she and Ri get along so well. She's just as bossy and strong as Ri but in her own way.

"You really love her, don't you?" Lucy asks as she cleans my wound.

"I do."

"I'm sorry." Lucy doesn't meet my gaze as she puts ointment on the thin wound.

"Sorry for what?"

She shakes her head. "I don't know why I said that."

"You're sorry that Ri is gone, and I'm hurting?" I lift her chin, forcing her to look at me, but I don't think that's it at all. There's something she's not telling me.

"Is there something you know, Lucy? Do you know what happened to Ri?"

"No, I don't."

"What aren't you saying?"

Lucy exhales, and her blonde hair flies. "I've always wanted her to find love, to find someone she could share her shitty life with outside of me. We are great friends, but she deserves to experience all that life has to offer. But now, I realize it was a mistake. It's just going to lead to terrible heartbreak for both of you. No matter how much you want each other, no matter how much you love each other, it will never be enough. You can't be together, not in the end."

I frown. "If one of us wins the game, then we will. If I win, I can be with her. If she wins, she can choose me. The odds are actually in our favor."

Her lips thin. "I wish it were that simple."

I'm about to question her more when Lennox pokes his head in. "I have Caius."

Lennox pushes his phone into my hand, and Lucy skirts out of the bathroom before I have a chance to question her further.

"What do you want?" Caius asks.

"I want a meeting. You, me, and Odette."

"I can't do that. I don't trust that you won't tie us up again or try to kill us. And the others won't let us out of their sight. We can't just leave."

"Figure it out because I have a deal that will make it worth your while. Odette especially will want to hear the deal I'm offering."

I'm not sure if Caius will take the bait, but it's my only option.

"Where?" he finally asks.

"I'll text you the address. Be ready to meet in an hour." Then I hang up the phone before Caius can make any demands.

"What are we doing, boss?" Lennox asks, a little weary.

"We are getting Ri back."

———

We spent the next hour finding the perfect location and getting everyone ready. Lucy and Loki are staying at the house by themselves. Hopefully, it's safe enough, but I can't leave any men behind to watch her. Honestly, she was happy to see us go. She seemed to want to be alone.

I never got a chance to ask her any further questions, but I'm not sure if Lucy knows what she's talking about anyway.

We load up with every weapon we have before climbing into two cars to head to the restaurant. We considered an emptier building but figured Caius and Odette would better behave in a more public space. We're still prepared for an all-out war the second we leave the premises, though. I hope it's just Caius and Odette alone, but I suspect they will have brought backup just like I did.

We get to the restaurant. "I'll stay with you," Lennox says.

"No, I told them just the three of us, and that's what it needs to be—just the three of us. Gage said he can tap into the security cameras at the restaurant."

"The images aren't the best, though, so if you need us, you have to alert us. It will be hard for us to see exactly what's going on via the cameras," Gage says.

I nod.

"Are you sure you don't want a mic?" Hayes asks.

"Yes." I don't want anyone to hear the details we are about to discuss. It's too important.

No one—not Lennox, Gage, or Hayes—likes the plan. They say I'm setting myself up to be captured. I probably am, but I'll only cooperate if I get what I want first.

Ryker is the only one who doesn't seem upset with my plan. He doesn't care about my safety at the end of the day. His only goal is to find the best plan to get Ri back. And since this is currently the only plan, he's going with it.

"I'll make sure these assholes stay out here so you can get whatever info you need," Ryker says.

I nod.

"If this doesn't work, follow Ryker's lead. If he says it's worth fighting to try and get me back, then do that. But if he doesn't think you have a good shot at rescuing me, then leave me and save yourself. I need you all safe to go after Ri," I say.

"But—" they all say at once.

"Ryker is the only objective person in this car. If I'm captured or killed, you follow his lead. For the next two and half days at least, you are all on the same side with the same mission—rescue Ri at all costs. If I have to be sacrificed, so be it."

"You'll get whatever information you need, boss," Lennox says.

"Ryker is your leader until I come back. Everyone agree?"

I wait for them to all nod their heads in agreement.

"Good."

I climb out of the car and head inside the restaurant without telling them the most important part of my plan. Whether my negotiations are successful or not, I don't expect to come back.

The restaurant is swanky. I'm dressed in a suit. It's uncomfortable but surprisingly easy to hide all my weapons, so I'm not complaining.

My entire focus is on my plan to save Ri. I'm hoping for a miracle, a chance that Ri will somehow appear completely unscathed in the next five minutes, and I won't have to do this. But that's not my life. I don't get that lucky. In fact, I get unlucky. It won't shock me if Ri is found safe and sound five minutes after I do this.

Every minute that passes is a minute she might not survive. Another minute passing that I could lose her forever, so I can't waste another single minute.

"Reservation should be under Monroe," I say to the hostess.

She smiles brightly at me like I'm her favorite person she's ever seen. "Right this way, Mr. Monroe."

I vomit in my mouth when she calls me Monroe. Technically, that's the name that I said I'd go by as leader of the Retribution Kings. At the time, I wanted a connection to Odette, but now I can't run far enough away from it.

The hostess leads me to a small hidden table on the second floor. It's private, which is what I wanted, and it appears that Odette and Caius haven't arrived yet.

I take a seat and order a bottle of Odette's favorite wine while I wait. I'm not sure if they'll come, and if they do, I suspect it will be with a dozen Retribution Kings set on killing me. None of that scares me, though. What does scare me is a life without Ri.

Every time I think I've gotten Ri back, someone else takes her or puts an obstacle in our path. Every. Fucking. Time.

I drink my glass of wine without Caius or Odette showing up.

Fuck.

I realize they aren't coming after sitting for almost forty-five minutes.

I throw some cash on the table and am about to stand up when I hear her voice. "So sorry we're late, darling! My sandal strap snapped, and we had to stop by a store to pick up some new shoes."

Odette whisks over to me and kisses me on the corner of my mouth like we are a happily married couple, not a couple on the brink of war.

I let her kiss me. I don't flinch as her lips touch my skin, burning me like a hot coal. Caius pulls out a chair for her opposite me, which she graciously thanks him for before sitting. He sits in the chair next to us both a moment later.

I loosen my jaw as I look at the woman sitting across from me. The sight of her is such a stark difference from the kindergarten teacher I once thought she was. She's wearing a skin-tight red dress with her boobs popping out of the top. I'm not sure how she can breathe with how it seems to be constricting her ribs. Her hair is curled in big Hollywood waves, and she has red painted lips. Odette always liked dressing up, but I've never seen her get dolled up to this extent, except at our own wedding.

I glance at Caius out of the corner of my eye. He's in a tailored suit with his hair gelled back. They look like they planned on attending a grand gala, not just dinner with me.

They want me to feel small like I'm out of my league. This is their world. They are used to dressing up, to playing the part. I'm not.

It doesn't matter. I didn't come here to determine who was better at playing dress-up.

"Nice of you to show up forty-five minutes late," I say.

Odette reaches across the table and brushes my hand spinning my glass of wine.

"I told you, babe, my straps snapped."

"You couldn't just wear a different pair you owned?"

She licks her lips at me as she smiles. "I needed black; silver just wouldn't do with this stress."

I roll my eyes in my head, but outside I'm stone. I don't show her any affection, but I also don't dismiss her—not until I get what I need from her.

Our waiter returns and pours Caius and Odette wine from the bottle I ordered.

"Oh, you got my favorite wine! How you know me so well, hubby."

I wince just the tiniest bit when she calls me 'hubby.' She doesn't seem to notice, but I'm sure Caius did.

"Are you ready to order?" the waiter asks.

After we all order, it's time to get to business. I've stalled long enough.

"So why are we here?" Caius asks, not happy to just have a pleasant dinner like Odette apparently is.

"First, I need to know you have no listening devices on either of you. This conversation needs to be completely private," I say.

Caius nods, assuming I would want to check. Odette just laughs. "Of course, this is a private conversation."

"Then you won't mind that I check." I pull out a small device and scan them both. To my surprise, they're clear.

"We didn't bring any men either in case you were wondering, although we did see a car of your men outside. But I do have a gun, and I have no problem using it if I need to," Caius barks.

I don't blame him for being upset with me. I took his three most loyal men and turned their loyalties to me. He would be the leader of the Retribution Kings if it wasn't for them wanting to take down my brother for some reason. My life would have been far simpler if it had turned out that way too.

"I have a proposition for you, one I think you'll both be happy with."

Caius frowns.

Odette bats her eyelashes at me.

My heart beats fast in my chest, begging me not to say the next words. It's a mistake, but this is the only way. This is the only thing I can offer that will be enough for them. This is the only way to guarantee that Ri comes back unharmed.

"I need your help getting Ri back safely."

Caius snickers.

Odette looks annoyed as hell.

"And why would we do that?" Caius asks.

"Because…" I stumble over my own words. Reluctantly, I finally force them out in a whoosh of breath and hope to god I'm doing the right thing.

BACK AND FORTH, I rock like a baby in a cradle. I drift left then right. For a few minutes, it's rhythmic, but then it shifts just slightly, and I realize where I am. I'm on a boat. That's what the rocking is.

How did I get on a boat?

What happened?

I furrow my brow, trying to think of the last thing I remember. Beckett had a gun aimed at my head. My heart broke. I was pissed at him.

My head pounds, and my lips are dry and cracked.

How long have I been out of it? Long enough to be severely dehydrated.

I sit up slowly, afraid the light-headedness is going to cause me to pass out again.

I'm below deck in a small room, only big enough for a twin bed and a nightstand. There are no clues of who took me.

I put my hand over my chest. It hurts. It fucking aches like something I've never felt before. The loss of him, of the man I love, rips through me, breaking me in half.

I want to sob and scream and lose my mind.

But I don't feel safe here—wherever here is.

I pat my clothes for a weapon, but I find none. I open the night-stand drawer, but all I find is an old condom wrapper and a pen. Gross.

I close it quickly.

I need to leave. I need to find a weapon, something to defend myself against whoever is on this boat.

Carefully, I stand. My legs are shaky from lack of water and food. That may need to be my first mission—food, water, then a weapon. I need to find a kitchen. I can find all of those things there.

I stumble to the bedroom door and pull it open an inch to peek through the crack. There is no one in the hallway outside my door. Whoever has me has shitty security too.

I move quickly into the hallway, up the stairs, and find a small galley. There's a small fridge containing a box of pizza. I grab a slice and shovel the cold food into my mouth. Falling into the sink, I throw my mouth under the faucet for water—too exhausted to find a glass first.

After I finish a slice of pizza and have had a few gulps of water, I'm feeling well enough to search for a weapon. I open drawer after drawer, looking for a steak knife or chef's knife. I find neither, not even a butter knife.

"You were always deadlier with a knife than a gun. I couldn't take any chances."

His voice sends all the hairs on my arms into a standing posi-tion. The last man I want to be captured by has kidnapped me. I've been running from this man for years, and somehow I failed.

He must have taken advantage of my broken heart.

"You never did want a fair fight," I say, slowly turning to face Kek.

He grins at me. His jet-black hair is cut short on the sides and longer on top; his eyes are just as black as his hair. Pits form in my stomach when he looks at me.

The rest of him is just as fit as the last time I saw him too.

Muscles protrude from beneath his fitted black T-shirt and beneath his jeans.

"I don't have a knife either, so it seems fair enough to me."

"Not really when you haven't fed me or given me anything to drink in days."

He shrugs. "It's only been one day, not days. And you seem to have found enough food and water to replenish you for now. Besides, I don't want to fight with you."

I raise an eyebrow and stay alert as he walks further into the galley. I'm standing next to the island in the center of the room, keeping it between him and me as he gets closer. It won't do much to protect me, but it makes me feel better to have a chance to get away if he attacks.

"You're always looking for a fight."

"That was the old Kek; the new Kek just wants to talk."

"You kidnapped me so we could talk? You could have just sent me a text or left a voicemail; that would have been easier."

"This conversation needed to happen in person."

"So you kidnapped me and brought me to the middle of nowhere so no one will be able to find me. You do know Vincent, not to mention countless others, will be looking for me."

At least, I hope that's true. I think back to my last memory of Beckett. He wanted to kill me. He might not care about saving me. How did I escape? How did I not end up dead? Kek didn't save me, but who did?

I can't make sense of my fuzzy memories, so I suspect someone fucked with my head. I'm guessing the culprit is the man standing in front of me.

"I know, which is why we don't have a lot of time. Someone will come for you soon enough," he says.

"Vincent?"

Kek laughs. "No, but someone will."

"Are you afraid you'll lose?"

"No. I don't plan on fighting."

I frown. "So you're going to finally kill me?" I take a step back, away from him, trying to plan my escape.

Kek chuckles louder. "I'll never kill you, Princess. What fun would that be?"

"You really brought me here to talk?"

He nods.

I suck in a breath. "What do you want to talk about?"

I'm on high alert. I don't trust Kek; I never will. He killed someone I loved. I've barely survived his past games, and I can't imagine what game he's playing now.

He opens his mouth, and I know the phrase he's about to say.

Fuck.

I cover my ears and start screaming at the top of my lungs. I refuse to let him control me anymore. I run out the galley and up the stairs to the top deck of the boat, not really sure what I'm going to do next. But I'll jump in the water and start swimming if it comes to it.

I'm hoping to find a weapon, anything I can use to kill him once and for all. Or something to kill myself with because I'd rather die than let him torture me again.

Kek is right behind me. I keep screaming and yelling, trying to block out any words when I hear the rumble of an engine. Someone is nearby.

I change my screams to cries for help. I don't know who the nearby boat belongs to, and I may be signing their death sentence if the boater isn't from this world and prepared to fight, but I have to try. It's my only hope.

I wave my hands frantically in the air as the boat nears, and I see blonde locks sticking out from under a man's ball cap.

I let out a sigh. It's not entirely who I was hoping for, but he'll do.

Kek grabs my arms and whips me around to face him. I'm still yelling, still trying to block out his words—just a few seconds longer, and I'll have help. Kek is a good fighter, but his best strength is being able to control me. He already said he doesn't plan on fighting. I have to hope he was telling the truth.

Kek's eyes are wild and desperate. There's a flicker of fear in them.

I've never seen him like this. I don't understand it.

"Stop, just listen. I won't use the phrase. I just need you to hear me."

"I don't trust you."

"I know, and you shouldn't."

The boat lurches—Caius's boat must have hit ours. We have seconds, not minutes, until he'll be here.

Footsteps make their way onto the top deck, and I know Kek is about to make his grand disappearance.

"Don't trust them, any of them." Kek pushes me away toward Caius when he says one last phrase that doesn't make sense to me. "Give him up."

And then Kek is gone.

I frown. *That was what was so important? For Kek to tell me not to trust anyone?* I already knew that. There had to be something else I'm missing.

Caius runs to me and pulls me into his arms. I let him. It feels good to be held again.

"Are you hurt?" Caius asks.

"No."

"We need to go after him." He pushes a gun into my hand.

I take it, but it's no use; Kek is gone. It's one of his greatest abilities—to be able to disappear without a word. He can just be gone like a shadow in the night.

Caius won't believe me, though, and I want to see with my own eyes that Kek is gone.

"Stay close to me. I don't want to let you out of my sight," Caius says.

I want to argue that I can defend myself, but when it comes to

Kek, I don't feel comfortable being by myself. So I follow Caius as we check the top deck and then the rooms below.

"I don't understand; he's just gone," Caius says.

I nod. "I never understood it either, but he's very good at disappearing when he wants to."

I look at the boat Caius brought. "Anyone else come with you?"

He shakes his head. "Just me. We all followed separate leads. The Retribution Kings are doing everything they can to try and find you."

He doesn't mention Beckett.

"Even when they almost had me killed before?"

"They realized their mistake." Caius looks at me with longing eyes as he searches mine for something. He's probably looking for any amount of affection that I might have toward him.

"Thank you for saving me," I say.

He holds out his hand toward me, and I take it. "Anytime."

He helps me onto his boat and wraps a blanket around my shoulders. I sit down in one of the two captain chairs, and we start driving toward shore. Looking around now, I realize we're on Lake Michigan.

"What do you remember?" Caius asks.

I stare out at the water. "I remember Beckett almost killing me and then nothing. I don't know how I got from that point to Kek taking me."

Caius sighs. "We helped you—Lennox, Hayes, Gage, and me. Beckett didn't tell any of us his plan, but we knew it couldn't be true. We got you out of there, and then Odette came back, so we knew we were right."

I'm holding my breath, I realize.

"And Beckett?"

He turns his head to look at me slowly out of the corner of his eye as he holds the helm. "He only has eyes for Odette. They've been inseparable since he got back. I think he realizes his mistake when it comes to you, and he's sorry, but all he cared about was being with her.

"Odette's the love of his life. He thought he lost her. It broke him in a way we didn't think was repairable. He used you as a distraction and to help get her back. But now that she's back, he's consumed with her and making sure that no harm comes to her."

My throat closes up, and my heart seizes. I'm not even sure if it's pumping blood anymore; it doesn't really see the point.

I close my eyes, trying to remember, but I can't find anything in my memories that could contradict Caius's words.

"I'm so sorry," he says, slowing the boat down until he can walk over and wrap his arms around me.

It's then that I release the tears—full out sobs into his shoulder. I can't hold them back any longer.

I'm embarrassed with how long I cry, but it's nice to have Caius holding me in his arms. It's nice to feel loved even if I don't love him back.

"I'm sorry," I say, rubbing the tears and snot on the corner of the blanket.

He chuckles. "Don't be. I care about you, Princess. I'm here for you whenever you need a friend or more."

There's so much hope left in his voice when he says 'more.' I don't want to squash the hope of my savior, but I'm not sure anything can change my feelings for Caius. He's a nice guy, but not someone I could love. Maybe that's what I need, though. A man who's strong and kind, but not a man I could fall in love with. A man who can't hurt me. A man who could be a partner, not a lover.

There aren't many men left in the game. If I had to choose one of them, Caius wouldn't be a bad choice. I wouldn't be surprised if Beckett bowed out of the game now that Odette's back.

It's between Caius, Ryker, and three others.

Caius might be my best choice.

I lean into his shoulder, now damp with my tears.

"What would I do without you?" I ask.

He pushes my hair back and then kisses my forehead. "I don't know what I would do without you either."

It feels right and wrong at the same time to be in his arms, but I need the strength right now. I need the support, so I take it.

Then Caius whispers something into my ear that I can barely make out. If I wasn't sure where Caius's loyalties lie, I am now.

BECKETT

WAITING SUCKS.

I have no idea if my plan is working. No idea if Ri is safe. No idea if the sacrifice I made is worth it. And I don't know how long it's going to take for her to be safe.

I can't breathe until I know Ri's safe. I did something crazy and ruthless to get her back. And if it doesn't work, I still have to keep my end of the deal. I'm trapped, and it would all be for nothing if she wasn't safe.

"Honey, you've hardly touched your food," Odette says from my left. We're sitting at the center of a long table, looking out at the Retribution Kings celebrating our union.

The crowd is jubilant. They drink and eat and laugh like this is a true celebration. I'm the only one who knows the truth.

Hayes, Gage, Lennox, and Ryker sit to my right at the long table as my closest men. All of them stare at me like I've lost my fucking mind.

Hayes keeps shaking his head at me in disappointment.

Gage shoots daggers in my direction.

Lennox can't stand to look at me, and anytime anyone makes a toast, he laughs instead of cheers.

Ryker is the only one who keeps his emotions to himself. He either doesn't care about me as much as the others, or he knows—he knows the only reason I'm sitting here acting like Odette is my queen is because I did something to get Ri back.

It's better that they don't suspect, though. It's better that I'm the only one who knows. I'm going to have to keep this up for days, weeks, years—locking my secret away in my own mind will help keep me up the charade.

My heart is Ri's, not Odette's, but I can never show that truth. It's the only way to keep Ri safe from Kek, from the Retribution Kings.

Odette leans into me. I do everything not to stiffen. I smile lovingly back at her because I know what she wants, and I'm forced to give it to her.

I've given Odette everything of me—my body to do what she pleases with, my kingdom I fought so hard to win, my power, my very soul—it's hers.

But I kept my heart. It's locked away for Ri, for the hope that someday it could be hers in a real way. But that's a lost hope.

I lean into Odette and kiss her for the hundredth time tonight. She's insatiable, and every second I'm kissing her is pure torture. I'd rather be stabbed repeatedly in the chest than kiss her, but this is the sacrifice I made, and soon, I should know if it was worth it or not.

I pull my phone out, waiting for a text or call from Caius to let me know she's okay. But there's nothing.

I put the phone on the table next to me so I can see the second he sends a message. Odette gave Caius the info he needed to find Ri. She knew more about Kek than even I suspected. She knew the phrase to help unlock Ri's mind. She knew how to find Kek. It only makes me more suspicious of Odette, but I don't give a shit what lies Odette has told me if it saves Ri.

If I'm to live this life, I need to know that Ri is alive and her mind is her own. Ideally, I need her free of the dangers, free to chose her own husband, free to be her own woman. But that might be too much to hope for her. Alive and her mind uncontrolled might be the best I can do for her.

Caius may not be my greatest ally, but he cares about Ri. He'll do everything he can to find her.

At least, that's what I keep telling myself. Caius will find her. He'll call. He wants Ri safe, and he wants his sister happy. He'll do the right thing.

The back door of the banquet hall opens. I barely pay attention to it; people have shown up late all night through that door. But this time, raven-colored hair catches my attention.

My heart stops when I see them. Caius has his arm and a blanket around Ri's shoulders. She looks exhausted. I can tell her eyes are red and swollen from here. She leans her head into his chest like a lover. Despite her eyes, she has a soft smile on her lips.

Caius looks concerned as if now that he's brought her back, I won't keep to my promise. But I know what will happen if I don't.

Odette says something that the others at the table laugh at, so I join in. It's a deep, belly laugh, the kind that Odette used to swoon at. Swoon she does when she hears it again.

"It's so good to hear you laugh again," Odette says, resting her hand against my chest.

"It feels good to laugh again now that you're back in my life." I grip her hand, pretending it's Ri's, and then I kiss her.

I don't look at Ri. I don't watch for her reaction. I'm not sure if Ri will believe my act, but I'd rather break her heart now than slowly over days. It was never going to be me. I was never going to be enough.

Ri calls me a hero. I guess I am, and she'll never know it. I saved her from the worst, but now she's going to have to find a way to save herself from the rest.

When I break from Odette's lips, I put my classic shit-eating grin, complete with dimples, on my face and laugh like this is the greatest day of my life.

Man, I'm sick. This is my life now—playing politics and pretending to care for the woman who betrayed me. All while the real woman I want is sitting in the same room.

I can feel their eyes on me, the guys next to me.

"Are you not going to go check on Ri?" Hayes, the closest to me, asks.

"Nah, she looks fine from here. Ryker should be happy that Corsi isn't going to kick his ass now that she's back safe and sound."

None of them blink as they stare at me, trying to find out what demon is inhabiting my body right now. It's me guys; I'm just saving Ri the only way I know how.

Slowly, one by one, they all get up and walk over to her.

I refuse to look in her direction. I refuse to torture myself. And I have to play the part of disinterested leader who's elated to have his wife back.

Wife—ugh. What the hell was I thinking, getting married when I barely knew her?

Ri is safe. Ri is with the men who care about her the most. They'll help her get through this, probably fuck her again like last time—the bastards.

And then Stan walks over, ruining my fake pleasant mood.

"What do you want?"

"For you to get retribution against the Black Empire for your incredible wife," Stan says.

I frown as I wrap my arm around Odette's shoulders. "I have her back; we're happy. I'm not going to start a war."

He smirks. "I'm glad to see the happy couple back together, but you don't have a choice. If you want to stay married to Odette and, you know, breathing, then you have to get retribution. We are the Retribution Kings. We didn't get that name from just living happily ever after with our wives. We got the name from exacting revenge. Now, declare war or I'll have you killed tonight in your sleep."

He walks away and talks to someone else at the head table before I have a chance to argue back.

"Can't you tell everyone you made a mistake? My brother and his family had nothing to do with your disappearance," I hiss to Odette.

She bats her long eyelashes in my direction. "And why would I do that when it's not true?"

"I'm giving you everything you want. I'm being the doting husband. I'm leading the Retribution Kings. Isn't it enough?"

Her eyes drag up and down my face before she says, "No, it's not enough."

I blink, not believing I'm hearing the coldness in her tone. I thought she was the sweet, kind woman I fell for. I thought she genuinely cared about other people. I couldn't be more wrong.

"If you love me, you'll do this for me," I say.

"I would if you really loved me, but you still love her. I'm glad you made the right decision to be with me, but I won't be made a fool of. You're not as good an actor as you think. I can see through you easily enough, so I'm sure others can too. Now, declare war, or you won't be the only one dying in your sleep." Odette's eyes slither to Ri, and I realize just how trapped I am. I'm going to have to declare war with my brother to save the woman I love.

Forgive me, brother.

BARELY ANYONE PAYS us attention when we walk into the banquet hall. It's strange not to be the center of attention, but I like it.

The only people who do see us are the table at the far end of the room. Everyone is staring in their direction, which is why they don't notice Caius and me.

Beckett, Odette, and the guys notice me.

Beckett pretends he doesn't.

Odette pretends I don't phase her.

And the guys stare at me like they've seen a ghost.

Beckett laughs. It's a beautiful laugh, the kind I don't think I've ever seen.

Hmmm...

Then he pulls Odette against his lips in a big show of their love and affection for each other.

I stop walking when they kiss and study them like animals in a zoo exhibit.

Caius stumbles to a stop next to me. His arm is draped around me, shielding me as best as he can.

"You okay?" he asks, looking from me to the happy couple.

I check my feelings expecting to feel immense pain, heartbreak, or rage. Instead, I feel nothing—just nothing—no feelings whatsoever watching them.

Strange.

I nod. "I'm hungry. Let's find a table to eat."

Caius leads me to an empty table toward a quieter corner of the room. He flags a waiter down and orders for me, so I don't have to think. He probably thinks I'm in shock.

He thrusts a glass of water in front of me and tells me to drink. I comply.

Next, a plate of food is brought over. Chicken, potatoes, macaroni—comfort food.

I dig in, not caring what the food is.

I'm mid-chew when I hear footsteps approaching our table. I look up to see them all stop suddenly, staring down at me like I'm an alien.

"Are you going to join us or just stare?" I ask.

They all take a seat at once.

I look from each face to the next. All of them look solemn and frightened of me like I'm going to punch them.

"What's wrong?" I ask before shoveling more food into my mouth. I'm starving; I can't believe how hungry I am. I don't know what tomorrow is going to bring, but I need to regain my strength.

Hayes looks from me to Beckett. I let my eyes follow his gaze. "Are you okay with..."

I reach across the table and grip his hand. "I'm fine, just hungry."

"Are you really okay? Kek didn't hurt you?" Lennox asks, worry threading his voice.

I nod. "I'm fine. He locked me in a room. Maybe fucked with my memories a little, but otherwise, I'm perfectly fine. No broken bones. No scars. No bullet wounds."

They all look at me suspiciously, and I can tell the question they want to know, but none of them have the balls to ask.

"He didn't rape me," I say, putting them all out of their misery.

They all exhale at once as if they couldn't breathe until they knew.

I roll my eyes. But it's nice how much they care.

Caius rubs my back, and I don't flinch away.

Gage especially stares at the contact like he can't believe what he's seeing. Ryker is the only one who hasn't shown strong emotion.

"I need to talk to you," I say, putting my fork down.

"We're here to listen," Hayes says, with a tiny playful smile.

"Individually," I say, looking from him to the others.

Everyone nods, and Lennox, Gage, and Ryker all stand. I look to Caius. "Leave us."

He frowns but then stands. "I'll get you something to drink. What do you want?"

"Red wine."

He nods and then heads to the bar. Hayes is left at the table to speak with me alone first.

"Has Caius—" Hayes starts.

"No, Caius has been a perfect gentleman. He rescued me."

"That's why you are being so nice to him?"

I nod but don't say more. I don't know who to trust anymore.

"So why do you want to talk to all of us alone?"

"I want to know about Beckett."

Hayes frowns. "I'll tell you anything you want to know. But why do you need to hear from us separately?"

"I just think my heart will believe it more if all of you tell me on your own that Beckett is in love with Odette."

Hayes's shoulders slump. "I can't tell you who he loves. Honestly, I don't understand a thing about him anymore."

I raise my eyebrows at him, imploring him to get to the point.

He sighs, rubbing the back of this neck. "I don't know. He either loves her, or he's putting on quite an act." Hayes must read the disappointment on my face because he adds, "That doesn't mean he doesn't love you too. You could still win him back! It just—"

"It's okay, Hayes. Can you call Lennox over?"

Hayes gets up, and I let Hayes's words settle into me before Lennox sits down.

"You want to talk about Beckett?" he asks.

I nod. He could always read people better than anyone else.

He considers his words carefully. "Let him go, Princess. Whether he loves you or her makes no difference. He's made his choice."

"Thank you for your honesty."

"I'll send Gage over."

A few seconds later, Gage is sitting in front of me.

"Does Beckett love Odette?"

"Yes," Gage answers in a single word. No other explanation. No sugar coating it. No 'but he loves you too' speak.

I nod.

He doesn't say more. He just gets up and tells Ryker it's his turn with me.

Ryker is the only one who smiles at me when he sits across from me. "It's good to see you, gorgeous."

"That's only because you needed to save your own skin."

He laughs. "Partially, but also because I've become fond of you, kiddo. And I want to finish the games. I think I have a good shot at beating Charming over there." He points to Caius.

"And the dickhead on the throne." He motions to Beckett.

"I doubt the dickhead on the throne will be competing much longer. Why compete for me when he already has a wife?"

Ryker falls back in his chair. "That's what you wanted to ask us. Do we think Beckett loves her or you?"

I grit my teeth, feeling stupid asking them all the question, but I need to know what Ryker thinks, perhaps more than the rest.

He studies me for a moment as if somehow, I have the answer displayed somewhere on my body.

"I think you're asking the wrong question."

"Huh?"

"I don't think it matters who Beckett is in love with. It matters who you love. You have a lot more power and control over your destiny than you realize. If you love him, go get him."

I frown. "That easy, huh?"

"Of course."

"And I don't suppose you love anyone?"

"That is a moot point. We aren't talking about me; we're talking about you. Stop listening to everyone. Stop paying attention to his actions. Listen to your own heart. If you want him, go get him. If you don't, let him go."

"What if I want him, but it would hurt more people to go after him than it would if I let him go?"

Ryker frowns at me. "I can't answer that for you. That's something only you can decide."

The others join us, and we all drink wine together. Hayes makes jokes. Caius rubs my back. The others alternate glares between Caius and Beckett.

That is until Beckett is handed a microphone.

He stands with Odette at his side. She holds onto his shoulder as he holds the mic with his one hand.

"Thank you all for coming here to celebrate me getting Odette back. I don't know what I'd do without her."

Beckett leans over and kisses her forehead as she beams.

I notice that no one at my table claps.

"I hope you have all enjoyed yourselves tonight, and you've gotten plenty to eat and drink."

Everyone mumbles their agreement.

"Good, because I have a serious announcement to make."

The room goes silent, and I stop breathing. *What could he announce that's worse than being married to her?* She's pregnant—that would crush me. It would mean he's been with her while he was with me. What a fool I've been.

"As you all know, Enzo Black was one of the men responsible for taking my wife from me. We are going to get retribution for those weeks of torture where I thought the love of my life was dead. We are going to war with the Black Empire."

The room breaks out in cheers. Everyone is happy except our table, once again. My table looks at him in disgust, like they can't believe what they are hearing. Even Caius seems disturbed.

Then Beckett's eyes land on mine. They are empty and vacant. I don't know if he loves her or me, but I know he loves his brother. I know he played a part in Caius finding me.

Ryker told me it didn't matter what Beckett felt; it matters what I feel. He's right. I still love Beckett, even if I want to kill him.

My final act of love will be trying to stop this war.

19
RI

"READY TO GO TO BED?" Caius asks me as the ballroom slowly starts clearing.

The others glare at him.

"What? I didn't mean go to bed with me, just go to sleep," Caius snaps back.

I put my hand on Caius's arm. "I knew what you meant." I yawn, stretching my arms. "And yes, please."

I'm not sure where we are all going to sleep, but I'm more than ready to stop watching Beckett and Odette's displays of affection, real or fake.

I stand up, and Caius leads me outside, followed by the others. The sun set hours ago, and there's a chill in the air. I shiver, and Caius is right there to put the blanket I left behind in the banquet hall around me.

"Thanks," I say with a soft smile.

"Of course." He puts his hands in his pockets as we walk toward a nearby hotel where Caius has rooms reserved for the night. The others follow behind.

No one speaks about Beckett's declaration of war. No one knows what's going on in his head anymore, and no one wants to speculate. That, or they don't want to bring up his name around me in case it hurts me.

We reach the hotel, and Caius goes to the desk to collect our keys.

He returns and holds out a key for me.

"What about everyone else?" I ask.

Hayes runs up to me and puts his arm around my shoulders. "We aren't letting you out of our sight again."

"Since that worked so well the last time," Lennox grumbles.

Hayes frowns. "Well, this time, we'll do shifts, so someone is awake at all times. We won't let anyone through, not this time. We promise."

"Don't make promises you can't keep," I say.

Hayes's scowl deepens.

Caius starts walking toward the elevators, and I follow. Then we are all riding up to the top floor, where we will all be sharing a room. But when Caius opens the door, I realize it's a suite taking up half the floor. There are plenty of places for the guys to crash that aren't two feet away from my bed—thank god.

"I'm going to shower," I say, walking through the suite to the main bedroom and ensuite bathroom.

Every guy in the room starts following me.

I snap my head back toward them. "Alone."

Lennox and Hayes chuckle. "We aren't going to stand in the bathroom with you, but we need to do a quick sweep first. Then someone will be outside your door at all times," Lennox says.

I roll my eyes but let the guys pass. Every single one of them heads into the bathroom like they don't trust the others to do a security sweep.

Finally, one by one, they file back out. "All good?" I cross my arms over my chest as I smirk at them.

"All good," Gage says.

I walk into the bathroom. Apparently, Hayes got bathroom duty because every five minutes, he hollers into the bathroom, and I have to holler back to keep him from breaking down the door.

I sigh as the hot water pours over me. So much for a hot, relaxing shower in solitude to wash away the pain of the day.

I find a robe on the back of the door and wrap it around me rather than putting my dirty clothes back on. I open the door to find all five of the guys inspecting the bedroom or lounging on the bed.

"You do know this place has a lot more space than just this one room, right?" I say, toweling off my hair.

Their eyes zero in on my body, peeking out a little too much thanks to this loose-fitting robe, but I don't care. I'm not Beckett's. And I'm comfortable. I'm not ashamed of my body, but it doesn't mean I'm going to fuck any of them either.

I walk over to the edge of the bed and climb up as no one responds to my snarky comment.

"What?" I finally ask, knowing there is something they aren't telling me.

"Corsi called," Ryker says.

I frown, and all the warmth in the room leaves. "What did he want?"

"To talk to you."

I take a couple of deep breaths. I don't know if he was behind Kek kidnapping me. I don't know what crazy thing my father demands of me now, but I need to talk to him.

"Get him on the phone," I say.

Caius pulls out his phone and dials a number, then hands the phone to me.

I take it, unsure if the others should be listening to this conversation or not, but I doubt I'll convince any of them to leave. Even if I do, Gage will just fasten something to listen through the door.

"Hello," Vincent's deep voice comes through the phone.

"Vincent, you called?"

"I did. I'm surprised you returned my call so quickly. You have a tendency not to follow my directions."

"Just trying to keep you on your toes."

He ignores me. "I thought you'd like to know that you get to pick the next game."

My eyes shoot out of my head. I wasn't sure my father really considered me part of the game. I didn't think if my name was selected, he'd actually let me choose the game.

"Do I need to tell you ahead of time?" I ask.

"I'll summon you about an hour before the game is supposed to start. That should give us enough time to set up whatever you have planned."

Suddenly, the phone line goes dead.

He ended the call without a goodbye or a chance for me to ask any other questions.

I lower the phone, still in shock.

"What did he want?" Caius asks.

"I get to choose the game."

Everyone's mouth drops.

"I know," I say, my own mouth hanging open.

"Do you know what game you'll pick?" Gage asks.

I shake my head. I honestly don't.

"If you could give me a heads up, Princess, I'd appreciate it. I'd like to not die this week," Ryker says.

I smile at him. "I'll make sure it's a game that won't end in your death. Maybe just seriously injured," I tease.

He laughs.

I get to pick the game.

I could pick something that plays to my strengths. Something I could win and have all the power. If I won, would I get to take care of myself for the week instead of having to live with others?

I don't know if Vincent would ever allow that.

I climb into the bed, exhausted and tired of violence. Whatever game I choose won't be violent. It will be civilized, maybe something to help my father actually see the men's merits. See why they would or wouldn't make a good husband for me.

It probably won't help, and the next week someone else will come up with another violent game. But at least this time, I can do something that won't end in death this week.

I close my eyes as ideas start spinning in my head. The guys make themselves comfortable on the floor around me in silence.

"This bed is big enough for at least one or two more. Not everyone should sleep on the floor," I say.

There's some hushed mumbling, and then I feel two bodies climbing into the bed, one on either side of me.

I smile and peek my eyes open to see Hayes on one side and Caius on the other.

I'll sleep well tonight.

The sounds come. They're muffled at first, but they grow stronger with every bang of the bed against the wall.

I can't breathe, I'm suffocating, this is my worst nightmare.

I don't think the others realize who it is at first. They, after all, are not intimately familiar with the sounds one of them makes like I am. But after a minute of the sound coming through the wall, there is no denying who is on the other side and what they are doing.

How could they end up in the room right next door?

My memories are fuzzy about the last couple of days. I thought I was okay with Beckett choosing Odette. As long as he's happy, I'm happy for him. But this...this breaks me—every moan, every bang of her head against the headboard, every cry of his name.

The tears fall, and they don't stop.

ODETTE IS in the bathroom doing god knows what. I quickly climbed into bed and am hoping to be fast asleep before she comes out. I doubt I'll ever sleep again, though. I have too many thoughts in my head—about Ri, about my brother.

I declared war tonight. If my brother wouldn't talk to me before, he won't talk to me now.

And I don't know how to put a stop to any of it.

I need to find a way to send a message to Kai and Enzo to warn them, to tell them I don't want this.

I can try to delay things as long as possible. I can convince the Retribution Kings we need to see how the game plays out with Ri and what Corsi does. We may need his army. I doubt they will let me keep playing in the game, though.

Delay—that's all I can hope to do. I've decided my fate. I've done all that I can to save Ri, *but will it be worth the cost?*

How do I protect Enzo and Kai?

I smirk. I don't.

They are more than capable of winning a war against these idiots. And if I help steer the Retribution Kings in the wrong direction, their odds increase. Kai won't let anything happen to her family.

My head falls back on my pillow, a bit relaxed for the first time. My family will destroy the Retribution Kings, and then I'll be free. They'll be pissed at me, more pissed than all the other stupid shit I've done combined, but I'll willfully spend my life making it up to them.

The bathroom door opens; I squeeze my eyes shut and calm my breathing. I meditate to stay as still as possible, so Odette thinks I'm asleep as she comes to bed.

She doesn't say anything, not even a whisper of my name. Maybe she's had a long day too and just wants to sleep.

I feel the bed shift and the covers move as she climbs into bed. I don't move. I don't know if I'm a snorer or not. I don't know the typical sounds I make when I sleep, but I'm hoping it's silence.

Odette rolls over to me and kisses me sweetly on the forehead. Thank god. She's just going to kiss me goodnight.

"If you want her to live through the night, you'll stop faking sleep and fuck me."

Her words are ice cold and delivered to make an impact.

I open my eyes but still don't move.

"Ri helped you. She helped you escape when you thought you had no options. Why would you kill her?"

"Because you prefer her to me. You don't belong with her; you belong with me. You don't want a girl who can hold her own on a battlefield right next to you. You want a girl who will be waiting at home with a good meal and warm bed when you return."

"You can't cook."

"I can learn."

I grunt. "Don't threaten her life. If you want something from me, then figure out how to convince me."

I roll on top of her, pinning her to the bed and tightening my hand around her throat, making it difficult for her to breathe. "Don't threaten Ri ever again, or I'll kill you. Understand?"

I scare her like the monster I am. She's destroyed my life, and I want to end her. But I can't—at least not until Ri is completely safe. Ri needs to have run away or married a man who is strong enough to protect her.

I cringe at that thought.

She nods, but when I release her throat, she becomes maniacal. Her nails dig into my skin, and she cackles like a cartoon villain.

"I own you, Beckett. You can't threaten me without threatening her. You needed Caius's help to save her. He did that, but he's also getting close to her. He might have even fucked her in her misery over losing you. He's slowly gaining her trust. And he's got the best shot of winning the game and marrying her."

If I could kill her with a look, then I would. My eyes brand my hatred into her body.

"If you don't do exactly what I say, if you so much as lay another finger on me, and most definitely if you kill me, Caius will end her. Caius likes her. He'd love for her to be his wife, but he loves me. He's loyal to me. He'd do anything to avenge his sister's death. So threaten me again and see what happens. Mark me again, and I'll let him know exactly where to put the same marks on her body."

My eyes well with tears, but I don't let them out.

"What do you want?" I ask with as much strength as I can muster.

She grins, knowing she's won. And she has, but she won't always.

I don't regret tying her life to Ri's. It means Ri is safe. Caius and the Retribution Kings will do everything to keep her safe. But someday, Odette will get what's coming to her.

"I want you to fuck me like I'm her."

I swallow hard against my throat. That's impossible. I can't fuck anyone like I do Ri. It will never be the same.

Odette undoes the robe she's wearing, revealing some red lacy lingerie. There was a time when I would have found her sexy as hell. Now I want to throw her into the depths of hell.

"Beckett, I'm waiting." Odette just lies spread out on the bed, waiting for me to do all the work.

Fuck, it would have been so much easier to just let her ride my dick. I should have let her take from me and not be an active participant.

God, how am I going to do this?

I'm just wearing my boxer briefs as I position myself over her body. Just two thin pieces of fabric separate us.

It's just sex. Just fucking, I try to convince myself.

It's just putting my heart and soul in a shredder. This will destroy me. I'll never forgive myself. Ri won't either. I won't ever be able to fuck a woman without thinking about this moment. This mistake. This...

Odette sinks her nails into my chest, drawing blood. I curse.

"Get on with it, baby. I've been waiting a long time to have you again."

My cock is anything but hard.

I remove it from my briefs and close my eyes, thinking of Ri. Of what snarky comment she might say to me. Of her red lips wrapped around my cock. Of her whimpers and cries when I touch her.

A hand reaches out and strokes my length. I squeeze my eyes shut tighter.

It's Ri. It's Ri. It's Ri.

I moan as the hand pumps me. It does feel good.

And then I'm guided toward her entrance.

I keep my eyes shut, my arm trembling against the headboard. The second I feel a drop of moisture on my cock, I thrust hard, ripping through her. I thrust viciously. If I don't, I won't be able to stomach it.

I pound as hard as I can. I'm out of breath, so is she. I hear her head hitting the headboard.

Ri.

Ri.

Ri.

I force myself to think of her, not reality.

Every part of my body knows it's not her, though. No matter how tightly I squeeze my eyes shut, I can't keep tears from dripping down my face and onto hers.

She cries out, and I know she's orgasming.

"Come with me, baby," she purrs.

I can't. There's no fucking way I can or will. But I go through the motions. I make the fake sounds, the fake grunts, and jerks into her body.

She doesn't call me out.

I open my eyes to see her smirking in victory up at me.

I pull myself out and off of her as fast as I can, heading to the bathroom before she can protest. I intend to shower to wash her stench off me, but I don't make it that far, vomiting violently into the toilet first.

I'll never forgive myself. That was too much. I made too many mistakes that led me here. I've never felt so much despair, emptiness, darkness. All I really want to do right now is find Ri and tell her to hold me as she drives a dagger into my heart to make the pain stop.

"I WANT to take you somewhere before we leave to meet Corsi tonight," Caius says.

We've been eating breakfast in the hotel room, taking our time drinking several cups of coffee and a couple of rounds of breakfast. No one slept very well last night between Beckett and Odette fucking, half of them sleeping on the floor and waking up at various hours all night to change security shifts.

I set my third cup of coffee down on the kitchen table. "Okay."

"Where are we going?" Hayes asks.

Caius frowns. "I meant just Ri and me."

Hayes looks baffled with his unkempt hair and glasses sitting crooked on his face. "But—"

I give Hayes a look. "I'm supposed to meet Vincent in two hours. Nothing is going to happen to me between then and now."

Hayes looks to Ryker for help.

Ryker looks at me. "Wear a tracker? And don't get kidnapped. I need to meet with some of my guys before tonight anyway."

He kisses my cheek.

"Thank you," I whisper, knowing he's ultimately the one who gets to decide. It will be his ass if anything happens to me.

I need a moment away from everyone's pity glances, anyway. I'm the foolish girl who fell in love with a man who always loved someone else.

Hayes turns to the others. "Help me out here. She shouldn't be going anywhere alone, especially not with hi—"

"I think it would be good for you to get some fresh air," Gage says to me.

"I agree. You two should talk; clear the air. We need to find Beckett and see what the hell he wants us to do anyway," Lennox says.

Hayes looks at both of them like they've lost their minds. "We're not still going to do what that idiot says, are we?"

Gage and Lennox ignore him.

Ryker brings me a simple bracelet with a small emergency button to wear as a tracker. If I take it off, it sets the alarm off as well.

After gulping down the rest of my coffee, I'm ready to go.

Caius and I walk out of the building silently. I did my best not to look at Beckett and Odette's door as we walked by, but it was hard. I didn't hear any sounds from their room this morning, thank god.

"So, where are we going?" I ask as soon as we're outside.

"For a walk."

I raise my eyebrows. "A walk?"

He nods with a shy smile.

"Lead the way."

We walk a couple of blocks before the sidewalk leads to a creek. The trail along the creek turns more rugged; soon, trees and water surround us instead of buildings.

The sun feels nice on my face as we walk. So does the silence, but Caius brought me here to say something, and I need to hear it.

"So...? What do you want to talk about?" I ask.

He takes a deep breath. "I'm sorry for being pushy with you before. It was wrong of me, and I shouldn't have. You clearly wanted Beckett, and I kept pushing. I just wanted to say I'm sorry."

"You're sorry because now that Beckett has proved what an ass he is, you still want a chance with me?"

He chuckles. "No, I just needed to tell you I'm sorry. I saw how much pain you were in last night, and I never want to be the cause of you being in that much distress. I like you a great deal, but I'm not the right man for you.

"But if I win the game, or if you chose me, I'll do everything in my power to help you—escape or be a good husband, if that's what you choose. Whatever happens, I just want to apologize. I fucked up, and I don't want to do it again."

"Your apology is accepted."

His shoulders slump in a relaxed manner. "Thank you."

"Is that all you wanted to talk about?"

He opens his mouth like he wants to say more. I know he does, but sharing his feelings is hard for him, and I'm not exactly making it easy.

"I want to help you, but I don't know how. Tell me what you want. You want me to go kick Beckett's ass, kill him for hurting you? I will," he sputters out.

"You would kill the man your sister loves for me?"

He shrugs. "She could do better."

I smile at that. "Probably, but I still don't think you would do it. You love your sister too much, and I'm not blaming you for that."

"Then how do I help you with your father? Do I help you run? Do I help you win? What do you want?"

I sigh. "I can't run."

"Then how do I help you win?"

"Not sure, exactly. I doubt Vincent will let me win. Just ensure you and Ryker are the best choices for Vincent to pick. Show how strong you are. How good of a leader you are. How you won't take any crap from me and will be able to protect me, not how much you love or care for me.

"Show him how you can take over his place, how you're cruel and heartless. Ryker has that public image down. You could work on that some more. Stop coming off so charming and be more menacing."

His eyes are dark and sorrowful. "I'll do anything I can for you, Ri—anything."

We lock eyes, and there is so much unsaid between us—so much that will never be said.

I nod.

We finish our hike, talking about less serious things. We talk about which of the guys snores and which will find a girlfriend next. We talk about how nice the weather is. We talk about our favorite movies and books. We talk about anything that can distract us from our pain. His pain at losing his father and regaining his sister. My pain at losing the love of my life.

As we start heading back, I turn the conversation serious once again. "I've thought of something else you can do."

"Anything," Caius repeats.

This is going to test his promise to me. "Try to find a way to stop the war between Beckett and his brother."

His smile drops, and he looks down at the dirt path we're walking on.

"I don't know why Beckett declared war, but he loves his brother, his family. He would do anything for them. Don't let him go to war," I plead.

Caius looks at me, dumbfounded. He wants to help me, but he can't promise me this.

"If not for Beckett's sake, then for your sister's. If Beckett goes to war, he'll never be the same. He'll be lost forever. If she wants a man who will love and protect her all her life, then he can't go to war. You have to help him put a stop to it."

Caius chews on his bottom lip for a second as my words sink in. "I'll see what I can do."

It's the best I'm going to get from him, so I don't push him further. We leave the creek trail and are back in town. It's a little early, but I don't want to return to the guys. I'm tired of saying goodbye.

"Take me to Vincent."

———

It feels strange stepping foot back in Vincent's swanky downtown penthouse. My head pounds—either from the pain of being back here or the fuzziness of my memories after Kek took me. I still don't remember much from the time Beckett almost killed me to when Kek took me. The guys filled me in some, but I feel like they all left out huge chunks of time, and I have no idea why.

What are they hiding from me?

I pour myself a glass of the nicest bottle of wine I can find and then make myself comfortable on the couch until Vincent makes his presence known.

I wait twenty minutes, but I don't mind. The silence is nice. I haven't had much of it since Caius rescued me. The guys are too afraid to leave me alone for a single second. I look down at the bracelet. It will stop working soon now that I'm safe. Ryker will have no need to protect me. I don't think the others will stop, though.

"So let's hear the brilliant game you've come up with," Vincent says, sitting on the edge of a nearby couch with his own glass of wine.

"I want the man I'm forced to marry to be the right man for me, not just the best man with a gun. So my game is a simple one— impress me with your words. Tell me why you deserve to marry me. What qualities do you possess that should make me pick you? Impress me. Tell me you love me if it's true or that you could love me. Declare your feelings for me."

Vincent just sips his wine. He hates my game and is going to come up with one of his own. This was a mistake. I should have come up with something more dangerous, then he might have gone along with it, and I would have some control.

"Or we could—"

Vincent cuts me off. "I like it. Simple, but an important task. We need a man who can speak, as well as he can shoot or lead. A leader's job is much more about speaking than shooting anyway."

"Really? You don't hate the idea?"

"Not at all." Vincent drinks more of his wine.

"And you'll let me choose the winner?"

"Of course, I think your opinion matters a great deal." There's a pause just long enough for me to feel like I've won. "But my opinion matters too."

My heart drops. "Of course," I mutter. I down the rest of my wine before standing and walking to the kitchen to pour myself another glass.

When I return, Vincent feels ready to drop a bigger bomb on me.

"Sit," he commands.

I take my seat again, afraid of what he's going to say.

"War is coming."

"Between the Retribution Kings and—"

"No, not just them. War in general. I've seen it come enough times now that I know when it's coming, and it's coming. You don't think I know why all these leaders entered this ridiculous game?"

"To win me?"

He chuckles. "To have a shot to take me down. They could either win and get my kingdom or try to use the game as a way to get close to me. Infiltrate my organization and kill me from within, but they've all failed so far."

"There have been attacks on you?" my mouth drops open at that thought.

"Of course. I made sure they all paid the price in the game. There is no need for these wars."

He sighs. "But war is coming. I've grown too powerful, and

these young ones, especially, want more and more power. They aren't satisfied just to rule over their gangs and crews; they need more."

Vincent stands and walks over to a window, looking out. I can see the wrinkles on his face, the hairs that have all but turned grey, and the age that he used to carry so well weighing down on him. He's tired of leading, tired of being the ruler with great, terrifying power.

"What are you going to do?" I ask.

"We are strong. We can't be defeated by one or two rogue gang leaders. The only way we can be taken down is if they all work together. Only then will our armies fall."

"Do they realize that? Are they—"

"Yes, they are all cocky sons of bitches that think they are strong enough to take me down. They are starting to band together. I've seen the evidence of them meeting, of them trying to kill you in order to end my line. So far, their attempts have been futile. The ones leading the attacks aren't the smartest, but all it takes is one smart leader to join them, and then we'll fall."

I frown with my heart thumping wildly in my chest because I know how my father handles threats. I know how he handles attacks. And I don't like where this is headed.

"We need to take down as many leaders as possible. The strongest are left in this game, and we need to take as many down as possible before an uprising happens. We are so close to the end; I can't let anything interfere with my plans, not after everything we've sacrificed."

"I don't understand."

"Tonight, we kill half of them. We kill any that are a threat to us. We kill any that aren't on our side, any that could lead the others in war."

I gasp—*half.*

Half could include Caius.

It could include Ryker.

It could include Beckett. *No, Beckett won't come. He'll bow out.*

I suck in a breath. I need to change his mind. This is too much, too high of a chance of death.

"But the best leader among them is exactly who we want to lead the Corsi mafia. Wouldn't we be killing the best among them?"

"No, we don't want the best. We want the most loyal."

I stand and pace now. I can't let them die. I have to find a way to stop the death. None of the men left deserve to die.

"Won't their number twos come after us if we just kill men willy-nilly? It's one thing for them to die in competition, but it's another for us to just shoot them point-blank."

"We aren't going to shoot them; you are."

I frown. "I won't agree to shoot innocent people for no reason."

He laughs. "None of these men are innocent."

True. I'm running out of arguments.

"Why me?"

"I'm ready to unleash you, for the rest to see who you really are."

"And if I refuse?"

Don't say you'll kill Lucy, don't say you'll kill Beckett, don't say you'll kill...

"I'm not going to threaten you anymore."

"Then, what are you going to do?"

Vincent snaps his fingers, and Kek appears. I guessed he was working with my father to scare me or control me, but then I glance down to who he's holding in his arms—a limp Lucy, beaten and bruised.

"Lucy!" I run over to them.

"What happened?" I brush her hair out of her face and try not to wince when I see a large gash over her eye.

Lucy's bottom lip trembles, and she shivers in Kek's arms.

"Did you...?" I snap at Kek, assuming he's the monster behind this.

"It wasn't him," Vincent.

Lucy leans into his body like he alone will protect her, and I believe that Kek didn't hurt her.

"Then who?" I demand.

"That's what we are going to figure out. Only a limited number of people knew about the safe house—Ryker, Caius, and Beckett are at the top of the list."

My teeth grind together, but I know Vincent is right. One of them betrayed us. One of them did this to Lucy.

"I'm—" Lucy starts and then passes out in Kek's arms.

"Lucy!" I scream louder as I check her pulse. "I don't think she's breathing."

Kek lowers her onto the floor and starts performing CPR. Vincent calls for a medic, and I stand frantically by watching my only friend in the world—the only one I can truly trust—have her heart stop beating. I have no idea if she'll survive.

My blood rages through my body. Without a doubt in my mind, I'll kill anyone involved. It may play into my father's plan, but for once, we are on the same side.

THERE HAVEN'T BEEN many times in my life when I felt like I made the right choice. A sense of calm washes through me as I step into the restaurant; today I decided correctly.

Caius is on my left as we walk into the Italian restaurant owned by the Corsi family.

It took a lot of convincing the Retribution Kings to let me come, to keep competing since Odette is alive and I no longer have a need to win Rialta as my wife. But I told the Kings we still needed to finish the game, and I'd do everything in my power to help Caius win. I promised them if I somehow won, I'd have Caius or another member of the Retribution Kings marry Rialta. Corsi and controlling his kingdom are too important for me to bow out.

Ultimately, Odette was actually the one who convinced everyone I should go. I don't know what her motivations are. Maybe she wanted me to help protect her brother. Maybe she wants to see me dead. Or maybe there's something else going on I don't know about, but once she said I should go, there was no more discussion about it.

So here I am.

I have no idea why this game is taking place in one of their

Italian restaurants, but at least we aren't decked out in tactical gear or arriving in the middle of the forest.

That has to be a good sign, right?

One of Corsi's men leads us through the empty restaurant to a back room where a large table has been set up. A few men are already sitting at the table as Caius and I take our seats. Ryker shows up next, but he pretends he doesn't know who we are. He sits next to one of the most ruthless men still in the game.

The table quickly fills up. Wine is poured. Bread is brought out. But still no sign of Ri or her father.

"Something's not right," I whisper to Caius after the main course is brought out.

"I agree. Do you think the game has already started, and they didn't tell us the rules?" Caius stares down at his food. "Like they poisoned the wine or food and want to see who has the strength to survive?"

"That seems farfetched. I more meant they were planning on starting the games at seven, like the text said, but had to move it back because something happened."

"You think something happened to Ri?" Caius asks, his face turning white instantly.

"I don't know, but something just doesn't feel right."

"Ryker put a tracker on her; maybe it's still active."

I glance across the table to where Ryker is. He laughs at something the man next to him says, acting like he doesn't have a care in the world.

But then Ryker's eyes meet mine.

I don't know how to communicate with him to tell him we're worried about Ri.

He looks down at his lap, and I realize he's on his phone. I wait a minute to pull my phone out after I feel it buzz in my pocket. I don't want anyone to notice we are communicating. Before I can pull my phone out, the back doors open, and Corsi, Ri, and a third man enter the dining room.

"Holy fuck, that's Kek" Caius whispers next to me.

What the hell is going on?

All three of them take a seat at a table on the other side of the room facing us. I study Ri carefully, looking for any signs that her mind has been messed with, that she's been hurt, or is scared to death and sending signals for someone to help her. Instead, all I see is a ruthlessness in her eyes as she scans the room.

She starts her perusal on the other side of the table, looking at each man one by one. I don't know what she's so pissed about. I don't know what she's looking for in each of our eyes, but a small silence falls over the table under her gaze. Each man is being judged for his sins in her eyes.

She looks at Caius, and even he sinks down into his chair. She holds nothing back.

And then she looks at me. For a split second, her eyes widen and soften. There isn't the same hatred and pain she gave the other guys.

She's surprised I'm here.

A second later, that look is gone, replaced with the same heartless stare she gave everyone else. I've never seen Ri so furious.

She continues on until she has stared down every single one of us.

Corsi clears his throat, and the room goes silent. He doesn't move from his chair as he says, "Tonight's game is simple. You will meet with us, one at a time. Your task is to convince us that you should win, that you are worthy of my daughter. Only the top half will be advancing."

They are eliminating half of us. *The question is will the losing half get to live?*

Caius swallows hard next to me, and I suspect he's pondering the same question.

A name is called to their table, and then another course of food and wine is brought out. Conversation returns as the man takes a seat at the table and begins his interrogation—because I'm sure that's what it feels like.

Five minutes later, the guy returns to the table, looking completely unfazed. This is how it continues down the line. No one can really hear what the others are saying. The tables are too far away, and the sound of us chatting while we eat and drink drowns everything else out.

It's Caius's turn to be followed by mine.

I consider what I'm going to say.

What can I say?

I love you, Ri. I'm only staying with Odette to try and protect you from the guy you're currently sitting next to. The only reason I'm staying married to Odette is because she and Caius know the phrase that can be used to undo whatever Kek does to you.

Caius walks back to the table. He gives me no clue what he said or what happened. Now it's my turn.

I still don't know what I'm going to say as I approach the table. I came here to see if she's okay. Clearly, she's not okay. Something terrible happened, and I have no idea who to save her from.

"Have a seat, Beckett," Corsi says as I approach.

I take the seat across from them. Corsi doesn't show any emotion. Kek looks like he wants to murder me. And Ri—she looks completely lost when she looks at me.

It's then that I realize what I have to do. I have to stop leading her on. I have to put the final nail in her heart, severing her from me completely.

"You have five minutes to convince us why you should win and marry my daughter," Corsi says.

I take a deep breath, staring right at Ri. I came here to end this, to provide closure for both of us. I hope she can be with someone worthy of her, someone who deserves her.

"I shouldn't marry your daughter. I'm the last man who should."

Corsi's eyes raise, and Kek's face darkens, but Ri doesn't react to my words. She's strong and already knows what I'm about to say. I'm not even sure she needs to hear my words, but I need to say it out loud.

"I've betrayed her, hurt her, lied to her. I gave my heart to another woman who I thought had died. No, not died—I thought Ri killed her."

I look Ri dead in the eyes. "But I know that isn't true. My wife is alive. I'm a married man, which is one of the many reasons I'm not the right man for her. I'm not worthy of her. I'm not a good man. I suck as a leader. I let my emotions drive my actions. I failed to protect her time and time again.

"But the number one reason I'm not the one for your daughter —I'm in love with another woman."

I wait for Corsi to chew me out. I wait for Ri to ask me to resign from the games. Neither happens.

"Thank you, your time is up," Corsi says.

I stand and turn to head back to my spot, unsure what's going to happen until I hear Kek speak.

"He's a dead man."

I TRIED to listen to the men when they all stated they were the ones for me. Several insisted they were the best choice because they were the most vicious, cruel man around—not exactly what I wanted to hear. Some said they were madly in love.

Ryker was harsh and controlling with his words. He pretended to think of me as nothing more than a possession, something to control. He said we both have a role to play, and he knew his. Everything he said was the complete opposite of the man I knew.

Caius ignored my advice. Instead of acting like Ryker, Caius was sweet, charming, a love-sick boy who professed his love for me.

And Beckett was...honest, devastatingly honest.

Why did he come?

He should have just quit; now there's a strong chance he'll die for what he just said.

There has to be a reason Beckett came; I just can't figure out what it is. I can't figure out anything when it comes to him.

"So, who wins and who loses?" Kek asks us.

I stare at Vincent, unsure of what happens next. There was no obvious culprit who hurt Lucy, but someone here did.

"What do you think, Ri?" Vincent asks.

"I honestly don't know who hurt Lucy, and that's all I care about at the moment. Not professions of love. Not who is the strongest, badass guy around. I just want to punish whoever hurt Lucy; the rest can live."

Vincent nods. "It's not about killing the right person. It's about setting an example that we won't tolerate this. We will kill until we get answers."

I frown as a tear slips. "It matters to me."

"We'll make sure the right person pays, but for now, we just need to show our power."

I look at him, knowing what happens next. "Who do you want me to kill?"

"Three, any three."

I stare him down, shocked he's giving me this power.

"They're all armed. What do I do when they retaliate?"

"They won't. We'll make it clear we have evidence of them scheming together to kill Lucy. It will stop them from working together in the future against us."

I'm not sure it will, but I need to know who hurt Lucy.

"You'll let me do this my way? I'll kill whoever I think is responsible for Lucy's death?"

"You have my word. Show them how strong you are. Show them what won't be tolerated."

"What's changed? Why do I no longer have to play the princess part?"

"We are close to the end, and I need the men to see who you truly are."

I look to Kek, a man I fear. A man who can wipe my memories in a single second—I may need him to after what I'm about to do.

"How do I get them to confess?" I ask.

Kek has tortured me, and I'm sure countless others. He knows how to pull confessions out of people.

He smirks. "You already know how."

I frown, not really sure what he's saying.

"If everyone could line up against the wall, we'd like to announce the winners," Vincent announces.

The men stand casually and walk to a wall to be picked as the winner. Only a couple seem weary. Ryker, Caius, and Beckett all know what's about to happen, but they do as they're asked. I doubt they will fight their fates. All of them are prepared to die.

Kek, Vincent, and I take our time standing and walking over in front of them.

"Rialta will do the announcing of winners. Rialta," Vincent says, giving me the floor.

Two of the guys give me a flirtatious wink; I ignore them.

"Listen up," I snap with my full voice, and I know I've got their full attention. "My best friend, Lucy, was seriously injured. Right now, she's unconscious, fighting for her life." My voice pours with pain and desperation.

I walk up and down the line, staring at each of them. "I'm giving you one chance. If you know anything about who hurt Lucy, tell me now."

I continue to walk up and down the line of men. I stare at Ryker, Caius, Beckett. One of them has to know something. One of them might have even been the one to hurt her.

A man, I think his name is Nigel, steps forward from the line. I don't know much about him, except he's a cruel man. From the speech he gave me, he doesn't think highly of women.

I don't hesitate.

I pull my gun and fire into his chest.

I watch the shock appear on his face, the whites in his eyes grow wider, and then he falls hard to the ground.

No one moves.

I expect them all to reach for their guns. I expect an all-out war to start. Vincent was right, though—show my power, and they all fear me.

"Anyone else have anything to say about what happened to Lucy?" I ask.

No one moves a muscle.

I'm not sure what I should do next.

I turn, and Vincent looks at me sternly, egging me on. If I don't choose more to kill, he will, and that scares the shit out of me.

I grab Kek's arm, and we take a step back, far enough away from the line that they can't hear me.

"I don't know what to do," I say.

Kek looks at me. "And you're asking me? The guy you fear more than anything?"

"I don't fear you, not anymore."

I look over my shoulder and see Beckett out of the corner of my eye. He's the only man I care to save, even if it kills me.

"Is he a good man?" Kek asks me, talking about Beckett.

"The best." Even if he doesn't always seem like it, I know who he is deep down.

"Then he can never be yours."

I turn, staring back at Kek. "What do you mean?"

He sighs. "You have to give him up."

"What if I can't?" I whisper, tears coming, assuming he means give him up to Odette.

"Kill him now if you can't give him up. He'll never be yours."

It's the most honest thing anyone has ever said to me.

He puts his fingers under my chin and looks deep into my eyes. "For what it's worth, I think you're strong enough to give him up, strong enough to let him live with another."

I blink back my tears, refusing to cry.

"I need you to erase my memories. Erase him completely from my head. That's the only way I'll survive watching him with another woman."

Kek looks at me sadly. "I already tried and failed. Even when I erased the best of him, you still loved him."

I frown. "What do you mean?"

"You need to kill two more men."

"I don't know how to choose."

"You do. You know exactly who your greatest threats are. You know who hurt Lucy. You know. Deep down, you know."

I run my hand through my hair. I do, but...*can I do it?*

We walk back toward the line of men, and I look at each of them again.

Ryker looks bored.

Caius looks concerned.

Beckett looks at peace, ready to die.

Two more men have to die.

I know exactly which two.

Then Kek whispers in my ear the phrase I hate. But this time I'm thankful because he gives me everything back. "Kill all those who are a threat to you and trust your gut."

I know which two have to die.

Both deaths are hard.

But one I know to be a sinner. He's hurt me time and time again.

The other, I'm just realizing how much of a saint he is.

Both are threats to me.

Both have to die.

I thought one didn't love me.

I was wrong.

And now two people are going to die for my mistake.

I lift my gun and fire twice.

Two lives have ended.

And I'll never be the same again.

———

TORTURED HERO

RETRIBUTION GAMES BOOK 5

TRUST MY GUT.

The words vibrate through my body as I stand in front of a row of men. I want to destroy them all for their roles in my life. For thinking they can control me, just because they're men. For thinking I'm a piece of property, only good for sticking their cocks in and producing male heirs.

But there are also kind men. Men who are just doing their best to lead a group they inherited. Those men simply want to keep their men alive and out of jail.

This group is comprised of men I hate, men I have to kill, and a man I love.

Vincent wants me to show strength. Now that my mind is my own again, I realize why. I remember my purpose, my goal in life. Why I am the way I am—I remember it all.

I also remember why I had to forget for so long and why now is the time to remember. It's a lot to process, a lot to feel, but I know what I have to do.

The gun feels heavier in my hand, heavier than it's ever felt before. I've been trained how to use a gun my entire life for as long as I can remember. Vincent did a lot of the training, but it was nothing compared to what Kek did.

He trained me to not feel emotions, to just do the job. Kill relentlessly to protect, and always protect.

These kills may look like an attack from an outsider's perspective, but they are all about protecting those I love. It doesn't make it any easier for me to pull the trigger, though.

Ryker is my friend. He's protected me even when he didn't have to, but his allegiance is ultimately to his men. He'll throw me under the bus every time if it means protecting his own. But he's a good man, too good of a man—a man who needs to find a way out before an inevitable war starts.

Beckett is the man I love, but he'll never be mine. He's Odette's. Even if he came here to prove he can win me too, it doesn't matter. He's chosen her time and time again, and he'll always choose her over me. But he doesn't deserve to die for loving another woman. I'm not sure I could shoot him even if he did deserve death—I'm too infatuated with him. He'll always feel like my other half, so I need him alive for me to survive what's coming.

The next two men remaining aren't contenders in my head. I skip down the line to my greatest enemy here, and yet the greatest saint.

I turn the gun to him, my eyes welling. He has been kind, way too kind toward me. He's saved me, and I've protected him. He's pushed his limits with me, making it clear he wants me. If I chose him, he'd do everything to make me happy. I thought he was a lovesick, charming man who wanted me while mourning his sister.

I was wrong.

He has betrayed me more than anyone here.

He knew the phrase to fuck with my memories and mind.

I almost died during one of the games because he used the phrase to control me. I couldn't move, couldn't fight back because of him.

He helped Odette escape. He knew from the start she was

never dead. He knew exactly where she was and what had happened to her.

He used Odette's death and Beckett's family to start a war.

He pretended to want me when it was so obvious that what he really wants is to kill Vincent and me. The only thing he cares about is putting an end to the Corsi name once and for all.

The Retribution Kings are the enemy. They are the ones wanting to start a war. They're greedy assholes who just want more power.

Caius is my enemy.

But it's harder than it should be to pull the trigger. I've been wrong before, and I could be wrong here. I could be killing an innocent man.

Trust your gut; Kek's words push through me.

I know what my gut is telling me.

Caius is responsible for Lucy's injuries. He's responsible for all of this drama.

I take one deep breath and pull the trigger.

Caius drops, but I don't let my eyes follow him down—part of my training to stay unemotional.

I don't meet anyone else's gaze. I don't want to see the judgment. I don't want to see their fear that I could turn the gun on them next. I could shoot them dead before they could even attempt an attack.

This is what they signed up for when they entered the game, though. Vincent and I are strong. Between the two of us, we could continue the Corsi line. We could control all of these motherfuckers and all of their armies. We are that strong. We are Corsis.

But I'm going to need the strength of all my ancestors to make the next kill. This next one is going to hurt. Not just him, but for me.

He knows it too. He's been begging me to do it for a while. It's his job. It's always been his destiny to protect just like me.

He's not standing in the line against the wall but next to me.

He's a saint.

My saint.

He protected me even when I thought he was trying to kill me. He protected me by training me for the worst situations possible. My nightmares told me he was the enemy, but he was saving me. He was making me stronger, ensuring that when I faced down a dozen men, I would win. He made me strong enough to do the task I was assigned.

And I am because of him.

He's been warning me this entire time, trying to prepare me for the inevitable end. Our destiny was written when I was five years old.

Kek is my saint.

I turn to face him, not sure if I'm doing the right thing. I don't lift my gun right away, and I look Kek in the eyes.

It's a mistake, I know.

Don't get emotional. If you feel threatened, follow your gut. It won't fail.

He's a threat to my goal. He knows too much, a loose end that has outlived his purpose.

But god, why does it have to be me? Why do I have to be the one to kill him?

Why couldn't Vincent do it?

Why couldn't any man here kill him?

I look into Kek's eyes and see him smiling down at me. I know the words he would say if he chose to speak.

This makes you stronger. And these men need to see your absolute strength.

I look at Kek one more time. I remember the darkness of his eyes. I remember the life we had before we had to deal with the real world when we were just training. Before things got messy and complicated, and I needed to forget everything we shared.

I'll never forget you, Kek, never.

He doesn't stop smiling as he gives me the tiniest of nods.

He's ready even if I'm not.

I pull the trigger and turn before the bullet even hits his body. I can't watch. I can't, or I'll no longer show strength. I'll reveal how incredibly weak I actually am. They'll see how much that devastated me, how I'll do anything Vincent wants.

But they can also see how I protect but at the cost of everything.

Everything I love.

Everything I want.

Everything I am.

Anyone in my life who doesn't serve my life's purpose will pay the cost as well.

I walk out the back door of the restaurant's private room. I hear Vincent's voice boom at the remaining four men behind me.

"If you betray us, you die. If you hurt Rialta's friends, you die. If you start a war, you die—at her hand or mine."

I keep walking. I don't know where I'm going, just far enough away so my show won't be undone a minute later.

I walk out of the building, pausing in an empty alleyway.

Then I fall to my knees and sob.

THE ROOM IS silent as Ri walks out of the room. I can't even hear anyone breathing. The reaction is raw, full of shock and heaviness as we all collectively watch Ri strut away.

The mafia princess.

She's supposed to spend her time in fine dresses, attending balls, and bearing heirs. The woman who has mostly hidden her true talents from everyone at her father's orders now shows her true abilities.

She can wield a gun with the best of us.

She can hide her emotions to complete a terrible task.

She can decide for her own who lives and who dies.

She's willing to defy her father when the rest of us cower.

She is strength, and intelligence, and ruthlessness.

She's not just a princess; she's a fighter.

She isn't just owned by the mafia; she is the mafia. We should fear her the same as her father.

That's the message that was sent today. Rialta Corsi is as powerful as any mafia leader, and she's just as vicious.

I don't know why that message needed to be sent so clearly

today when Vincent has been doing his best to make her appear weak so far, but we all got the message.

I stare at the two men dead on the floor. I'm glad Kek is dead, although I'm surprised she killed him. Corsi shockingly didn't step in and scold her for the action. From where I was standing, it appeared Kek was on her side.

Then I turn my gaze toward Caius's body.

My chest swirls with relief but also something else—sorrow. It didn't have to be this way. He helped protect her, but I also suspect he was behind many of her close calls. It wouldn't surprise me if Caius hurt Lucy, if he knew where Odette was the entire time, if he used the phrase to control Ri. He's been pining for her this whole time while also working against her.

But still, I feel sorry for him because I don't think he's the mastermind behind his actions. I think he was just protecting his family, doing what he had to do to be loved by his father and sister.

What a waste.

Ri knew he was a snake, and she killed him. She protected me. She could have just as easily killed me for what she thinks is a betrayal.

She didn't.

She still cares—at least enough to let me live.

She may have done the hard part, but Caius's death is going to be a pain in my ass to deal with.

Corsi steps forward, not the least bit shocked by his daughter's actions. He takes his time, staring each of us down in the eye before he speaks.

"Don't ever try to take my kingdom, my daughter, or my life from me. Ri has been trained for years to defend and kill. She is my right-hand man. I trust her with my life. And if you want to marry my daughter..."

He motions toward the door. "Then you have to accept Ri for who she is. She's not going to let you walk all over her. She's not going to let you control her; she's the fiercest motherfucker here.

She will have no problem killing every single one of you, going to the sperm bank, and raising an heir all by herself."

I smirk, knowing he's exactly right. If she needs an heir, she'd rather do it herself than with any of our dumbasses.

"If you want the power of my kingdom, then the game is where you fight for it. There will be no war, no more attacks on people in my family. If you're idiotic enough to ignore these rules, you'll be the next one with a bullet in your head."

Corsi looks at me. "Dispose of your man's body. I have enough to clean up."

I nod.

Corsi starts to walk out the door his daughter just left. "There will only be one more game. I'll be in contact soon." And then he's gone.

Two of the remaining men start cursing and practically run out the door, not able to get out fast enough.

Not me, and not Ryker.

Together we walk over to Caius's body.

"What are you going to do?" Ryker asks me.

"What I've always done—protect Ri."

Ryker nods.

We bend down and lift Caius's lifeless body. She shot him in the heart; he bled out in seconds. His death was quick, which was more than he deserved. Ryker helps me position his body on my back. I'm covered in his blood, so I'll have to explain that I didn't do this.

Dammit, Ri, it would have been easier if you had just killed me.

But then I wouldn't be around to protect her, and I refuse to leave her unprotected.

We start walking toward the door but stop at Kek's body.

"What about him?" Ryker asks.

I frown, still not sure why Ri killed him. I'm missing something because I swear killing Kek was harder for her than killing Caius.

"Leave him. There is nothing we can do for him now."

Ryker helps me load Caius into the back of my car. He doesn't immediately leave. He lingers, something he needs to say on the tip of his tongue.

"Spit it out, Ryker. We don't have all night."

"It has to be you."

"What does?"

"You have to be the winner. You're the one she loves. You're the one she wants. You're—"

"I can't."

"You don't have a choice."

"I'm married to someone else."

"Doesn't matter."

"I have to stay married to protect Ri."

Ryker scoffs like he thinks I'm batshit crazy or something. "Find another way. You two are destined for each other. The only way this ends is with you two together. If you don't, we're all doomed."

Finally, he walks away. He doesn't give me a chance to argue, to say that he's wrong. She should be with him. He hasn't betrayed her, broken her heart, or ruined her for all others. He's a good man. If he loses, he'll end up dead, and he doesn't deserve that.

I'll do everything I can to see Ri happy, and Ryker is her best chance of happiness.

———

I drive back to our hotel. I haven't talked to Gage, Lennox, or Hayes since I returned to Odette's side, but I'm going to need their help now. I send them a group text when I get closer to meet me in the parking lot.

I pull into an empty parking spot at the back of the lot, against some bushes and trees. Only someone standing directly behind my car will be able to see what's in the trunk.

I stand outside, leaning against the side of the car while I wait for the guys. I don't know how any of them are going to react. They've all known Caius a lot longer than I have. They've been friends since they were kids. And yet, they've chosen me over him many times.

But after my recent actions, I'm sure they hate me. Surely, they're going to think I killed Caius.

Finally, I see three shadows approach.

I stiffen as they get closer. All of their faces read undeniable frustration and rage.

My shirt sleeves are rolled up, and my jacket is currently under Caius's body in the trunk, but their eyes roll through me like I'm naked. As if they already know what happened and judge me responsible.

None of us speak. I walk to the back of my car and pop the trunk. I step back, waiting for the attacks, punches, and guns to be pulled on me in vengeance.

Hayes, Gage, and Lennox all walk closer as they stare down at their dead childhood friend.

I open my mouth to say I'm sorry, *but what is that going to do?* It's not going to bring him back or change any of my actions.

So I'm silent. They are too.

A strong wind brushes through us before Hayes finally breaks the silence.

"Ri?"

"Alive," I respond.

He nods; that's all he cares about. Apparently, that's all any of them care about anymore—Ri. She's the only thing pure between us.

I swallow down the dryness in my throat. "She killed him."

Hayes nods as if he already knew that.

Gage stiffens.

Lennox swears under his breath.

"Well, it's not like he didn't deserve it," Gage finally says.

Everyone chuckles through wet tears.

Their feelings toward Caius were complicated. He was a friend and an enemy; their leader and their villain.

"What do we do now?" I ask as I realize a tear has escaped my eye as well. I wipe it away quickly before the others notice that I mourn Caius's death just like they do.

"We? Are we a 'we' again?" Hayes asks with a grin.

"We were never not a 'we,'" I growl back.

He chuckles. "Sure seems like we haven't been a 'we' since you took Odette back and cut us out of the loop. What the hell?"

I rub the back of my neck, not sure if I should tell them what happened or not.

"Really? Are you still not going to talk to us? Fine, you can figure this out yourself," Hayes grumbles, starting to walk away.

Lennox grabs the back of his shirt and pulls him back. "You aren't going anywhere, and Beckett will tell us what he needs to tell us."

Gage is quiet, but he just stares at me with disappointment in his eyes.

"I did it for Ri, okay?"

"What?" Hayes spits out.

"I'm with Odette to protect Ri. I can't tell you more than that without risking the deal and Ri's life, but that's why I'm with her."

The tears are back.

Damn, fucking tears.

I push through. "I love Ri with everything inside me, but I can never be with her. I'm not good for her, and the circumstances... If I chose Ri, she'd end up dead, and I refuse to let that happen."

Hayes's mouth drops.

Lennox and Gage stare silently, taking in my words.

"I can't tell you more. I can't give you the specifics. If you knew them, you wouldn't want to know because I know you all care about Ri too."

They nod.

"You have to trust me. If you want to protect Ri, then you have to trust me."

"Okay," Gage says first, followed by begrudging agreements from both Hayes and Lennox.

"Thank you."

"What now?" Hayes asks.

"Now, we help Ryker win, and we keep protecting Ri in the process."

"Ryker? Really?" Lennox asks.

I nod. "He's the best guy left in the game, you all know that. He won't pressure her. He just wants to protect his own. She'll have as much freedom as she wants."

All three of them stare back at me like I'm insane.

"Dude, all she wants is you. Anything less won't be enough for her," Hayes says.

I frown. "She loves me, sure, but she's strong enough to find a fulfilling life without me."

"Maybe, but she'll never love again," Lennox chimes in.

"Love is overrated," I say.

We all turn back to Caius's body.

"Now, what do we do about him? Everyone is going to think I killed him."

"So let them," Gage says.

We all turn to him. I cock an eyebrow. "How does that help me stay in control of the Retribution Kings and not get killed?"

"For one, you don't really care about either of those things, but neither of them will happen. And two, your main job is to protect Ri. If you tell anyone that Ri killed him, then you'll start another war for sure. Then you can't guarantee Ri's safety."

He's right.

I need to do everything I can to protect Ri, even if that means telling everyone I killed Caius.

"They won't kill you. You are the leader. You're going to war with your brother in retribution. If you say Caius was attacking you or threatening that goal in any way, they'll have no choice but to believe you. If you said Caius needed to die, then Caius needed to die."

I agree, although sometimes I think an all-out war is exactly what we need. Ri is strong and capable. She could win in a war—even get free, real freedom, if her father and other mafia leaders died.

But it's too risky. I won't risk her life for a chance of freedom.

I do sometimes wonder if it's time the whole world burns. Only the strong and worthy would survive the fires of hell.

"There is only one problem—what do I tell Odette? She's going to want to kill me either way."

"Will she? She needs you. And you have a deal with her to keep Ri alive and safe, so use it."

I nod, but it's easier said than done. I'm the only one who knows the real Odette and just how vengeful she can be.

I WALK DOWN the long hallways smudged with tan boring paint. I don't know why anyone would choose this color for a place supposed to be full of hope and healing. Instead, it makes me want to puke and run in the opposite direction.

Maybe that's actually what they're going for here. Instead of giving you hope and peace, they terrify you to convince you to heal faster and get your ass out of their hospital bed.

I'm a mess. I should have changed out of my dress. I should have washed the ruined mascara off my face, or at least first washed off the stench of death before coming. But I couldn't wait. I need to see how she's doing. I need more truths.

One of Vincent's men is stationed outside her room, ensuring her safety as long as she's here. At least she'll be protected from physical threats, although no one can help much with whatever is happening internally.

He nods at me when I walk past him. I don't speak to him as I reach for the door handle.

Does he know what I've done? Was he friends with Kek? Did they train together?

I can't think about that.

What's done is done.

I did what I had to do. I'm no better than anyone else, but at least I serve a purpose. I've always had a goal, and I'll do everything I can to achieve it.

I push the door open and carefully walk inside. I don't want to wake Lucy if she's asleep. But before I take more than a step inside, Loki greets me, full paws up on my chest and almost knocking me back.

"Hey, boy," I say with a smile, glad that Vincent found Loki to keep Lucy company. "How's she doing?"

He wags his tail at me as I enter the room.

Lucy is asleep in the hospital bed. Tubes are connected to her arms and chest, and yet she looks so peaceful.

I could check her chart or ask a nurse what's wrong with her, but that won't help Lucy. Instead, I sit in the chair next to her bed and hold her hand. Loki jumps up on the bed next to Lucy and curls up.

I sigh as I stare at her.

"Oh, Lucy. Why didn't you tell me the truth? Why hide everything from me?"

I already know the answer. It's the same reason I made myself forget.

To protect something greater than both of us, something that we love more than life itself, something pure and worthy.

Protection will cost us everything, but it's worth it.

"You need to hang on, Luce. Just a little longer, and then this is all over. Then you can live your life again."

I swear I hear her moan. It's so soft I'm not sure I actually heard it, but it doesn't seem that she agrees with me.

I frown.

She needs to live. She's the only one left in this world with me.

I don't know why Caius attacked her. I don't know what he was looking for, what information he thought he could get out of her, but I know she didn't tell him. She hid the truth just like I did.

I hear the door open and close. I expect it to be a nurse or doctor, but I know from how silently the person is moving that it's Vincent.

I stare up at him. He probably wants to talk to me, punish me for killing Kek.

I stand without him asking and follow him out of the room. We walk a bit down the hallway until he turns into what appears to be a staff break room but is completely empty. Vincent starts pouring us cups of coffee.

"I'm sorry—" I start.

"Don't be," Vincent responds.

I open my mouth and then slam it shut, flabbergasted. I blink.

Maybe I'm hallucinating?

Every time I blink, he's still standing there looking at me with approving eyes.

Huh.

I take the cup of coffee he offers me, even though I need sleep, not caffeine, to stay awake.

"You did the right thing. Kek was a weak link. He was tortured by keeping our secrets and the darkness he had to become to help you. He hated himself for what he did to you, hated all the pain he inflicted. He would have snapped eventually. You did him a kindness by killing him and ending his misery."

"He didn't deserve to die."

"I know, but he needed to."

Kek needed to die.

I'm not sure anyone needs to die.

"I didn't do it because I was upset with all the things he did. I did it because I saw his pain, and I knew he was tired. He couldn't do the job anymore."

Vincent nods. "As I said, you did the right thing. And the others respect you more for shooting your own man when he went against you."

"Kek never went against me."

"I know that, but the men will assume he did and respect you even more for it."

"So now I get to be who I truly am? Do I get to show off all my skills? Show how strong I am?"

"Yes. Make the men fear you."

I let that thought settle as I sip the cheap coffee.

"You remember everything?" Vincent asks.

"Yes, Kek released me before I killed him. Was he wrong to do that? Should he have waited?"

"No. Now is the time."

I look past him to the door. All I want right now is to go check on Lucy, curl up in the chair next to her, and sleep.

"You still on board with the plan?" Vincent asks.

I frown. How dare he ask me that after everything I've sacrificed. "Yes, I've always been a good soldier."

He smirks. "That you are."

"How are we ending this game?"

"I'm not sure you're going to like my plan."

"I never like any of your plans, but I still follow them."

He gives me a condescending look. "Until you take matters into your own hands."

I shrug. "That's why you like me."

He smiles, and I know it's true.

"There will be one final game. We are running out of time, and I want everything settled—"

A dog's bark in the distance stops him mid-sentence.

"Lucy!" I scream in a panicked voice.

I run into the hallway and down to her room.

I'm not the only one running. Nurses, doctors, and other medical professionals all flood into her room.

I try to run inside, but one of them stops me.

"Loki, come!" I yell into the room, knowing he's not helping.

For once, he listens to me.

"Good boy." I kneel next to him outside the door and rub his neck. We both listen intently to them working on Lucy, unsure if she's going to live or die.

I look over at her guard.

"Did anyone enter?" I ask.

"No, of course not," he says in a frantic voice, afraid I'm going to kill him if I find out otherwise. Apparently, news of what I've done travels fast.

I ignore him. I'm not going to kill him, but Vincent might if he fucked up.

Vincent finally makes his way down the hallway to where I'm crouched against the wall feeling helpless.

"Lucy thought she was safe. She thought no one would harm her, no matter what. That's what she told me. Why did she think that?"

I look up at Vincent.

He looks down at me sternly. I'm not going to get an answer from him, at least not right now.

I hear a loud flat beep; Lucy's heart gave out.

I hear frantic words of doctors and nurses trying one more time to save her.

I hear the exhaustion in their voices, and I know the outcome.

"She didn't want you to worry. I tried to train her as I trained you, but she didn't have your raw talent or strength. Since she couldn't protect herself, all she wanted was to ensure you were happy and could do your job.

"Just like Kek, she was willing to make the ultimate sacrifice. Death meant nothing to her if it meant keeping you safe. You're the only one who needs to stay alive now."

I hear a doctor call out her time of death.

Tears drip down my cheek in a flood.

Lucy gave her life to the cause, just like Kek. Vincent will one day, too, as will I.

We all need to stay alive until we don't.

I'll be the last to die, but I'll die too. Maybe then I'll learn if all of our sacrifices were worth it.

$$4$$

BECKETT

"ODETTE?" I whisper into the darkness of our hotel suite.

"You don't have to whisper. I wasn't going to sleep until you got back." Odette walks over to me and kisses me on the lips before I have a chance to react. This is my life now—being kissed and touched by a woman I hate to protect a woman I love.

"I'm glad you made it out safely. Now you can pull out of the game. I'm sure my brother can win without your help. There can't be that many rounds left."

I hold out my hand to her, a gesture I only do in public when I need to play the part. "Come with me."

She frowns. "It's the middle of the night."

"I know." I continue to hold my hand out, insisting she come with me.

I may not like Odette very much right now, and my feelings for Caius were complicated, but I still feel sorry for her. This is going to hurt her. She and her brother were close, and losing him will wreck her.

Reluctantly, she takes my hand, and I silently lead her out of the hotel. She doesn't ask any questions. Somehow, she senses what awaits her. If she's silent for a little longer, then she can avoid the pain for a few more seconds.

I understand. I've been in that situation countless times.

But this time, she needs to face the truth—the faster, the better. The morning will be easier if she deals with the bulk of the pain now, in the darkness.

I lead her to the back of my car and pop the trunk.

For most people, showing them their dead loved one is the wrong move. It's harsh, and the memory they keep is not one they want to remember. But in this case and in our world, we want the truth. We don't shy away from reality, from the pain.

And usually, the only way we truly believe someone is dead is if we see the body—maybe not even then. I look at Odette and think of the picture and the body we buried I thought was hers.

She doesn't fall apart right away. She's stronger than that.

She reaches her hand out and strokes Caius's hair off his forehead. His face looks peaceful, like he's just asleep, not dead. The rest of his body is what carries the marks of reality. The blood and open wound in his chest explain what really happened.

She lets her hand run down his face and then over some of the blood.

I take a step back, giving her space to process however she needs to—cry, scream, anything.

It turns out Odette is stronger than I thought. She doesn't let any emotion out at all. She's as solid as ice. Her heart doesn't break at all, at least not from where I'm standing.

It takes longer for reality to set in for some people, maybe what's happening here. But I don't think she'll break later either—at least, not in the traditional tears and wailing kind of way.

"How?" she asks, her voice low and deep.

"We were playing the game. He attacked me. I had no choice but to defend myself. I'm so sorry, Odette. He was like a brother to me. I never meant for him to die." The words aren't the complete truth, but they're what she needs to hear—remorse.

She laughs.

Laughs.

She's diabolical.

I grip my gun, ready for anything.

She turns and looks me dead in the eyes. "Don't lie to me."

"I'm not lying."

"For one, Caius and I were blackmailing you into doing what we wanted. Don't feed me that bullshit about him being like a brother to you."

"Fine, but I still cared about him. I didn't want him to die. I don't think Caius was an evil man; I just think he was being pressured to do what you said."

"More lies."

I frown.

"You know what I think?" she asks, stepping closer to me, outrage threatening in her voice. Apparently, her depression from losing her brother is going to come out as anger, not sadness. Unluckily, I'm the one she plans to take her wrath out on.

I don't move. I won't cower in front of her. I won't show fear. She wants a fight; I'll win.

Me, not her.

She's won too many times, way too many fucking times. Just give me a reason to fight, and I'll take it.

"I think your precious whore of a girlfriend killed him."

I cross my arm over my chest, not looking the least bit fazed. I can't let her know she's right. I'll protect Ri at all costs. "She's not a whore, and she's not my girlfriend. Why would she kill Caius? In fact, I'm pretty sure she likes him a lot. She did fuck him after all."

My face wrinkles at that thought. The dead bastard fucked her before I did. She wanted him, even liked him, but she had to kill him. She realized he knew her secret. Odette shared it with him, and neither of them is on our side.

"I don't care who the whore fucked or not. Although, I'm

guessing I should get tested because who knows where her cunt has been, and your dick has been inside her."

I glare at her. "Don't call her a whore."

She cackles like a witch. How did I get so fooled by this woman? She couldn't be further away from the angel I thought she was.

"The mafia princess killed him. She found out he knew the truth, and he hurt her friend. She had no choice."

"What do you mean Caius hurt her friend?"

Odette doesn't answer.

"Do you mean Lucy?"

"Is that the blonde bitch's name? Then yes."

"Why did her hurt her?"

She shrugs, looking bored with this part of the conversation. "We needed information from her. But now that he's dead, I have no idea if he got it or not."

I growl. I'm going to kill her.

"I should talk to Stan. We'll figure out a plan to take down the Corsi mafia now that we know for sure they are working against us."

I pull my gun out, no longer playing with her.

Her mouth snaps shut at the sight of the gun.

"You're not going to kill me," she says, staring down the barrel of my gun. Anyone else would say she looks fearless at the moment, but I can see her terror. I can see the way her pupils widen for just a second. She's afraid of dying just like anyone else, and she's not sure what I will do.

"What's stopping me from killing you right now? I got what I needed from you. Ri's safe, and you're the only one left alive who knows how to control her. With you dead, I can get what I really want."

Her mouth curls up in a wicked grin. "You think I'm the only one who knows?" Then there's that damn cackle again that sends vicious tingles down my spine.

"Who did you tell?"

"And why would I tell you that?"

"If you want me to keep you alive, you'll tell me."

"I don't think I will."

"Fine, then I'll kill you."

"That's how you're going to kill me? With your gun? Not very personal. I thought if you did kill me, you'd do it with your bare hands at least. That way, I would feel the heat of your breath on my neck as I take my last breath."

"I wouldn't give you that satisfaction. You mean nothing to me."

She cocks an eyebrow. "Nothing? I thought I was the love of your life? Caius told me about how you wailed when I died, the pain you felt. You mourned me. That is until your whore came along. But before that, you cared. Don't act like you didn't."

"That was before I knew who you really were. You're nothing more than a greedy snake, just like your father and brother."

She laughs. "You don't understand the Retribution Kings at all. We don't want power; we want revenge."

I frown.

"What did my brother ever do to you?"

She licks her bottom lip, but it's a ploy to keep the pain out of her eyes.

I stare at her curiously. He did do something to hurt her. Or at least, she thinks he did.

"What did Corsi do?"

"His sin is more straightforward. He punished my father by taking away a drug shipment that was our main source of revenue. No one trusted us after that. We had to make money the old-fashioned way from that point on—siphoning money from our rich clients. The drugs were so much easier to make money from."

"So what? His daughter deserves to die for that?"

"No, she deserves to die for seducing you into sinking your cock inside of her."

I roll my eyes.

"You don't get to kill her. That's the deal. If you want me to stay your husband and start a war for you, she lives happily ever after, untouched."

"I know, but our deal doesn't extend to her father. You keep playing the game to get close enough to take him out."

"That is if I don't kill you first."

"You won't. If you were going to kill me, you would have already done it. You don't know what precautions I've taken. You don't know who I've instructed to kill her if I die. You can't kill me without killing her."

I frown. I can't tell if she's bluffing or not, but I wouldn't put it past her.

"Tell me the truth—did Enzo hurt you?"

She bats her eyelashes like she's innocent. "He didn't kidnap me. Everything I told you was a lie. But that doesn't mean he doesn't deserve to pay for what he and his family did to me."

"Tell me what they did, and maybe I'll help you willingly."

She shakes her head. "You won't. You're loyal to your family to a fault. It was the same with Caius and me." She looks at his body, and finally, a tear falls. "I never betrayed him, even if he deserved it."

I can't fault her for that, I guess.

"So are you going to kill me and take the chance that Ri will die next? Or are you going to let me clean up your mess, so your sweet princess gets to live a day longer?"

I hate my choices. I want to kill her. But I can't, not until I know if she's speaking the truth. I won't threaten Ri's life.

I lower my gun and then slowly pocket it.

"That's what I thought." She holds out her hand to me like I did to lead her outside.

I brush past her hand, and we walk together back towards the hotel. The whole time we walk, I'm terrified of what Odette is going to demand of me next.

5
RI

I'VE BEEN RUNNING for an hour now. I don't know where I'm running; I just let my feet carry me.

Loki is at my side, and he seems just as content to simply run. It keeps our mind off the people we lost.

After Lucy died, I had her guard go get me some running clothes and shoes. Instead of getting the sleep my body needed, I needed to run.

Vincent told me his plan to end the game.

I agreed to it, no matter how difficult it might end up being for me. It is the best way to end the game, so I agreed.

But I'm not thinking about the game as I run.

I'm thinking about Caius.

Kek.

Lucy.

I'm thinking about all the friends I never made.

About all the family I never knew because of who I am and what I chose.

I chose this.

It may not seem like it now as I run through the darkness. I have no idea what time it is, but the sun must be coming up soon. It's been dark for too long.

I keep running until I finally realize where I'm running, or more likely who I'm running to.

I stop on the edge of the woods—the same woods I hiked in with Caius before his death.

I should replay his conversation in my head, find out if he was trying to tell me anything before his death. But I can't. It's too painful, even if his death was the easiest of the three I care about.

I slow once we get to the woods. It's dark; only a bit of moonlight lights the path. It's not enough to clearly see where we're going.

I'm panting hard, as is Loki, so we need a break anyway. I don't know where Beckett is. I don't know if he's asleep in the hotel room nearby. I don't know if they went to the cabin or some other secret Retribution Kings headquarters.

Somehow, he penetrates my thoughts despite everything that's happened, despite all the pain.

He confuses me more than anyone.

I thought he loved me.

Then I saw him with Odette and knew I was wrong.

But then he came to the game...*why come to the game?* The prize is me. He already has a wife.

Unless it's to fuck with Vincent somehow? Or help ensure Caius won?

"Are you really there? Or are you a figment of my imagination?" His voice breaks through the thin air. It hits my chest like a sledgehammer, waking me back up from my despair.

"I'm really here. The question is, are you?"

I turn toward the voice, and I can barely see him through the shadows, but he's there.

I step closer.

He does the same.

Finally, we are close enough to make out each other's features.

He's shirtless, wearing running shorts, and is dripping in sweat.

"Seems like we had the same idea," I say.

"It seems that way."

We don't say anything else to each other. *What else is there to say?* I don't trust either of us with the truth.

Loki seems to have a different idea. He pushes forward, giving me no choice but to step closer or yank on the beast's leash.

Loki greets Beckett happily, even though he just lost his best friend. He doesn't let the grief overtake him. He licks Beckett's hand and then jumps up against his chest.

Beckett smiles. "It's good to see you too." He rubs his head and then tells Loki to get down.

He listens and immediately sits at his feet, wagging his tail like he just found his favorite person. He found my favorite person.

And then Beckett looks at me, really looks at me, and he can see everything—straight to my soul.

I think he can see all of my secrets, the truth I've kept hidden my entire life. I think he's going to figure out who I am. He's going to put all the pieces together.

That would be a disaster, but a part of me wants him to. I want to share my secret. I want a life with him, even if it's the one thing I can't have.

He sees me, but he also sees another secret.

"Is Lucy...?" his voice is soft and gentle, begging me to tell him, most likely so he can help me.

But I can't accept his help. If I do, I'll cave. I'll let him manipulate me again. I'll fall for him and give up everything else. But I don't want to lie either.

"She's gone," I say flatly, folding my arms across my chest before he gets any ideas about hugging me.

"I'm sorry. She didn't deserve to die." He takes a deep breath. "None of them did."

"Are you telling me I shouldn't have killed them?"

"No, you did the right thing. I'm saying we all should have lived a much different life. The boys should have been in college, not fighting for their lives."

"And you, what would you do if your life was different?" I can't help but ask.

He takes a deep breath, staring out into the woods. "This," he says when he finally turns back to me. "I'd do this. I'm not a good man, Ri. I lost my arm. I lost my family. This life cost me everything, and yet, I can't imagine doing anything else."

"That's not true; you just don't think you deserve anything else."

The truth bounces back in his eyes. He thinks of himself as a monster, but he's not. I'm still trying to figure out exactly who he is, but he's definitely not a monster.

"I love Odette," he says, seemingly out of nowhere. I know why he said it, though, to get out of the awkwardness of this conversation.

"You do?"

"I do." His eyes pierce mine convincingly. He loves her. He wants her. Even after all the horrors she's done, she's his first love. I'm nothing but a fling to get over her. I should just walk away. I shouldn't stay and listen to anything else he has to say, but I need to hear more. I need to be sure.

"Why did you come to the game then? You have a wife; go live happily ever after with her," my words are harsh and rip through me quickly and sharp.

I take a deep breath while I wait for his answer to calm myself. When I look at Beckett, I expect to see pity in his eyes or the need to hug me. Instead, there's a look of disinterest, like he couldn't care less about my feelings. Maybe he is heartless.

"The Retribution Kings decided we want it all. Even though you didn't hurt Odette, your family has still hurt the Kings in the past. The best way to get revenge is to win the game."

I frown. "If you win the game, then you have to marry me. You can't do that if you're already married."

"No, but I can tell you to marry Gage or Lennox or Hayes. Any one of which would make a good number two in my command."

"They are all back on your side?"

"They were always on my side. They are Retribution Kings until death. Nothing will change that."

I narrow my eyes, not really believing him, but I doubt I'll get a more honest answer from him.

"Why are you acting like a monster?"

"I am one. I'm going to war with my own brother. I'm taking over the Corsi mafia empire. I'm going to rule this world."

Loki tucks his tail and ears back as he makes his way back to my side, not recognizing this new version of Beckett either.

I'm usually a good judge of character. I can usually tell when someone is telling the truth or not. I don't think this is the real Beckett at all, but there is some reason he's pretending it is. I just can't figure out why he's acting this way.

"So you're going to keep playing the game just so you can win and force me to marry one of your friends? Did I get that right?" my voice is bitter and angry.

"Yes."

"What makes you think me or Vincent will go for it?"

"Vincent will agree when there are no other men left. He'll see how powerful I am and won't want to start a war. He said as much at the last game. He'll accept my offer."

"I won't."

He laughs. "You won't have a choice, Princess. Besides, I don't believe you. You've already fucked all of them. From where I was standing, you seemed to enjoy it. So don't tell me you wouldn't want it."

I glare at him. I hate this version of him. *What are you hiding?*

"Good luck with your plan, but it won't work. You can't control three different empires at once."

"Watch me," he growls.

"You won't win. I know what the final game is, and there is no way you can do it."

"I'm stronger than any of the men left, smarter, and more determined. I'll win."

His nostrils flare, and I swear I see a bit of fear. He needs to win. *Why? Why is he so desperate to win?*

I'm done with this conversation, but there is one part left that I need to discuss with him. I'm not sure how he's going to react, though. He may try and kill me right here, right now.

"I need to speak to your wife when she has a moment."

"And why the hell do you need to talk to her? She hates you."

The feeling is mutual, but I don't say that out loud. It won't help anything.

"She has the phrase that can control my mind. I need to ensure she will never use it." She's the only one left who knows it unless she has gone around telling others. But that's a secret too juicy for her to share. She would want the power all to herself."

Beckett grits his teeth, and I can tell he doesn't want to talk about Odette. He doesn't want to drag her into this. He loves her. He truly loves her.

Fuck.

So many fucks.

I should kill Odette. She knows the secret, or if not, she can figure it out.

But I can't, not if he truly loves her.

"Odette won't say anything. She won't do anything. You have my word. She won't use the phrase. She wants nothing to do with you. She won't hurt you in any way."

His words are calm and sincere, but it's not enough.

"Tell me again why you love her. Why you'll do anything in the world for her?"

"Why?"

"Convince me that you love her more than anything else in this world."

"Why?"

"Beckett, just trust me and tell me."

He brushes his hair back in frustration. Apparently, it's torture to share the depths of his heart with me. He opens his mouth and closes it several times before he finally decides where to begin.

"I love Odette because she's the first thing I think about when I wake up. She's my light, my reason for living." He smiles as he thinks about her, spilling his guts.

"She has this beauty—this incredible beauty. It starts with her outward appearance. From her hair to her curves, to her skin—everything about her is radiant. But it doesn't stop with her appearance; it runs deep, all the way to her heart. She cares deeply about those she loves. She cares about those she shouldn't. She connects with me on a soul level that I can't explain. It's like I've known her my entire life. It's like she was hand-selected for me and me her. She has this fierceness and determination that matches me."

He chuckles, thinking about it. "No, it outdoes mine. She is the strength. She's the boss, the one in control. Though don't tell her that. It will go to her head, and then I'll never hear the end of it."

I smile and nod.

He smiles brighter, thinking about her.

"I love her because she saved me. Time and time again, when I was in my darkest places, she found me there. She made me believe that life was worth living. She kept me from falling over the edge. She's the only reason I would give up this life. I'd give up the Retribution Kings, the game, the war, everything for her. All she'd have to do is ask, and I wouldn't question why; I'd just do it.

"She wants a mansion; it's hers. She wants a tiny house in the middle of the Swedish Fjords; it's hers. She wants a dozen kids; I'll have them with her. She wants none; then she's more than enough for me. Whatever she wants, whatever she needs, I'd give her everything I have. I'd die a million deaths for her to live."

He looks at me darkly, "Don't you dare threaten her life because I don't care who I have to kill to protect her. I'll do anything to protect her, anything to save her. She won't spill your secret. I'll make sure of it. But if you value your life, you won't go near Odette."

His words flood me with the strength of his emotion, of his love for one woman. That's what I've been looking for my entire adult life but never found.

I'm in awe, suddenly feeling tears stinging my eyes. I'm happy for him, really I am.

I grab Loki's leash, and I turn around, ready to jog back home. I got what I subconsciously came here for. On a night where I was left utterly alone by everyone I cared about, I needed to hear this. It solidifies my purpose. It reminds me of what I was born on this earth to do.

"Ri!" Beckett yells.

I turn and look at him, finding fear and complete desperation in his eyes.

"I won't kill Odette," I assure him.

His eyebrow shoots up. "You won't?"

"No, she'll stay alive as long as you love her. But I still need to talk to her," I say against my better judgment.

Then I disappear into the night before I realize my mistake and take it all back. Odette should die, but I won't kill her. I fell in love with a man who will never love me. My happily ever after is different than everyone else's. I don't get to be with the man I love, but I can protect the woman he loves. That will have to be enough to sustain me.

I WANTED to pick her up and drag her away and tell her all my truths. I wanted to kiss her, fuck her, make her mine, let her know she's the only woman for me. But I couldn't do any of those things.

I could love her forever if the world were different. Instead, I'm going to be tortured the rest of my life living with a woman I hate. She has the power to destroy the love of my life, and she'll hold that over my head forever.

No, I can't spend the rest of my life tied to Odette. I'll find a way to get free. I'll find a way to make Ri safe once and for all. By then, Ri will be married, though, so Ri will never be mine. But I can still save us both from a lifetime of misery.

As I watch Ri walk away, I realize I'm kidding myself. A lifetime without Ri is a lifetime of misery for me, with or without Odette. Maybe I can be the cool uncle to her kids, still in her life even when she's married. I'm good at playing the uncle role.

God, even that would be torture. Everything about my life will be torture, but it would be better to have her in my life than out.

Slowly walking back to the hotel, I consider returning to my shared room with Odette, but I can't. I can't deal with her touching my body again. Instead, I end up at the room next door.

My knuckles knock against the door, and I'm unsure if anyone is awake. If no one answers, I'll sleep in my car. The guys were dealing with Caius's body, but I suspect they passed out after that.

The door opens to reveal Lennox looking at me. He's fully dressed, not like a man who was just sleeping. He holds the door open for me, and I step inside. I walk straight to the living room couch and flop down on it.

Hayes, Gage, and Lennox all look at me from various spots in the living room.

Hayes looks to the door. "Why aren't you with Odette? Is she sleeping here?" He wrinkles his face in disgust.

Gage hits him in the back of the head.

"Ow!" He rubs the back of his head. "What was that for?"

Gage rolls his eyes. "You know why he's not with Odette. Don't be stupid."

Hayes looks confused as he looks from Gage to me, finally letting out a quiet sigh of understanding.

"The look on your face just now when you thought Odette might be coming here is the same look I have every time she touches me and demands for me to fuck her," I snap.

My heart thumps hard in my chest as silence stretches. I can't believe I just told them that. Slowly, I look to the three guys that have become brothers to me just as much as my own brother.

"Damn, Beckett. We're going to figure a way out of this mess. And from now on, we're running interference. We aren't letting that witch touch you again," Hayes says.

Gage's eyes darken with a murderous glare.

Lennox looks away uncomfortably. Maybe he has a secret or two of his own to share, but now isn't the time.

"Thank you, but it's my burden to bear. You don't need to worry about it. I shouldn't have said anything," I say.

"Why do you let her touch you at all? I would—" Hayes starts before Lennox gives him an angry look.

"Really? Do you not think before you open your mouth? He has to sleep with Odette to protect Ri. Odette could have Ri killed if Beckett so much as gets into a lover's spat," Lennox answers.

I sit up. "It's okay, really. Anyone got any liquor?"

"Coming right up." Lennox goes to the kitchen and pours a glass of an amber liquid before handing it to me.

"Thanks." I take a sip. I don't want to spend my life drunk, but tonight I need enough liquor to pass out and not run after Ri.

"What happened?" Lennox asks, noticing my mood isn't just about Odette.

"I ran into Ri, and I had to lie to her. I told her I love Odette. I said she can't kill Odette because I love her. When in reality, killing Odette would only kick off whatever contingency plan she has in place to kill Ri." I drink the rest of the glass, letting it burn down my throat, but it's not enough to make me feel. "I played the part, and Ri believed me."

I think about our conversation, about Ri asking me why I love Odette. I couldn't come up with anything, so I told her all the reasons why I love Ri instead. Each word was a dagger to her heart when my words should have been music to her heart. But she got to hear my words, even if she'll never know that they were for her.

Lennox brings the bottle over and pours me another glass, then takes a sip straight from the bottle himself. Hayes grabs the bottle and takes a long sip, passing it to Gage next, who does the same.

"Don't give up hope yet. We all love her—" Hayes starts and then sees the grimace on my face. "I don't mean like that. Yes, we've all fucked her, but that's not what I meant about 'love her.' We know how special she is. And we all know that as much as any of us would be lucky to have her, she's yours. We'll do whatever it takes to make that happen."

"I'm going to need another drink before I tell you my plan." I hold out my hand, and Gage passes me the bottle.

I take a long sip until my head gets a little dizzy. "As much as I want that to be true, I don't know if we have the time to figure out how to take Odette down before Ri gets married. She said there is only one final game."

"Shit. Well, we'll have to work fast," Hayes says.

Lennox stares through me, already knowing what I'm about to say. His jaw tightens. Gage looks to Lennox, the one who can read people the best. Even Hayes eventually looks to Lennox.

"I'm going to keep playing the game. Even Odette wants me to. She wants the Retribution Kings to control everything, starting with the Black Empire and the Corsi Crime Family."

"But you can't marry Ri if you win; you're already married to Odette," Hayes says.

I nod slowly.

"I told her if I win, I'll choose her husband for her," I say.

"Will Corsi go for that?" Gage asks.

"He won't have a choice. I'll make sure there will be no one left in the game for him to choose instead. And I'll threaten war with him if not."

"So, who would you choose?" Hayes asks.

I look from Hayes to Lennox, to Gage. "I'd choose one of you three to marry her."

———

No one really talked after I announced my plan to win and pick one of them to marry Ri. I don't know how I'll choose. I'd let Ri choose, but I don't think she would pick any of them. And right now, it's not my problem. I have to worry about winning first; then I can figure out how to choose.

I have to win—to save her from the other monsters left in the game. Any one of my men would treat her right. Any one of them would let her live her life and have as much freedom as she wanted. Any one of them would do a good job of helping her lead the Corsi mafia. Any one of them could fall in love with her and help her grow to love him in return. Any one of them could make her happy.

Any of them except me.

We walk into the banquet hall where the Retribution Kings are gathered. Odette is talking to one of her friends and scurries over to my side as soon as she sees me. I barely acknowledge her. Hayes, Gage, and Lennox flank me as we walk to the center of the room.

We have to tell everyone what happened last night. We have to lie about why Caius is dead.

I give Odette enough time of day to notice she's decked out in all black and is already letting tears fall for her brother. I'm sure some of the tears are real, but others are part of her performance.

Thankfully, as the fearless leader, I won't be expected to show emotion. I need to appear strong and unbreakable.

"There is an unfortunate reason for our gathering today," I say loudly, drawing everyone's attention. I never thought I'd be able to command an entire room with just my voice, no microphone to make it louder. I never thought I'd be strong enough to endure the stares, but for the first time, I feel like maybe this is what I was born to do. If it wasn't for all the other shit, then maybe I could even enjoy it.

Odette snuggles her way into my chest, and I play the good husband by holding her against me.

"I have to announce that my dear brother-in-law, Caius Monroe, has died."

Murmurs and shock work through the crowd.

"How?" someone shouts at the same time as someone else cries out for retribution.

Odette sobs loudly into my chest, and that seems to quiet them.

"There will be no need for retribution," I say sternly, once again capturing the crowd's attention.

"I killed Caius during Corsi's game. I killed him. I did everything I could, but I didn't have a choice. I regret it bitterly. Caius was like a brother to me. He helped me grieve when I thought I had lost my wife. He helped me become a better leader. He was a good friend."

I see tears in many of the men's and women's eyes as I speak.

"I will finish the game in his honor. I will win to gain us control over Corsi's empire, and I will select one of my closest men to marry Rialta. I will not let Caius die in vain."

Many nod and murmur their agreement. For once, I feel like I'm their leader, and they agree with me.

"Caius is going to be buried in the plot next to his father. I invite you all to follow us to the gravesite. Then return here for food and mourning."

The guys brought Caius's body to the morgue last night to be prepared for burial today.

Odette doesn't say anything, just sobs into me. But it's enough to sell the lie. If she's not arguing with me or saying anything differently, then they believe my story. I killed Caius. I didn't have a choice. I'm devastated that he's gone.

They will never know the truth—Ri killed him. He was a bastard who tried to manipulate her. They will think of him as a loyal Retribution King who would do anything for the cause.

We travel to the gravesite in a caravan. It's strange coming back here. The last time I was here, I thought I was burying Odette. This time, I know for sure I'm burying Caius.

We walk to the site, keeping things simple and not doing a traditional funeral. There wasn't time to do much planning, and this seems right anyway.

Odette's gravestone has been removed, but I still look at the spot on the other side of her father, and my blood boils all over again. I have to let go of Odette for a second when I see her now unused gravesite.

Odette seems to understand and gives me my space.

The ground has already been dug for Caius on the other side of their father. His casket rests suspended above the hole.

Lennox, Hayes, and Gage each say words about losing Caius. They are all truthful, even though they knew what a snake he was in the end. He was still their friend first.

Odette speaks through sobs.

I say a few more words before we lower Caius's body into the ground. We each sprinkle a handful of dirt over his lowered casket.

It's then that I find my eyes have watered.

I look at Odette standing in front of Caius's lowered casket. His death is because of her. She orchestrated everything. She is the one who wanted power, control.

I vow right now that she will be back where she belongs—in the ground next to her father.

VINCENT GAVE us a couple of days off before the next game. I think after the last one, we all needed it.

Time to mourn.

Time to collect our thoughts.

Time to regroup and strategize.

Just time to live.

I stand in front of Lucy's headstone while Loki lays in the grass in front of it. My time to mourn is up; I have a job to do. But in a way, I'll never stop mourning what I've lost.

"I'll never forget you," I say, putting my hand on the stone. "Caius initially hurt you, but the doctor said you were fine before you crashed. I'll make sure whoever killed you pays."

Loki moans.

"And I'll take care of Loki for you, don't you worry." I scratch his head, and then we start heading back to the car.

I pass Kek's grave as I walk back to the car, but I don't stop. His death is so much more painful because I had a choice. I could have let him live—I didn't. I'm not ready to face that reality yet.

I open the car's driver-side door for myself but find Loki jumping in first. He climbs over to the passenger seat, even though he has a lot more room in the back seat. I roll his window down after he paws at the window, and then we're off.

I don't have any guards. Vincent is no longer pretending that I need them. He knows I'm more capable than any guard he has.

And despite not wanting to play the last game, Vincent knows I'll show up. I won't run. I won't shirk my responsibilities. As much as I'm tired of playing games, I'm ready for this to all be over.

It will never be over, though. This is my life, and it will never stop.

At least there won't be any more games.

Today is the final game. I drive to the same restaurant where the last games were held, where I shot three people dead. I didn't want the next game to happen here too, but Vincent said it would remind the men of what happened last time and how strong I am.

I didn't argue, although I don't know how they could forget me killing in front of them. All it's going to do is mess with my head.

I park in the parking lot and look at Loki.

"Ready?"

He wags his tail in response.

I open my door, and he jumps out after me, landing awkwardly as he does. It makes me smile.

"Come on," I say, not bothering to put a leash on him. He hasn't strayed from my side since Lucy died. I'm guessing he has separation anxiety, but I haven't had time to bring him to a vet to see how to help him.

We walk side by side into the restaurant just as the clock strikes seven. I didn't want to show up a second early or a second late.

I hold my head high, walking into the room where the remaining four men stand.

The room is silent; all eyes are on me as I enter. Thankfully I haven't cried today, so my eyes aren't puffy. There is no sign of the mourning I've been going through this week, nor are there any other signs of weakness.

Loki stares down all the men, baring his teeth at some of them as I walk to Vincent's side. Loki growls at one of the men, and he flinches.

I smile and pat Loki's head. "Good boy."

We stop next to Vincent.

"You ready?" he asks me.

"I was born ready."

He gives me a knowing smile. "I know; that's why I picked you."

I turn solemnly to the crowd of men who are spread out in front of us. They're all dressed up again in suits and tuxes. *Maybe they think they're making less work for the mortician after I kill them?*

I spot Ryker, who is, as usual, playing his part of acting like he couldn't care less, and he's above this all.

Next to him is a guy I wouldn't let near me—Hogan. Cruel and ruthless, he has no redeeming qualities. His men are loyal to him strictly out of fear, not loyalty. He has no chance of winning this game or my heart.

And then there is Beckett. He winks at me when I look at him. *Does he think he's somehow doing me a favor by being here?* He has no idea that he can't win. Vincent would never allow him to choose one of his friends for me to marry instead of him. If he wins, Vincent will make his marriage to Odette disappear. That's not what Beckett wants, so I won't let it happen.

The final man, standing off to the side, is one I barely know. He doesn't look intimidating, but he's not cowering in terror, afraid I'm about to shoot him. He's the only one whose name escapes me. Maybe I need to take a closer look at him.

"Thank you all for keeping to the rules this week. I'm glad to report no scheming or wars have been started this week, so there's no need for Rialta to kill anyone to start off the game."

I give the room a seductive, disappointed smile that says I'd love to shoot and kill again.

Hogan swallows hard, sweat beading off his forehead.

I smirk; he's a dead man.

"We have decided there will be one final game. Rialta's birthday is coming up soon, and she's anxious to get married," Vincent continues.

Ryker and no name both grin cockily, thinking they will be the one I marry. They're probably right. Either of them is the current front runners in my book.

Unfortunately, I don't know what the exact rules of this game even are. I get the general idea, but I don't know if Vincent or I will be declaring the winner.

"The game is simple. In fact, it's the easiest game we've played so far. Scoring is very objective, and soon we will have a clear winner," Vincent says, drawing out the men's anxiety.

"Although the game is simple, it's not any less dangerous. There are no rules. Hurt, betray or kill anyone in this room. Do whatever you have to do to win. If you lose, you'll probably end up dead."

The men start eyeing each other with deadly unsaid threats. I roll my eyes.

"As I've said before, the winner gets to marry my daughter, Rialta Corsi, and take control of my empire as soon as they produce a male heir to continue my legacy." Vincent looks to me, silently waiting for me to back out.

I know how risky this game is; I know what's at stake. But we have to know who the right guy is, and this is the best way to figure it out.

If I had to choose right now, I'd pick Ryker. *But do I really know him? Could he have tricked me all along? Could I have been blinded by his good looks and my need to get back at Beckett?*

Could the mystery man be better?

And then my gaze turns to Beckett. He would have been perfect. One tiny thing got in the way, unfortunately—he loves another woman.

Choosing the man to win isn't about love. It should be about finding the best man for the job. The man that will make the best husband. The man who will fight to the death to protect his family.

The man who will do the best job in following in Vincent's footsteps. The man who will become a leader feared by the outside world but also supported by unending respect earned from his own men.

If I listen to my heart, Beckett is that man. But that's why I'm not listening to my heart anymore. I'm listening to my head.

Ryker.

It has to be Ryker.

I should talk to Vincent about my thoughts, see if he agrees.

"There are two ways to win the final game," Vincent speaks again.

I lock eyes with Beckett, wanting to see his reaction more than anything. I know Ryker won't break face when Vincent announces the game. I should look at the mystery man to see his reaction, but I don't know him well enough to know if he can fake his emotions or not. But Beckett—he can't hide from me. He can't hide his reactions, not fully.

"The first way to win is the most straightforward."

Here it is—the moment I've been dreading.

I suck in a deep breath so I can keep my own reaction flat.

"To win, you have to be the one to get her pregnant," Vincent says, motioning to me.

I don't see anyone's reaction but Beckett's. His is the only one that matters. His eyes dilate. His nostrils flare. His hand fists so hard that I think he's going to break his own bones.

He's pissed.

If he doesn't get control over it, he'll start fighting every man in this room to the death right here.

It's the action of a man who cares—*a man who might even love?*

Curious.

Quickly, he regains control of his emotions. The rage and fury are still there under the surface, but anyone else looking at him would think he doesn't care. His eyes are now scanning my body, thinking about strategy. His eyes land on my arm, where I told him I had birth control implanted. The same place where he shot me.

His eyes examine my body, maybe trying to figure out if he already got me pregnant. *Does he think he's already won?* Or maybe he's considering how low his chances of winning might be since he's fucked me numerous times without protection and didn't get me pregnant.

Beckett says he loves Odette, and after that impassioned speech, I believe him. But this will be the ultimate test of that love. If he loves her, he won't touch me, even to win. And if he doesn't...

"Any questions?" Vincent asks the room.

"So, we're supposed to kidnap her and then rape her until we get her pregnant?" Hogan asks.

Vincent shrugs. "That's one option."

I feel everyone's eyes on me, reading my reaction. I'm stone-cold; I won't be getting raped. At least, I'll do everything I can to not be. And I'd bet on my skills against any man here.

They can try, but I'll cut off their dicks for daring to touch me without my permission.

"How do we prove we're the one that got her pregnant?" Hogan asks.

"Don't worry about that. We'll know. And if it isn't obvious, there are always tests that can be done," Vincent answers.

I stare down the men, just teasing them to try and fuck me without my permission. Loki is doing the same thing next to me, almost like he understands the words Vincent spoke and won't be letting any man near me.

Ryker steps forward. "You said there are two ways for us to win. What is the other objective?"

Vincent looks at me out of the corner of his eye, and I can read what he isn't saying. I know the other way to win instinctually. If it's up to me, this will be the way the victor will win.

"The second way you can win will remain a mystery. It's something you will have to figure out for yourself."

"That's not fair; how are we supposed to win if we don't know all the rules?" Hogan asks.

"This game was never designed to be fair. It was designed to find the best man for the job. You want to win? Then figure it out."

Vincent quickly exits the room, leaving Loki and me standing in front of the men alone.

I can see Beckett's eyes again, this time asking a million questions. *The most important one is why? Why would I agree to a game where I could end up raped?*

I don't answer him. I don't give him any more clues than the other guys.

The guys expect me to run, to shriek in terror that they may gang up on me and all take turns raping me right now just to get the game over with. But I'm done running. I'll never run again.

"Good luck, boys," I say. Then I turn and casually walk out the door after Vincent with Loki by my side. The men are left speechless with their mouths agape, not having a clue what to do next. But they'll figure it out soon, and then the game will really start.

WHAT. The. Hell.

What the hell is happening?

Impregnate her? That's how we win? That's INSANE.

It's even more insane when you consider how calm Ri was about it. She knew it was coming. It was clear that she and Corsi had talked about it beforehand. She should have argued with Vincent after his announcement and tried to stop it from happening.

She didn't.

She accepted it as easily as she did any of the other games.

I'm missing something.

I must have misheard the rules.

Yes, that's it.

Except, I didn't.

I heard correctly.

The game is simple—get Ri pregnant by any means.

Fuck!

Now, what the hell do I do?

I can't let Ri know I still love her, that it's always been her. I have to convince her I'm in love with Odette. It's the only way to protect her until I figure out how to take down Odette without harming Ri.

Does Ri already know? Or at least suspect?

The way she looked at me just now made it look like she thought I was full of shit. But before she seemed so convinced—I don't know.

Still, I can't get Ri pregnant while married to Odette. Odette would kill her if she found out what I did, even to win the game. And it's not like Ri would let me touch her anyway.

Unless...

Ri hasn't been on birth control since I shot her in the arm. I could read the truth in her eyes when I stared at the scar on her bicep.

Is she already pregnant?

That's even more of a nightmare. I don't want kids. I've seen my brother and his friends try to raise kids while being involved in organized crime, and it never works out. They are never safe.

I love being an uncle. I love watching the kids and taking care of them, but I'm not sure I'm cut out to be a dad.

But if Ri was carrying my kid...fuck, I would do anything for that kid.

Anything.

I just don't know what the truth is.

We all stand in shocked silence, silently watching Ri walk out of the room like she's not about to have six men and everyone who works for them come to rape her.

My stomach curls at the thought.

Fuck.

Suddenly, I feel everything coming up. The acid in my stomach hits me first and then the pasta that Hayes cooked for dinner.

I push it all down, ignoring how I want to do nothing but vomit. I have to figure out a plan before these bastards do.

Smack.

I feel my jaw come unhinged as pressure builds in my face, and

I fall back. The only thing keeping me from falling on my ass is the wall I slam into behind me.

Another punch connects with my eye socket before I can react. If I wasn't in such a state of shock about what just happened, then maybe I would have been better prepared for this outcome—but I wasn't.

I throw my own arm up, blocking another punch before I kick the asshole's legs out from under him. He falls hard, but I don't let up, continuing to kick him as I realize an all-out brawl has broken out. Weapons are being drawn—it's a fight to see who is going to get their hands on Ri first.

I pull out my own gun and duck as a bullet whizzes past me. I squat, trying to use Hogan's moaning body on the ground as my shield while I fire back.

The last remaining man is firing right at me. It seems he thinks I'm his biggest threat.

I can take him down, though.

A dozen men start filing into the room, and now I'm not so confident. My team is nearby, but I won't call them into a situation where they are vastly outnumbered and have a high probability of dying. I'm on my own.

"Beckett!" I hear someone shout.

I flick my head in his direction but keep firing to keep from being shot to death.

Ryker.

He has three men around him firing.

"Let's go!" he shouts. I realize he's waiting to help me escape. Ryker deserves to win, not me, not anyone else—him. I just need to figure out if that's what Ri wants—Ryker. Or if she'd rather have Lennox, Hayes, or Gage. I'll give her any man in the world she wants; it just won't be me.

I stay low to the ground as I run as fast as I can toward Ryker and his men. They cover me, and then I'm out the door just as his men slam it shut.

We sprint out of the back of the restaurant and into the alley-way. That's when my team finds us.

"What the hell happened to you? I thought you could fight better than that," Hayes says.

"I can," I growl.

Hayes motions to Gage, who is wearing a backpack full of gear. The next thing I know, Hayes has an ice pack out and is pressing it against my face.

"I'm fine," I say, pushing his hand away.

"You won't be able to see tomorrow if you don't get the swelling down. And you might need your sight, so you don't lose another fight."

I roll my eyes but press the ice pack against my face.

"Thanks, Ryker. You didn't have to save my ass back there," I say.

"I did because I don't know what the hell to do next. I need an ally."

I nod. "Then you have one."

"Good, now what?" Ryker asks.

I chuckle. "I have no fucking idea. We have to be missing some-thing, right?"

"I would think so, but nothing about this whole game makes any sense."

"What happened? Is the game over already? Who won?" Hayes asks.

We ignore him.

"You going to fuck her?" Ryker asks.

I smirk. "She wouldn't allow it. You?"

"Not unless she begs me to, but that won't stop the others. I know she's tough. I've seen it first hand. She's stronger than any chick I've ever met, but this is different. This is the final game. This is between winning everything—her, the empire, ultimate power—and most likely death. Everyone who has lost is now dead. This round won't be any different."

He's right, but I don't say that. Ri can take on a lot of men, but if all of a gang is after her, she doesn't stand a chance. She can't fight and take down an entire organized crime family as much as she thinks she can. She does have weaknesses, and eventually, one of the men will catch her. Once they do, she's screwed.

She needs a hero.

I'm no hero.

I've told her time and time again; I'm not hers.

But maybe it's time to play the hero. Maybe it's time to knock some sense into her. I'll give her a choice—Ryker, Lennox, Hayes, or Gage. Any one of them will do, but she has to pick. She has to tell us how to win without impregnating her. Because I can't fuck her while married to Odette if she wants Lennox, Hayes, or Gage. And if she wants Ryker, it could take months for him to get her pregnant. It's too risky to let the game go on that long.

We need to find the fastest way to end this game.

"We go after her and catch her before the others," I say.

"You mean kidnap her against her will?"

I nod.

Ryker laughs. "I'm going to enjoy watching her castrate you."

9

RI

A BATTLE BREAKS out behind me. I hear guns going off and the scuffle of hands and fists hitting each other. Maybe they'll all kill each other, and I can forget this stupid game.

No, we need a winner.

Had Nico not died, we wouldn't have had to do these games. *Was he perfect?* No, but he would have done the job well. He was loyal and trustworthy. He was vicious when he needed to be, but not too power-hungry. He wasn't horrible to look at either, but there were no butterflies, no passion. It would have been only a job arrangement.

That's how I need to think of this—find the best business partner.

I cringe as I hear more bullets flying behind me. The best business partner needs to be able to survive a little fight. I can't think about who might be hurt, injured, or dying in there right now.

"They're all still boys. None of them are acting like men," Vincent says.

I nod and pet Loki's head next to me to keep from thinking about the guys. I want to ask Vincent the exact rules. I want to know how much power I have in deciding my fate, but I'm too scared to ask.

Vincent looks me in the eyes, and I know...I have all the control I could possibly want. Just get through this final game, and I'll have my life back. Or at least, my role will be more settled.

The battle gets louder behind me. I don't want to be here when someone emerges from the door. I have to make it a little harder for them than that.

I look down at Loki. I won't let him get hurt in the process.

"Stay," I tell him and then look purposefully at Vincent.

He sighs and rolls his eyes, but he'll take good care of Loki.

I smile and then jog off.

———

Apparently, I made it too hard for any of them to find me because it's been three days, and I'm bored to tears. I've been renting an extravagant, fully furnished condo for the last three days, ordering room service, going to the spa every day, and soaking in the over-sized tub every night.

But I'm getting tired of not having a purpose during my day. I'm getting tired of waiting to find out which guy will find me first. I'm getting tired of chocolates, wine, and watching Netflix.

Lying on the bed, I'm staring up at the light fixture in the bedroom. It's a chandelier with hundreds of little lights. It's night-time, and I've turned the light off, but I can see the reflection of the moon through the window hitting each light individually. *Why does a fixture need so many lights? What's the purpose? To just look pretty and produce heirs?*

Some women want this—a life of luxury and pampering where their only job is to look pretty and get pregnant as soon as possible.

I scrunch my nose at that, not me.

Giving up on sleep, I get up and walk outside to the balcony overlooking the river below. I rest my forearms on the railing. I've never been afraid of heights, but there is something about being so high up when you're at a crossroads in your life. It would be so easy to end it on my own terms, to not let anyone control me ever again.

A shadow moves behind me—finally.

I glance down at my arms. No hairs are raised. I don't have goosebumps, no chills race down my spine. I know who it's not—only one man gives my body that reaction.

So who is it?

I turn just as his hand grabs onto my neck, and I grab onto his.

"Mystery man," I say.

He raises a cocky eyebrow. "You don't remember me, sweetheart?"

I shrug. "There have been a lot of guys. Sorry, you weren't that memorable."

"Then I did my job well. My goal was to make it to the finals without being noticed. Only now will I fight to win."

"Do I get your name?"

"Sure, but only so I can have the pleasure of hearing you yell it out over and over again when I fuck you. It's Elias Roberts."

My features turn dark. "I won't be calling out your name, and you won't be fucking me."

"I think I will. I want to win. I don't want to die. If I lose, I die. So I won't lose. And you'll be calling out my name, alright. Either out of pleasure or pain—I'll take either." His lips curl until I see the whites of teeth. His front teeth are crooked, just like him.

"Then you should have brought more men to capture me, Elias." I break his hold before kicking him hard in the stomach. I enjoy the sight of watching him double over in pain.

I was hoping that Elias was some saint, the perfect man for the job. It would make things less complicated, but he's not. He's a monster, just like the rest of them.

Actually, he's scared shitless and will do anything to protect his own skin—the exact opposite of what you want in a leader.

I run inside and stop in my tracks. My apartment is flooded

with armed men. I can't even count all of them. There has to be at least twenty, no thirty, plus men—all with their guns pointed at me.

I roll my eyes. Well, this is way more than what was needed.

I turn around just as Elias walks inside.

"I brought plenty of backup," he says with a sly smirk.

I slow clap like I'm impressed. "Good job. You did one thing right. It doesn't mean you're going to fuck me. And it doesn't mean you're going to win."

"Actually, it does," Elias says as I feel hands descend on me.

———

I wake up freezing cold. My entire body is trembling so violently that my teeth are chattering. My head is fuzzy; they must have drugged me. But I'm not sure that's the source of my shivering body.

I force my eyes open to face the reality of my situation. It's as perilous as I suspected.

I'm naked.

Chained.

Drugged.

The room is spinning, and my stomach is ready to hurl. The drugs haven't left my system. Elias took all the precautions, using heavy chains to tie me to the wall and stripping off my clothes. The room looks like a dungeon, and my cell is meant to be unbreakable for their worst enemies.

There are metal bars surrounding me and then a thick wall and door surrounding the bars. I glance around the room, looking for cameras I'm sure are there to keep a constant watch on me.

My heart starts speeding, and sweat pours from my brow. This was always the risk I took in this game—someone could be clever enough to outsmart me, and I would lose. Unlike the guys, losing doesn't mean death for me. I'll be violated in the worst way, and to me, that's worse than death.

You've been in situations like this before. This is what I trained you for. You won't fail, Kek's voice penetrates my fear.

I can't break literal metal. I can't break free of the drugs. I'm not strong enough.

I can hear Kek's vicious chuckle in my head. It's a haunting sound that both comforts me and fills me with dread.

If you fail, what was the point? Of my training? Of my death? Of your life? Of everything? You can't fail.

I can't fail.

He's right.

It will all be for nothing if I fail now when we are so close to the end.

What do I do?

You take a deep breath. Calm your fucking heart, your breath, your spinning head—everything needs to become still.

Right, breathe.

I close my eyes, blocking everything out as I take a breath and then another and another.

Everything slows. Everything stills.

And then I open my eyes.

Elias is staring back at me, watching me from the shadows like the coward he is. I can barely make him out.

"Why are you hiding? You had your men drug me, tie me in chains, and you're still afraid of me?" I taunt.

Elias takes a step forward from the shadows. "Just giving the drugs time to work their way out of your system. I don't want to fuck a corpse."

"Unlock the chains, and you won't be fucking a corpse." *You won't be fucking anything.*

He cocks his head as he studies me. "You shouldn't resist. The sooner I do this, the sooner this can all be over, and you can go back to a life of luxury and protection."

"I don't want that. I can take care of myself, thank you."

He grins. "It doesn't look like it from where I'm standing. You were far too easy to kidnap."

"Then why did it take fifty men?"

"You can never be too cautious. You're my future wife, and soon, you'll be carrying my future child. I had to do everything to protect you. I didn't want you to get hurt."

"Raping me is hurting me," I bite back.

"I'm sorry, Princess. If we had more time, I'd wine and dine you first. But you'll realize when this is all over that I was right. I'm the only man you want to marry, and you'll be happy with me."

I laugh at the absurdity. "I will never be happy with a man who takes what he wants from me without my permission."

He studies me a minute. "Maybe I should sedate you so you won't remember."

I don't have a smart comeback. Drugs are the hardest thing for me to beat. But if he does inject me more, I'll have to do my best. I won't fail. I won't let him touch me.

He starts removing his jacket. "Don't worry; it will only be this way one time. Tomorrow I'm flying in a fertility specialist. From there, it will all be needles and IVF and anything that gives me the best chance of getting you pregnant this cycle."

"Then why fuck me now?"

"Because I want to increase my odds."

I shake my head with a grin. "No, you're afraid I'll escape, or someone better than you will kidnap me before tomorrow. You think this might be your only shot to get me pregnant, so you're taking it."

He frowns; I've guessed correctly. His eyes turn wild, on the verge of losing control.

I take another deep breath, calming myself.

And then he's in front of me—touching me, trying to grab my throat.

It's always the throat with men who need control—always about trying to cut off my oxygen, my ability to breathe, think, exist. I'm ready, though. I've prepared my entire life for moments like this. I won't fail.

Elias has one hand on my throat and the other on his pants. He's trying to hurriedly get his pants off so he can thrust inside me and show me how much of a man he is, show me how much power he holds over me.

All of my urges tell me to fight, to try and stop him. That's how I win this fight, though, so I do the opposite.

With his head bowed as he fumbles with his pants, I kiss his forehead.

He freezes, confused about what I just did. Slowly, he looks up at me. I lick my lips, although I'm barely able to get enough oxygen in my lungs with his tight grip.

My lips beckon him to me; he's unable to resist. He doesn't speak—I'm not sure he can right now anyway.

Then he's close enough so my tongue can touch the corner of his mouth. I refuse to kiss him, but teasing to get what I need from him—that's different.

He leans into the touch of tongue against his skin, releasing his grip on my neck enough for me to lick up his jawline. His eyes drift close, and I nudge his head, getting him into the perfect position. Slowly, I move my tongue further up his jawline.

I feel his erection between my legs, and I try not to cringe. I try not to think about how close I am to failing. I do what I have to by pretending I want this, by seducing him with the only part of my body I can control at the moment.

He tilts his head, and my tongue finally makes its way to his ear. I take my time, licking around the outer shell, getting him completely under my control.

Then I bite down—hard.

His high-pitched scream is exactly what I expected. He's a weak coward, terrified of a little pain.

I don't have much time before his men will notice, so I have to do this quickly.

"Key," I say through my gritted teeth, his earlobe still between my teeth.

He flails around, trying to push me off, but I just bite down harder.

"You fucking bitch. Let me go!"

"No! Key or I bite your ear off."

He groans as I clamp down harder.

I just need to get one chain undone—one limb free, and then I'll be able to break free. I hear footsteps above us—I don't have much time left, so I bite down harder and the taste of blood fills my mouth.

"Key," I growl.

Slowly, Elias reaches into his pocket and pulls out a key. He reaches up and puts it in my hand.

"Release me," he commands.

I let him go at the same time he releases the key.

He scrambles back a few feet, acting like I just shot him instead of barely biting him—wuss.

But I don't focus on him. I concentrate on undoing the chain at my wrist. I fumble once, but the second time I get the key into the hole.

The footsteps grow louder, but I don't see anyone coming down the stairs yet. I still have time.

I get my left arm undone.

I grin.

Quickly, I work on unlocking the other chains. By the time I've freed myself of every chain, there are still no men running down the stairs.

Odd.

"Your security team really sucks," I say.

Elias frowns, looking at the door behind him. He locked it when he came in, so I doubt he can just leave.

I'm still naked, but I don't care. I'm about to kick his ass for touching me. For thinking he could take from me, for his slimy penis touching my body in any way.

He's still gripping his ear like I almost cut off a limb. His limp dick is barely poking through his jeans. Despite what just happened, the gleam in his eyes says he thinks he still has me. He thinks he can overtake me himself, or he'll have time to call down his men to restrain me.

I let him think that. I let him think he's about to get payback for making his ear bleed. His lobe is dangling, barely hanging onto the rest of the ear. I might have gone a little too far. Then again, he deserves to never be able to hear again.

Or see.

Or touch.

Or breathe.

He charges toward me at the speed of a raging bull. He reaches into this pocket at the last second, and I see the glint of a blade.

But he won't be touching me with that knife.

I wait until the last second. I let him get as close to me as I dare, and then I make my own move.

I evade him and grab his wrist, twisting the knife around until it drives into his stomach. The move is quick, and it takes him a second to register the pain before dropping to his knees like he's dying.

I doubt he's dying. The knife isn't that big, and he's barely bleeding. But he's groaning like death is seconds away.

It should be. I should end him.

Suddenly I feel familiar feelings of goosebumps on my arms and my speeding heart. I decide I have more important things to deal with than this man.

I lean down to get one last final word into his broken ear. "I'm letting you live, but only so I can torture you the rest of your life. Don't ever come near me, touch me, or even try fuck me against my will ever again. In fact, don't touch any women ever again. If you do, I'll be the one doing the kidnapping next time. And I'll enjoy ripping you apart limb by limb. Do you understand?"

Elias wheezes.

Huh, maybe I did puncture a lung?

I examine him closer and realize there is no way I punctured a lung; the wound is far too low.

I reach into his pocket and pull out his phone. "Call for help. You won't die tonight, but I'd sleep with one eye open if I were you."

I walk away toward the cell entrance, and the outer stone door slowly opens until only the metal bar door separates me from freedom.

Beckett is standing on the other side of the bars. His eyes are locked on my eyes, but they slowly start drifting down, taking in my naked body. There's heat behind his gaze. He may be checking to see if I have any injuries or for evidence of what Elias has done to me, but he can't hide the heat in his eyes.

"You have a wife. You shouldn't be here," I say, crossing my arms and at least blocking some of his view of my bare breasts.

He chuckles. "Doesn't mean I can't look at a beautiful naked woman in front of me. Odette won't be upset with me for just looking."

"What are you doing here? Saving me, Hero?"

"No, I've learned my lesson where saving you is concerned. You're far better at it than I am."

"Then what are you doing?"

"Kidnapping you." That's when I see the others behind him— Ryker, Hayes, Gage, and Lennox.

I shake my head, and my eyes glisten with a taunt. "Go ahead and kidnap me. But take a close look at what happened to the last guy who tried. That's your fate."

HER THREAT IS music to my ears. Whatever happened here, she'll get over it. Any trauma from this place that won't destroy her if she's able to make threats like that.

That's all I want for her—a life free of the traumas of her past. A life where she can feel fulfillment. A life where she can one day find happiness.

Elias is lying on the floor, barely moving like he's already dead. He was brave to be the first to kidnap her, but it was a foolish move that will ultimately lead to his death.

"You going to make this easy? At least, until we get out of the house? We've taken out most of Elias's men, but we don't know what other security he has," I say.

Ri smiles at me. "When have I ever made anything easy for you?"

I grin back—still so feisty and full of life. I don't think anything will ever bring her down. I yearn for her, for the strength she contains, for her will to live and shine above everything else.

"Would you at least like clothes? Or should we kidnap you while you're still naked?"

Ri looks behind me to where the others stand gazing at her. I try to ignore the fact that they've all fucked her, and one of the lucky bastards will get to marry her.

I try to keep my rage and jealousy in check, but I'm sure it's all over my face. How long can I keep up the ruse that I love Odette, not Ri? Somehow I have to manage until I figure out how to take down Odette or until Ri is married.

"No, I don't think I'd like clothes. My body is a good distraction," Ri says.

Jesus.

She's right, but my job is hard enough trying to protect her. I don't need her naked body teasing me to make it even more difficult.

There are five of us and only one of her, but she could take us all down. She'll only go with us if she wants to, but I'm not sure if she does. I'm not sure of her motives at all. It seems like she's going along with her father's plan. She's not really fighting it, which is strange in and of itself.

I glance back to the guys, readying them for what we are about to do. They all give me a slight nod. I turn around to face Ri again and unlock the cell's inner metal door.

Here goes nothing.

We all push inside the small cell. It makes my stomach curl at the thought of what could have happened if Ri couldn't save herself. Even with how strong she is, it's clear she came very close to having everything taken from her. There is still the tiniest hint of fear in her eyes at what she could have lost in this dank cell.

We all draw our weapons even though none of us will be using them against her, at least not to seriously hurt her. We won't even mark her skin. None of us can stand to hurt her.

She looks amused at the gun in my hand, raising her eyebrows. "You're going to shoot me if I don't go with you?"

"Maybe."

She glances quickly around the room, taking in the guns and knives drawn in everyone's hands.

We slowly surround her and then start inching closer to her. She doesn't seem fazed. She's been trained for years how to get out of situations like this, so I know it won't work.

Feigning bored, she waits for us to get within striking distance and then attacks. Hayes and Gage are the first to lose their guns. She kicks them out of their hands before they have a chance to even touch her.

Lennox grabs her wrist and holds his knife up to her throat. She quickly knocks his knife out of his hand and tosses it in Ryker's direction. It's a lazy throw, not one actually meant to hit him.

"Aw, come on, Princess, your aim is better than that," Ryker teases.

She smirks back. "Why are all the men around me so eager to die?"

"Oh, are you going to kill us, Princess? It doesn't seem like it. If you were going to, we'd already be on the ground next to Elias here moaning and taking in our last breaths," I say.

She lunges for me at the same time the guys move in. I aim my gun at her and fire, but not before she knocks the firearm away.

A loud groan ricochets around the room, far louder than the pathetic moaning still coming from Elias.

Ri turns and sees Hayes collapsed on the floor, gripping his chest. Ri falls to her knees as Hayes's eyes roll back in his head.

"Hayes!" she screams, putting her hand over his chest to stop the bleeding. "Hayes, hold on. Just hold on."

Tears are threatening her eyes as she turns to me. "Call for help!"

She immediately goes back to him, trying to apply more pressure, but the bleeding doesn't ease.

It's then I look to the others and nod.

We all descend on her—grabbing her arms and legs to start tying them behind her body.

"What are you doing? Save Hayes! I'll go with you willingly; just save Hayes!" Ri screams.

Only once we have her secured does Hayes open his eyes and stand up.

Her mouth drops as she stares at him. "You're—you're okay. But—"

"Sorry, Princess. We knew the only way to get you was to play to your weaknesses. I was voted most charming and the man we thought you'd care most about if I pretended to die," Hayes says.

Gage rolls his eyes. "He's just the best actor."

Hayes pulls out the fake blood to show her the truth. I didn't accidentally shoot him.

She slowly looks between us all with a wicked grin. "You cruel bastards."

———

We drive all night until we cross the border into Canada. Ryker found a large, secluded place in Toronto to give us some space and time alone with Ri. Ryker says it's completely secured. We rented a camper van, and each took turns sleeping.

Ri slept the entire time while someone also stood guard over her. The watch was more because she could escape at any second than because we were afraid someone was going to kidnap her.

Despite everyone sleeping most of the night in the van, everyone is exhausted when we arrive. Together, we carry Ri into the house covered in blankets. We never did convince her to put on clothes. She'll probably spend the entire time here naked just to spite me.

The house is a massive old stone exterior with modern interior renovations.

"This way," Ryker says, leading the way.

Gage, Lennox, Hayes, and I all follow, carrying Ri in our arms. To our surprise, she doesn't fight us. She lets us carry her, even though she's finally awake. She's probably as exhausted from the road trip as the rest of us.

Ryker leads us to the center of the house. "I picked this one because it has the least amount of windows. The walls are literally made of stone, practically bulletproof, but the inside is modern with a full security system."

"I'll get on updating the security system right away," Gage says as we enter the most central room in the house—it only has one door and no windows. The room has two couches, a bookshelf, and a grand piano in the corner. It will do perfectly until I can talk some sense into Ri.

We set Ri down on one of the couches. She doesn't say anything. She doesn't try to leave immediately.

"Leave us," I say to the others.

They nod, and everyone but Hayes leaves quickly. He lingers for a second, his eyes downcast and his movements heavy. "I'm really sorry, Ri. I didn't want to hurt or scare you."

She smiles weakly. "I know, Hayes. I'm just glad you're alive."

"I always knew you liked me the most." He winks at her.

"Get out of here so I can kick your boss's ass."

He laughs and then jogs out, the door locking behind him on the way out. Then it's just Ri and me.

I pull out a knife as I inch closer to remove the rope still tied around her wrists and ankles.

She stares at me with weary eyes as she watches me kneel in front of her. She doesn't budge as I cut the rope from her wrists and then ankles.

I wait for the punch, the kick, the threat—nothing comes. She doesn't move except to lift her blanket higher over her shoulders.

I stand.

"You going to rape me?" she asks with a hint of teasing in her voice.

"Why would I need to do that? If I wanted you, I could have

you willingly." I lick my lips and watch as her mouth waters at the sight, proving my point.

She scoffs. "I would only let you touch me to get you close enough to castrate you."

I walk over and sit down on the couch opposite her. It seems like we are going to have a long conversation, and I'm not going to stand the whole time. It truly feels like we are on opposite sides, battling it out as we face each other.

I look her up and down. "Maybe I already got you pregnant. We've fucked several times since your birth control was removed. There's a good possibility I've already won the game."

"So cocky. But no, I'm not pregnant."

"I think you should pee on a stick since you aren't exactly trustworthy at the moment."

"If I am pregnant, it doesn't mean that you're the father."

I glare at her. "You haven't fucked any other man but me. The guys pleasured you, but they didn't fuck you. And you wouldn't have let anyone else go near you."

She bats her eyelashes at me. "You have no idea what I've done when we aren't together, just like I don't know what you've done. Don't act like you know me when you don't."

"I do know you, just like you know me," I say before I can think better of it. Ri knows me better than anyone, which is why I'm surprised she hasn't seen my true feelings for her yet.

"So, what's your plan? You're going to impregnate me to win? I don't think your dear wife will be okay with you fucking me and me carrying your firstborn child."

"I'll handle Odette. She knows I have to go to great lengths to win the game. All she cares about is that I win and survive. She'd much rather I cheat on her and live than be loyal to her and die."

"You're going to need some major marriage counseling after this is all over."

I chuckle. "Probably. But the state of my marriage isn't what I brought you here to talk about."

"What do you want to talk about?"

"I want to give you as much choice in your future as possible. We'll figure out what it means to win or lose later." I take a deep breath because her answer to the next question is going to hurt. "I want to know who you want. Do you want to marry Ryker, Lennox, Gage, or Hayes?"

"DO you want to marry Ryker, Lennox, Gage, or Hayes?"

Beckett thinks I have a choice, a say in my own fate. I guess I do, just not in the way he thinks.

My mind is still spinning with their ploy to get me here. It was a smart move to play on my emotions, my feelings for Hayes. I care for him like a brother, and thinking he was dying in front of my eyes was terrifying.

But I shouldn't have reacted that way. I've let my emotions cloud my judgment for far too long.

I sit on the couch opposite Beckett. It feels like we're squared off for a fight, except I'm naked. He's leaning back casually on the couch; his leg crossed over the other knee while he casually waits for me to tell him which of his friends I want to marry.

Why is Beckett trying to help me?

He says he doesn't love me, that he loves Odette.

Is he that worried about losing? Does he really think I'd let him die?

Or is he doing this because even though he doesn't love me, our friendship is real?

"Since three out of the four are not eligible, I don't think it really matters," I say.

"Let me handle the details. For now, just dream. Tell me who you'd choose to spend your life with if given a choice."

Just dream—that's not something I can do. My entire life has been a nightmare.

If I answer honestly, I would choose Beckett. He's my equal, but I have to stop with my emotions and think logically. Dreams and emotions are what have gotten me into this mess.

"I can't dream. I have to be logical," I answer.

Beckett frowns. "Fine. Then logically, who would you choose?"

I just stare at Beckett and pull the blanket tighter around my body. I can't imagine choosing one of them. I can't imagine choosing anyone.

"We aren't leaving this room until you start talking."

That's not really a punishment. It means that reality can be put off for a few more days. It means I get to spend more time with Beckett in this fairytale.

We stare at each other, neither of us speaking. His gaze is warm and comforting, even when he's trying to force me to talk to him. He's begging me to tell him how he can help me; I can see the desperation in his eyes. And yet, I won't give him the answer he wants.

We sit.

We stare.

A silent standoff.

There's a knock on the door, and even then, we don't tear our eyes from each other.

"It's been a few hours; I thought you might want food and drink," Hayes says, bringing in a loaded tray.

We don't look at him. We don't speak to him. We only continue to stare at each other.

He sets the tray down on the coffee table between us.

"Really? You're not even going to talk to me?" Hayes asks as he tries to squat down between us to block our views, but we both crane our heads and continue to stare at each other.

Hayes sighs. "Fine, ignore me. I didn't slave away cooking you a gourmet meal of steak, crab cakes, and a side of asparagus for the last two hours or anything," he mumbles under his breath as he walks away. He pauses at the door, mumbling something else I can't make out before finally locking the door again.

"Poor Hayes," I finally say.

Beckett breaks out laughing as he grabs the bottle of red wine and starts pouring it into two glasses.

I take a deep breath, taking in the smell of the food. "It smells delicious."

"As you know, Hayes is an excellent cook. I'm sure it tastes as good as it looks."

We both reach for our own plates. I settle mine on my lap while Beckett balances his on his knee.

Steak isn't the easiest thing to eat without a table to eat at, but Hayes did leave us each a knife.

I grab the fork and knife. "Do you think Hayes is trying to start something?" I twirl the knife around in my hand.

Beckett chuckles. "Probably, but the food is too good not to eat first." He pops a bite of steak into his mouth and then moans in delight. It's a seductive sound meant to rattle me. I won't let him shake me.

I cut into my own steak and take a bite. As I do, I realize Beckett wasn't faking moans to drive me mad. He was making delighted noises because he couldn't resist. The sound that leaves my throat is primal and deep too.

"You're going to be the death of me," Beckett says.

I look at him and see darkness in his eyes. It's a lustful look he shouldn't have, not when he's married. Not when he's in love with another woman.

He's a conundrum I can't understand. Just like Beckett wants answers before we leave this room, so do I.

My main question is who does Beckett love? Or does he love anyone at all?

Even though it's not the smart move, I let myself enjoy every bite of food, every drop of wine that touches my lips. The sounds that leave me are not something I can control. I let myself feel every emotion, possibly for the last time.

When I've finished my plate of food and curled up on the couch with my wine, I finally feel the heat of Beckett's stare.

"You are impossible," he says, his eyes perusing my body.

I glance down as I realize the blanket has pooled at my waist, and I'm naked from the top-up. The way Beckett looks at me makes me never want to put clothes on again.

It has to be my imagination. He loves Odette. I heard his speech. I've seen them together. This is just a dream.

I stand up, letting the blanket fall all the way to the floor.

He swallows hard at the sight of me. His body tenses, and I swear I see a bulge in his pants.

He wants me.

I lick my lips, letting him know that I, too, want him.

He stands to move closer to me, I think. He wants to touch me, to possibly try and fuck me.

His hand reaches out, and he touches my cheek.

I close my eyes, leaning into his touch.

And then he's gone.

The door slams behind him on the way out.

I smirk. He may have succeeded in kidnapping me, but I just won our first battle. I drink down the rest of my wine.

I plan on winning a lot more.

I'M SO FUCKED.

So fucking fucked.

I slam the door behind me as Lennox jumps up from his seat with raised eyebrows.

"You okay?" he asks.

"No, I'm not fucking okay. The woman I love is probably going to marry you while I'm stuck married to a monster for the rest of my life."

I punch the wall just to feel something other than my unending lust for Ri. My knuckles redden but don't break. It's not enough to take me out of myself.

I punch again, but Lennox grabs my arm, stopping me.

I growl at him, but he doesn't let go.

"I need to talk to everyone." I start walking down the hallway. "Now."

"But Ri—"

"Ri won't leave that room, trust me." She's too intent on seducing the truth out of me.

Lennox stifles a chuckle as he follows me into the main living area of the house.

I march into the living room, where Ryker is stretched out on a couch. Lennox goes in search of Gage and Hayes.

Ryker's eyes widen as he looks at me. "She take your balls already?"

"Don't start," I grumble.

He grins as he sits up. The others make their way into the living room, sitting down on various pieces of furniture.

I stare at the four of them. Ri will be married to one of them in a month's time if I don't figure out a solution.

But I need to accept that reality. I need to help Ri choose; it's the most likely outcome.

"I'm in over my head," I say finally, letting my head fall back against the couch.

"No kidding," Gage says while the others chuckle.

I lean my head up and glare at them all. "None of you are helping."

"Well, we can't have that. What do you suggest we do?" Lennox says with a coy smile.

"Help me solve two problems at once."

Hayes raises his eyebrows. "Which are?"

"I need to find out Odette's plan. I need to find a way to take her down without hurting Ri."

They all nod back at me.

"And I need to find out who Ri would choose among you four if I fail and can't marry her myself."

No one responds to that.

I sigh and stand up, knowing I need their help and they'd rather be anywhere else, discussing anything else.

"I need two of you to go back to Chicago. I need you to spy on Odette. I need you to figure out who she told about Ri. I need to know everything about her plan—everything."

I run my hand through my hair as I stop pacing. "And I need the other two here with me, talking to Ri and trying to convince her to pick you. She has to pick. I can't keep her safe here forever. The faster one of you can charm her, the faster she'll be safe."

Silence meets me.

I stare down each of them individually. Ryker just narrows his eyes at me. Gage looks away. Hayes pouts in disbelief. And Lennox gives me a disappointed shake of his head.

"If anyone has anything to say about my plan, now is the fucking time!" I growl.

They all look at each other as if having a secret conversation without me. It's annoying as fuck.

"Speak!" I snap.

Lennox is the one who finally speaks. "The four of us should all go back."

"What? Why? If Ri tries—"

"She won't run. You said it yourself. She's too curious and wants this settled as much as any of us do. If she is to choose one of the four of us, then you two need to work out your shit. She will never marry any of us as long as she thinks there's still hope that you love her."

I frown, but I understand. I just don't know what to do.

"You aren't one to give up so easily. We will all return and devote all of our efforts to figuring out Odette's plan. We'll find out who she has told about Ri, and we'll find a way to stop Odette before the game is over. As much as any of us would love to marry Ri, we would never be able to enjoy it with you glaring at us every chance you get."

I look from Lennox to the others. "Odette is a ruthless woman. I don't understand why she's so focused on power, on going to war, on staying married to me. She will threaten you, and she has the entire Retribution Kings willing to do her bidding. If she realizes what any of you are doing, she will have you killed. That's something I'm not willing to risk."

"Odette doesn't have the entire Retribution Kings at her

bidding. At least not the most handsome ones," Hayes says, standing.

"Or the smartest ones," Gage says, rising.

"Or the strongest ones," Lennox says, standing.

"You'll also have the help of my men as well. We can take down Odette," Ryker says, standing next to the others.

"Soon, you'll get your happily ever after. Just don't kill each other before we get back," Hayes teases.

If only it were that simple, but they give me hope I don't deserve. This hope is going to come crashing down and destroy me.

THE PLAN IS SIMPLE—GO back and give no clue as to where we've been or what Beckett's plan is. That's easier said than done. None of us trust anyone in the Retribution Kings anymore, and Odette is going to be suspicious as hell, but we have to try. Beckett's happiness, and ours, depends on it.

As much as I and the others care for Ri, she's not ours. She hasn't given us her heart. She's not our match—she's Beckett's.

Any one of us would marry her if we had to in order to protect her. We would try our best to make her happy, but we could never make her happy like Beckett could.

Beckett is our boss, but he's also our friend. We will do whatever it takes to give him his life back.

While Ryker is checking in with his men, the three of us are regrouping at our Chicago hotel.

"What's the plan again? I think we should stay as far away from her as possible—do some snooping or spy work instead," Hayes says as we walk down a hallway.

"The best way to uncover Odette's plan is to get close to her. Get her drunk or something to divulge her secrets. She's our best chance; we don't even know who else to start with," I say.

"I agree. We get to Odette. We've known her all our lives. We grew up with her. We used to be friends. We know her better than almost anyone. We can get her to talk," Gage says.

"Exactly, we know her better than anyone. You're both forgetting how annoying, self-righteous, and vicious she is, though," Hayes says.

"I don't remember her being anything but sweet, kind, and caring," Gage frowns.

Hayes laughs. "That's because she liked you. She hated me. She thought I wasn't smart enough to be friends with her brother. She teased me endlessly."

"And you teased her right back," I say.

"This will get us nowhere," Hayes says.

"You don't know that. We have to try everything unless you are volunteering to marry Ri and face her and Beckett's misery for the rest of eternity," I say.

"We need her to think we hate Beckett; we're angry and upset that Caius died. He was one of us, our closest friend. We can say we're playing double agents, pretending to be on Beckett's side when really we are on hers. Let's convince her we need to know her plan so we can help her," Gage says.

"Good thinking," I say as I knock on Odette's door.

"It's not going to work," Hayes mumbles under his breath.

I shoot him a glare, and he shuts his mouth just as Odette opens the door.

"What are you doing here? Where's Beckett?" she asks, standing in her robe.

"We're here to talk to you and make sure you're protected," I say.

"Protected? I'm pretty sure you are the ones I need protecting from."

I ignore her and push my way into her hotel room. The others follow me.

Odette follows me. "Where is Beckett?"

"He has to finish playing the game. If he doesn't, they'll kill him."

She sighs. "And when will the game be over?"

"A month, most likely," Gage answers.

"I have to be without Beckett for an entire month?"

"Yes," Hayes answers.

"Luckily, you get the three of us in the meantime," I say, flashing her wistful smile.

"Get out," she grumbles, not even wanting to hear us out.

Hayes gives me a look as if to say, 'I told you so.'

"You want to take down Beckett?" I ask, and she pauses, turning back around to face me. "Then let us help you."

She narrows her eyes as I stand and approach her.

"We know the truth—Beckett killed Caius in cold blood. We want revenge, same as you."

"There's just one little problem." She pauses, her finger working its way down my chest. "I don't want revenge against Beckett."

I frown.

"Then what do you want?"

She smirks. "Right now? I want you all to leave."

Then she walks into the bedroom and slams the door.

Hayes snickers, resting his arm on the back of the couch. "That went well."

I look to Gage. "Now what?"

He shrugs. "Get her drunk or..."

"Or?" I ask.

"Or play rock, paper, scissors to see which one of us tries to seduce her," Gage answers.

"Nah, I'm out of here," Hayes says.

I stare at the door, knowing one of us needs to at least try. We need to try everything. That's what being a Retribution King is really about. It's not about revenge and murder. It's not about payback. It's about being loyal to those you consider family and friends. We have to try everything to help Beckett.

I stare at the door. "No need. I'll sacrifice myself."

"Thank god," Hayes mumbles.

Even Gage says, "Good luck."

Then they both leave, walking out of the room.

Fuck, what have I gotten myself into?

I have no idea what I'm doing, but I have to figure out a way to get through to Odette and get her to trust me.

I walk into the kitchenette and grab a bottle of champagne, popping the cork. I would love something stronger, but this is all I find, so it'll have to do.

Maybe I should wait until tomorrow? I can wait for her to have had more time to realize that we are on her side.

No, we are running out of time. And giving her any time to think is just letting her plan and scheme to find more ways to attack Beckett.

It has to be now.

And if this plan fails, then we try again and again and again. We cannot fail.

For Ri's sake.

For Beckett's.

For our own.

We are a family, and I will not let anyone destroy it—especially not when Beckett is so close to happiness. Gage, Hayes, and I may never find a love like theirs. We may never have a chance for that kind of happiness, but dammit, I'm not going to let Beckett squander his future because of his fear of losing Ri.

I knock on Odette's bedroom door.

I don't expect an answer.

But a moment later, she slowly opens it with a half-smirk on her face. Her hair was up before, but it's now down in loose waves.

"I figured you'd be the one they'd send," she says.

"What do you mean?"

"You were always the leader, even when my brother tried so hard to be it. You were the responsible one, the one that carried the weight of the group on your shoulders. If Hayes got high and failed a mission, you took the blame. If Gage took apart a computer and couldn't put it back together, you said it was you. You're always cleaning up everyone's messes. It doesn't surprise me you're the one still here, trying to convince me of whatever scheme you've concocted."

She's right. I'm the one who always takes the blame. It's why I'm so cynical most of the time.

"I just came here to drink and do my job," I say, holding up a glass of champagne.

"Which is?"

"I told Beckett I'd keep an eye on you. I have to have something to report, so here I am."

She snatches the bottle of champagne from my hand as she turns away. She walks back into her bedroom and sits down on the edge of her bed before taking a long sip directly from the bottle.

I lean against the doorframe, trying not to be too obvious. She was always a talker when she drank, so hopefully, that hasn't changed.

She holds up the bottle. "Trying to get me drunk, so I'll talk?"

I frown. Apparently, I'm too obvious.

I walk over to her, take the bottle from her hand, and take a long drink.

She cocks her head to the side as she looks up at me. "You can't trick me, Lennox. I've known you all for years. None of you have ever liked me."

"Hayes least of all."

She grins at that. "Then I did my job well."

"Maybe we did our jobs well too. Caius wouldn't let any of us like you even if we wanted you." I chuckle. "He threatened us plenty of times with murder if we so much as touched you, let alone fuck you. He was beyond protective of you."

Our eyes meet. "Maybe now that he's gone, it's time to protect you in a different way. I know your relationship with Beckett is strained. But if you tell me that Beckett should live, then I'll let him live. Just let me help you with whatever you have planned."

She snatches the bottle back and takes another gulp. I watch as the liquid goes down her throat. I try my best to seem attracted to her. I lock onto her luscious red lips like I want to kiss them, but all I want to do is tape them shut.

I let my gaze linger on her thin throat as she swallows slowly. But all I can think about is how I want to choke her for threatening Ri.

I lick my own lips and think of her naked in bed, trying to seduce her with my gaze. But all I want is to torture her until I find out the information I need to help Ri.

I can't torture her, or she might set her plan into motion. Ri might die if I screw this up. Or Beckett might stay married to this monster forever.

Suddenly, she laughs. Throwing her head back, she laughs and laughs and laughs. She laughs so hard that tears drip out of her eyes. She falls back on the bed laughing, somehow keeping the Champagne bottle upright and not spilling a drop.

Her body trembles with laughter. Then the snorts start, followed by the hiccups.

"What am I missing?" I ask when it's clear she's not going to stop.

"You're a terrible actor, Lennox. I don't know what game you're playing. I don't know who you're loyal to, and I don't care, but please spare me your sexy eyes again. It just looks like you're constipated, not trying to seduce me."

"I'm not playing a game. I'm sorry if you don't find me attractive, but I've always found you attractive and—"

She makes a zipping motion with her fingers, and I stop talking, realizing I've failed. I'm going to have to try a different way to get information from her. Or I could let Gage try; Hayes would just end up killing her.

I'm not beyond trying torture. Beckett thinks if anything happens to her, the same or worse would happen to Ri, but I can't let Odette win. I'm a good friend, and I'd marry Ri if that is what everyone thought was best, but I don't plan on marrying, ever.

Everyone thinks I'm the one who always steps up, who takes on the responsibility when the others fuck up. But this time, I'm doing this for myself. As much as I like Ri, I can't get married.

Even though I may not believe in happily ever afters, Beckett and Ri make me believe that for some small percentage of people, the one percent of the one percent, they're real.

That tiny bit of hope is enough for me.

I'M LYING on the carpet in the middle of the room, spread eagle when the door opens again. I don't move. I couldn't have planned this better myself, even though I was just getting comfortable on the floor.

I feel a lump of fabric hit my stomach.

I peel an eye open to look down and find a pile of clothes.

"Put them on," Beckett commands.

"You know, I'm really tired of your commands. If you want me to do something, you should ask. Otherwise, I'm just going to fight you."

Beckett grits his teeth as he stands over me, clearly on his last nerve with me already. This is going to be a long few days together if he's already riled up at me.

"Ri, will you please put on some clothes?"

"Thank you for asking, but no."

Beckett's glare turns downright diabolical. I'm pretty sure I'm about to find out if he has any real feelings for me right here, right now. If I live, then he does care.

I raise my eyebrows and grin up at him as he stands over me with a sigh.

"Can we at least sit on the couch?" he asks.

"You can. I'm going to lie right here."

"Why do you have to make everything so difficult?"

"Why do you have to make everything so boring?"

"I should just hire a doctor to shove some of everyone's sperm up in you, and whoever's sperm takes wins. Or he loses because he has to put up with you for the rest of his life."

He's grumpy today. Lack of sleep and being tortured by someone he can't have will do that to a person.

I sit up and grab the shirt on top and slowly put it on. I don't bother with the bra or panties or even pants. The shirt is the only compromise he's getting out of me.

"Better?"

"Yes, thank you," Beckett sighs as he sits down on the rug next to me. He doesn't lie back like I do, but I'm guessing this is his compromise.

He sits in silence for a minute while I continue to stare up at the ceiling, counting the dots on the popcorn ceiling like I would stars.

"Tell me who you think I should pick," I say suddenly.

Beckett looks over at me. "Why do you think I have any idea who you should pick?"

"Just humor me."

"I guess whoever was best in bed," he teases.

"Hayes wins then," I say.

He gives me a dirty look.

"What? You thought I was going to say you? Sorry, but Hayes is bigger, and he's a more selfless lover. You're far too selfish. I don't know how Odette puts up with you."

He growls. "I am not a selfish lover."

I laugh.

He falls back, exhausted with me.

I laugh harder.

Beckett is by far the best I've ever had, but I won't be admitting that out loud ever again, and definitely not to his face.

"Come on, give me your pros and cons list. Tell me why you think I should or shouldn't marry each of them," I say.

I need help. Beckett is off the table. I need to think of the others objectively, and Beckett can help with that. And his plan will work. If I want Lennox, Hayes, or Gage instead of one of the main four remaining, then Vincent would honor that if Beckett technically won.

Beckett puts his hand behind his head. "Who should I start with?"

"Gage."

"Well, the pros are Gage is the smartest. You would never have to worry about security with him. He would always have you covered. And he's good at keeping secrets."

"All good points. And cons?"

"Cons are he doesn't want to lead an organization. He's too quiet and possibly too nerdy for most of the men to take him seriously. He's too serious for you, and he's not in love with you."

I laugh at his last one. "Alright, Hayes next."

"Hmm, well, apparently, he's the best in bed. He's loyal to a fault. He's kind, sweet, charming."

"He's a good chef. I'd never go hungry."

"You'd never go hungry. And he's lovable, like a puppy. You'd laugh the most with him."

I nod, agreeing.

"But he's also the easiest to trick. You would spend as much time protecting him as he would protecting you. He's a pushover, and the Corsi men would eat him for dinner. And he's not in love with you."

I analyze everything Beckett said, and I know it to be true. Although he's the sweetest and easiest to love, I can't marry Hayes because he would be the worse protector. Gage remains in the running simply because he's a better protector.

"Okay, what about Lennox?"

Beckett takes a deep breath like this conversation is taxing him. "Lennox...where to start with him? He's a born leader. He's better at it than me, better Caius ever was. He's intelligent and level-headed. And he'd approach a relationship like a second job."

"But?"

"He's too serious, and he's always hated you."

"Hey, he doesn't hate me anymore."

"Still, he held a grudge against you, and that doesn't go away easily, even if it seems like it."

"Fine, point made."

"And if he leaves, there will be no one left to lead the other two."

"You wouldn't lead them?" she asks.

"Yes, I'm the leader of the Retribution Kings, but I mean the three of them specifically. I do my best, but he's known them the longest. He's who they depend on. And he's hiding something dark; I can tell."

"You're probably right. But then again, I'm guessing all of them have dark secrets."

"And he's not in love with you." Beckett's eyes meet mine, and I can see that's the most hurtful part for him to say. He desperately wants one of them to be in love with me. That would somehow make this all easier—if one of them just loved me or if I loved one of them.

I don't want to tell him it would actually make it much harder. Love clouds everything. I need to think logically about the man I'll spend the rest of my life with, and love has nothing to do with it.

"And Ryker?" he asks. "I've spent the least amount of time with him, but he's an excellent pick. Already a good leader. A good actor. He's already feared. You two have chemistry together. Maybe even more so than with the other three. I've seen it with my own eyes."

I blush at that.

"But the only way a man can act as cruel as Ryker is if he's experienced torture or has a small streak of viciousness inside him. He's the biggest wildcard. He'd protect you, but I'm not sure if he would challenge you. He'd put his men and empire above you. And—"

"And he's not in love with me," I say.

He nods.

"So, what do you think? You've heard my opinions; what are yours?" he asks me.

"I think any one of them could do the job, even with their faults. But I'm still not sure who the right guy is."

"How are you going to choose?"

"I don't know."

"Do you feel like you need to spend time with them? Should we form our own little game to see who knows you the best or who's the strongest or something?"

I laugh. "God, no, that's the last thing we should do." I smack Beckett. "Thanks for giving Vincent the idea of the game in the first place—just a brilliant idea," I say sarcastically.

"I stand by it. It's still a brilliant idea."

"How exactly? We've both almost died. Everyone who has lost has died even if they didn't deserve it. Two of my friends died. Caius died."

His face drops. "I'm sorry. I still can't get over Lucy and Kek— I'm sure I'll never know the full story on him, but I'm sorry that you lost him."

I sit up, hugging my knees against my chest.

Beckett slowly rises next to me, mirroring my moves.

"I still need to talk to Odette. Whether you love her or not, I need to know she can't hurt me. I need her to forget."

I expect Beckett to argue with me. I expect him to tell me to leave her out of it.

"I know. I'm working on it," is all he replies.

I ALWAYS GET the worst jobs. I huff as I walk into the bar.

Okay, maybe that's not fair. Lennox spent the entire night with Odette, and judging by his grumpy mood this morning, he failed miserably at getting close to her.

Gage is too occupied playing spy by reviewing every security camera and trying to hack into the computers and phones of her and every other suspect in the Retribution Kings.

And I won't go near Odette unless we've agreed on the torturing her route. Then I'll be happy to coerce some information out of her.

Instead, I have this crappy job that definitely won't work. But as Lennox said, it's my turn to do something for once. He acts like I don't do any work, *but who do they ask when they want to eat? Me.*

I've barely sat down at the bar before I sense him.

"Ryker," I say with a genuine smile. "So glad you could make it."

"You didn't exactly give me a choice." He frowns as he sits down at the bar next to me.

It's a crowded bar. There are people sitting the entire length of the bar, and the bartender is overwhelmed, so it'll take a while to get anything to drink. But that's never stopped me before.

I reach over the bar and snap up two glasses and the closest bottle before quickly pouring the liquid into the glasses and putting the bottle back.

Ryker stares at me incredulously and sniffs the drink. "This smells horrible."

"Do you want a drink in the next hour? Then this is what you're getting."

He rolls his eyes. "Or I could go home where I'd find a lot better to drink there. Why are we in the most crowded bar in the city?"

He stares me down. "So I can't make a scene when you tell me whatever you're going to tell me."

I shrug as I take a sip of my drink before almost spitting it out. I must have picked a bottle of the cheapest tequila in the bar.

"Why am I here, Hayes?" Ryker asks again.

"We need your help with Odette."

"I've been helping. I've been using my own resources to look into her and surveil her. And I've come up with three guys who seem to be working with her—Stan, Keith, and Dominic. I should have contacted you guys sooner, but I wanted to be sure I didn't miss anyone. I—"

"Gage has already come to the same conclusion."

"Okay, so then why do you want to talk to me?"

"If it were as simple as just surveilling her, we'd already have taken the three of them out and brought Ri home. But it's not. Odette is far from simple. She's secretive, sly, and most of all, a liar."

Ryker frowns. "I still don't know what you want me to do about it."

"Lennox was our best chance of someone getting close to her. He failed. Gage is better behind a computer, and I can't stand the woman. So..."

"No," Ryker says before I even finish speaking.

"We have to try everything. We have too much history with Odette. But you—you have no history with her."

"So you want me to what—fuck her? Coerce her? Get her to divulge all her secrets to me just because I have a big dick and am good in bed?" He tosses back his drink. "You really think that a woman who is as sly as you say she is would so easily divulge her secrets to a stranger? Do you really think a woman who holds all her power from being married to Beckett would cheat?"

"We won't know until we try. You're charming. You got Ri to like you even though she loves Beckett. How is this any different?"

"It's different because I like Ri. This Odette seems like a pain in my ass."

"Just try; that's all we're asking. Try."

"No."

"Fine, then you'll marry Ri knowing she loves another man? Knowing you can never make her happy? Knowing she'll be miserable the rest of her life?"

Ryker glares at me, narrowing his eyes as he reaches across the bar and grabs the same cheap bottle of tequila. He pours himself another glass, tossing the liquid back before refilling his glass and taking another shot.

I have him. He'll do whatever needs to be done because he cares about Ri just like we do.

"I don't know what you expect from me. Odette isn't going to give me the time of day, but I do care about Ri—enough not to marry her unless it's the only way to save her.

"Fine, I'll try for her. But I wouldn't hold my breath on the outcome. And I'd start planning a plan B."

I throw some money down, and we both walk out of the bar. "You are the plan B, and I'm not sure we have time for a plan C."

"SHE KILLED LUCY," Ri whispers.

I narrow my eyes but don't let any of my feelings out. I'm not sure where she's going with this. I'm not sure why she hasn't attempted an escape yet.

I don't know why she's sitting here so relaxed and acting like we are just two friends having a pleasant conversation. I've very skeptical. I'm pretty sure she has a plan, an angle; I just haven't figured out what it is yet.

"Odette—she killed Lucy," Ri says while watching my face closely, so I keep it as nonchalant as I can. I don't even speak.

I know Ri's right. Odette and Caius killed Lucy, but I don't know why. I don't know her motives except that she wants to hurt Ri, hurt me, hurt everyone in her life. I don't understand Odette, but hopefully, the guys are figuring it out.

I can't stay married to her forever, not when Ri walks this earth. I don't deserve her, but I want a real chance to fight for her, to be honest, tell her everything, and see how she feels.

Ri grits her teeth when I don't try to defend Odette or even disagree with her.

"Do you agree? Odette killed Lucy?"

I clear my throat, knowing she won't give up until I answer her. "Maybe. I don't really know. I wasn't there. You'd have to present the evidence against her for me to believe it. But Odette is a strong woman. She's capable of many things. She's capable of murder just like you are. And I'm sure if she did, she had her reasons."

"Unbelievable." Ri stands abruptly and starts pacing the room.

I remain seated on the floor. If I stand, I'll get worked up right along with her. I'll show my emotions, and I need to guard them carefully until Odette has been dealt with. Odette could have anyone prepared to hurt Ri. If I was Odette, it would be someone close to Ri.

Fuck, someone close to Ri. That would mean Gage, Hayes, or Lennox—even Ryker.

Fuck, fuck, fuck.

I can't trust any of them.

Ri tilts her head, noticing the anger rising in my chest. "How could you love her?"

I stand—it's a mistake. I know the second my blood rushes through my veins, but I can't help it. I'm too frustrated with myself for not realizing that one of them is most likely working for Odette. *But who?*

Ri moves in front of me, stepping into my space.

"How could you love her when she killed someone so innocent?"

"I doubt Lucy was innocent," I snark back.

Ri punches me—hard across the cheek. My head snaps to the side as the hit lands, and my eye feels like it's coming out of its socket. It's probably fair considering she just lost her friend, and I basically said she deserved it. But I'm not thinking logically. All I'm thinking about is how I fucked up.

"Lucy was my best friend, the only one who stuck by me. Don't you dare say Lucy wasn't innocent. She was the only person who ever cared about me. She didn't deserve to die!"

Ri charges at me.

I blink, still struggling to see out the eye she just clobbered, but I'm not going to let her hurt me without consequence. I attack at the same moment she does. Her hand flies to my face again, but I block her fist at the same time I knee her hard in the stomach, knocking the breath out of her.

She takes a step back, gripping her stomach and catching her breath. "I can't believe you just did that."

"No kidding, since it was such an obvious move, you should have easily blocked. It seems like you're letting your emotions get the best of you."

Her nostrils flare and her hands fist, ready to punch again.

"Why did Odette kill Lucy? If Odette is the love of your life, then she would have told you. You would have known. You would have been okay with it. Why did she do it?"

I shrug. "I don't know. Odette and I have this thing between us called trust. It's why we work. I don't question her every move, and she doesn't question mine. It's why you and I would never work. No trust between us."

"That I believe, but the other statement is just plain bullshit." Ri circles me, her fists up, ready for a fight. She throws a jab, I duck.

"Lazy punch."

I throw another kick. She avoids it easily this time, rolling her eyes. "That was lazy." She throws out a combination of punches and kicks—this time stronger than before. I dodge most, but she gets a punch into my shoulder.

"You know what I think? I think she killed Lucy because she thinks Lucy knew something. She thinks Lucy knew her secrets and was willing to spill them, but I don't think Lucy deserved to die," she says.

"Any more than Caius deserved to die? Sometimes death is inevitable. Sometimes it's our destiny to die young," I reply.

"You're a fucking asshole. Is that why you love her? You two are evil fucks together?"

This time when she punches, she doesn't let up. I'm too riled up and focused on my own idiocy, so I instinctively punch right back, acting like she's my enemy instead of the woman I'd die for.

I hit her in the throat.

She retaliates with a kick to the groin.

Another punch to her stomach.

And then she gets one in my sternum.

We're both panting, frustrated as hell with each other. It's clear what her goal is—she's trying to push me to admit I don't love Odette.

But I won't slip up. I love Ri too much for that. I need her to think I'm head over heels about Odette, at least for a little longer. At least until I solve the mystery that is my wife.

She takes a step back. I take a step forward.

Another back.

Another forward.

And then my hands reach out to her. But instead of grabbing her throat or throwing another punch, my hand lands on her waist. She grips my shirt as she yanks me close.

We're still steaming mad, but there's also an undercurrent of lust that always exists when we're together.

I glare down at her.

She cocks her head back, licking her bottom lip seductively; she thinks this is where I'll break. With my hand on her hip bone, standing so close that we are breathing the same air, I'll give into my lust and kiss her.

I won't break. I can't. I have to remain strong to save her.

"I'm tired of your games, Princess."

"And I'm tired of yours," she hisses back.

"Then end this. Tell me who you want to marry, and this will all be over. We can go our separate ways and never see each other again." Just don't pick the man who is on Odette's payroll. Then you'll be in even more danger, and I'll never be able to keep you safe.

"How can you love her? She's a monster," Ri's voice breaks. Her eyes water as she thinks about her lost friend, probably also thinking about losing me.

I raise my hand, placing it under her chin so I can see all of her tears, all of her pain, all of everything I deserve to feel.

It ruins me seeing her like this—in so much fucking pain, pain I'm causing. But it's moments like this that I remember why even if I solve my Odette problem, it doesn't really matter. The other guys are better—kinder, sweeter, more compassionate. We've all killed, but so far, I'm the only one who has proven to betray her. I'm not the man for her. I never will be.

"We're all monsters. Love doesn't care if the person is a monster or not; it just exists. Everyone deserves to be loved. I'm her person, and she's mine."

Ri's face falls in defeat.

"Plus, between Odette and me, I'm the bigger monster."

Maybe it's time I explain to Ri why.

17

RYKER

WHY AM I DOING THIS?

This is so stupid. It's not going to work. They couldn't get Odette to talk to them; she's not going to talk to me, a complete stranger.

I'm doing this because of Ri, because I love her.

I'm not in love with her. Although, I could easily fall for a woman like Ri if she wasn't already in love with another man.

For now, Ri's like the girl next door that I like to look after. The hot 'could kick my ass better than any man' girl next door. I'm not even convinced Ri needs my help.

I'm still in favor of Beckett just telling Ri the truth and them working together to get rid of Odette and any other attacks against them. But nobody listens to me outside of my own men. I'm ready for this to be all over so I can spend my time just doing my damn job instead of playing stupid games.

I'm staked out outside the Retribution Kings' office downtown. This is the office that handles what the world sees—the real estate and law offices that claim to make the millions while they're really smuggling drugs and weapons and every other criminal way they can make money.

I know Odette is coming. Hayes texted me her schedule, and this is where I agreed to try and meet her. Hayes didn't understand why I wouldn't try to run into her at the bar she frequents at night, but that's the worst place to try to pick up a woman who doesn't want to be hit on.

Her driver pulls up, and she steps out in a fitted black dress that covers her curves but is somehow still sexy as hell. She's clearly going for boss lady vibes with her attire all the way down to her black pumps and perfect blonde bun.

I start walking as soon as she opens the door into the office building. I'm several feet behind her, but I'll easily catch up. She can't take very big strides in her heels. Plus, I want to time it perfectly.

I enter the building behind her and flash the guard a fake badge as I follow her to the elevator banks. She steps into an empty elevator, and just as the door is about to close, I put my arm between the doors.

She has her phone out, typing away on it, but her eyes look up to flash me a death stare as my arm holds the door open, delaying her from getting to her meeting on time. She's about to be in for a rude awakening if she thinks five seconds is a delay.

I step on, and Odette goes back to typing on her phone as I hit the button for two floors below hers.

The doors close, and the elevator takes off.

I ignore her but don't take out my own phone. I just act completely disinterested, like her long legs, red lips, and heavenly perfume do nothing for me. If I didn't know who she was, I might want to hit on her just because I could. She's not exactly my type, but she's hot, strong, and in charge. I can work with that.

She licks her lips and makes this soft purring sound, almost as if she needs the attention, thrives on it.

I ignore her harder, staring at the floor numbers as we rise, acting like they are far more interesting than her.

I can practically feel her pouting next to me as she holds her hand out next to mine, probably going for the casual move of letting our fingers brush together to see if there is any electricity between us.

I put my hands in my pockets, and her pout intensifies. It's adorable. I want to laugh at her, but it would ruin my act of not giving her any attention.

I don't think Odette would actually cheat on Beckett with me. I think too much is at stake for her to be seen as a cheater right now, but she's a woman used to being fawned over. I'm not that type of man, though. I only give someone attention if they deserve it, and Odette doesn't deserve it.

We get to the fifteenth floor, and the elevator stops, but the doors remain closed just like I planned.

She huffs, immediately annoyed, even though she has no idea how long this will last. She has no idea if it will last five seconds, five minutes, or five hours. For both our sakes, I hope I break her before we get anywhere close to the five-hour mark.

She stomps her foot down as she approaches the elevator panel. She presses the button for her floor incessantly, like that will somehow get the elevator button moving.

"Fine, I'll just take the stairs. I could use the exercise anyway." She presses the button for the doors to open, but they don't budge.

She stares at me incredulously, but I continue to ignore her. I don't show any displeasure or any emotion. She has no idea what's going on in my head.

"You're supposed to say I look great and don't need the exercise. That's the polite thing."

I can't help it; I chuckle at that. "Really? That's what you're mad at? I didn't tell you your ass looks good."

She gives me a scathing look as her blue eyes shoot daggers in my direction. She turns back toward the elevator panel and presses the help button.

Nothing happens.

Nothing is going to happen until I give the cue to get us moving again.

"What the hell? Why isn't this working?" This time she looks at me with slight panic in her eyes.

I don't respond.

"Hello! Are you are going to talk to me or try to fix this?"

I chuckle again. "I assumed your question was rhetorical. And I'm not an elevator technician. How would I know how to fix the elevator?" I raise my eyebrows.

"Because you're, you know…"

"Because I have a dick? Isn't that sexist?" I grin slyly at her.

She crosses her arms and sticks out her hips. "No, that's not sexist."

"Oh, so you're one of those women who believe that sexism only exists if it happens to the woman, not the man."

She bites her bottom lip, and I can practically see the steam coming out of her ears. I don't know if this is the right way to get her to talk to me or not, but I sure as hell know that flattery won't get me anywhere. And I'm quite enjoying arguing with her and teasing her, so I keep going.

"You're probably one of those stay-at-home husbands married to a woman who works all the time and brings home the dough while you sit on your ass and pretend to cook and clean, aren't you?"

I hold up my left hand. "Not married."

She narrows her eyes looking for a tan line.

"Fine. Boyfriend, fiancé, whatever."

"Nope, not currently in a relationship."

"Then, get over here and try to figure out how to work this damn elevator and stop acting like someone is going to be upset if you stand within a foot of me."

I take a step back. "Maybe I just don't want to help you. You seem like the uptight kind, and I'm more of a chill guy. I don't think we would work well together."

"I'm not asking you to marry me or even like me, just fix the damn elevator."

I take another step back until I feel the elevator wall behind me. I slide down to the floor until I'm sitting.

"What the hell are you doing?"

I close my eyes and stretch my legs out. "I'm waiting for the elevator technician to come and fix the elevator instead of having a coronary like some people."

She frowns. "Do you think this imaginary elevator technician will be coming soon?"

I shrug, not opening my eyes. "Maybe, maybe not."

"And that doesn't bother you, that you have no idea how long it's going to take for him to come? Don't you have something important to do?" She pauses for dramatic effect. "Oh, that's right. You don't work or do anything important. You mooch off your parents, most likely."

I chuckle. "You're really wound up; you know that? But if you must know, yes, I do have somewhere important to be. I just don't believe in getting worked up and anxious about things I can't change."

"How do you know you can't change things when you haven't even tried?"

"As I said, I'm not an elevator technician. I watched you press the buttons; they don't work. I might as well meditate or nap or do something useful."

She rolls her eyes at me and pulls her phone back out.

"Unbelievable, I don't have reception in here."

I can feel her eyes on me, and then she kicks my foot. "Hey you, want to try your phone and see if it has any reception?"

"I don't have a phone."

"Yes, you do; I can see it in your front pocket."

"What are you staring at my crouch for?" I smirk.

"You stared at my ass and tits; now we're even."

I laugh. "You're really full of yourself; you know that?" That's when I pretend to notice her ring for the first time.

"Especially for someone who's married," I say with a disapproving look.

"Like a guy like you cares that I'm married."

"A guy like me? What's that supposed to mean?"

"I don't know what you do, but it can't be important. You're not wearing a suit, your jeans are from Kohl's, your watch is a knock-off, and your shoes are covered in mud. You don't work in an office; you work in the field, which means you don't make much money, you didn't go to college, you're not that smart."

I raise an eyebrow and shake my head, disappointed in her. "So a guy like me would take any attention from a woman like you whether she's married or not? A guy like me has no morals and knows the only way he can ever fuck a woman like you is if she feels like cheating? Because what could I possibly offer a woman like you except a quick fuck?"

She shrugs. "I'm not wrong. You don't have enough money to satisfy me."

I let my eyes run up and down her body, evaluating her in the same way.

"Prada shoes, a designer dress, well-manicured hands. I get it; a girl like you takes a lot of money to be made beautiful every day."

She scoffs. "I'm beautiful without all of this."

I look at her in disbelief. "I doubt that, sweetheart. But you say I don't have enough money to be able to afford a date with you anyway."

"You don't. It's a fact."

"The problem is you don't know how to judge men. You think just because I don't wear an expensive designer suit that I don't have money. Honey, I have more money than you can dream of. Money I've earned with my hands, not in an office."

"Prove it."

"Why should I? I don't want to go on a date with you."

"Don't you? You should know I'm more than just a pretty face. I have plenty of power and money of my own."

"Good for you, but that's not what I look for in a woman."

"What do you look for?" she asks, far too curious.

Maybe I will be able to do this. I won't make her fall in love with me, but I can get her to go out with me long enough to learn some of her secrets. Or at least I could get her into her bed so I can explore her shit when she's asleep.

"A woman who doesn't care about my wealth, for one."

"You still haven't confirmed that you're wealthy."

I look up at the corner of the elevator and give a slight nod of my head, indicating we should move again. I have her captivated; that's all I can hope for.

The elevator starts moving again.

I stand up, but Odette holds her ground in front of me. We're face to face, exchanging oxygen with each other.

The door opens on my floor.

"This is my floor," I say.

"Uh-huh," she says, not able to get any other words out.

I put my hands on her hips.

She sucks in a breath as I lean in close like I'm about to kiss her. She licks her lips and then parts them, readying herself for a kiss.

Then I gently move her to the side and walk past her out of the elevator. I don't need to turn around to see if she's following me; I can hear her heels clicking on the ground as she does.

I grin like an idiot as I keep walking through the office floor. I stop suddenly, and she slams into my back. It amuses me to no end.

I turn and face her. "Can I help you?"

"You're one of them," she says suddenly like she's figured it out."

"Hmmm?" I play dumb.

"You're playing the stupid game to win the Rialta girl. You're an organized crime boss. You don't make money; you steal it."

I bow. "That's me, Ryker Parks. And you—you're no better than me. You married a boss and are manipulating him to try and start a war."

She glares at me.

I hold her gaze right back.

"I can't believe you manipulated me like that! You're just trying to fuck with my head, just like all the rest of them! You—"

I lean forward and press my lips against hers. It's a tame kiss for me, but I'm shocked to see how her lips feel against mine. My heart thumps wildly, and I feel warm and hot inside, something I haven't felt before.

It's probably just because I've been told how bitter and cold she is, so I was expecting her kiss to make me feel cold, not warm—that's all. There is nothing else to the kiss.

I pull away, and her lips stay puckered as if she was hoping for a longer kiss.

Her eyes land on mine, and finally, she says, "What was that for?"

I grin. "I needed to shut you up somehow."

Quickly, I walk away before she can truly process what happened. Hayes will be mad that more didn't happen, but if he wants this to work, I'm going to need to move slowly with her. If I push her too far, too fast, we won't get anything. I just hope Beckett's plan to stall gives me enough time to crack Odette and hopefully not fall victim to her schemes.

A chill runs through my body, one that unsettles me and makes me think that falling victim isn't what I should be worried about. I should be worried about a very different falling.

I'M TRYING to push Beckett to break. I get close, but every time I do, he pushes me away—so close and yet so far.

I need to know for sure how Beckett feels. He's the best choice by a million miles. I suspect I know the truth, but if he is the best choice, the right choice, the only choice—then I need to hear it from him. He needs to be the one to say it. That's the only way I'll choose him.

I have to push him to his absolute limit because he thinks he's doing the right thing. While he's amazing for doing it, the best thing for him to do is tell the truth. Tell the truth, and then I can make the best decision for all of us.

We're still standing close, my back to a wall and Beckett's hand tucked under my chin. Tears water my eyes for everything I'm about to lose—I know my fate. I'll lose practically everything no matter what Beckett chooses, but I can help him pick the best option for him.

His eye is already swelling from where I hit him, and I'm sure my ribs are turning black and blue from where he got me. We are so volatile together. It might be better if we aren't in each other's lives anymore, but I have to be sure.

"You really love her?" I ask my question quieter this time. He's sick of me asking, but until I'm one thousand million percent sure, I won't choose anyone else.

He doesn't answer. He doesn't blink. He just stares at me.

"I just need to know the truth, whatever it is. I can take it. Please."

His teeth slowly scrape along his bottom lip. I'm not sure if I've pushed enough or if I've pushed too far, but it's not in my nature to give up. So I keep pushing, keep hoping he'll answer me.

"How can you love a woman who betrayed you? Who's trying to start a war with your brother? Your family?" I whisper.

My eyes glide back and forth over his, and I can see the darkness brewing there. I see the pain, the need to talk to me, but also the pull to keep everything inside, so it doesn't break him. I don't know why the truth would destroy him.

After everything I've seen him go through, I think it's impossible for him to break. He's stronger than he realizes. He can endure anything; I've seen him endure hell. Whatever is eating him up, he'll survive that too.

"We all need this to end. We need the games to end and the wars to hopefully stop before they start. But we can't do that until this game is over. I'm trying to decide, but I can't until I know the truth. Just tell me the truth, and then I can move on. No one else is here. There is nowhere else for us to go. Just be honest with me, Beckett. You owe me that."

He doesn't move for a heartbeat. I assume, once again, I'll get nothing real from him, nothing more than I've gotten every other time.

But then, his hand drops from my face, and he takes a step back.

"Do you want wine or something harder?" he asks.

I look at him in confusion.

"You want the truth? Then we're both going to need a drink."

"Wine, please." I'm afraid of anything stronger. He may need a drink, but I need to be sober, so my feelings don't affect my decisions. My emotions have always failed me.

Beckett nods and leaves the room.

I pace for a second, full of nervous energy, but then decide to just sit. I don't want to scare Beckett off now that he's decided to talk, and my nervous energy might do just that.

I sit, but soon I realize my legs are bouncing up and down.

Jesus, I'm a mess.

I'm getting exactly what I want, though.

I put my hands on my knees and force them down to stop my legs. But unless I hold my hands down the entire time, I'm not going to be able to hold still. Just as Beckett reenters the room, I decide to just curl my legs underneath me.

If I'm still shaking or showing any nervous energy, he doesn't seem to notice as he pours us each a glass of red wine. He hands me one, barely looking at me, and then takes a seat across from me.

We take long sips before finally staring at each other.

I'm silent. I've pushed, and now it's time for him to open up, to tell me his secrets. And soon—he'll learn mine.

"About two years before I met Odette, I fell in love for the first time."

My eyebrows shoot up before realizing a neutral reaction is probably more helpful than a shocked one to get Beckett to talk. Quickly, I tone down my reaction and take a small sip of my drink, not interrupting him. I'll give him all the time in the world to tell his story.

"Her name was Jennifer. She was from Seattle. She ran a boat club, and that's how we met. I rented a boat for an afternoon. As soon as I saw her, I knew she was the one for me. She was the most beautiful woman I had ever met—long auburn hair, fit body, striking green eyes.

"But it was her personality that got me—bigger than life. Her laugh was infectious, her smile entrancing. Right away, I could tell she was the most caring woman I'd ever met." Beckett's face brightens as he talks about Jennifer, about this mystery woman he supposedly loved before he met Odette.

I can't help but skip ahead and assume that the only way he lost a love like her is if she died and he blames himself. I brace myself to hear about his heart being broken and the tragic story about to unfold.

"She was the one. She was my one. But my life was complicated. I'd done terrible things, killed people. Not everyone is strong enough to handle hearing that. Not everyone would accept my family with open arms. Not everyone would care less about my past, just about the man I have become.

"But Jennifer...she did. She was able to put everything aside. Not only that, but my sister-in-law, Kai, even started training her on how to use a gun and fight. She got quite good at it in the end."

Beckett sighs.

I take another drink, waiting for the bomb to drop and my heart to break for him.

"Jennifer fit in completely. She loved all my nieces and nephews. She loved being out on the water. She loved me..."

Beckett looks away at the wall.

Here it comes.

"And then one night, Enzo came to me. Some money was missing after some of our men had disobeyed Kai's orders. They said it was just a mistake, but Enzo didn't think so. He suspected Jennifer, saying something just didn't add up."

Beckett shakes his head. "I told Enzo he was crazy. I loved Jennifer, and I was going to marry her. I said he needed to accept her or get out of my life."

He swallows hard. I'm gripping onto my glass so tight I think it might break.

"And then the worst happened—Enzo's kids went missing. We'd had scares before, but never like this. They just vanished. Enzo immediately accused Jennifer. I defended her. I would have defended her to the death."

Beckett downs the rest of his drink, liquid courage to continue. "I took Jennifer, and we left to elope. I was completely blind. I did anything she said. I let love blind me. I did whatever she said, not knowing I was helping her conceal my niece and nephew. I didn't realize I was helping her blackmail my family for millions of dollars."

He's silent for a moment, but he's not done talking. He needs to finish.

"Did you eventually figure it out?"

"Yes, but it was too late. The damage had been done. The kids are traumatized by the experience. Enzo and Kai will never look at me the same. They'll never trust me; I don't even trust myself. I'm a monster for believing a woman I barely knew over my own flesh and blood. I should have believed my brother."

"You're not a monster, Beckett. She was. You figured out the truth, and then you fixed it."

"That's just it—I didn't fix it. Enzo and I never reconciled. We never talked about the situation. I continued to work for Kai as penance. When I met Odette, I found a way out. At least, that's what I thought.

"I thought the lesson I should learn was to not bring the women in my life into my world. So when I fell for Odette, I swore to never tell her the truth. I'd never work for my brother and sister-in-law again. I'd start over, and my punishment would be a life without my family."

He looks at me with a crooked grin and disgust in his eyes. "My judgment sucks, doesn't it? I keep choosing the wrong women. I keep letting people I love get hurt. I keep learning the wrong lessons. The lesson was that I can't let love be my guide. Love isn't what makes a couple work. It's not real. It's not how I should decide if I'm with a woman or not. And it's definitely not how I should decide if I spend forever with them or not."

"I couldn't agree with you more. Love isn't worth it. You should choose with your brain, not with your heart. The person who is loyal, honest, and fits you best on paper—that's how partners should be chosen."

I return Beckett's intense stare, seeing each other clearly for the first time. It doesn't matter who either of us loves. Love isn't enough, not for people like us. We need a partner. We need someone ready to take on this world. We need someone who will stand by our side as we take bullets and have our families' lives threatened.

"So who do you choose? Odette?" I ask.

For once, I'm not sure what his answer is going to be.

I STARE at my phone as I sit in my office. I reach for it but quickly pull my hand back into my lap—repeat times infinity. That's how I've spent my afternoon—debating whether or not I should call Ryker.

He didn't leave his number, but I had Gage get it for me. I'm sure that led the guys to a lot of questions, but I'll deal with them later. They're mostly harmless, even though I don't know whose side they are truly on. It doesn't matter. Once the war starts, even they won't be able to stop it.

Then why am I sitting here in my father's office contemplating whether or not I should be calling Ryker when I should be planning a war?

That fucking kiss.

What did the guy put into it? It wasn't tantalizing. He didn't use his tongue. It wasn't an exceptionally good kiss. It wasn't even about the kiss. When we touched, something happened. I can't explain it, but I want to understand what the hell that was.

I pick up the phone and dial Ryker's number before I change my mind again for the millionth time.

I tap my heel incessantly on the floor while I wait to see if he'll answer or not.

"Hello, Odette. I thought you'd at least wait twenty-four hours before you called me. Apparently, I made quite the impression on you," Ryker says.

I roll my eyes and consider hanging up. This was a mistake.

But I push through. More than just our connection, I need to know what his motivations are. Our interaction earlier wasn't just an accident. I don't believe in coincidences.

"What do you really want, Ryker? What was that yesterday?"

"I like it when you say my name."

I make fake gagging sounds. I hate romance. It's not real. It doesn't exist.

Beckett is a nice guy, but he was always a target. I never intended to stay married to him long-term. My plan was always to use and lose him. My father needed an heir, and I needed retribution against Enzo Black and his family.

I set everything in motion, everything that would be needed for the Retribution Kings to go to war against Enzo Black. And everything was going perfectly until Beckett fell in love with that tramp, and my plan went to hell.

So I returned from the dead to ensure my mission will be completed. Beckett was my key to doing that. Beckett and Enzo were fighting. I'd been watching them for a while, and it became clear Beckett is the key to beating Enzo. But what happened with Enzo is why I don't believe in love. I'll never believe in love and romance and happily ever afters.

Love has nothing to do with why I'm calling Ryker. I'm just making sure he's not going to ruin the plan I've been working on for years.

"Why did you plan that run-in? Why stop the elevator? What did you hope to gain?"

"Not just a pretty face. Yes, I stopped the elevator."

"Why?"

"Your bodyguards wanted me to ask you questions to find out what you're up to."

I assume he means Lennox, Gage, and Hayes, who have all been keeping close to me ever since they returned.

"Then why didn't you ask me any questions?"

"I don't take orders from them. I owed them a favor, so I met with you. But that's all I'm going to do for them. Any other questions?"

I frown. That's it? Is he not going to try and pressure me for more? He's not going to ask me what my plan is?

"Nope, just one request of my own—have dinner with me tonight," I say.

There's a pause. "Why?"

"Maybe you'd like to come work for me."

"I don't work for anyone but myself."

"Then come because I need someone to bicker with, and I think you could blow off some steam as well before the final game ends you."

"Oh, I'm going to win that game."

"Sure, you are. But in case you don't, let me buy you dinner before you die."

"Jeez, you really know how to convince a man. The answer is no."

I huff. "Fine, what do you want from me to have dinner with me?"

There's a pause.

"And I'm not sucking your dick or anything degrading," I add.

He chuckles.

"I'm not sure yet, but when I do, I'll let you know. I'll meet you at Alinea at seven-thirty."

"Wait, what do you mean you'll let me know? That's not how negotiations work. You tell me now or—"

He ends the call.

"Bastard."

He knows I'll show up; I'm too curious. But fuck him for playing games.

I'M SITTING at a private table at Alinea at seven-thirty sharp. I doubt she will show, and if she does, it will be late. She won't give me the satisfaction of her showing up on time. I order a drink and prepare myself for a long wait.

I consider if my decision to not let the others listen in was correct or not. But I've been going with my gut as far as Odette Monroe is concerned, and so far, I've gotten further with her than the others. So I stand by my decision.

Odette would know if others were listening and I was communicating with them. She's smarter than any of us give her credit for. I just wish I could figure her out. There's still a lot of mystery around her, and all the others are too blinded by their hatred of her to actually get to know her.

"Your whiskey, sir. Is there anything else I can get you?" my waiter asks as he sets my drink down.

"No, thank you. The drink will do until Odette arrives."

He leaves, and no sooner have I taken a sip of my drink is Odette standing in front of me.

I blink rapidly, surprised to see her here so early. So much so that I choke on my drink as I stare up at her slinky red dress, striking and fierce.

She grins at my reaction.

"I'm pleased you can tell time correctly," I say.

Her smile drops as she pulls out her chair and takes a seat across from me at the white table-clothed table. "I can tell time just fine, and I'm punctual. It's just good manners not to waste someone's time. You didn't even pull out my chair for me or wait to order your drink until I arrived, so apparently, I'm the only one with manners."

I smirk at her. This creature is so fascinating to me. She's strong and independent, and her sassy mouth is beyond entertaining. I could argue with her for hours, but that's not why I'm here. I'm here to get her to spill her secrets without revealing that's actually my only goal.

"What can I get you to drink?" the waiter asks as he returns.

"I'll have what he's having," Odette says.

The waiter nods.

"So you're a whiskey girl? I took you as a white wine girl."

She rolls her eyes. "So cliche. I'm more than I appear."

"That's what fascinates me about you."

"So you're fascinated by me?" She grins and bats her eyelashes at me. *Why wouldn't every man be fascinated with her?*

"In the same way that I'm fascinated about how airplanes stay in the air. I'm not sure I'd take it as a compliment."

The waiter returns with her drink. She immediately grabs the glass, realizing she's going to need plenty of alcohol to put up with me. But it's an act. She likes bickering with me just as much as I enjoy it with her. If she didn't, she wouldn't be here.

"I didn't expect your manners to be very good after you hung up on me without answering my question," she says.

"It's killing you, isn't it? Not knowing what favor I'm going to ask of you in return for me showing up tonight," I reply.

She runs her hand over the rim of her drink. "I hate giving up control, so yes, it's bothering me. If you want me to stay, you'll tell me what favor I owe you."

"I'm not worried about you leaving. It was you who called for this dinner. It seems you are the one fascinated with me, so I think I'll hold onto the favor for a bit longer."

"One—I wanted this dinner so I could find out more about why you trapped us together in an elevator. Two—I'm fascinated with you in the same way that you are fascinated with you. And three— you can hold onto the favor you want me to do all you want; it doesn't mean I'll do it."

"You will," I tease.

She gives me a sly look. "If you're so confident, you don't know me very well."

"Or maybe I know you too well."

The waiter returns, and we inform him we're ready to begin the night's tasting menu.

"So what questions did my dear bodyguards want you to ask me?"

"The usual. Just trying to find out all your secrets so they can blackmail you. Same reason you invited me here tonight—find out dirt on me to use. Just because you are the wife of a mob boss instead of the leader yourself doesn't mean you aren't just as conniving and savage as the rest of us."

"Glad you would put the two of us on equal footing. Most men don't see me as anything more than a trophy wife."

"Again, I think I know you pretty well."

"Because you spent twenty minutes trapped in an elevator with me or because you had me surveilled?"

"Does it matter?"

"Yes," she snaps.

"I guess you'll have to keep wondering. I won't divulge all my secrets."

She shifts her weight in her seat, and as a consequence, her foot bumps against my knee underneath the table.

I raise a brow. "You trying to give me a massage?"

She frowns. "You're a disgusting man. I'm a married woman. And you still need to apologize for that vile kiss."

"You didn't seem to mind. You didn't pull away. You didn't push me or chastise me in the moment."

"I didn't give you permission to kiss me either."

"Fair enough. I do apologize."

Her eyes widen when I apologize. "You apologize just like that?"

"I always apologize when I'm wrong. Although, based on my knowledge of you, it doesn't appear that you are happily married. It seems more like a business arrangement than a love match."

"My marriage is none of your concern."

"It is actually, seeing as I'm on a date with a married woman. I should know what I'm getting myself into. Is your husband going to hunt me down for merely having dinner with you?"

"Don't worry about that. If I want you dead, I'll be the one doing the killing."

I grin, flashing her my dimples. "I have no doubt of that."

The waiter brings out several dishes, and we both take a moment to enjoy our food before returning to interrogating one another.

"So what should we argue about now?" Odette grins at me. She enjoys arguing with me as much as I enjoy arguing with her.

"Maybe we should focus on what we have in common."

"We have things in common?"

"I think a great deal," I say.

She scoffs. "Do tell."

"We are both incredibly good-looking."

She blushes.

"We are both intelligent, witty, and both enjoy good food and a glass of whiskey," I continue.

"That's true. We're also incredibly ambitious, great leaders, and likable," she says.

"I don't find either of us very likable. But otherwise, I would agree."

She laughs. "Fine, we're very unlikable, but only because we know what we want and have high expectations of others."

We finish the last of our food, and the waiter clears our table. We both decline the dessert courses.

Looking across the table, I can see her practically bouncing in her seat with nerves. I tilt my head, smirking at her.

"You can't stand not to know, can you?" I ask.

"Know what?" she bats her eyes at me in fake confusion.

"You want to know what you owe for the enjoyment of having me at your dinner," I say.

She pulls out her purse. "I have more than enough money to pay."

I chuckle. "The task is simple."

"I'm not going to take off my underwear in public or flirt with the waiter if you're going to dare me to do something stupid like that."

"I would never insult you by asking you to do something stupid."

"Then what are you asking?"

"Simple. All I want is for you to tell me something no one else knows," I say.

She blinks at me. "That's so vague. I could answer that with practically anything, and you wouldn't know if I was telling the truth or not."

I nod. "I know you well; you won't lie to me. I know you will answer because everyone has at least one secret they want to tell. Share something real, not something small and shallow. Share something you're dying to share, something deep in your soul that needs to come out."

She stares at me for a long while. "You just want to know what scheme I'm plotting. You want to know about Beckett and Rialta and all the others."

"No, actually. I don't care what you share; just share a part of your soul so I may better know and understand you. That's all I've ever wanted as far as you're concerned," I say.

"And you'll tell me a secret in return?"

I chuckle. "If I feel like it. But since your secret is payment for me being here tonight, I'll have to see if your secret is worthy of one of my own."

She stills for a moment, and I think I was wrong. She's not going to divulge anything.

"I'll tell you a secret, but not here."

She stands, and I follow.

"You're going to owe me an awfully big secret if I'm to follow you to a second location," I say.

"I know, but you'll come."

"How do you know that?"

"For the same reason you knew I'd tell you a secret."

"Which is?" I ask.

"Fascination."

ODETTE

RYKER WALKS me out of the restaurant, and for once, I don't feel completely in control. Not because he's taken control from me, but because I feel myself losing it. I want to give up a bit of control when I'm with him.

Fuck, what am I doing?

We make it outside when I say, "You can follow me in your car."

"Or I can ride with you," he says back.

I swallow hard. "Or you can ride with me."

We walk to my Maserati, and Ryker slides into the passenger seat while I slide behind the wheel. I start the car and begin backing out of my parking spot.

"Odette!" Ryker yells and I slam on my brakes.

I look in my rearview mirror and see that I about backed into a couple walking into the restaurant. The woman flashes me a dirty look, and the man flips me off.

"Maybe I should drive," Ryker says.

I run my hands through my hair and shake the nervous energy off. I tilt my head side to side and roll my shoulders back. I look Ryker dead in the eyes. "No, I've got this."

He nods, his eyes skimming over me before he buckles his seat-belt and lets me take control.

Most men would have insisted on driving after that little blunder, but not Ryker. He still trusts me. That or his desire to get answers far outweighs his will to live.

I make it out onto the road and start driving through downtown streets. We aren't going far. We just need to go somewhere the three idiots won't have already set up cameras to record us, somewhere where we can truly be alone.

Ryker doesn't ask any questions. He also doesn't show any signs of nervousness or distress as I drive through the city streets. He seems completely at ease next to me.

After driving for twenty minutes, I pull the car into the valet of my favorite hotel chain.

Ryker's eyes dart up at the tower above us and then looks at me. "If I knew we were getting a hotel room, I wouldn't have argued about coming."

I shake my head. "Just because I brought you to a hotel doesn't mean you're going to score."

"It doesn't mean I'm not going to either." He winks at me.

I glare back.

He shrugs. "It doesn't matter where you take me. I can make you want me in a dark alleyway next to a dumpster if I want."

"So full of yourself." The valet opens my door and helps me out.

"Do you have any bags I can take for you?" the valet asks.

"No," I reply.

Then Ryker is by my side. He holds out his arm, waiting for me to decide if I want to take it or not.

I hesitate for just a second before I hook my arm through his, and we walk inside. Ryker leads me to the front desk.

"Hello, Mrs. Monroe. Your usual?" the woman behind the front desk asks when she sees me.

I nod.

Ryker studies me closely out of the corner of his eye as she slides a key to me.

"Enjoy your stay," the receptionist says.

And then we are in the elevators riding up to the top floor.

"You take men who aren't your husband to this hotel often?" Ryker asks.

I grin. "You'll never know."

He narrows his eyes. "I'm going to take that as a no."

"Take it however you want; it doesn't make it true."

The doors open, and we begin walking down the hallway to my suite as I continue holding onto Ryker's arm. Once inside, I let go of his arm, and he takes a minute to survey the spacious room.

"Still think you have enough money to compete with me?" I ask teasingly.

He smirks. "I own real estate properties that are more expensive than this entire hotel. Yes, I can compete with you on money, but I'm not going to."

I start walking toward the living room. I want to talk. I need someone to talk to, someone to hear my story. Someone who has very little to no reason to hate me.

"Do you think I'm a monster?" I ask before I sit down on the couch. There are plenty of stories to tell him, but the one I need to share the most depends on his answer to this question.

He stares out the floor-to-ceiling windows a second while he debates his answer.

"You could say we are all monsters."

I hold my breath, waiting for him to continue.

"But I prefer to think of us all as humans doing our best to survive in a world where many won't. We all do what it takes to survive as long as we can. We all do plenty of immoral things. We all steal, threaten, and murder. Only true monsters take without need. They hurt others out of pure enjoyment. They murder not out of protection or need but just because they like to see the light leave people's eyes."

I swallow hard, not sure where he considers me on this scale.

He stares me down as if reading my soul.

"You, Odette, are not a monster. Everything you do is for survival."

"And revenge," I add.

I wait for him to say that makes me a monster. I've forced Beckett to fuck me almost every night we were together, even though he hates it. That is the very definition of a monster, according to Ryker, and he'd be right.

"Do you think that makes you a monster? Seeking revenge on those who have hurt you?"

"Yes. I enjoy the pain and suffering of those who have hurt me," I say.

He smiles. "You aren't a monster."

"How do you figure?"

"A monster wouldn't admit they are a monster and feel guilt about it. You do."

"How do you know?" I ask.

"I can see it in your eyes. You're disappointed by what you did, ashamed even. We are all human. We all do things we shouldn't; that doesn't make you a monster."

I take a seat, and Ryker mirrors me, sitting on the couch opposite me. Everything he just said could have been because he wants me to open up to him. He could have an ulterior motive.

But just like he senses things about me, I sense things about him. And I need to talk to someone. Everyone who knows about my past is dead—my father and my brother. I'm all alone in this world.

"I was kidnapped, assaulted, and raped," I say.

"That's common knowledge. Although, I'm so sorry for what happened to you," he says quietly.

I shake my head. "What I shared was a lie. Enzo didn't kidnap me—this time. But he has before."

Ryker's eyes widen ever so slightly, but he doesn't react otherwise.

"When I was eighteen, Vincent Corsi's men took me from my home. They didn't hurt me, didn't touch me, really. They held me in a clean hotel room. They fed me, let me watch TV. It was all very civil. I just thought they were ransoming my father or upset with something he did. I wasn't afraid. I knew my father and brother would come for me. They'd pay whatever price Corsi demanded."

I close my eyes, trying to remain emotionless as I speak, but it's near impossible when the images flood my brain again. The trauma lives in every fiber of my body. I can pretend the memories don't exist, but they are always there, just hovering below the surface, ready to overwhelm me at any time.

"My father never came, neither did my brother. Someone else far more sinister did," I continue.

I keep my eyes closed as I speak. I keep the pain in, the tears in.

I don't care about Ryker's reaction. I don't care if he believes me or not. I just need to tell someone. I need to remember why I'm doing this.

"Enzo Black was the one who showed up. He paid for me like he was buying a horse. And for the first time, I knew what it felt like to be terrified. He tied my arms, my legs, and he gagged me. He tossed me in his trunk like a piece of garbage, not a human.

"For hours, we drove, and I could barely breathe stuffed in that trunk. He didn't care. He didn't check on me. He didn't feed me. Nothing."

I swallow down the lump in my throat as I get to the next part, the worst part, the part I wish I could forget.

"Enzo carried me from the car. I barely had any energy to fight. And even if I could, my father never taught me how to get out bindings like that. I was helpless.

"Inside, things got worse. He removed my bindings only to tie me to a bed. I heard Enzo and his father talking. I was a daughter of a crime boss. Enzo wanted to sell me as quickly as possible. He didn't want to start a war, but his father wasn't afraid of a fight. He wasn't afraid of the Retribution Kings. He wanted to send a message that he was far more powerful than my father."

The tears slip, but I don't open my eyes. I let the water streak down my cheek as I carry on.

"I was there for five days, but it might as well have been five years. I was assaulted and raped in every way imaginable. I thought it would never end. I thought I would be there forever. Then one day, I was dropped back off in front of my father's doorstep.

"Naked.

"Beaten.

"Abused."

I clear my throat.

"I woke up before my father did. I paid for a hotel room, and I stayed there until I healed. I didn't tell my father what happened, at least not until a few years later. That's when a plan started to form."

I open my eyes. "I want to destroy them all. I need to destroy them all. Everyone involved I need revenge against. Beckett is the weak link. He didn't hurt me directly, but he's Enzo's brother. He works for him, has done horrible things for him. He was my way in, and I don't feel guilty about punishing Beckett and everyone in Enzo's family for Enzo and his father's crimes."

Finally, I look at Ryker. There are tears in his eyes. His nostrils are flared. His face is a deep red. His hands are fisted at his side, and his knees bounce anxiously.

"Don't pity me. I don't want or need your pity," I spit.

He opens his mouth and then closes it. Over and over, he does this before I see tears streaming down his own face.

I stand up abruptly, not able to face his sorrow. "I told you not to pity me."

"I don't pity you. I'm heartbroken at what you went through. But I'm also so incredibly awestruck by how brave and strong you are, how much of a fighter you are."

I turn and face him. He doesn't retreat even though we're standing so close that a strong wind could push us into each other.

"I don't need you to be in awe of me. I'm just a human who has been hurt and betrayed, and I want revenge. It's the only way to squash the nightmares."

He grins down at me in his sexy way. "You should get the revenge you seek. But are you sure that revenge is the only way to get rid of the nightmares?"

The next thing I know, he leans in and kisses me. It's a soft and tender kiss at first, giving me plenty of room to pull away. But when I don't, he grabs the back of my neck and kisses me hungrily.

And as soon as our tongues touch, I never want him to stop.

I'VE NEVER BEEN SO ATTRACTED to someone in my life. Her strength, her courage, her beauty—everything about her I want.

She's like me in a lot of ways. We're both leaders that do what we have to in order to survive. We don't share our plans with many others. And although she didn't share her exact plan when it came to Ri, she shared an awful lot.

Odette shared her darkest secret, a hidden piece of her soul. It's the part that defines her, the part that explains everything.

Everyone sees her as this evil adversary who wants to take them down for the sake of hurting them, for power and money and control.

In reality, she's a woman who's been hurt in the worst possible way seeking retribution for what happened to her. And I can relate to that.

Ri doesn't deserve to die for what happened to Odette, though. Enzo deserves to pay for what he and his father did; so does Corsi. And Beckett...I'm not sure what his role is exactly yet in all of this, but if he knew and did nothing, then he deserves to pay as well.

I kiss Odette with everything I have, assuming she's going to stop me at any moment. She doesn't want my pity, so kissing her is the only way I can think of to show her how incredible I think she is.

Fuck, she tastes amazing.

Her body leans into mine, and I about lose it. I want to rip her dress off. I want to fuck her against the window and claim her as mine.

But she's not mine...

I gently pull away, stopping the kiss and everything else before this goes too far.

"I'm sorry," I say.

Her grin is so wide I must be hallucinating. "You have nothing to be sorry for; that kiss was incredible."

"It was, wasn't it?" I smirk. "I'm not sorry about the kiss, even if you are a married woman. I'm sorry about my intentions. I am here to try and find a way to protect Ri, but there's something more here. Something has shifted between us. I still want to protect Ri, she's my friend, but I also understand everything about you."

Odette stiffens at the mention of Ri, so I continue.

"Thank you for sharing your story with me. I'll protect it with everything I have. I don't want to be your enemy anymore; I want to be honest with you."

"I already knew that's why you approached me. Rialta will be safe as long as the others don't interfere with my plan for revenge."

I nod. "Thank you."

We stand awkwardly in front of each other as the tension grows.

"I should go," I say.

"Or you should kiss me again." There's a twinkle in her eyes, a wanting only I can fulfill.

"You belong to Beckett, and I've already touched someone who belonged to him once. I'm not sure I have the strength to do it again."

"I don't belong to Beckett. He belongs to me. But if it helps, I won't touch him again," she says.

I bite the back of my knuckles as she pushes out her chest and licks her bottom lip.

God, do I want her. I want her so fucking badly. But then what? We can't date. We can't even fuck regularly. I still want to protect Ri. And I can't lead my men to war, but...

"Fuck me, Ryker. I'm not asking you to marry me or fight in a war; just fuck me tonight."

I growl and then attack her.

"Tonight, you're mine, Odette," I bark.

I kiss her just as she's about to respond, catching her mouth open. Our teeth clash together in an aggressive kiss. Our bodies collide, and my hand goes to her ass, yanking her to me. My other hand grabs her neck, tilting her head to deepen the kiss.

Her hands are clutched tightly around my neck as if she's afraid I'm going to break the kiss again and run out the door. She needs this as much as I do. She needs a connection to someone who actually wants her, not stuck in a marriage for revenge.

I don't know what this is. *Just one night? The start of something more? The beginning of a friendship or alliance? Or a one-time reprieve before we fight on opposite sides of a war?* Whatever this is, I'm going to enjoy it. And I'm damn sure going to make sure she enjoys it too.

We're on the top floor of a high-rise building, but I need everyone to know that tonight this fearless and hot as fuck woman is mine. I'm the one making her scream, making her come.

I grab her ass with both hands, and she gladly wraps her legs around my waist as I walk us back toward the floor-to-ceiling windows. The lights are on, and it's getting dark outside. If anyone looks in our direction, they will be able to see everything.

I press her back against the wall as I devour her mouth. I'm not gentle. Maybe I should be, but I'm trusting my instincts here unless she tells me otherwise. My gut says to show her how much I want her.

With the window helping to support her back, I move a free

hand from her ass to beneath her dress. I don't waste any time inching my hand up her thigh until I feel the wetness between her legs.

"No panties, naughty girl."

She whimpers against my lips, and her hips shift, begging for me to touch her aching clit.

But I'm a cruel man, and I want to hear her beg first. Quickly, I remove my hand.

She pulls back from the kiss, and I realize I just made a huge mistake. She's about to tell me to take a hike since I didn't do things her way. Instead, she grabs my chin and glares at me.

"I don't like to be toyed with," she says.

I smirk and run a finger down her neck to the top of her cleavage. "You're going to have to learn to be patient if you want me to fuck you. I won't rush the time I have with you."

"Fine, but I can tease too."

"I look forward to it," I reply.

I lean in for a kiss, but at the last second, she turns her head. My kiss lands on her cheek instead of her lips.

I growl my response. This woman is either going to be the best or worst thing for me; I just can't figure out which. I wish I would know the answer before I fuck her and lose myself to her completely.

I lick down her cheek to her neck as her hand creeps down the front of my chest, lower and lower, until she reaches the top of my jeans. I fully expect her to stop and barely tease me. I try to keep my cock from getting too excited, but it's straining hard against the zipper in my jeans.

She undoes the snap, then the zipper, and I hold my breath, expecting utter denial of her touch. But then her hand dips down beneath my underwear and grazes the curve of my cock.

My head falls back as she strokes the top of my cock. It's not even the most sensitive part, but I feel like I'm about to explode into a million pieces.

I groan as she roughly pulls me out of my boxer briefs and wraps her entire hand around my cock. My eyes are closed as she pumps me, making me almost lose my goddamned mind.

And then I feel wetness being spread over my cock, warming me and making every touch that much more incredible.

I open my eyes, realizing what she's doing. She's using my cock as her personal dildo, rubbing it against her clit since I wouldn't give her what she wanted.

I grab her wrist, stopping her. "You play dirty."

She bites down on her lip, trying to hide a smile.

I lick over her lips until she lets my tongue in, swirling around to take control once again. I reach behind her and find the zipper on her dress. Quickly, I pull it down, tracing my fingers down her back as she trembles in my arms.

"Why do your fingers on my spine alone feel so good?" she wonders out loud.

"The same reason everything else does. You and I share a spark, a rare connection I thought wasn't real. Plus, I'm a damn good lover, baby."

She rolls her eyes and pinches my butt. "I've yet to see how good of a lover you are since you won't actually fuck me."

I shake my head. "So impatient."

And then I yank her dress down her body until it's bunching at her waist.

"No bra either." My eyes lock in on her gorgeous breasts.

Her eyes stare down at me as her chest heaves, and her breathing slows.

I lick my lips in a slow circle—the same way I plan on encircling her nipples.

She purses her lips, trying to remain in control.

And then, I slowly dip my head toward the closest nipple. Her hand grabs the back of my head, and she pushes me down until her nipple grazes my lips.

I laugh before licking around her pink point until she's panting. Then I make the same motion to the other nipple.

She arches her back into the window as she holds my head firmly against her breast.

"Do you want me to touch you?" I mutter in between licks.

"Yes."

"Then you have to beg."

"I don't beg."

I chuckle. "You will."

I press my cock between her legs, letting her clit feel the pressure of me there, but not more. I don't move, just hold firmly against her. And then I devour her neck, her breasts, her lips—everything but what she actually wants.

Her breath speeds, and she drenches me in wetness. I'm fucking aching to be inside her, to touch her, to give us both the satisfaction. But it's up to her. I can be patient. I can hold out until she begs. At least I think I can, but each second that goes by is harder and harder.

I can't take it any longer. I—

"Please," she begs.

One word.

One syllable.

But it's enough.

"Thank fuck," I groan.

I set her down and yank her dress off until she's completely bare in front of me.

"So fucking incredible," I gasp.

She rakes her teeth over her bottom lip as I spin her around so the entire world can see what I get tonight. This woman is mine.

My hand sneaks around the front of her body and finally gives her what she's been begging for—I stroke her clit.

Her knees give out as I stroke her. "Is it too much?" I tease.

"Don't you dare stop!"

I chuckle low and deep as I shift behind her, my cock pressing against her ass. My other hand fumbles with a condom from the pocket of my jeans. I slip it on as she moans loudly for me; I'm barely able to control myself.

"If you keep moaning like that, I'm going to come before I'm even inside you."

"Don't you dare! I need you," she moans.

That's all it takes for me to lose any resemblance of control. I grab her hips, and then my cock is inside her in one long stroke.

Her face and chest press against the window as my fingers continue to work her swollen bud. She rocks against me, meeting every thrust, her moans growing louder and completely unfiltered. She doesn't care if the entire hotel can hear her. It drives me to make it even better for her, to see what other sounds I can pull for her.

This woman deserves the best damn sex a man can give her. And I plan on giving her just that.

I pump into her faster as my fingers run circles over her clit. Her nipples are pressed hard against the windowpane, as is her cheek.

My lips brush over her earlobe, and then I kiss down her neck, eliciting more moans vibrating from her throat.

"How close are you, baby?" I moan, knowing I'm not going to be able to hold on much longer.

"Ryker!" she screams as she begins to fall apart around me.

I come right along with her, losing complete control.

She falls back into me, and I barely have the strength to catch her and keep myself upright. I carry her back to the couch behind us, where I collapse with her on top of me and my arms around her.

She doesn't struggle to get away. She lets me hold her, but I don't know how long this will last. I don't know what our future holds. I doubt we'll be together despite how I feel when I'm around her.

I do know one thing, though. I'm going to do everything I can to ensure she lets me fuck her again.

23
RI

"SO, WHO DO YOU CHOOSE? ODETTE?" I ask.

He doesn't answer me. He opens his mouth and then closes it like he can't bring himself to answer. That is an answer in of itself.

If he loved her like he's said in the past, if he would move heaven and earth for her, he'd choose her. If it's always been her, as he claims, this would be an easy proclamation.

Beckett takes a deep breath, and I mirror him. Our breaths start slow as we try to remain calm. With each passing second, our breaths quicken. Faster and faster until our hyperventilating is the only thing I can feel. We're out of control. Whatever we do next, it won't be something we planned. It won't be something we think all the way through.

It will be reckless, stupid, and carnal. We won't be using logic. Our brains are turned off—something that should never happen, especially now that I know the truth.

I can't be reckless.

I can't be selfish.

I can't...

And yet, I'm about to do or say something very stupid.

No.

It's smart.

Tactical.

At least that's what I convince myself.

It's clear Beckett doesn't love Odette. I don't know his motives exactly for why he stays with her, and it doesn't really matter. But I wonder...does he love me?

"You told me you loved me once. I'm sure you've said the same to Odette many times." My words come out gentler and calmer than I thought they would.

"How could you?" I snap.

Beckett tilts his head, looking at me with deep pain in his eyes.

"How dare you play with our emotions like that! How dare you lie to us!" My voice cracks as I toss my wine glass on the floor, and it shatters into a million tiny shards.

I stand up.

Beckett is on his feet instantly. He's not going to cower. He's not going to just take it. He's not going to just let me attack him.

"I did what I had to to get what I wanted. I'm a monster. It's not my fault if you didn't see that."

"Bastard."

His nostrils flare wide as he clenches his jaw. He's so close to breaking, to admitting the absolute truth. *But am I ready to hear it?*

"Fuck you, Hero!"

"I'm not your hero. You were stupid enough to think that. I'm your villain, the man who will take everything from you."

"You're right, you are my villain, and I'm tired of waiting to figure out what your next move is. You want to win the game? You want to choose my husband, control my father's empire? Then take it." I grab the hem of my shirt and lift it over my head, and I'm naked again in front of him.

His eyes bulge, and I can hear his teeth grinding together as he tries to hold it together.

"Take it! Take what you want from me! That's all I'm good for anyway—a hole you can fuck! A pawn in your game you can move and sacrifice and take whatever you want from. So take from me! Win the fucking game! End this!"

Beckett takes a step forward; I don't move.

"Ri," he says, his voice soft and breaking.

He keeps walking closer until he's standing inches in front of me.

What is he going to do? Kiss me? Fuck me? Threaten me? Tell me the truth?

He does none of those things. He bends down and picks up the shirt lying on the floor.

"Please," he says, not even looking at me as he shoves the shirt into my chest.

I grab his hand. "Look at me, you coward!"

His eyes drift in my direction, and I see unending pain, but I also see something else...*lust.*

That one look, and I know I'm going to do the wrong thing, the reckless thing, the regrettable thing. But it's my last chance to be selfish. And I can at least learn one thing from my impulsive actions...

I grab his cheeks, and I pull him into a hard kiss. It's a brass kiss, a kiss of pure desperation and need and...

He kisses me back—just as desperate, full of just as much need.

I can't breathe as the kiss consumes everything inside me. I forget how to take in air, but I'd gladly die in this kiss.

"Breathe, Ri," he whispers in between kisses.

I can't. If I take a second to breathe, it's a moment for him to come to his senses and put an end to this.

So as he pulls his lips off mine, I attack with mine, gasping into his lips as my body falls against his. I grab his hips, pressing them hard against mine, not letting him roll away.

Our tongues tangle, and Beckett grabs one of my thighs, hiking it up against his leg.

"I want this, Fighter. I want you," he says.

I don't know if it's the alcohol talking or the lust or what, but he won't back out now. Not an earthquake or a bomb dropping; nothing will stop us. That fact doesn't slow me down, though. I've spent too long without this man touching me, kissing me, fucking me. All because I thought he loved another woman. All because I thought he betrayed me.

I grab the collar of his shirt and rip, pulling it aggressively down in half and scraping my nails along his bare chest over the tattoo that claims his loyalty to the Retribution Kings. I trace the crown of the tattoo that is meaningless. He can mark his body all he wants, but no one knows where his true loyalty lies. I don't know. Odette doesn't know. His family doesn't know. His friends don't know.

He captures my hand in his and kisses the palm. I can feel the kiss through my entire body.

I grab his jeans and undo them just enough to yank them down his body until he's as bare as me. When our naked skin touches, it's all over.

Our animal instincts take over. Our minds cease to exist. Our bodies collide in a tangle of arms and legs as we fall to the floor together.

The shards from my wine glass stick into our backs, but the pain won't stop us—nothing will.

I straddle Beckett as I kiss him, starting from his lips, down his neck, and over his stomach until I reach his cock. Usually, I'd take him slowly, tease him and get us turned on. We're already both so turned on that none of that is necessary. And while nothing will stop us, plenty of things could try, and I'm not taking that chance.

I take all of him in my mouth, swirling my tongue around his tip as he lightly thrusts into my mouth, hitting the back of my throat. I love how he tastes in my mouth as I lick up and down the length of him, savoring every drop of him, feeling every ridge of his veins. I indulge in every moan he makes as I suck him.

As soon as I popped the head of his cock out from my lips, he's grabbed my hip and is pulling me up his body. He doesn't stop until my hips hover over his chin.

I won't deny myself any longer. I let my hips sink down on top of his face as his tongue slides up and down my slit. My wetness intensifies as he finds my clit and applies just the right amount of pressure with his tongue. His hand palms my breast, teasing my nipple.

I'm mush on top of him. My body feels like jello as he works me into a frenzy. I'm along for the ride but no longer in control. I can't move my limbs. I can barely keep myself upright as his tongue brings me closer to orgasm.

He doesn't have to say a word, not a single syllable. He doesn't have to tell me to come. He doesn't have to ask if I'm coming. He just knows.

Fuck, he knows everything about my body.

I love how he pays attention to me. I love how he watches for signs of what I like and don't like without asking. I love how he worships my body.

Suddenly I can't hold back my screams any longer.

I come undone on his face as his tongue dips in and out of me. I moan loudly but don't speak a syllable, afraid that if I do, the spell we're both under might be broken.

I collapse, slamming my hips down, my vagina covering his face, probably suffocating him. But he doesn't seem to care; he doesn't push me off.

I fall forward, grabbing the coffee table to keep me from collapsing completely face down.

Beckett gives me a second to regain my strength before he slides me down his body. My wetness coats his abs until I feel his hard cock at my ass.

I grab his cock, sliding it between my folds, coating him in my moisture. And then, with my eyes locked on Beckett's, I align our bodies and slide down onto his thick cock.

I groan as he fills me completely. It's more than just fulfilling a sexual need for me, but I don't let my mind go there. I focus on Beckett, on his reaction. *Is it more than just sex for him?*

He thrusts into me with everything he has. His hand grabs my hip, helping me move up and down on his cock. His eyes are glossy with lust and desire. The sounds he makes are animalistic and carnal. His actions all point to one thing.

I ride him harder, focusing more on the moment and my impending orgasm instead of Beckett's reactions.

His hand moves between my legs, rubbing on my clit as I get closer and closer to falling over the edge.

We still haven't spoken, still haven't shared any feelings. It feels more like a one-night stand than two people who know and care about each other.

As I start to get close, Beckett flips us over, pushing me beneath him and continuing his thrusts inside me. It deepens the angle and allows him better access to my body.

His eyes darken as he thrusts harder and deeper while his thumb rubs my sensitive clit. I'm about to come, but I try to hold it back, knowing that when I do, it could be all over. This is the last fucking time we are together. The last time ever.

I've thought that before, felt it. But this time is different. This time I know deep in my soul, I know in my barely functioning brain. This is the last time. There will never be another moment like this.

But Beckett is too good a lover; I couldn't hold back my orgasm if I tried. My orgasm explodes through my body, knocking me even more out of my body as I come. My head falls back, and my eyes fall closed as I just let myself feel everything happening in my body, as I get to experience him—all of him—one last time.

Beckett still hasn't spoken. I haven't either.

My eyes slowly open, and I see Beckett staring down at me with dark eyes.

No words are exchanged.

No feelings.

No mention of love.

Acceptance washes over me.

He doesn't love Odette.

And he doesn't love me. Our connection is one-sided lust, filled with my yearning. He doesn't return the sentiment.

And almost as if to prove my point, he stands and walks away without a word, leaving me naked on the floor.

I guess he got what he wanted. A chance to win the game. A chance to get me pregnant.

I sit up slowly as a warm liquid flows down my belly. I look down and am shocked by what I see—Beckett's cum covers my stomach. He didn't come inside me. He didn't try to win the game. He just fucked me.

I stare at the door he just left through, more confused about his feelings than ever. But I am closer to making a decision, and the games are about to end.

24

BECKETT

I CAN'T THINK. I have to get out of this room. I can't be in the same space as her for another second, or I'm going to crack. All I can do is get myself away from Ri, so that's exactly what I do.

I walk out of the room. I can't even tell her what I'm doing; I'm so close to the edge of spilling everything, even if it risks Ri's life. That's the opposite of what I want.

I run my hand through my hair as I pace in the empty hallway. I wish any of the guys were here; I need someone to talk to. I need someone to remind me why I can't tell her the truth. I need someone to talk some sense into me before I do something I'll regret.

I walk down the hallway and find my phone still lying on the kitchen counter where I left it. I need information. I need to know if the guys have figured out Odette's plan, or anything at all, yet.

After fucking Ri, being so close, holding her in my arm, I need some hope. I don't know how I'm going to give her up. I've known I loved her for a long time, but having her again after everything that happened, after sharing everything with her, after her still clearly loving me—it's much more difficult to let her go. I'm not sure I'm strong enough this time to give her up permanently.

I dial Gage's number and wait. He answers on the third ring. "Tell me you have something. Tell me you found out anything we can use to blackmail Odette. Tell me she spilled her guts. Tell me something good."

Gage hesitates; they have nothing.

"Well...Ryker made some headway with Odette," he begins tepidly.

"Oh, thank god."

"Yea, um, the two of them are real close...um..." he stutters.

I frown. "Gage, are you trying to tell me that Ryker slept with my wife? I don't care. In fact, I'd be grateful if he's with her. Maybe she'll find someone who isn't me to sink her teeth into."

"Yes, Ryker and Odette have become a bit of a thing, although not publicly. They're keeping their relationship secret," he says.

"Great. What has he found out? Any details? Has he gotten close to figuring out how to prevent her from attacking Ri?"

"Um...I'm not sure...I guess...I'm not...it's just..."

"Jesus Christ, man, spit it out."

There's a pause, and then Hayes comes on the phone. "You need to get back here, right the hell now."

"Why?"

"They're going to attack your brother at midnight," Hayes says.

"Who is 'they?'" My chest seizes at the thought of Odette going to battle with my brother. He and his family have been through so much. They don't deserve to have to go through another war. I'm having a heart attack at the thought of anything happening to my family. Despite everything that has happened between us, they're still my family. I'll do everything I can to protect my family.

"Odette is leading the Retribution Kings. She has practically everyone on her side. And..." Hayes trails off. If he speaks, it's barely audible, more of a mumble.

"Jesus, put Lennox on," I say, fed up with both Hayes and Gage.

After a moment, Lennox begins filling in the details for me.

"Ryker—he's leading his men to fight in the battle side-by-side with the Retribution Kings. He's also rounding up some of the other local crime organizations and rallying them to his side. They're trying to convince them to take down the great Enzo Black first, so they'll be strong enough to go after Corsi."

"Fuck! How could you guys let this happen?" Apparently, I didn't have to worry about the three of them being spies for Odette. I should have been worried about Ryker falling in love with the bitch. I should have seen it coming. It's what she did to me.

"You wanted us to get information any way possible. The three of us failed, so we sent in Ryker. We didn't think he'd actually fall for her schemes," Lennox says.

"Are you sure he's fallen for her? He isn't just playing her to get information?" I ask. It's the only thing left I can hope for.

"Maybe? He's not talking to us at the moment, so I don't think so."

"Fuck," I swear again.

That's when I hear her footsteps behind me on the wooden floor. I turn and look at Ri.

She's beautiful and still very naked in front of me. My cum is still dripping off her abs. All I want to do is drag her to the closest bedroom and fuck her again and again.

I don't care about the game. I don't care about getting her pregnant. I just want her to be mine.

She stares at me, trying to read the situation.

I'm sure I look hopeless as I stand naked in front of her. There's lust in my eyes when I look at her, but nothing in hers except careful examination.

"They're currently in a meeting planning their attack. Gage says he overheard via his cameras that the go time is midnight."

I don't respond at first. I don't want Ri to know anything is wrong, but I need to tell them something.

"Tell Gage to find out everything he can, and the rest of you need to stall as long as you can." I hang up the phone. I'm not sure what I'm going to do, but I can't stay here.

"Everything okay?" Ri asks.

I laugh. "Everything is never okay."

She smiles at that. Then she says, "I'm ready for you to take me back to Chicago."

"You are?"

"Yes, I know who I'm going to choose."

She isn't going to tell me. Her one-sentence terrifies me as much as Lennox's words. I can't fight two wars at once, but I don't have a choice.

"Then let's go home," I say.

25

GAGE

FIND OUT EVERYTHING, he says. Like we haven't been trying to do that this whole time.

Stall, he says. I don't know how you stall a war when the woman in charge has clearly been planning this exact moment, but I'll try.

I look to Lennox and Hayes; they look as desperate as I feel. Although Beckett is rushing back to do what he can to stop this, he's not going to make it in time.

"We failed at getting information from Odette, but we're not going to fail at stalling this," I say.

The other two nod their heads. "We don't even know where Enzo Black and his family are. Even if Odette leads the Retribution Kings out of here at midnight, it doesn't mean they will be able to attack anytime soon. We just need to stall them, make it harder for them to leave," Lennox says.

I agree. "We won't fail, not this time."

"So, what's the plan?" Hayes asks, looking at me. I'm not the one who usually makes the plans, but I know why they both look to me now. I'm the only one who can hack into any computer system. I'm the one that Beckett trusts the most among us three.

"Hayes, work on Odette. Lennox work on Ryker. I'm going to put cameras on everyone I can and see if anyone talks. We need to figure out their plan. Last we knew, Enzo Black and his crew were in the Caribbean. We need to figure out how they plan on attacking and getting there. Maybe we can stall them by blowing out some tires or engines."

"I'll trade you," Hayes says to Lennox.

"Not a chance in hell. It's your turn to work Odette," Lennox responds.

I attach tiny cameras to both men. "Go."

"What are you going to do, again?" Hayes frowns, clearly annoyed that he was put on Odette.

"What I do best," I grin.

He rolls his eyes.

After a short car ride, we park outside the warehouse that is the Retribution Kings' operations center. There was once a time when we felt like we owned this building. A time when we were the top of the Retribution Kings, set to be leaders. Now I'm not sure how any of them look at us.

Betrayers?

Accomplices?

Outcasts?

Nonetheless, we walk inside like we own the place. We keep our heads up, our chests out, and our eyes downcast like everyone is beneath us.

No one speaks to us; no one tries to kick us out. I'd like to see them try.

I divert to the right, to some of the gathered gang leaders, while Lennox and Hayes continue forward to where Odette and Ryker are.

I push my way through the crowd, putting small cameras on everyone in sight and making my way toward the side alleyway where I can monitor the feeds. I won't be able to hide forever without people getting suspicious of planted cameras now that they've seen me, but I don't need long. People like to talk.

I pull out my phone and check Lennox's and Hayes's cameras first.

"Buzz off, Hayes, I don't need you pestering me right now," Odette says.

Hayes doesn't budge. "I'm under strict orders from Beckett to protect you at all costs. If there's going to be a war, I need to make sure you're safe. Beckett would hate to lose you again."

She scoffs. "I'm sure."

I flip the screen to Lennox. "What the hell are you doing, Ryker?"

Ryker brushes past him.

"What would Ri say?" Lennox tries again.

Ryker stops for just a second but thinks better of talking to Lennox and keeps walking.

Dammit.

I flip to the other leaders. "I'm not going all the way to the Caribbean to fight Enzo Black, not where he has the edge. His yachts are indestructible. It doesn't matter how many men we bring. We'd never win there," one says.

Another man responds, "We aren't going to the Caribbean. Odette and Beckett lured them here with a meeting to talk peace."

They laugh together.

Shit.

We need info now.

I head back inside toward Ryker.

"Not you too," Ryker says.

"Just tell us what happened," I plead.

"I can't."

I pat Ryker on the shoulder, planting a camera. "Then, I just hope you know what you're getting yourself into."

Quickly, I walk toward the other exit. I pull my phone back up and flip to the feed of Ryker. He walks toward Odette, telling Hayes to go fuck himself.

Hayes eventually leaves, and then it's just the two of them.

They don't touch each other. After all, everyone thinks Odette is married to Beckett. But it's obvious how they feel about each other. They like each other a lot, maybe even love each other.

Fuck.

Ryker is no longer ours. He's on her side, and I don't know how to stop this.

Ryker gets close to Odette, and I think he might lean in to kiss her or touch her at least. He doesn't, but he says in a hushed tone, "If I do this, Ri lives. No matter what."

Odette looks at him and then nods.

Maybe I was wrong. Ryker just got us the one thing Beckett asked of us—stop Odette from hurting Ri. But it's at the cost of his family. Beckett wants us to stop this war, but if we do, Ri won't be safe.

I don't know what he wants us to do now that it's gotten even more complicated.

BECKETT IS an anxious mess as we drive back. He hasn't spoken since telling me to get dressed and hopping in the car with me. I haven't really talked either, but as we get closer to the city, my own worry grows. It'd be nice to hear from him why he's in a rush to get back.

"What happened?" I ask.

He doesn't respond.

I huff. "Really? You're not going to talk to me?"

"Who did you choose?" Beckett tosses back at me.

I frown, not ready to talk about that.

"Exactly," he huffs and keeps driving.

I don't ask any questions again, but it doesn't take long for me to get some answers.

"What, Gage?" Beckett snaps into his phone.

He listens carefully and then goes white. Beckett doesn't say anything, but I can read his face well enough.

"Did war break out?" I ask.

The look he gives me confirms it.

"Fuck," I whisper, hating it as much as he does. Even if my own family isn't involved—yet. Vincent Corsi always gets involved in war eventually, though. It's how he shows and keeps his power. It's only a matter of time until this is my problem too.

Beckett starts dialing numbers on his phone. "Pick up, pick up, pick up!"

Whoever he's calling doesn't answer.

"I need a gun," I say.

"Glove compartment."

I pop it open and find a fully loaded gun and knife. I take both.

We pull into a parking lot to the sound of gunfire.

"Holy shit," I say.

"What?" Beckett asks.

"That's one of Corsi's men. Apparently, we're already involved in this fight."

I step out of the car, and Beckett follows me.

"Beckett, what day is it?" I ask as chills creep over my skin.

"The fifteenth."

I start running.

"Ri!" Beckett yells. "Ri, slow down! You can't fight them all on your own!"

"Watch me!" I shout as I fire into the back of a man crouched down behind a car.

The parking lot is for a warehouse along Lake Michigan. Men are fighting in alleyways, from the water, and along the shoreline. Police won't be showing up to put a stop to this, as I'm sure someone has already threatened them to stay away.

I realize why this location was chosen. I'm scared to death—I failed. Vincent failed. Everything we've been working for all along was a massive failure.

I need to get to the shore.

I duck behind a car near the edge of the parking lot. There's a lot of fighting between me and the shoreline. Before I can make my move, Beckett crouches down next to me.

"What's your plan?" he asks.

"I need to get as close to the shore as possible," I reply.

"Me too."

I stare through one of the car's windows, but all I see is chaos. I can't make anything out; I can't even decipher who are friends or foes.

"Together," Beckett says, taking my hand and squeezing it.

I squeeze back.

He drops my hand to grab his gun, and we take off into the fight.

There isn't much room for cover, so the only thing we can do is run and try not to draw attention to ourselves. When we do, we fire back.

Beckett stays by my side as we run. Despite everything we've been through, we trust each other on the battlefield. I cover the left side. He covers the right. Neither of us worries about the other failing at their job.

I see Lennox fighting with a man, so I shoot that man in the head. Lennox whips around, sees me, and smiles his gratitude.

I wish I could do more. I wish I could help ensure everyone I love and care about is safe. But right now, I have to be focused on only one person.

"Duck," I yell, pushing Beckett to the ground to narrowly avoid a bullet.

We both start firing back as soon as we hit the ground. A moment later, Beckett grabs the collar of my shirt, and then we're back on our feet and taking off.

I run as fast as I can, trying to keep up with Beckett running faster than before. It takes me a second, but I see his intended destination. A row of cars is parked a few yards away.

I pick up my speed, and we dive down between two cars.

"You hurt?" Beckett asks, inspecting me closely.

"No, I'm fine," I say, out of breath.

He nods. "Catch your breath before we move again."

I carefully peer through one of the car windows. Beckett does the same.

"We need to go left," I say.

"No, right," Beckett says.

Our eyes meet. I'm sure his family is to the right, but I have to go left.

"Stay safe," is all I say. Then I run out from behind the car toward her.

She's riding in one of Vincent's SUVs, but they've been completely ambushed. She'll be fine as long as she stays in the car; it's bulletproof and safe. Just stay in the car.

I run, shooting down men left and right as I get closer. It's my job to protect her.

Suddenly one of the SUV's doors opens.

"No, keep the door closed!" I shout.

But she doesn't listen.

The door opens, and she takes off.

Fuck.

I run faster.

"Who is she?" Beckett asks suddenly from beside me.

"Someone who needs our help," I respond.

He nods and picks up his speed.

I stop running to get a better aim and quickly shoot down three men chasing her. But she's still not safe.

Beckett keeps running after her.

I keep shooting.

My adrenaline is out of control as I resume sprinting, trying to keep a perimeter around her while Beckett catches up to her.

"I've got you. I'm here to protect you," Beckett's words reach my ears.

Thank god.

"Get her back into the SUV!" I shout.

Beckett carries her as she shakes in his arm, connecting her eyes with my own.

"Stay in the car. You're safe there. Trust me."

She nods.

We jog to the car. I lead the way and Beckett carries her behind me.

I don't see people—all I see are enemies. I shoot anyone that comes near us regardless of their alliance. Enemies or allies—it makes no difference to me right now. I just need her safe.

Beckett quickly helps her back into the bulletproof SUV and slams the door shut. The driver immediately takes off, now having a clear path out of the mayhem.

I need a car. I need to go after her. I need to make sure she's okay.

Odette knew about her. She knew—that's why she chose this location.

If my decision wasn't made before, it is now.

"Who was that?" Beckett asks, confused as hell.

"It doesn't matter."

He stares after the car, though.

"Ask me again," I say.

"Who was that?"

I shake my head. "No, not that. Ask me what you asked me on the drive here."

His eyes widen, and he holds his breath.

"Ask me," I whisper, pulling him behind a building so we can't be seen or interrupted.

"Who do you choose?" he asks, his voice cracking.

"I choose you."

BECKETT

RI CHOSE ME.

She chose me.

Nothing is official yet, and I have no idea what it means, but she chose me. She wants me, and that's all I need.

It's been a week since I last saw her. She snuck away in the middle of the battle soon after she told me. I went back into the battle, looking for my brother and his family. They're missing, but the fact that Odette continues the war reassures me that they are alive and safe somewhere.

I haven't talked to Odette in person either. The only people I've been with lately are Gage, Lennox, and Hayes.

We've been searching for Enzo and his family. Trying to get Ri to talk to us. Trying to find a way to end Odette without hurting Ri.

We all agreed that we have to let Ryker continue to help Odette. If she was honest with him, then she won't hurt Ri as long as he's helping her.

But keeping everyone I love safe is a challenge when every criminal organization and gang in the area has decided to fight on Odette's side. Between her and Ryker, they've rallied them all. They convinced them it's time to take down Corsi and that she has a way to take over everything he has. She told them Enzo, and his empire have always been allies with Corsi, so they need to be taken down as well.

I feel torn between my brother and those I've always considered family, and Ri, a woman I love with everything inside me, who I've always tried to protect.

For now, I don't have to choose, but there will come a time when I will. On the battlefield, in the moment, I chose Ri. I stayed by her side and protected her, but that was only because I didn't know exactly where my brother was. *But who would I choose if I actually had to decide?*

The four of us are currently in a hotel room, gathering any intel we can on the whereabouts of my brother and his family while trying to get in contact with Ri. But she hasn't reached out, and neither has Corsi to finish the game. Her declaration is getting less and less certain with every day that passes.

I'm staring at a computer screen, tapping into security systems, phone lines, anything we can to gain info. It's the same thing I've been doing every day when suddenly my phone next to me buzzes. Hayes ran out to get coffee, so I assume it's him forgetting one of our coffee orders again.

I open a text, and my heart seizes.

Meet me at the church on tenth street. Midnight. Wear a nice suit.

I stand up, knocking my chair to the ground. "Holy hell."

"What?" Gage and Lennox say at the same time.

"I think Ri just texted me. She wants to meet tonight."

I hold out the phone to them. They both stand from their spots at the table and walk over to get a better look.

"Are you sure it's her? It could be a trap," Gage says.

I sigh and reconsider the text. He's always the one to bring me back to reality.

Lennox frowns. "Can you ask her something only she knows?"

I consider a minute before texting back.

What was the last question I asked you?

Her response comes a second later.

Who do you choose?

"It's her."

Gage nods, accepting my test.

"What do you think she wants? Should we go with you?" Lennox asks.

"Yes, I want you all with me, but I'm not sure what she wants."

"What who wants?" Hayes asks as he pushes through the door, carrying three cups of coffee.

"Ri texted me." I hold out the phone to Hayes, and he sets the coffee down before taking my phone from me.

He grins widely at me.

"What?" I ask, confused.

"Dude. She invited you to a church and told you to wear a suit. She chose you. What do you think she wants?"

I shrug, completely confused.

"She wants you there to get married," Hayes says.

"What? You're reading too much into this. Even if that's true, I'm still legally married to Odette."

"No, you're not," Gage says, holding his laptop up to me. "Your marriage to Odette has been annulled, effective two days ago."

My eyes widen. "Holy shit."

My heart starts hammering uncontrollably.

Are my dreams finally coming true? Do I really get Ri the rest of my life? Once we marry, can we find a way to stop Odette with the power of the Corsi empire behind us?

The guys all stare at me with smirks on their faces. Hayes is right. I'm getting married tonight.

———

My palms are sweaty as I walk into the church with Lennox, Hayes, and Gage behind me, all in our best suits. Soft piano music is playing as we enter, but otherwise, the church seems empty.

I spent the day pacing, sweating, and rereading the text message a million times, trying to figure out if I misunderstood. I bought a simple ring—one I think Ri will like, just in case it's true.

I didn't know how else to spend my day other than waiting and hoping.

I don't draw my gun, but the other three do as we walk down the aisle of the church. Beautiful stain-glass windows, wooden pews, and a stone floor give the moment a traditional feel.

Slowly, we make our way toward the front as my hopes drop of this being my wedding. This was probably just a secluded place Ri wanted to meet so we wouldn't be spotted together.

As we reach the end of the aisle, right in front of the pulpit, I see a man walk toward me. Before I can ask him a question, the music changes, and the doors at the back of the church open. Ri is standing in a wedding dress and a full veil over her face. She begins walking down the aisle with Corsi escorting her.

Oh my god. This is really happening.

The guys smile at me as they put their guns away and stand behind me as if they're my groomsmen. We all turn and watch Ri walk down the aisle.

Her dress is one for a princess—full and puffy. I'm sure she wore it to tease us for always calling her a princess, not because it fits her style. I can barely see beneath her veil, but her long, raven hair sticks out around the edges.

I don't think I breathe as she slowly walks down the aisle with her father. He looks at me stone-faced, emotionless. I have no idea what he thinks of all of this, but I'm thankful he's honoring Ri's wishes.

I won.

I get to spend the rest of my life with her.

I stare at her stomach. She said to win, you either had to get her pregnant or accomplish some other secret method of winning.

Did I win because I was the one who impregnated her? If so, it had to have been from before.

Or did I win because I won her heart?

I can't wait to ask her that and a million other questions soon. She's mine, and together we will conquer the world.

They reach the end of the aisle, and I hold out my arm for her to take it.

Corsi looks at me. "Protect Rialta with your life."

"I swear I will," I vow.

He nods and then passes Ri's hand from his arm to mine. Together, she and I take two steps toward the minister.

"Can I lift your veil? I want to look you in the eyes when I marry you," I ask her.

She nods.

Slowly, I lift her veil, careful not to mess up her hair or makeup. I'm expecting to see Ri's beautiful big eyes staring back at me with a teasing gaze, but that's not what I get. In fact, Ri isn't the one staring back at me at all—it's the woman I helped Ri save.

I blink in disbelief. This has to be a mistake.

"Who are you?" I ask.

"Rialta Corsi," she replies.

———

DANGEROUS PRINCESS

RETRIBUTION GAMES BOOK 6

1

BECKETT

DID *I win because I was the one who impregnated her? Or did I win because I won her heart?*

I can't wait to ask her those and a million other questions after the wedding. She's mine, and together we will conquer the world.

Ri and her father reach the end of the aisle, and I hold out my arm for Ri to take it.

Corsi looks at me. "Protect Rialta with your life."

"I swear I will," I vow.

He nods and then passes Ri's hand from his arm to mine. Together, she and I take two steps toward the minister.

"Can I lift your veil? I want to look you in the eyes when I marry you," I ask her.

She nods.

Slowly, I lift her veil, careful not to mess up her hair or makeup. I'm expecting to see Ri's beautiful big eyes staring back at me with a teasing gaze, but that's not what I get. In fact, Ri isn't the one staring back at me at all—it's the woman I helped Ri save.

I blink in disbelief. This has to be a mistake.

"Who are you?" I ask.

"Rialta Corsi," she replies.

I must have heard her wrong. This can't be the truth. This woman isn't Rialta.

No—my Rialta is taller, has darker hair, a fierce sparkle in her brown eyes. My Rialta's arms are toned and ready to beat any man in this room. My Rialta looks at me with love and lust with an undercurrent of hatred.

This woman is an imposter. She's a similar height but at least an inch shorter. She has dark hair like Rialta, but it's lighter with auburn highlights. There is no fierceness in her eyes. Her arms look like chicken wings—thin and scrawny, nowhere near ready to fight. And this woman looks at me with indifference. There's no emotion at all in her eyes when she sees me.

The woman standing before me was made to wear this dress with her model-thin frame. With a tiara in her hair, she looks like a fairytale princess—not the princess warrior I've come to know.

I blink several times, thinking this has to be a mistake. I have to be hallucinating this person. Maybe I'm hallucinating because I can't believe I'll ever actually get to marry Rialta. I don't deserve her, and my dreams will never come true.

But every time I blink, this imposter is still standing in front of me.

My mouth falls open, and I swear my heart stops. I can't breathe. I can't think. This can't be happening—not after everything. I can't go from being married to a woman I hate to a woman I don't even know, not while the woman I love walks this earth.

The imposter doesn't speak, neither do I.

We stare at each other in a desperate search for answers. I'm not sure either of us has a clue as to what is going on.

I don't know how I muster it or even where it comes from, but I finally get words out. "I don't understand."

She sucks in a breath but doesn't speak. I can see the hesitation in her eyes, along with fear and concern. She doesn't understand either.

I look around the church, looking for the real Rialta, for Ri. As I quickly search the pews, the aisle, the banisters, the stage behind us, I find her nowhere. She's not here.

I look to the three men standing behind me as my best men—Hayes, Lennox, and Gage. They finally get a full look at her face and seem just as shocked as me. None of them say anything. It will take them some time to process this before they can be helpful, so I'm on my own.

I look to Corsi sitting in the first pew on Rialta's side, and he returns my gaze with stern eyes. Then I see the gun he has laid out casually on his lap.

We all have guns. It's four against one, so I don't know what he thinks he's going to accomplish with that threat.

Corsi looks to the minister and nods his head.

The minister begins speaking, but I don't hear any of his words —I can't. I keep looking at Rialta, urgently trying to process everything.

What am I missing?

Did the real Ri try to warn me?

Did she give me some clue?

Is she in danger? Is she dead, and this woman was hired to take her place as a shitty impersonation?

"Where is the real Ri?" I ask her.

She blinks at me but doesn't even bother to open her mouth and offer me an explanation. I assume it's because of Corsi. She's as terrified of him as everyone else in this city.

What do I do?

I need answers. I need to know what happened to Ri. That's all that matters right now. I need to stop thinking of myself and save her. If I can't get answers from this woman, then I need to try Corsi.

I don't care if I start a war with him. A war has already been started.

I'll do anything for Ri. I'll do anything to protect her. If I have to die to keep her safe, then so be it.

I take a step toward Corsi before I hear Lennox shout, "Beckett, don't move!"

I stop, confused as to what he's seeing. But as I turn in his direction—a flicker of red light on my chest catches my eyes.

I stare down at the red dot—a threat to stay put. To get married to a complete stranger. To do as Corsi wants.

I quickly glance around the church, trying to find the person who has me in the crosshairs of their sniper rifle. I don't see anyone, but the red dot doesn't move, so neither do I.

I look to Corsi, and he raises his eyebrows at me in a challenge.

"I'm not going to marry her. This wasn't the deal. I was to marry Ri, not this imposter," I say, cutting off the minister and not looking at the woman in the wedding dress next to me. I don't know if I've offended her by saying I won't marry her, but I really could care less about her opinion right now. All I care about is finding out what happened to Ri.

"Actually, the deal was that if you win, you get to marry my daughter—Rialta Corsi. You get to produce an heir with my daughter, and my kingdom is yours. That was the deal."

"This isn't Rialta Corsi!" I protest.

Corsi only gives me a sly smile. I've been betrayed. Somehow everything I've believed turned out to be false.

"Beckett Monroe, let me introduce you to Rialta Corsi, my daughter," Corsi says.

My eyes cut to the woman in front of me, and I see moisture welling in the corner of her eyes. She's about to cry. She looks the same age as Ri but somehow feels decades younger. She's timid where if Ri were here, she'd be outspoken, demanding what she wants from the room.

"Where is Ri?" I ask through gritted teeth. My hand fists as I consider my options to stop this.

"It doesn't matter where she is. What matters is that you won. You won the games; now you have to accept the reward. Marry my daughter and fulfill the contract you entered into when you started the games."

"I won't be marrying anyone today."

Another red dot appears on my chest, followed by a third.

I look Corsi straight in the eyes—leader to leader.

"Marry her, or you die," Corsi says simply.

"You won't kill me. If you do, you won't have anyone left to marry your daughter. You obviously need someone to marry your daughter very badly. Why? I don't know or care, but you need me. You won't kill me."

Corsi frowns, but the dots don't leave my chest. He studies me carefully, thinking of another way to manipulate me.

"Fine, you leave me no choice. If you don't marry my daughter, then I'll kill Ri," he says.

My eyes widen, and a knot forms deep in my stomach. "You wouldn't. I don't know who she is to you, but you care about her."

"I'm a cruel man, Beckett. You know this. It's why I'm the leader that I am. Leaders in this world have to do some pretty horrible things. You've killed men that didn't exactly deserve it for the greater good. This would be no different. Ri knows her place. She would willingly die if it ensured your marriage to Rialta."

"Ri wants this?" I say in words barely audible. I can't believe it.

"Let me talk to Ri," I plead, needing to hear it from her lips. I need to understand what I'm not understanding.

"No," Corsi says flatly.

I glare at him. "If you want me to consider marrying Rialta, then let me talk to Ri." It's the most ridiculous thing I've ever said. I still can't believe I'm talking about two different people, that Rialta and Ri aren't the same person.

"No, you'll marry my daughter. If you don't, then Ri dies. Simple as that. You don't get to talk to anyone. You don't get to talk to Ri. You'll do what I say, or she dies," Corsi dictates.

My heart stops cold at the thought of Ri dying, but he's at least confirmed to me that she's alive—I think.

"How do I know Ri's even alive? How do I know you haven't already killed her?" I ask.

Corsi narrows his eyes at me. He doesn't like being challenged. He doesn't like that I'm pushing back.

"Rialta, would you like to confirm that Ri is still alive?" Corsi asks her.

I turn toward her, looking her dead in the eyes. She's much easier to read than Corsi or Ri, so I'll be able to tell if she's lying.

Rialta doesn't meet my gaze initially. She stares down at the floor as her bottom lip trembles just slightly.

Please, God, please let her be alive.

"Rialta, please," I whisper in a prayer.

She finally looks up at me. I don't know what she sees when she looks me in the eyes. I don't know if whatever she sees is the reason she finally gives me an answer.

"Ri—she's alive," she says in the softest voice. I stare at her closely. Her eyes are sincere. Her voice is honest. She told the truth. Ri's alive.

"But she won't be if you don't marry her," Corsi barks.

I swallow down the lump in my throat. I just got out of one loveless marriage, and now I'm about to be locked in another. I was the leader of the Retribution Kings, but I'm sure that became void the second my marriage to Odette was annulled.

If I marry Rialta and she produces an heir, I become the leader of the Corsi's mafia—an even stronger group. At least I will no longer be at direct war with my brother and his family. And after I marry Rialta, Corsi will start grooming me to take over. I'll have resources to help my family.

But can I go through with another fake marriage?

No, I can't.

I look down at the dots on my chest. I don't have a choice but to marry Rialta, this imposter. I'll die if I don't. Ri will die if I don't.

I turn back to the minister and hold out my arm to Rialta. Marriage doesn't mean anything. It's just a contract I can dissolve later. I just need to stay alive and keep Ri alive. I'll figure out how to get out of the marriage later.

I don't glance at her, but I feel Rialta take my arm, and we step up to the minister, who looks in Corsi's direction. Corsi must nod at him to continue because the minister resumes speaking, and this time, I listen.

The minister is brief in his opening remarks, quickly getting to the vows part. I feel uneasiness in waves coming off Lennox, Gage, and Hayes. I don't have to look at them to know they all have their hands on their guns, ready for a fight to break out at a moment's notice.

The red dots are gone from my chest, but I'm sure they're on my back. They won't shoot me dead, but they won't let me walk out of here either without finishing this ceremony.

"Do you, Rialta Corsi, take Beckett Monroe to be your husband?" the minister looks to Rialta.

I look straight ahead, giving Rialta space to answer the question. It feels far too intimate to look her in the eyes.

I wait for her to say 'I do,' but if she said the words, I didn't hear it. Although maybe I didn't want to hear it. If she said 'I do,' then I'll have to go next, and it's going to kill me to say it, even if it's the only way to keep Ri alive.

But she must not have said anything because the minister keeps looking at her in earnest, waiting for her to say the magic words.

Finally, I look over at Rialta, wondering why she hasn't spoken. I'm a complete stranger to her, but I expect she wants this since she walked down the aisle willingly.

When I look at her, I see a scared woman. Her face is white, her bottom lip is trembling, and her throat is tightened. There is no way she will be able to speak; she's in too much shock.

I don't know how to help her. I don't even know if she is truly Rialta or what Corsi's endgame is. I don't know why this marriage is being forced. I don't understand any of it.

"Purse your lips and try to breathe," I try to encourage her, just hoping the woman will calm down and not have a full-blown panic attack. Although, maybe a panic attack will help me stall to figure a way out of this wedding.

She purses her lips like I told her and is about to breathe when I feel her swaying.

"Rialta, are you okay?" I ask, but she can't answer.

She's falling.

Her grip on my arm releases as she falls back. I barely have time to reach behind her head and cradle it to keep her skull from hitting the hard stone.

I don't know what just happened. *Was she shot? Did she faint to avoid marrying me?* I don't know. What I do know is that whatever happened, I've been spared my worst nightmare—at least temporarily.

I won't let the chance go to waste.

I'M HIDING in the shadows of the rafters when Beckett and the guys walk into the church. I wasn't sure they would show or if Beckett would realize he's about to get married. The fact that he showed up in a suit tells me he knows exactly what he's in for.

Well, not exactly. He doesn't know the whole truth—far from it. But I have no doubt that by the end of the night, he'll be married. The plan will go off smoothly, but not without my heart breaking.

I'll be surprised if everyone in the church doesn't hear my heart shatter into a million pieces and fall all over the floor when Beckett says, 'I do.' But it is my duty to arrange this. It is my honor. My job. My life. And I will do it without shedding a tear.

But when I go home tonight, there will be floods of tears. I'll cry uncontrollably without being able to stop, but not now. Now I have a job to do.

I watch as Beckett happily walks down the aisle with the others. I don't know how to feel about his attitude. *Would he really have been that happy to marry me? Or did he really just want Vincent's power and the ability to stop the war against his brother?*

I don't allow myself to think too hard about the answers. The answers don't matter. What matters is getting them married, getting her safe.

Beckett waits with his men at the end of the aisle, and the church doors open a moment later. Vincent and Rialta start walking down the aisle. She's beautiful in her fluffy dress, complete with tiara. It's not my style, but it suits her.

How long will it take Beckett to realize I'm not the woman in that dress?

I get my answer seconds later when Beckett lifts her veil. I told her not to let him do that. I told her not to speak, wait as long as possible. But of course, he realized something was off the second she got near him.

I expect the shock on Beckett's face. What I don't expect is the rest of his emotions. In addition to shock, there's disappointment, fear, and brokenness. There's something else too, something I dare not name—not now. It doesn't matter anymore. It's all done, or it's about to be.

But the question sneaks into my head—*did I make the right choice?*

I'm in a haze of feelings when Beckett takes a step toward Vincent, and I automatically aim my rifle's laser at his chest. I would never shoot him, not unless he was threatening her life. But the threat alone will keep him in place long enough for Vincent to convince him he has no choice but to stay.

Lennox yells out, and Beckett notices the red dot on his chest. Beckett looks in my direction, trying to find his assailant. He can't see me—I'm too well hidden in the shadows. But for a second, I think he knows it's me. We can always feel each other. We can always sense when each other is near. I have no doubt he feels my presence as I always feel his.

Hopefully, those feelings go away soon enough. We will be living too close together to be feeling such things for the rest of our lives. I hold my breath, remaining as still as possible until Beckett finally looks away.

Beckett talks to Vincent. I barely listen. I focus on keeping the laser pointed at his chest. I'm not the only one up here. I might be Rialta's main protection, but on a night like tonight, we have a full army protecting her.

I look to the three men standing to Beckett's right. All of them have hands buried beneath their jackets, most likely gripping a gun should a battle break out. Their eyes circle around the room, looking for the threat. They know we're up here in the church rafters, but they can't see us. What they can see is Rialta—and they look at her like she's the enemy.

I sigh. It's going to take a while for them to trust her, to want to protect her. But if Beckett protects her, then they will too. I have no doubt about that. They are no longer loyal to the Retribution Kings. They are loyal to Beckett. Any man who can earn the loyalty of others like that is worthy of marrying Rialta.

I'm focusing on Beckett's men when Vincent's words draw me back into his conversation.

"If you don't marry my daughter, then I'll kill Ri."

My heart stops.

I'm not afraid to die; I never have been. In fact, I'm surprised I've survived this long. And Vincent doesn't make a threat he's not willing to act on. If Beckett doesn't marry Rialta, then Vincent will kill me.

I wish I could shut my ears off because I don't want to hear Beckett's response. I don't want to hear if he cares about me. I don't want to hear he has any feelings for me.

His feelings will change. They will grow to love Rialta. She's incredible and worthy, and he will find a way to love her. He's fallen in love countless times. I have no doubt he will again.

Beckett is a romantic, though. He believes in his one true love. He's never said that, but it's why he's so disappointed and heartbroken when his relationships end. He always thinks she was the one for him. What he doesn't realize is there is no such thing as the one, no such thing as one great love. We can love many people. We can fall in love with our enemies or our friends. We can fall in love without meaning to, but that doesn't mean that person is worthy of our love.

No, he will fall in love with her in time. What is more worrying is whether or not she will fall in love with him. *Will she ever accept him?*

I fell in love with him easily, even when I shouldn't have. It's not my fault—not really. I had no memories of my role in Rialta's life, and Beckett is so damn easy to fall in love with.

I look down at Rialta standing at the end of the aisle, looking at Beckett carefully. She doesn't give any indication of how she feels. I was surprised when Vincent told her she was to get married tonight, and she didn't protest. She didn't cry, throw a tantrum, or demand to at least meet the man a handful of times first. She didn't do any of those things. She simply heard her instructions and agreed to them.

Vincent seemed pleased, but I had my suspicions. I still do. I haven't seen Rialta in years. She's grown and matured a lot in the time since I last saw her, but she's still young. Marrying a man you don't know, even a good man like Beckett, is still a big deal.

But Rialta did as she was told without a fuss, without even the slightest protest.

As I study Rialta now, I can see a hint of the truth. She's terrified. Her skin is pale, her eyes are dilated, and I'm pretty sure I can see a bead of sweat dripping down from her forehead through my rifle scope. She's going to be a problem as much as Beckett will be.

As Vincent finishes threatening Beckett, a fight doesn't break out, surprisingly. Beckett simply holds out his arm to Rialta, and she takes it. They turn to face the minister, and he continues with the ceremony.

I can't breathe. I don't know what to think.

I'm not going to be able to shut out this next part. I'm going to hear them speak every vow. I'm going to hear them speak every promise to each other. They will be with each other forever—until one of them dies.

Beckett will never be mine.

I will have to spend my life watching the two of them as a married couple.

Even though my heart is bursting with agony now, it will heal. There is no such thing as one great love anyway. I will find another man to love or lust after. Beckett wasn't special in that way, but he will be a good fit for Rialta.

"Do you, Rialta Corsi, take Beckett Monroe to be your husband?" the minister asks.

Please, ears, turn off.

I stare down at Rialta, waiting for her to say the magic words. It will kill me, but Beckett's 'I do' in response will end me.

The words never come—from either of them.

Instead, Rialta falls to the ground.

No!

I want to run to her, jump down from my hiding spot in the rafters and scoop her up in my arms. My instincts are yelling at me to do that, but my training tells me to wait. I shouldn't reveal myself. Vincent can help her as easily as I can. My job is to stay here and watch from the rafters until a more clear need presents itself.

If she was shot, I need to stay up here to return fire.

If she just fainted, then I'm not really needed, even if it's difficult to stay away.

Then Beckett does something that proves his value to Rialta more than anything else. He catches her head, preventing her from hitting the ground.

He whistles for his men to surround her, and he drapes his body over hers. If she is under attack, no more bullets will hit her. He leans in close, quickly checking her vitals, assessing what happened to her.

My breath eases. My pulse relaxes.

Vincent catches my attention and gives me a pleased nod.

I chose the right man for Rialta. Beckett will do everything he can to protect her; that's who he is. He's a good man. He's a man who falls in love a little too easily. Most importantly, he's a man who protects the innocent. He protects those who are worthy of protection.

Beckett has claimed time and time again that he isn't my hero. He was right—I never needed a hero.

But he sure as hell is hers.

3

BECKETT

WITH A QUICK WHISTLE, all of my men surround Rialta,
ensuring no harm comes to her. I may not want to marry her, but
she doesn't deserve to die. She's young, innocent, and most likely
being as forced to marry me as I am her.

"Is she bleeding?" Hayes asks.

I feel over the back of her head and dress. "I don't see anything
obvious."

"Other than Corsi's snipers in the ceiling, I don't see anyone
that would be attacking us," Lennox says.

Gage pulls up his phone and types furiously. "There aren't any
security cameras in the church, and I don't see anyone from the cafe
across the street."

I nod. "If we were under attack, the snipers would be shooting
like crazy right now. I think she just fainted."

"I don't blame the poor girl after she took one look at you,"
Hayes teases.

"Jokes right now, Hayes?" Lennox barks.

I ignore them both as I place my hand on Rialta's neck to check
her pulse. My eyes cut to Vincent, who is still seated in the first
pew, watching us closely. He doesn't run to his daughter's side. He

371

obviously doesn't feel like whatever happened is very serious. That or he trusts me—like really, really trusts me. He trusts me with his daughter's life. I suck in a breath at that thought.

That's what the games were about. He wanted to figure out who among us could be trusted with his daughter, not just who would be the best leader. In fact, it wouldn't shock me if the main reason I won is that they think I'm the best at keeping her safe.

Ri has called me a hero numerous times. It hits me now that she wasn't looking for a hero for herself, but for this woman, whoever she is, and whatever relation she has to Ri.

I frown as I continue to feel her pulse.

"What's wrong?" Hayes asks.

"Her pulse is extremely weak, and her breaths are too shallow. We need to get her to a hospital ASAP," I snap.

Hayes's eyes widen, and Lennox helps me scoop Rialta up in my arm.

Vincent is finally on his feet as he realizes this isn't about a scared girl fainting. This is some sort of medical emergency.

"I'll call an ambulance," Vincent says.

"No, it will be faster if we drive. We have a first aid kit in the car," I say.

Vincent pockets his phone. "My men and I will follow you. Don't let her die." He eyes me, and the threat is obvious. If she dies, so do I.

I nod and run behind Lennox and Hayes as I carry Rialta against me. Gage takes up the rear with Corsi behind him.

I see men starting to drop from the rafters and running after us. For a second, I want to stay and see if Ri is among them. I'm still not entirely convinced she's alive. I still think this could be a switch. Ri died, and Corsi found a lookalike to take her place, not accepting that he doesn't have an heir.

But this woman in my arms, whoever she is, deserves to live. I'll have to find Ri later.

We race to our SUV parked outside the church. Lennox is

already in the driver's seat. Hayes has the first aid kit out and the back door open. I climb inside with Rialta in my arm while Gage hops into the front seat.

The second we are all in, Lennox steps on the gas.

Hayes reaches across and tests her pulse. "She still has a pulse; it's just really weak."

I nod. I can't really assess her with most of her body resting against my arm, but I feel her chest rising slowly against me.

"What do you think is wrong with her? Did she just faint?" Hayes asks.

I look down at the woman. She's skinny, far too skinny, now that I have a better look at her. Her skin is still pale, almost yellow, and I can't find muscle anywhere on her body.

"I don't think this is just about fainting. I think this is something else," I say ominously.

All eyes in the car land on me, but no one says anything. Less than five minutes later, Lennox pulls the car in front of an emergency room. Gage has my door open before I can even move for it, and he helps me get Rialta out of the car.

We are met at the door by medical staff pushing a gurney. I gently place Rialta on the bed and run by her side as they roll her through the hospital doors. The others are right on our tail as we enter the hospital. Their guns would be drawn if it wouldn't draw too much suspicion.

They push her into a private room, and a nurse turns to us immediately. "Everyone who isn't family, get out," she says.

Lennox, Hayes, and Gage all look to me, waiting for me to tell them what to do.

I nod. They can protect her just as well outside the room as they can inside it. And the nurses and doctors need room to work.

They leave the room, and the nurse turns to me.

"I'm family," I say, keeping it simple.

She examines me in my suit and then looks at her wedding

dress, piecing things together. She pats me on the shoulder and then turns to begin helping them work on Rialta.

I slink into the corner. I'm guessing whether they believe I'm family or not, it's just a matter of time before I'm kicked out too if things turn south.

I watch as an IV is placed, her dress is cut from her body, pads are placed on her chest and hooked up to wires, and an oxygen mask is placed over her face. There is no obvious sign of what's wrong with her. I can see her chest still rising and falling, and her heart rate is starting to show up on the monitor, so she's still alive.

I should want her dead. That's the easiest way to get out of having to marry her, but I can't wish death on someone so innocent. And whatever it means for me, I won't allow her to die.

A second later, Corsi appears in the doorway of her room. He quickly walks to the side of her bed and takes her hand in his, moisture pooling in his eyes.

He tries to speak to her, but the second he opens his mouth, tears start streaming down his face. He gets choked up and can't get the words out. He's still gripping her hand as her heart starts to flatline.

A nurse pushes him back into the corner opposite me as they go to work on restarting her heart. The paddles come out, and they shock her heart.

Corsi nearly collapses in the corner at the sight. I've never seen him so broken, so vulnerable. He's supposed to be this fearless, ruthless leader, not a stumbling man consumed by his emotions.

I turn my attention back to the screen, but it's still flatlining. My eyes widen as I look at the beautiful woman, so young and on the brink of death. It's not fair. I don't know who she is, but she doesn't deserve this.

A nurse performs CPR while they wait to try again to shock her heart. It can't be more than a couple of seconds before the paddles come down on her chest again, but it feels like a lifetime to me. I can't imagine what it feels like to Corsi.

And then—life.

The line goes up and down on the machine, and if I look closely at Rialta, I can see her chest rise and fall.

An uneasy relief washes through everyone in the room. She survived this time, but there is no guarantee she'll endure the next incident.

One of the nurses looks to Corsi, then me. "We need to clear the room, so we have more space to work."

Corsi's eyes widen, and he opens his mouth to protest, but his throat runs dry. No words come out of the most feared leader in Chicago.

The nurse is right—Corsi shouldn't stay here. Whatever happens, he shouldn't see any more.

I walk over to Corsi. "Go. I won't leave her side no matter what happens; you have my word."

Corsi's eyes narrow at me; he'll hold me to my promise. But it's a promise I'd make whether I want to get in Corsi's good graces or not.

Rialta doesn't deserve to be alone right now.

I push Corsi toward the door as I take Rialta's hand.

The nurse who ordered us to leave gives me a look.

"I'm not leaving. You can call security, but they'll be knocked out on the floor before they even enter the room. You've seen the guys outside. You know who I work for. I'm not leaving," I threaten.

The nurse frowns but doesn't argue anymore. I remain by Rialta's side, holding her hand while the doctors and nurses work. I'm not sure Rialta is going to make it until twenty minutes later, when I feel her squeeze my hand back. It's then that I know she's still in there. I realize Rialta and Ri do have something in common— they're both fighters.

An hour later, Rialta is finally stable enough to be moved to a recovery room. We're left alone after they've settled her.

She hasn't woken up fully yet, and I haven't let go of her hand.

I can't help but wonder what's wrong with her. Normal twenty-something young women don't faint like that. Their hearts don't just stop like that. They don't have to get rushed to the hospital like that.

I hope I can have a moment alone with her to ask. Although I'm sure Gage has already pulled up all her medical files and has all the answers.

There's a soft knock on the door, though. My time alone with Rialta is about to be up. I assume it's Corsi or one of the nurses coming back to check on her. But familiar chills race up my spine, telling me it's not Corsi standing at the foot of Rialta's bed.

I turn and see Ri—she's alive.

BECKETT IS HOLDING Rialta's hand as she lies unconscious in her hospital bed. He's already so good at protecting and taking care of her. I know I chose the right man for the job.

I thought it would hurt seeing him take care of her. But right now, all I care about is that she's alive, and he's holding her hand when I can't.

"Is she okay?" I ask, my voice unusually soft and timid.

Beckett blinks, not believing his eyes that I'm here.

I take a step closer and can see Rialta take deep, slow breaths in her sleep. She's going to make it.

"You're alive," Beckett says in shock.

"Yes, why wouldn't I be?" I ask.

He shakes his head, and I can see tears welling in his eyes. "When I lifted that veil and saw it wasn't you, I was so terrified you were dead. I thought Corsi found a lookalike to replace you as quickly as possible before word of your death spread."

I swallow the lump in my throat. "Well, as you can see, I'm very much alive."

The air between us changes, supercharging with tension.

I should leave.

I don't even know why I came. I just needed to see Rialta is fine with my own eyes and—

In the next second, Beckett has his arm around me, pulling my head tight against his chest and holding me so tight I'm afraid he'll never let go.

"Lennox!" Beckett hollers out into the hallway.

Lennox appears at the door, staring at me like he's seen a ghost.

I sigh.

"Hold Rialta's hand and watch over her until I get back," Beckett orders him.

He nods and takes Beckett's place by Rialta's bedside.

I raise an eyebrow.

Beckett doesn't say more as he takes my hand and drags me out of the hospital room. He doesn't stop to let me talk to Gage or Hayes, who guard the door and give me questioning looks as we walk by. Beckett is on a mission to get me alone, and I don't resist. Maybe I should, but I don't.

He continues to yank my hand, leading me out of the hospital. Once outside, he doesn't stop until we've reached an empty alleyway around the corner. With a tug of his hand, he spins me to face him. We are all but touching, staring each other down.

"Start talking," he orders.

I furrow my brow, annoyed with his tone.

"You're not pregnant?" he asks.

I shake my head. "No, I'm not."

"You're not hurt?"

"No."

His eyes roam my body, looking for any evidence of injuries. Once he's satisfied, he makes his move.

I don't anticipate it, so I'm taken off guard when his lips crash down on mine. I should push him away, but I'm so desperate for the kiss that I literally can't. Not only do I let him, but I kiss him back.

Our bodies slam together, and my hands lock around the back of his head as I deepen the kiss. I love everything about kissing him.

I love how his tongue tastes, how his lips feel, and the deep throaty growls that vibrate through his neck. My panties soak with every swipe of his tongue against mine under the moonlight.

In the dark, our kisses are hidden. But once dawn arrives, there will be no hiding.

I put my hand on his chest and gently push him away. I can't keep letting myself fall for this man. I can't keep letting my emotions get in the way.

Beckett grasps my hand in his, but he doesn't fight me. He doesn't try to kiss me again.

He looks deep into my eyes, searching for the truth I've kept hidden from him. It's a truth I've hidden for a long time.

"My job is to protect Rialta Corsi. It's been my job practically my entire life," I say.

Beckett's eyes dart side to side as he looks into mine. His eyes alone ask a million questions.

I'll answer some of them, but probably not enough to fully satisfy him.

"Vincent decided early on that the best way to protect her was to hide her away, while I agreed to pretend to be her."

Beckett frowns but doesn't interrupt or ask any questions.

"I went along with being hypnotized by Kek so I would truly believe I was her, to keep her hidden. I only recently remembered the truth when Kek reversed the hypnotization."

Beckett takes in my words, only revealing the most basic outline.

"What's wrong with Rialta?" he asks.

"Nothing."

He narrows his eyes. "Why would you agree to living a fake life? Why risk your life to protect her? Why find a husband for her?"

"She's worth protecting."

"What about you? Is your life not worth protecting?"

"I can take care of myself." I rip my hand from his grasp.

"I know that, but it doesn't mean you should take extra risks for someone else."

"It was worth it," I protest.

"So everything between us, it was all a lie? You never felt anything for me? Were you just trying to find a good husband for Rialta? Someone who could take up your mantel and protect her?"

"Yes," I breathe.

That single word is more of a lie than anything I've ever said or done before. I do love Beckett. And I love Rialta, that's why they're perfect for each other.

His head drops in disbelief.

"What's your name? Ri? Something else?"

I open my mouth but hesitate. It's been so long since I've used my own name since anyone actually said my name aloud. I lick my lips and speak.

"My name is River."

"River," Beckett tests my name on his lips, and my heart explodes.

"River what?"

I shrug. "I was adopted. I never knew my last name, but I guess it's Corsi now."

"River Corsi," he says hesitantly, still getting used to the way it sounds, just as I am.

"You can keep calling me Ri, though," I say.

He bites his bottom lip, considering it—likely considering a lot of things.

He circles around me as he thinks.

I close my eyes as I feel his gaze on me, trying not to let him see how he affects me. How my body heats with his gaze on me. How my skin crawls, itching for him to touch me again, to kiss me.

That was the last time I'll ever kiss him, and it wasn't enough. It's never enough. I could kiss him a million times, and it wouldn't be enough.

Fuck.

"Open your eyes," he says.

I do, hoping I'm not giving away any feelings.

He once again searches my eyes, but if he sees anything, he doesn't tell me.

"So what now?" he asks.

I clear my throat. "You marry Rialta Corsi. I continue to protect her as one of her guards, and you slowly fall in love with her. In the meantime, Vincent will teach you how he runs things and prepare you to take over for him. I assume the Retribution Kings have already disowned you. Luckily Vincent's empire is bigger than the Retribution Kings's, so you'll have plenty of power over them."

"You think I'm after power?" His eyebrows shoot up, and he scowls.

"No," I say.

"Then why would I marry Rialta? What do I get out of it?"

"You believe in one true love, don't you?"

"Yes," he says.

"She's it. I've spent weeks getting to know you. I know you better than anyone. And I know her better than anyone. She's your match in every way. She needs a hero—and whether you want to admit it or not, you play the hero role well, Beckett."

His face darkens. "I don't believe I'll ever fall in love again—not after all my failed attempts."

I wince, knowing he's including me.

"I don't want love. I don't want power," he says.

"What do you want?"

His heated stare is his only response. My throat tightens, my skin warms, and my pulse races through me. *Please stop wanting me. It would be so much easier.*

"I won't marry Rialta."

"You won the game. That was the rule. You win; you marry her. Then, once you produce an heir, you take over Vincent's role as leader of the mafia."

"Well, you should offer the position to the runner-up because I don't want it."

I frown, glaring at him.

"You'll marry her," I say.

"I won't."

"You'll marry Rialta, or I die."

He frowns. "Corsi wouldn't kill you. You've been too invaluable to him for far too long. He would be killing his daughter's protector —one of his most valuable assets. I don't believe he'll actually kill you."

"You're willing to take that risk?" I ask.

He sucks in a hiss; he'll do anything to keep me alive. His feelings for me haven't changed yet. But soon enough, Rialta will be his whole world. He'll do everything he can for her, and I'll be nothing but a distant memory.

"Trust me when I say that Vincent will do anything to protect Rialta—anything. That includes killing me, so think twice before you refuse to marry her," I beg.

RIVER—THAT'S her name. Not Ri, not Rialta, not Princess, not Fighter—River.

River Corsi.

I always knew she was a Corsi, but I didn't realize how deep the bonds run. I'm still not sure I fully understand. It's not about blood—there's some other reason she stays and works for that man and his family.

Ri—River—will die if I don't marry Rialta. That's what she says. That's what Corsi said.

I don't want to believe either of them, but I do. Corsi is a brutal, ruthless man. The lengths he's taken to protect his daughter make it clear how much he loves her. He's willing to do anything for Rialta.

River and he have the same goal—to protect Rialta at all costs. They think I'm the man who can keep her safe. I don't understand why, but they will stop at nothing to ensure our marriage happens.

I know what I have to do.

I return to the hospital on my own; River doesn't follow me. Although, I'm sure River at least plans to hide in the shadows with a sniper rifle on me in case I don't follow through.

I head back to Rialta's room. All three of the guys are standing outside when I approach.

"I thought I told you to stay with Rialta until I got back," I snap at Lennox.

"Corsi is in there with her. I didn't think it was appropriate for me to stay," Lennox answers.

I nod and then rap my knuckles against the door before entering.

Rialta is still asleep in her bed, with Corsi sitting in the chair next to her bed. He looks up at me with tears still in his eyes. He doesn't wipe them away or try to hide in shame at showing his weakness so clearly to me. His greatest weakness is his daughter.

I stand at the foot of her bed, unsure if this is the appropriate place to have this conversation or not.

Corsi stands to lead me out of the room but stops a few feet away from me, facing me.

"River chose well. I wasn't sure, but I trusted her. She has a sixth sense when it comes to things like this. You and Rialta will make a good match," Corsi says.

"Why? Why not trust Rialta to find her own husband?" I pause. "Actually, why does Rialta need a husband at all? She seems plenty strong enough. And if she isn't, then River and your men seem more than capable of protecting her."

"I don't have to explain myself to you," he snaps.

"Maybe you should if you're willing to pass your daughter and everything you've built to me."

Corsi frowns but doesn't open his mouth. He doesn't speak. He doesn't offer me any explanation, and he probably never will. But it doesn't matter; that's not what I came here for.

"I'll marry Rialta under one condition."

"You aren't in a position to be making conditions."

I glare at him. "Actually, I am. You need a husband for your daughter. And your threat to kill Ri, while real enough, is something you'd really like to avoid. So I'll make this easier on both of us.

There will be no more death threats or manipulation. We will work together in a partnership."

Corsi doesn't say anything, giving me his full attention. I don't understand why he wants his daughter married so badly, but I do know he doesn't want to spill any more blood. He just wants this game over, and Rialta married.

"I'll marry Rialta if you protect my brother and his family. Put a stop to the war between the gangs. Stop Odette. Then, I'll marry your daughter."

It's a lot to ask, I know. But if I'm going to marry Rialta, I might as well get something worthy out of it. I need my family to be safe.

I have three amazing guys who would die for me outside this room, but they alone aren't enough to stop the war. The Retribution Kings are no longer mine to control either. I need an army to stop this war and ensure my brother, Enzo, and his family are safe.

I won't marry Rialta for anything less.

Corsi looks me up and down. "River was right. You drive a hard bargain. But I can see how clearly you're a perfect fit for my daughter, so I'll do you this favor."

I let out an exhale of relief.

"But...I can't stop the war. I won't send my men to their deaths."

I frown. "If you don't, our deal is off."

"I can't stop the war, but I can ensure that Enzo Black and his family are safe. Is that good enough for you, Beckett?" Corsi says.

I consider his words, making sure I'm not missing anything. Corsi is careful with his words, and he'll hold me to the deal whether it's a good deal for me or not.

It would be better if he stopped the war, not just ensured my family is safe, but I doubt I'll get a better offer from him.

I don't know what will happen after I marry Rialta. I don't know if I'll grow to care for her. I don't know if I'll ever get over Ri. I don't know what Corsi will require of me to take over his position— not that I want it.

But I'll do anything to protect Ri and my family. This deal will ensure that Ri isn't harmed and that my brother and his family are safe.

I hold out my hand to Corsi.

He takes it, and we shake.

"I'll ensure your family is safe," Corsi says.

"After my family is safe, I'll marry your daughter."

As we shake, I feel eyes on us. I turn and see Rialta sitting up in bed, wide awake.

I lock eyes with her for the first time since she passed out in the church. She looks at me suspiciously, and I don't blame her. I gaze back at her in equal measure, unsure of what our future holds. There's a very good chance that we are going to end up as husband and wife, whether either of us wants it or not.

She doesn't know if I'm a good man, and I don't know the kind of woman she is. Yet, I don't see fear in her eyes. I see determination.

If she learned that look from Ri, then I should be terrified. That look can only mean she's as strong-willed as Ri, and I know I'm no match against the two of them.

I PULL into the driveway of a countryside house while Rialta sleeps in the backseat. Beckett sits next to her, staring out the window. His eyes never made contact with mine in the rearview mirror as we drove, but that could be because I rarely look in the rearview mirror.

I don't know what changed Beckett's mind. *Was it our conversation? Or did he have a different talk with Corsi?*

I park the car in the driveway. Rialta is still asleep.

"I'll go secure the house before you two come in," I say, getting out of the car and not waiting for Beckett to reply.

I'm relieved to be out of the car. It felt stifling in there, trapped with the two of them. It's going to be worse trapped in this house with them, though. I'll be trapped forever as I watch them get married and share their lives together.

If I'm lucky, they'll fire me, and I won't have to suffer much longer.

I head into the house with my gun drawn, ready for anything. The house is small—only two bedrooms, one bathroom, an eat-in kitchen, and a small living room with a fireplace. But it's in the middle of nowhere and safe—that's all that matters.

I take my time clearing the house. It gives me more time before I have to see Rialta or Beckett. We're here for her to heal and for them to get to know each other before they get married.

This trip is also giving Vincent time to fulfill whatever end of a deal he struck with Beckett to get him to agree so easily. There has to be a deal; that has to be the reason that Beckett is here without a fight. That or Beckett is just buying time to find an out.

After I've checked every room twice, I finally head back out to the car. They're right where I left them—Beckett looking out the window deep in thought and Rialta asleep next to him.

"All clear," I say as I open Rialta's door and gently wake her.

She opens her eyes, and Beckett finally looks in my direction.

I ignore him and give Rialta all my attention. That's my strategy for surviving this hell.

"How are you feeling?" I ask her.

She yawns. "Just sleepy."

"Well, let's get you into the house and into bed. Then you can sleep until you can't sleep anymore," I say.

Rialta smiles at me. "I've missed you."

"I've missed you too," I say.

I offer her my hand to help her out of the car. She takes it easily and seems steady on her feet. I barely have to help her.

I hear a door slam behind us and assume Beckett is right behind us. I turn my head to look when I feel Rialta's grasp slipping.

I try to catch her to keep her on her feet, but Beckett beats me to it. He catches her in his arm.

"Dizzy?" he asks her in his deep, inviting voice.

She nods.

"I can carry you if you want?"

"That's probably for the best if we don't want to have to immediately turn around and head back to the nearest hospital," she says.

He nods solemnly. Then he effortlessly scoops her up in his arm and carries her up the three steps to the front porch of the house.

I run ahead and hold the front door open as he carries her into the house. I can't help but notice how intensely Rialta looks at Beckett. I can't help but notice that he doesn't seem annoyed by her stare.

Jesus, I'm reading way too much into a look. He's just being nice and carrying her into the house.

"Which room?" Beckett asks me.

"The primary is on the right," I answer.

I take my time following after them, although I don't wait long enough. Just as I walk into the room, Beckett tucks her into bed and kisses her forehead. He sits down on the edge of her bed, clearly with no intention of leaving.

"I'll just leave you two alone. Holler if you need anything, Rialta."

"Wait," Rialta says.

I stop. "Need something? Food? Water?"

"Actually…" Rialta looks from Beckett to me. "I need to talk to River by myself."

"I'll start working on dinner," Beckett says, standing and walking toward me, toward the door.

The room is barely big enough for the queen-sized bed and dresser. When Beckett gets to me, there is nowhere for me to move out of the way.

He looks at me as he brushes past me, seemingly holding words back. Our shoulders nudge each other, and our fingers graze ever so slightly, sending a tingling of electricity through my body.

I ignore the feeling and walk to the side of Rialta's bed as Beckett closes the door on his way out.

I force a smile. "I'm so happy you're back. We have so much to catch up on."

"We do, but since our father thinks I need to get married immediately, we should focus on that," she replies.

I nod. "You're probably right." Although, her marriage to Beckett is the last thing I want to think about.

Her head falls back against the bed frame, and she yawns again. She's still exhausted from yesterday. She needs to sleep for a couple of days, and then she'll feel a lot better.

"Tell me about Beckett. Tell me what he's like. Tell me why you chose him for me," she says.

Oh, fuck me.

I don't want to have this conversation even though I love her to death. She's my best friend, the person I would die for, but this will be complete torture.

"Beckett is stubborn. He thinks he's right and everyone else is wrong. He won't let you win an argument with him. He doesn't express his feelings easily. In fact, you have to work really hard to get him to open up at all. He's loyal to a fault. He likes being in control and is bossy as hell," I start.

"You're not really making a case for why I should want to marry him."

"I'm just telling you all the facts. You need to know the good parts and the bad. But I was just getting to the good part." I smile. "Beckett is the best friend you'll ever have. He would take a bullet for you."

"Don't you mean he'd take a bullet for his friends?"

"No, he'd take a bullet for you because he knows you're inno-cent. He'd take a bullet for anyone he considers innocent. He protects his family and those he loves even harder. He's funny, sweet, and a great kisser." I wiggle my eyebrows, and she laughs.

I consider telling her he's an even greater lover, but I don't know how much she knows. And admitting you've fucked some-one's future husband probably isn't a great way to restart our friendship.

"Beckett's good-looking," Rialta says in a dreamy voice.

"That he is," I agree, but try not to think too hard about his rippling muscles and sexy smirk. I clear my throat.

"He lost one of his arms a few years back in an explosion, and that makes others look down on him like he's weak. But he's not weak—in fact, he's the opposite. He's a better fighter than almost any man I've ever met."

"A better fighter than you?" she asks.

"Well, no one's better than me."

She laughs. "You haven't changed much."

"Neither have you." I sit on the bed and pull her against my body like she's my little sister. I guess, in many ways, she is.

"What else?" she asks.

"He's not looking for power like most of the men we know. He's a good leader when he has to be, but he'd prefer to live a life without all the power."

"Good. I'd hate for him to be too much like Father."

"He's nothing like Vincent. Beckett is kind. He's gentle. He'll treat you like a princess," I say.

He'll probably call her that too. My heart takes a stabbing as I think about him using the same nicknames on her as he did me. "He'll pamper you, take you on romantic dates, and be a great husband."

Her face sobers. "How do you know? What if he hates me?"

I grab her chin and turn it gently to face me. "You, Rialta Corsi, are a great catch. In fact, dozens of men fought to their deaths to date you."

"They fought to the death for you," she says.

"No, they didn't. They fought for you. They didn't know who I was. As soon as they learned I know how to use a gun, they hated the idea of me. You were born for your role. You are meant to be a princess, Rialta. Beckett is your prince. He's a great hero."

"Maybe."

Beckett is going to have to do some of the convincing himself, but I have one last thing to add.

"Beckett is a romantic. He's been searching all his life for his one true love. He's failed, married the wrong person even. But he still wants it. All you have to do is let him in. Let him see how amazing, sweet, and caring you are. Let him see how big your heart is.

"Show him how you'll make an excellent mafia queen by his side. You'll be an incredible mother to his children. Let him see the real you, and I have no doubt he'll fall in love with you. And this time when he falls, it will be with the right woman."

A knock at the door makes us both jump, cutting off Rialta's response to my speech.

"Come in," Rialta says once she regains her composure.

Beckett opens the door and holds out a bottle of pills and water. "It's time for you to take your medications."

Rialta smiles at him brightly. "Thank you."

He walks in and over to her side of the bed. He helps her open the bottle and take her pills.

But his eyes are on me. He heard at least the last part of what I said, and he's not happy about it.

"NEED ANYTHING ELSE?" I ask Rialta as she yawns hard again. She's tired, and the meds make her even more tired, so she's not going to last much longer. Any conversation the two of us need to have will have to wait. Besides, she's not really the woman I want to talk to anyway.

"I'm good," she says, smiling at me like I'm her angel.

Fuck. I'm not her angel. I'm not her hero. I'm not her anything.

I nod and leave the room, my blood boiling from what I overheard River say.

I'm barely out the door when I hear the bedroom door close and footsteps behind me.

I'm back in the kitchen, pulling out vegetables to chop when River walks in.

"Rialta's asleep," she says.

"She couldn't possibly fall asleep that fast."

She laughs. "Then you don't know Rialta very well. Even before all this, she could fall asleep at the snap of her fingers and in the most uncomfortable of places."

"That's just the thing—I don't know Rialta. Just like I don't know you," I snap.

She stills at my words but doesn't give a quick retort.

I carry carrots, celery, and onion over to a chopping board. I go to work on the onion first, chopping away hard and fast. It's harder to chop vegetables when you only have one hand.

I could lean forward and use my residual limb to hold the vegetable while I chop. I could put something next to the vegetable to keep it from moving. But I do neither. I chop wildly, letting the onion fly around the chopping board. The pieces I chop won't be pretty, but I don't give a damn about that right now.

"Stop trying to make her like me," I say, chopping down so hard that a piece of onion juice flies at my face. I welcome the sting in my eye, wiping it off with the back of my shirt before chopping some more.

River looks at me with concern, but she knows better than to say anything while I have a knife in my hand.

"Why? Isn't it better if she likes you?"

"No," I say.

She frowns defiantly, crossing her arms in front of her chest.

"You made a deal with Vincent. I know you did; it's the only reason you intend on marrying her. And if you plan on marrying her, then I'm going to do everything I can to make the marriage work. I'm going to help her like you. And if you weren't so stubborn, I'd help you fall for her too," she lectures at me.

I slam the knife down harder, making her jump.

"What was the deal you made, Beckett?"

Of course, that's all she cares about. "Corsi will keep my brother and his family safe."

"Good, they should be safe. I was worried about them," she confesses.

I stop chopping and slowly put the knife down, lifting my head to glare at her. "Don't feel sorry for them. Don't feel sorry for any of my family, River." I say her name like a curse. To me, she'll always be Ri, short for Rialta. I don't know who this River person is.

"I don't feel sorry for them. I just don't like that they got twisted up in this whole mess."

"A mess you started." I pick up the knife and point it in her direction.

She sighs. "I was just protecting my family, the same as you."

I shake my head and begin to hack at the celery, but it's not enough to avoid the daggers she's shooting my way with her eyes.

"What are you making, anyway?" she asks.

I don't lift my head to look at her. "Chicken noodle soup. I thought it would help Rialta feel better."

She doesn't respond, but I feel a shift in her gaze. I don't want to look at her, but eventually, I can't resist. When I look up, I see admiration and love in her eyes.

"You're such a romantic, Hero."

"I'm not a romantic or a hero. Besides, I love chicken noodle soup. This is as much for me as it is for her."

"Uh-huh."

Great, now she thinks I'm already halfway in love with Rialta just because I'm making her this damn soup.

"Need any help?"

"No," I snap.

She sighs but doesn't say anything else. I keep chopping furiously, trying to remember how I got here and trying to find a way out of this situation.

The first step is to wait for word that Enzo and his family are safe. Until I get verification from Lennox and the others, I won't trust anything Corsi says. I need them safe; then I can figure out my predicament here.

I'm deep in thought when I feel pain rip through my index finger.

"Fucking hell," I curse as blood spills down my hand onto my wrist.

River is by my side before I even realize what happened. She grabs several paper towels and bunches them around my finger, applying pressure.

"The first aid kit is in the bathroom. Although, I should put a first aid kit in every room of this house. You two are the clumsiest people I know," she groans.

I frown. "You know I could lose my finger while you're making jokes."

"Drama queen. You're not going to lose your finger." She yanks on my hand, and I have no choice but to follow her to the bathroom.

The tiny, desperately needing renovation bathroom.

There's a small tub but no shower head. The toilet is smashed up right against the edge of the tub. The single sink looks like it hasn't been used in years, sitting atop a cabinet falling off its hinges. The rest of the house is mostly functional, except for this room.

"I know, I wish the bathroom was better, but this is the best I could find to rent without drawing suspicion," River says, applying pressure with one hand to my wound. She opens the cabinet door, sticking her hand inside to search for the supposed first aid kit.

"Found it!" Thankfully the first aid kit looks a whole lot newer than this bathroom. River sets the first aid kit on the sink before opening it. She quickly takes stock of the supplies before turning her attention back to my finger.

"Alright, let's see how bad it is."

She unwraps the paper towels now saturated with my blood. She cocks her head to the side as she examines my index finger.

"It's pretty deep. It could use stitches, but there aren't any in this first aid kit. I think I have some in the car—"

"Just bandage it. I'll be fine," I quip.

She raises an eyebrow as she yanks my arm under the sink and turns on the water to rinse the wound.

I wince as water pours over my cut.

She turns the faucet off and grabs an alcohol swab. "Don't scream in pain. Rialta is a deep sleeper, but she's not that deep of a sleeper."

"I won't scream," I sigh.

She rubs the alcohol on the wound, and I shift uncomfortably, wincing and biting my bottom lip to keep from making a sound.

When she stops, it's with a knowing grin. "Stings, doesn't it?"

"Nope," I lie. It burned like hell, worse than the initial injury.

She simply shakes her head. She pulls bandages out of the first aid kit and wraps them around my finger until the blood is no longer leaking down my hand. Then she finds a washcloth under the sink, wets it, and wipes the dried blood from my hand and arm.

"I still can't figure out how you cut yourself," she says.

I shrug, not really sure either. My hand must have slipped forward as the blade was coming down.

"You know you should really be more careful. You only have five fingers—none to spare. And you were always better at making me come with your fingers instead of your tongue. I wouldn't want you to lose your best feature," she teases.

"Seems like you'll be missing out either way unless Rialta is into an open relationship."

River's face drops as if, for a split second, she forgot. She forgot about Rialta. She forgot that we can never be together again if I marry her. She forgot everything and just let her guard down with me.

River clears her throat. "Well, you know how I feel about group sex, but I'm pretty sure Rialta doesn't like to share. You don't like sharing either. It's another reason why you two are perfect for each other."

I don't say anything. I try to look past her words. I try to understand the game she's playing.

She said she never had feelings for me. Everything between us was just a job. Her affections were all lies. She was just finding the best man for the job.

And yet...

I know the truth. She can't hide it from me any more than I can hide my feelings from her. Ri may be River, and I may have a monstrous past, but it doesn't stop how we feel about each other.

In another life, we'd be together. We wouldn't have lied, fucked up, or hurt each other. We would have just loved each other. Our love would be simple and pure.

It's clear in the way River looks at me that she still has feelings for me. And it's clear in the way my heart speeds in response to that look that I still love her. I may also want to rip River's throat out for lying to me, for hurting me, for pretending she doesn't love me, but then I'd desperately want to put all the pieces of her back together.

I want to yell at her to stop protecting others and, for once, just do what she wants. If she wants me, we'll fight every army in the world for our love.

But I know she can't stop protecting. It's one of the reasons I love her, and it's why she loves me. We protect those we love. We protect those who deserve our protection. We protect. We're both heroes, both protectors.

She's a bodyguard for her adopted sister.

I've always played the guard for my brother and his family.

I don't see a future without River in it. Rialta is great, and I'm sure I could learn to enjoy her company, but she's not River. She's been hiding away while River's been fighting to keep her alive.

There is only one River, and I want to give her the world. I just have to find a way for us to keep all the people we love safe before we can admit our love out loud again.

8

BECKETT

RIALTA SLEEPS THROUGH DINNER, and River and I keep our distance from one another after the incident in the bathroom. River's been on her phone, constantly monitoring the security system and cracking Rialta's door occasionally to check on her. She's been asleep every time.

I leave River in the living room while I slowly clean the kitchen with my bandaged hand. River found me some pain pills to pop if I want, but honestly, the ache in my finger is nothing. But I'm starting to run out of things to clean in the kitchen, which means I might have to interact with River.

I walk into the living room to see my worries are unfounded. River's snoring softly on the couch.

I smile down at her. When she's asleep, she can't argue with me. I like the arguing, but being able to look at her honestly is nice. Right now, I can look at her like I love her, and no one is here to stop me.

Her neck is craned on a pillow, and her feet are hanging over the edge of the small couch that isn't really large enough to sleep on.

This two-bedroom house is limited on sleeping arrangements.

399

River fits better than I would on the only couch, but I'm not going to let her wake up with a backache and a crick in her neck.

I decide to risk waking her and carrying her to the second bedroom. I'm not sure how much I'm going to sleep tonight anyway.

I try to be gentle as I lift River, but it's a little difficult with only one arm and a bandaged finger. She doesn't stir when I lift her; she must be exhausted.

I carry her into the other bedroom only to find the couch may have been better. I have to turn sideways to carry her around the tiny bed that barely fits in the small room.

As I lower her to the bed, River stirs. She blinks as I pull back the covers under her legs and try to cover her with them.

"What are you doing?" she snaps.

"Putting you to bed."

"You can't do that. I have to stay awake. I have to make sure Rialta is safe. I have to—"

"What's your plan? Never sleep? It's after one in the morning. You're not going to do a very good job protecting her if you don't get some sleep," I say.

"But I haven't set the alarm system yet. I haven't—"

"You need to sleep. I'll make sure Rialta is safe."

"But—"

"Stop. You chose me because you thought I would make a good husband for Rialta. You chose me because you thought I could keep Rialta safe. So trust me."

She frowns, debating further argument in her head, but her escaping yawn forces her eyes to grow heavy again.

"What about you? Don't you need sleep?"

"I'll sleep after you've gotten some sleep," I reply.

She can't keep her eyes open any longer, and they drift all the way closed. A moment later, she's snoring softly again.

I shake my head. "Always have to argue."

I pull the covers up over her and kiss her forehead. I want to kiss so much more, but I won't push my luck.

I tiptoe out of the room and close the door carefully behind me when I hear Rialta say, "River?"

"It's Beckett," I say softly back, turning and cracking Rialta's door open.

"Come in."

I walk into the room. "How are you feeling? Are you hungry?"

Her stomach growls before she can respond, and she giggles. "Yep, I should eat."

"I have chicken noodle soup. Is that okay?"

She nods.

"Do you want to eat in here or the living room?"

She stretches her arms over her head, causing her shirt to ride up and reveal her flat stomach. I look away, not wanting to see any part of her naked body.

"Living room, I think. I don't think I'll fall back asleep for a little while, and there's no TV in here."

I walk over to her side. "Is it okay if I carry you again? I don't think you should try to walk until you've had some food and liquids in your system. I don't want you to get dizzy and faint again."

"That's probably for the best," she agrees.

I scoop her up and carry her to the living room couch River was just on. It feels different carrying the two women. Carrying River is about doing something nice for her. She is more than capable of walking herself, but I want to do it anyway as an act of love. Carrying Rialta is about necessity. She feels fragile, weak, and young.

I should ask for River's real age because she seems decades older than Rialta. The gap is not in terms of looks or beauty, but rather wisdom and experience. Rialta feels like a young woman, still figuring out who she is. River knows exactly who she is.

I help Rialta onto the couch before heading to the kitchen to warm up the soup. I return a few minutes later and sit down on the couch next to her, holding the bowl out to her.

"I couldn't find a tray. Do you want me to hold it, or can you hold the bowl yourself?"

Rialta reaches out to grab the bowl, but her hands are shaking.

"No worries, I can help you," I say.

She smiles tightly. I'm not sure if she likes being helped or not. I set the bowl on my lap and lift a spoonful of the soup up to her lips.

She leans forward and takes a small sip. "Oh my god, that's delicious. I was expecting that stuff you get out of the can, but this is homemade. Did you make it?"

I nod. I don't tell her it almost cost me a finger.

Her eyes twinkle as she looks at me.

"I'm not that good of a cook, so I wouldn't get used to it."

She laughs. "Don't worry; I won't get used to anything when it comes to you."

"What do you mean?"

She shrugs. "My life is not my own, not really. I've never made any decision for myself. I've never been given a choice in how I'm to live my life. Whether we marry or not, the decision isn't mine. And even if we get married, men don't survive long in our world. I can't count on anything."

I frown. "You can count on me, no matter what happens. You can count on me always being there for you."

Her eyes water. "Thank you, Beckett." She puts her hand on mine. Her hand is warm and clammy, nothing like River's. But I can tell she feels something when she touches me. "You really are a good guy, aren't you?"

I clear my throat. "I'm not sure I would say that."

She lowers her lips, and I lift another spoonful to her mouth. She bats her eyelashes down at me while eating the spoonful. "I would," she says.

I help her eat the rest of the bowl of soup. We don't speak, but she keeps flashing me looks that make me uncomfortable. Her flirty looks tell me she'd have no problem marrying me.

I set the bowl down on the end table. "You want to go back to bed?"

"No, I'm not really tired."

I nod. "How about a movie?"

Her face lights up at that. "Okay, what movie?"

I pick up one of the remotes. I flick the TV on but realize we don't have an internet or cable connection. There's a stack of DVDs in the corner, though.

I pick up a couple of boxes. "Are you a rom-com girl or an action girl?"

"Whatever you want."

"No, you choose," I say insistently. I don't know what this woman's life was in hiding. I don't know why she feels she has so little choice in her life, but I can at least let her pick the movie.

I hold up two DVDs I'm pretty sure she'll like based on what limited information I have on her. There's a stack of about fifty behind me, but we'd spend the whole night picking a movie if she had that many choices.

She scrunches her nose, looking between the two. "The one with the woman in the wedding dress."

I grin, knowing she'd pick that one. I pop the DVD in and sit next to her on the tiny couch that leaves no room for me to not touch her.

Our shoulders graze each other, and our hips touch as the movie starts.

I have so many questions to ask her, so many things I want to know. Mostly about River, but I don't ask any of them. I'll have time to ask questions—at least, I hope I will.

Right now, it's just about Rialta recovering and us getting to know each other. There will be time for us to talk.

The movie starts, but not five minutes later, Rialta's eyes start drifting closed. She won't last long out here.

I don't say anything as her eyes close, and her heavy head falls to my shoulder. Her breathing is slow and deep; she's already asleep. I'll move her soon back to her room, but I let her stay for now. It gives me a minute to look at her without her staring back.

She's a beautiful woman, just like River. Her long dark hair cascades down her neck, her lips are a stark contrast against her pale skin, and her eyes are full of life, even though her life has been a hard one.

I don't know what her wants and dreams are. I know she's not used to making choices for herself, but I suspect she still has dreams. She's hidden them well, possibly even from herself.

She doesn't have a choice in her life. Neither do I. Neither does River. But I vow then to find a way to give us all a choice in our futures. It's the only way any of us will be happy.

My phone buzzes in my pocket. I carefully shift so as not to wake Rialta as I pull my phone out. It's a text from Lennox.

Lennox: Corsi hasn't found your brother yet, but there is no sign that Odette or the Retribution Kings have found them either. I'll let you know when I have more to report.

Me: Thanks. Keep me updated.

I put my phone back with a sigh. I want to know Enzo and his family are safe. I want to know they have the protection of Corsi and the entire mafia.

But I also know that as soon as that happens, Corsi will be calling on me to hold up my end of the deal, and I'm not ready to marry Rialta. I need more time to figure out a plan.

HIS FINGERS RAKE through my hair before he balls my hair into a fist and yanks back hard. His lips crash down on mine before I can cry out—mixing the pain and pleasure just the way I like it.

"You have to be quiet, baby. We can't wake anyone. We can't get caught," he says.

He's right; this is forbidden. It's wrong, but that doesn't mean I can control the sounds leaving my body, not when his fingers are slipping down my body between my legs. One pinch of my clit between his fingers, and I'm screaming again. The only thing keeping us from getting caught is his mouth pressed down tightly over mine.

I shouldn't want to get caught; I really shouldn't. But doing this while it's forbidden somehow makes it all so much hotter. I want to see how far we can push this.

We're currently hiding beneath the covers in the darkness of the night. I want to push us to the limits of our control. I want to drive him so wild with need and desire that he damns the consequences. That's how much I want him to want me; it's how much I want him.

His fingers continue to tease me. He pulls every drop of my wet desire from my body until I'm so close to the edge there is nowhere to go but over it.

He smirks against my lips, knowing how fast he can make me come.

It's okay; I'll give him this win. It's not really a win for him after all since I get to experience the first of many mind-blowing orgasms. And I'll make sure I win the next round.

Another circle of his finger over my clit, and I come undone—I lose it. I lose my mind to him. I scream. I cry. I go to some other-worldly place where he barely exists in my mind. I explode with pleasure.

When I finally come back down to earth and look at him, his expression is priceless.

"You enjoy that?" he asks, knowingly.

"Yes. Was I too loud?" I grin knowingly as well.

"Never."

His lips start to work their way down my body. But he doesn't get to have all the fun.

I push against his chest, needing to get to my favorite appendage of his between my legs. But damn does he want to kiss down my body; he barely budges.

I push harder—too hard, and suddenly he's a heap on the floor.

I giggle uncontrollably before jumping down on top of his naked body.

"You're ridiculous." He shakes his head.

"And you love me."

He flashes me a bright smile but doesn't say the words. He never says the words, and neither do I. The words are forbidden, given our situation. *How can we love each other when he's promised to another?*

I run my nails down his chest as punishment for not saying the words I'm so desperate to hear. I'll get him to say them. I'll get him to say he loves me so loud it wakes up the world; fuck the consequences.

He seems suspicious of me, but he wants me too badly to resist. *Can he resist not saying he loves me too?*

I'm betting no. I've been disappointed before, but I rarely lose. I'll hear those magic words by the end of the night.

I move my nails down his body until I get to his cock. It's already standing at attention, in desperate need of my touch. I drag my nails up his shaft, lighter than before but still enough to inflict a little pain for not giving me what I want.

He groans, but it's so low I can barely hear it, not loud enough for the house to hear.

"You can moan louder than that," I purr.

Then I lower my mouth over his cock, taking him all in at one time.

He gasps in shock.

I grin around his cock as I deep throat him and then run my tongue up and down his entire length.

His eyes roll back in his head, and his hand fists as he tries to hold onto what little control he has left.

So close, you're so close. Just let go. Give me one last good night. Just one night where you tell me the truth. One where I know you love me for sure. One where we've told each other all the truths, all the lies, and we still love each other.

I just need this once so I can survive a lifetime of not getting him.

That's what I keep telling myself. I only need one time to know this is completely real. A night of real feelings, not fake, where neither of us is holding back.

He's getting close, starting to lose control, starting to near admitting the truth.

His hand goes to my neck, trying to pull me off him, but I won't stop. I'll give him as many orgasms as I can tonight. This is just the first of many—the night is still young. Every orgasm I pull from him is a chance for him to admit the truth.

His growl is loud, ruthless, and powerful when he comes deep in my mouth—his warm, salty cum spills down my throat.

I release him, licking my lips as I do.

He breathes hard and fast. He was loud but still far too quiet.

His eyes open, locking on mine in worry.

But I'm not even close to being done with him.

I stand up and extend my hand to him, helping him to his feet.

But before I realize what he's doing, he tackles me onto the bed. My legs are spread wide, and his head is staring hungrily between them.

I hold my breath, knowing another orgasm is going to be the death of me. He knows it too. I guess I'll die from too strong a release.

Without warning, he dives between my legs, holding them open while his tongue devours me in delicious strokes. I'm so fucking sensitive already, and he's so damn good at what he does. I'm seeing stars way too soon.

And yet, he still hasn't said the words I'm desperate to hear. I might never get those words again. I might just have to accept this feeling—him worshipping my body like he loves me—may be the best I get.

"Beckett!" I yell as he makes me come again. "Beckett, Beckett, Beckett!"

———

"River!" I feel hands shaking my body, and I hear him speak, but I don't understand. "Ri! Wake up, Ri."

More shaking against my shoulders before I finally open my eyes. Beckett is over me, but he's not smiling like he should be. In fact, he's frowning.

Maybe I was too loud. Maybe I woke up the others. Maybe they know we still love each other. Maybe I did what was forbidden.

I don't say anything as he stares down at me with a mix of anger and confusion on his face. I look past his face and find him dressed.

I, on the other hand, am not. I'm in bed, covered in sweat, and I reek of sex. My hand is firmly between my legs, coated with my cum.

It takes me a minute to piece together what just happened. I had a sex dream about Beckett. None of it was real.

But now he's here.

Why is he in my room looking like a fucking god? A furious, hot god, but a god all the same.

Oh yea, probably because I called out his name.

"Something you want to tell me?" he asks.

I shake my head. "Nope."

I feel my cheeks heating. I'm sure they are a bright red shade of red. And I'm pretty sure he knows exactly what I was dreaming about.

"Are you okay?" he asks, his voice dropping, almost as if he understands, and he genuinely wants to make sure I'm okay. He's not scolding me for having the dreams. He's not upset that he's going to have to come up with some weird excuse to explain why I called out his name in my sleep to Rialta.

"I'm fine," I reply.

I'm anything but fine. I've been trapped in this nightmare for less than twenty-four hours, and I'm already failing.

He nods. His eyes roll down my bare chest, stopping where my nipples stick out from the top of the covers.

I grab the covers and lift them to cover my naked chest.

He turns his head to the floor next to my bed. I follow his gaze and find my clothes tossed haphazardly on the carpet.

He turns his attention back to me. He doesn't say a word, but he knows. God, he fucking knows exactly what I dreamed about.

He leans forward, taking a deep breath.

"What are you doing?" I ask.

Silently he lifts my right fingers to his mouth before wrapping his lips around them and sucking them clean.

It's fucking hot, seeing him lick my cum from my fingers. But it's also wrong, so fucking wrong. It feels like he participated in my sordid dream in the only way he could.

A second later, he turns and leaves the room without a word.

The second he's gone, I lift the covers over my head, like that will somehow ease my embarrassment and make things better.

Damn, damn, damn.

I want to scream, but I don't want to draw any more attention to myself.

I fucked up. I can't keep letting Beckett think I still want him. I can't give him any reason to doubt that he should be trying to fall in love with the real Rialta, not me. I'm a nobody. I'm an heir to no kingdom. I have no real money. I have no future except to protect the one woman I love as my sister.

And now, thanks to my stupid dream and stupid comment yesterday when I was tending to his finger, he thinks I care about him. Now I'm going to have to work twice as hard to convince him otherwise.

I throw the covers down and put my clothes back on, knowing I need to make an appearance out of my room sooner than later. And if I'm going to do my job, I need to go check in on Rialta.

I step out into the living room, but any worries about what happened in the bedroom are gone as soon as I see Beckett and Rialta together. They're sitting together on the couch, facing each other. Beckett has his arm around the back of the cushions, inches away from touching Rialta.

Worst of all, they're laughing—full out, hearty laughs. Beckett isn't faking either. They're real laughs.

"I would not like Die Hard; you're crazy," Rialta says.

"Tonight, we are watching it. No more of that bridesmaid shit."

"It was a great movie!"

"How would you know? You fell asleep five minutes into it," he replies.

Rialta opens her mouth to reply but laughs, having no comeback.

Beckett raises his eyebrows. "That's what I thought."

I walk past them, neither of them looking at me as I make my way to the kitchen. They have goo-goo eyes for each other, like two teenagers flirting with each other for the first time. It makes me sick.

No, this is a good thing. This is what I want. I want Beckett to like her and Rialta to like him. Just because I'm jealous doesn't mean anything.

I grab a mug and pour myself a stale cup of coffee.

Now what?

I can still hear them giggling together on the couch. Rialta is clearly fine. I pull out my phone to check the security cameras and any alerts from last night, but there is nothing.

"You stink!" I hear Rialta laugh again.

"So do you," Beckett retorts.

"Not as bad as you. You shower first. I can't stand the smell of you a second longer."

"Fine," Beckett grumbles. I hear him pad to the tiny bathroom, and I try to keep my thoughts from how good it felt to be in there with him yesterday. I wait until I hear the door close and the water turn on for good measure before making my way to the living room.

"Oh, River, you're awake," Rialta says with a bright smile.

I smile at her, too, knowing she doesn't mean anything by her comment at not noticing me, even though I walked right past her. She's just oblivious to the world sometimes.

"Did you sleep well?" I ask as I take up Beckett's spot on the couch. I quickly realize how close they really were to one another once I sit down.

"I did, thanks to Beckett."

"You're starting to fall for him?" I ask with a knowing smile.

Rialta shrugs. "He's a nice guy, that's all. I'm trying to get to know him. I wouldn't say I'm falling. I don't fall that easily."

My eyebrows shoot up, and I cough on my coffee. "Really? I seem to remember a girl who would fall for every guy. That was sort of the problem."

She laughs. "Maybe you're right. But you picked this one for me, so I can't go wrong this time, can I?"

I have nothing to say to that, so I just sip my coffee.

"You feeling okay?"

She nods tightly. "Just on edge after what happened. I still can't believe it."

"I know, I'm sorry. I'll make sure security—"

"It's not your fault. You did your job. It was the others who failed. That's part of the problem. You and father are the only ones I can trust." She pauses. "Well, now Beckett too."

Rialta studies my expression. "I can trust Beckett too, right?" she asks.

I nod. "Yes, no matter what happens, you can trust him. He's added you to his list of people he cares about, so yes, you can trust him."

"I have three people in my life I can trust; that's enough. I don't want anyone else on my security team—just you and Beckett."

"Rialta, I don't think that's a good idea. We need more people, or what happened yesterday could have been so much worse."

She shakes her head. "No. It's because of the others there was a problem. From now on, it's just the three of us."

Great...

The bathroom door opens, and Beckett steps out. We both turn, and I freeze. Beckett is standing, still dripping wet, in the tiniest towel I've ever seen wrapped around his waist, barely covering anything. He looks grumpy from the crappy arrangement until he sees my expression. Then he lights up like he couldn't have planned this better himself.

I look over at Rialta, and she's practically drooling at the sight of him. Maybe he's lighting up because of the way she's looking at him. He's happy his future wife finds him so attractive.

He is a very attractive man, even with his clothes on, but his nakedness takes it to another level. His muscles are built, the kind any hot-blooded woman wants to run her tongue over. He has a very defined V that cuts down beneath the towel. And there is a beautiful tattoo in the center of his chest. One that is most definitely going to have to change now that he belongs to the Corsi mafia and not the Retribution Kings.

He's absolutely beautiful.

I look over at Rialta, and she only has lust-filled eyes for him.

I know he's always concerned about what people think about his missing arm. But somehow, even the residual limb is all muscle and makes him even more attractive. He's a man that would risk everything for the woman he loves. It's built into his DNA, into every part of him. And he's going to be that man for Rialta.

"Eww, put on some clothes, Beckett," Rialta teases him. But the way she bats her eyes at him and licks her lips tells him exactly what she would do to him if I weren't here.

"I would, but I don't have any clean clothes," he says. When he speaks, he speaks to her, but he's looking at me.

"I packed a few things in a suitcase for everyone before we came. I left the suitcase in the car. I'll go get it," I say.

I hop off the couch so fast you'd think it was on fire. I take my time getting the suitcase, hating that I'm going to have to go back into the house and face them.

Thank god, at least I don't have a cock that can get hard and give me away at a time like this. Although, Beckett knows me well enough to know when I'm turned on.

Fuck, I'm not going to survive this.

I SLIP the black T-shirt that River packed for me over my head, hitting my elbow on the wall in the cramped bathroom. I curse as a jolt of pain radiates down my arm. I bite down and end up biting my tongue, spilling blood into my mouth, and causing more pain.

"Fuck," I groan a little louder than I probably should.

I hate it here, not just because this bathroom is tiny and the cramped house keeps finding small ways to injure me. I hate it because my heart is literally being tortured.

I'm so close to River, and yet, I can't touch her.

I wasn't sure if she wanted me. She even told me everything was an act. She was just doing her job, finding the best man for her sister. But that's not what it seems like.

River looks at me with a deep lust in her eyes. She watches me even when she should be watching Rialta. She worries about me. She tries to push me away but fails at every chance. And then this morning, she had a sex dream about me.

If it's just lust, then I'll give her up and marry Rialta. I'll save my family and learn to be a good Corsi leader. But if it's more than just lust, if it's love or something like love, then I have to know.

Because I'll...I don't know what I'll do, but I'm not sure I can give River up if she loves me too.

I spit blood into the sink, rinse the sink clean, and then stride back out into the living room. I plan on getting under River's skin to see how she reacts, but all I find is Rialta sitting on the couch alone.

"Where's Ri? I mean River." I'm still not getting used to calling her River. I'll probably always think of her as Ri, but Ri can just as easily be a nickname for Rialta as it is for River.

"She went for a run," Rialta says.

I raise my eyebrows. "A run? I thought she's supposed to stay here and protect you?"

Rialta grins. "Worried about me? Don't worry; River is keeping me safe. She's checking the grounds for signs of anyone. The security system is armed, and she left me here with you. She said I should trust you as much as her, so I'm perfectly safe."

I'm sure that's why she left, to check for intruders, not to get away from me. Her cheeks have been a bright red since I found her touching herself in her bed as she called out my name. She left because she's too chicken shit to face me.

I plop down on the couch next to Rialta. She looks at me schemingly. I can see her wheels turning with an idea.

"What are you thinking?" I ask.

"You know you're going to have to get rid of that tattoo before we get married."

It's the first time she's mentioned our wedding since our first ceremony resulted in her fainting. I almost choke on my saliva at how casually she said that like it was a forlorn conclusion.

"I do," I say. But whether thankfully or unfortunately, Corsi hasn't found and ensured the safety of my family yet, so the wedding can be held off for a little bit longer.

Her eyes glow mischievously.

"I don't like that look," I say.

She shrugs. "Get used to it. It's one of my favorite looks."

"You seem to be feeling better."

"I am. I can thank your excellent soup and caretaking skills for my speedy recovery," she says.

I shake my head. "I don't think I can take any of the credit. That's all you, but I'm just glad you're feeling better."

Even if no one will tell me why you fell ill in the first place.

The front door opens, and a sweaty River stands in the doorway. Her hair is pulled up in a high messy bun, her white shirt is covered in sweat, and her black leggings have sweat stains on them. She really pushed herself on her run to get that sweaty, probably trying to forget something.

She's panting hard when she enters but keeps her eyes on Rialta. She doesn't even acknowledge my presence. "How are you feeling?" she asks Rialta.

"Better than you," Rialta teases.

River playfully hits Rialta on the shoulder. "I'm fine, just out of shape."

"Or you pushed yourself too much because you're worried about something?" Rialta muses.

I agree with Rialta and turn my attention to River to see how she'll answer.

"I'm going to shower," River says through gasps for air.

"Perfect, then we can go," Rialta says, stopping River in her tracks.

"Go where exactly?" she asks.

"The closest tattoo shop. Beckett needs his tattoo fixed."

River looks at me with a glare.

"Don't look at me; this wasn't my idea," I say, throwing my arm behind the couch so I can watch the show that is their argument.

I'm still figuring out how the two of them interact together. It seems Rialta takes the role of a typical younger, spoiled sister who always gets what she wants. River takes on the responsible, older sister role, who can't say no to the younger, but I know River wants to keep Rialta safe too.

River snaps her head back to Rialta. "I'm not sure that's safe.

No one knows we're here, but if we venture into town, it will be harder to hide. Beckett can get his tattoo fixed later."

"I'm not going to hide away the rest of my life. I've tried that, and it wasn't any fun. I trust the two of you to keep me safe. Nothing will change after we're married. The three of us will live together, keeping each other safe, but I will not be locked away in a tower for the rest of my life. I'd rather live," Rialta says.

"The three of us will live together?" I ask.

"Yes, River will live with us as our exclusive bodyguard after we get married. I don't trust anyone but her, not even our father's men. She will be with us always."

River won't make eye contact with me, but I know it's true. We're expected to live together after Rialta and I are married. I've never thought of myself as one who would ever cheat once I make a vow, but with temptation that close, it's going to be near impossible for me to keep any wedding vows to Rialta. All the more reason this can't be the plan. If I do agree to marry Rialta, I'll be faithful to her, even if it kills me.

"Rialta, I know you want some freedom, but you have just started healing. Do you really think you're ready for a trip?" River tries reasoning with her.

"We're going. I'm in charge, and we're going. You can arrange the logistics. You decide the when and where and how, but we're going," Rialta stands and stomps off to her bedroom, slamming the door shut like a teenager demanding to out on a Friday night.

I look to River, who just shrugs. She's not going to argue with Rialta about it.

"We'll be safe about it. Wait until night to go. Find a tattoo shop hidden in the small town. It will be fine," I say.

River bites her bottom lip. "Nothing is ever safe and fine when it comes to Rialta. The bigger question is, why does she want to go so badly? Is this all really just about a tattoo?"

And before I can answer her, River heads into the bathroom and closes the door, leaving me wondering.

What is Rialta really up to?

———

We pull up to a suburban tattoo parlor a little after nine. We're not too close to the city, but also the town is not so small that anyone that sees us will be able to easily recall us since they get so few visitors.

River parks along the street about a block away from the parlor, and we all climb out of the car. Rialta immediately walks over to me, grabbing my arm like we're already a couple.

"So, what do you want to get to cover your tattoo?" Rialta asks.

I shrug. "It doesn't really matter to me, whatever the artist recommends."

"Really? So they could recommend getting a pink bunny to cover up that tattoo, and you'd be fine with it?"

"As long as the crown tattoo is gone, I'll be happy. If a big pink bunny tattoo is the best way to do that, then so be it. Although, I doubt that's going to be the best way to cover it up."

She laughs. "Probably not. Will you let me pick the tattoo then?"

"Sure," I say.

Rialta lights up and bounces as we walk to the tattoo shop. But I can't help but notice River's reaction. She trails behind us like a third wheel, listening carefully to our conversation. Perhaps the best way to learn River's true feelings is to act like I'm interested in Rialta. I should stop flirting with River and give Rialta all my attention to see if she cracks. That's my new plan.

I pull Rialta tighter against me as we walk to the front door.

"Shit, it's closed," Rialta says, slamming us to a halt.

"Darn. Oh, well, I guess we should head back," River says from behind us, almost like she planned for the shop to be closed.

"Or..." Rialta looks to River. "You could pick the lock."

"No," River says, turning around.

Rialta lets go of my arm and chases after River. She grabs her arm. "Please."

I can't make out Rialta's face, but I'm sure she's pouting and batting her eyelashes, pulling out all the stops to get River to help.

River sighs.

"Please," Rialta begs again.

"Fine." River walks past Rialta and toward the front door where I'm still standing. "Stand guard and let me know if anyone is coming," River says to me.

I raise my eyebrows. "You're really going to break into this tattoo shop?"

She rolls her eyes. "Like this is the worst thing I've done."

I pull Rialta to my side, afraid she's using this as a distraction to run off. I don't want to spend my night chasing a young woman.

"It's open," River says a couple of seconds later.

"That was fast. I'm impressed," Rialta says.

"You severely underestimate my skills if you thought that was going to take me very long," River says.

We all walk inside. None of us turn the lights on in case we draw attention to ourselves. The street is quiet, and there aren't many people out tonight, so us being in here shouldn't be a problem.

"We're in here, but one little problem. None of us are tattoo artists, so I don't know how you plan on covering my tattoo with another," I say.

River folds her arms across her chest as she looks to Rialta, waiting for her to answer.

"Well, I thought I'd do it," Rialta says.

River grins.

"Do you, uh, have any experience doing tattoos?" I rub the back of my neck nervously.

"No, I've never given a tattoo before."

"Then what makes you think you can give me a tattoo? Not only give me a tattoo but cover up the one I currently have?"

"My sketches are quite good, and I'm a fast learner. I can't imagine drawing and giving a tattoo is much different." Rialta grins at me, almost daring me to say no.

I spot River out of the corner of my eye, almost cracking up at the thought of letting Rialta tattoo me.

But we came all this way, and I'm not one to back down. If Rialta wants to give me a tattoo, then she can give me a tattoo.

I grab my shirt and pull it off over my head. "Go for it. You'll be the one that has to look at it every time I fuck you, so it'll be your fault if you screw it up."

Rialta gasps.

River freezes.

Now I'm the one smirking at the two of them.

"So, are we doing this or not?" I ask.

"Oh, we are definitely doing this," Rialta answers before walking into one of the rooms.

I follow after her.

"I'm going to stay out here to make sure we're not spotted," River says, staying in the lobby.

I frown, but I know I'm getting under her skin. Soon enough, I'll get River to talk to me.

Right now, I have to turn my attention to Rialta and her skills with a tattoo gun.

Rialta is standing next to a flattened chair. She taps it happily, waiting for me to lie down so she can go to work.

"I can't believe I'm doing this," I grumble under my breath.

She grins happily. "I can be very persuasive."

"Yea, that's it." This plan has nothing to do with me trying to drive the woman waiting in the lobby crazy with need for me.

I lie on the table and stare up at the bare ceiling while Rialta goes through the supplies and figures out what she needs. Before I know it, she's leaning over me, looking me in the eyes.

"Do you trust me?" she asks, looking sincere and heartfelt.

That's what this is to her—a moment of trust. She needs me to trust her as she trusts me.

She holds the tattoo gun in her hand. She drew no stencil. She hasn't done any practice runs with the gun. This is going to be a disaster, and yet, when I look into her eyes, I do have faith in her—far more faith in her than I probably should.

"Yes, I trust you," I reply.

"Good, don't move."

Slowly, she lowers the tattoo gun to my chest. The familiar prick of the needle and buzzing of pain lull me into a trance.

Rialta's tongue sticks out of her mouth, and her brows furrow as she concentrates on what she's doing. She doesn't talk or even look at me.

I close my eyes as she works, taking a short nap and feeling calmer than I have in days with her working on the tattoo on my chest. I'm not even sure I care what it turns into; I'm just happy for this peaceful experience.

"Beckett," I hear her soft voice.

I open my eyes, and Rialta is grinning down at me. "I'm finished. Want to see it before I bandage it?"

I nod, although maybe it would be better if I never saw it.

She holds out her hand to me and helps me off the chair. There is a full-length mirror in the corner of the room. I take a deep breath, preparing myself for anything before I look up.

My eyes pop wide, and my mouth falls open as I stare at myself in the mirror. I can't believe what I'm seeing, and I can't believe that Rialta isn't a certified tattoo artist that does this for a living. It's incredible; it really is.

I wouldn't call it a cover-up; it's more of an addition to the original tattoo. A second crown fit for a princess has been added. Details on both crowns make them look like they were done at the same time. It's very clear that the two are meant to be equals—equal strengths, equal in power, equal in love.

"River! Come look!" Rialta shouts giddily.

I'm not sure if River is going to come, but a moment later, she appears at the door. She doesn't come close enough to see all the intricate details, but she can see what the tattoo has become. She can see the additional crown.

"It's beautiful. You're very talented, Rialta," she says, forcing her words to grow louder than the whisper she started speaking in.

"Thank you, I know," Rialta says proudly.

"It really is amazing," I agree as River walks back out of the room.

Rialta takes my hand. "You really like it?"

"I do. I really do."

I study the crown closer, and I see the name etched across it—Ri.

Ri for Rialta or Ri for River?

I want to ask Rialta what she meant or if she forgot to finish the name on the crown, but I'm terrified of her answer.

She helps me cover the tattoo with petroleum jelly and a bandage to protect it. But that doesn't stop me from remembering every line of the tattoo and River's face when she saw it. She was in awe of how beautiful it looked but hated what she thought it represented—Rialta and me.

I'm not sure what it represents yet. I'm not sure if Rialta did it intentionally, keeping it open to both of us, or if she just ran out of room to fit her entire name. I'm not sure Rialta even realizes there's a connection between River and me. If she did, would she still want to marry me?

We leave the tattoo shop and head back to the house, returning with more questions than answers.

I FORCE my feet to move faster. Faster and faster and faster until my body can barely keep up with my feet. The wind beats at my face, and my heart struggles to pump enough blood through my body to keep me going. My lungs burn, and my legs feel numb from running so hard.

My foot slips on uneven pavement, and I fall to the ground, my wrists catching my weight. I pant hard into the ground, knowing I can't keep doing this to myself every day. I have to face reality.

My reality is the man I love is falling for my best friend. I'm going to have to get used to seeing them together every day. I need to adjust to thinking of them as a couple. Rip off the bandaid and just deal with the pain—the sooner I do that, the sooner this ache in my chest will start to heal.

Last night damn near killed me, though. Listening to the sound of the tattoo gun, knowing she was marking his skin permanently. She was repeatedly touching his chest. He put his complete trust in her. It was too much for me to handle.

And then when Rialta called me in there to see the work she did, and I saw the crown she added to represent her...I lost it. I wanted to cry, to scream, to throw something, but I couldn't because Beckett isn't mine. He never was. He was always hers.

It only got worse on the drive home. I drove while Beckett and Rialta flirted the whole way back, talking about everything from their favorite foods to movies to sex positions. I wish I had headphones to block them out, something I'll definitely remember to carry with me from now on.

And then, when we got back, they immediately went to her bedroom together.

TOGETHER!

I just stared frozen from the front door for a few minutes, waiting for Beckett to come back out. He had to be just tucking her in and making sure she had everything she needed for the night, right? But after thirty minutes of me just staring at the door, it became obvious he wasn't leaving that room.

I eventually walked to my bedroom and saw their lights were, in fact, off, but I could hear them on the other side of the door. I don't know if it was my overactive imagination or reality, but I swear I heard them kissing and moaning together.

I ran into my room, slammed my door, and wore headphones the rest of the night. But I didn't sleep.

I just kept playing images of the two of them together in my head. Of their wedding. Of them kissing in front of me. Of him carrying her up the stairs of their brand new house to go fuck her in every room and on every surface. Of the day she finds out she's pregnant.

It all played like a horror movie in my head. Every piece of their perfect life, with me by their side, watching and protecting and enduring it all.

I push myself off the ground and wipe the dirt on the sides of my leggings. But this is what my entire life has been for. This is what I wanted. I wanted to give Rialta her happily ever after. She deserves it after the life she's lived.

But don't I deserve it too?

I don't answer that. I don't compare my life to Rialta's. We've both been through a lot. The difference between her and me is that I know I'm strong enough to handle anything. Rialta is strong too, but she doesn't believe in her strength—not yet, at least. I know I'm strong enough. And like I've endured countless pains before, I'll endure losing Beckett.

I take my time walking back to the house, hoping the happy couple is awake and hopefully not too into public displays of affection this morning. At least, I hope they won't kiss and get all handsy when I'm around.

Maybe I should have some rules about what they can and can't do around me? If they want me to continue to be their security guard, that's the least they could do.

I open the door, and, to my relief, they are both dressed. Rialta is sitting on the couch, and Beckett is in the kitchen. They aren't kissing. They aren't even touching.

"Have a good run?" Rialta asks.

"Yep." I don't give her any details of what I've been thinking or any rules I might need them to abide by, not yet. The truth is I want them both to be happy, and if being together makes them happy, then I can be happy for them.

Maybe.

Eventually.

I'm working on it.

I sigh.

"I'm going to shower, but what's the plan for today? Movie day? Going for a walk? Baking some sugary treat?" I walk toward the bathroom.

Beckett walks back into the living room, carrying two thermoses of what I assume is coffee. He looks to Rialta, waiting for her to speak. It seems the plans for today have been decided without me.

"Actually..." Rialta runs her hands through her dark brown hair before twirling the ends around her fingers nervously.

I look to Beckett, seeing if he will give anything away, but he's stone-faced.

"Actually, what?" I ask.

"Actually, Beckett and I need some time alone. We are going to have lunch together."

"You're going to have lunch together where? I can drive you and keep a lookout outside the restaurant. Some places will be safer than others."

"No, we—just Beckett and I—are going to have lunch. We are going to drive ourselves. You can have the day off," Rialta says with barely-mustered confidence.

"The day off?" I raise an eyebrow. I haven't had a day off since I took this job when I was five. I don't even know what a day off means.

"Yes, a day off. I know this place isn't that glamorous, and there isn't much to do, but you can watch movies, eat any of the food Beckett cooked, take a nap, go for a walk, whatever you like," Rialta says.

I frown and look to Beckett. "Are you okay with this? You'll do whatever it takes to keep her safe?"

Beckett looks me dead in the eyes, but I still can't read him, not really. "Yes, I'll keep Rialta safe; you have my word."

Then he walks over to where Rialta is seated. She stands, taking one of the thermoses from underneath his arm, and then hooks her arm through his.

"When will you be back?" I ask, still not sure I should let them out of my sight. What would Vincent say?

I don't work for Vincent, not anymore. I work for Rialta.

They walk toward the door. "Before midnight," Rialta grins.

I roll my eyes. She always loved Cinderella.

Then they're gone, and I'm left alone in the tiny house, clueless if I've just been played and they're never coming back.

Worst yet, I'm pretty sure this is the moment I've been dreading. This is when they talk and agree to get married if they aren't disappearing to go elope right now. This is the moment they fall in love. This is the moment my heart shatters completely.

I sink to my knees on the floor as tears begin to fall. I could still stop them. I could go after them. Tell Beckett the truth—I love him, and I can't give him up.

But I won't. I can't. My entire life would be for nothing if I did.

I don't regret falling in love with him. No matter how much this hurts, I won't regret that. Loving him has reminded me that even though I am nothing more than a protector and a guard, I should find something I love beyond my work, and I deserve to be loved. And I'll find that love again.

RIALTA and I rush to the car to get away from that awkward exchange with River as soon as possible.

"So, where are we going?" I ask as soon as I'm settled in the driver's seat.

Rialta looks around. "Somewhere far enough that River can't see us, but close enough that we can come back if we need to in a hurry. Just somewhere nice to have a picnic."

I back out of the driveway and head down the gravel road until the house is no longer visible. I spot a nearby small hill overlooking much of the fields around and decide it would be a good spot to have lunch.

"You shouldn't have worried River like that," I scold as we drive.

Rialta looks at me with sad eyes. "I know, but it was necessary."

"Why?" I turn to look at her as I bring the car to a stop.

She shakes her head and gets out.

I follow suit, taking our thermoses from the car's center console. Rialta opens a back door where she pulls out a bag of sandwiches and fruit she packed out along with a blanket for us to sit on. Then we march up the small hill, spread out the blanket, and arrange our picnic.

We eat our sandwiches and drink our coffee, the whole time I'm burning with questions for her, but I resist. I remain patient, waiting to see if this is the moment she talks openly with me.

"Thank you for not asking," she says, finally.

I look up at her, almost dropping my thermos of coffee in my lap. I swallow hard, waiting to hear something of the truth, something of the pieces I've been missing.

"Did you know I'm not an only child?" she asks.

I shake my head. I'm guessing most of what I'm about to find out I don't know or I know very little about.

"I have an older brother and older sister—well, had," she says sadly.

I want to apologize for her loss, but it's best I remain quiet and let her talk. I don't want to scare her, and I'm pretty sure the only reason she's talking now is because I've given her so much space.

"My brother died when he was still a baby. My sister made it to three before she was killed, along with my mother."

My eyes widen. I had no idea she had siblings.

"We never figured out who killed them. If it was an internal job, someone who worked for my father, or one of our enemies wanting to see the Corsi mafia end and my father suffer as much as possible."

She takes a deep breath.

"I was just a baby when my sister and mother died. After that, my father never let me out of his sight," she continues.

I can understand his need for control after losing so many close to him. I wouldn't let her out of my sight either. But even that doesn't guarantee her protection; it doesn't guarantee her life.

"We were at a playground one day. I loved the slides. My father would spend hours with me at that playground, helping me up the stairs and then catching me going down the slide. He was amazing like that.

"But on one particular day, he got a phone call. He wasn't at the bottom of the slide when I came down. A strange man I'd never met was. My father was only gone a second, but it was enough for the man to shoot me once in the stomach."

Rialta lifts her shirt, revealing a scar to the left of her belly button.

"I don't know why I didn't blackout, but I didn't. My father came running, phone to his ear. He was already on the phone calling for an ambulance and probably calling on all of the mafia to find the man and kill him for what he did. As he was running across the parking lot, a girl found me first. She was maybe a year or two older than me if that—dark long hair and big deep eyes that held more wisdom than my frail body understood.

"Without hesitation, that girl took off her sweatshirt and applied pressure to my wound. She talked to me and told me it was going to be okay. She kept me awake by asking me all sorts of questions like my favorite color, favorite toy, and if I had any siblings. She kept me talking. She kept me conscious."

Rialta smiles. "That girl saved my life. When my father approached, he froze when he saw me. He thankfully had already called an ambulance, but when he saw me injured, he just froze. He couldn't help me. The pain and trauma overwhelmed him. But that little girl, she could help."

"River," I say, already knowing it was her.

She nods. "Yes, River saved my life that day. She stopped the bleeding until the paramedics got there. My father wasn't sure what to do. The girl was at the park by herself, and she was the only witness to what happened. So my father told her to get in our car with him, and together they followed my ambulance to the hospital. I'm pretty sure River asked him a million questions too, and that kept him from having a complete breakdown. She saved him too."

She saved her. She saved him. She saved me. *River saves people, but who saves her?*

"After that, River never left my bed in the hospital. We became best friends. We were inseparable. We shared everything together, and most of all, we helped each other heal. River grew up in foster care. She never knew who her parents were. And at the time, her foster father was beating and neglecting her. So she was more than happy to spend all of her time with me, even though Father rarely let me out of his sight."

I curse under my breath. They both went through so much.

"The attacks on my life kept coming. None were as close to succeeding as that first one, but they were enough to scare my father after what he'd been through. We rarely left the house. River started tasting my food before I ate it to make sure it wasn't poisoned. If I had to go to the doctor for an appointment, River would dress up as me and go out with one of the guards as a diversion." Rialta looks down like she's disgusted by what her father did and the risk River took even though she was only a child.

"There was a second bad attack. My wound had only just healed, and Father was afraid of his own shadow. He couldn't think straight. I was kidnapped, taken right under his nose," she goes on.

Rialta looks out at the vastness in front of us. She is speechless for a few minutes, most likely reliving whatever horrors happened to her while she was kidnapped. It's not my place to ask. If it helps her to share the memories, then she will. If not, then I don't need to know.

"It was horrible. It took my father three days to find me. When he did, he'd had enough. He wasn't going to take any more chances. He wasn't going to lose the last of his family." She wraps her arms around her chest in a hug. I would offer to hug her myself, but I'm not sure she'd want that.

"He sent me away to live with strangers, people outside this dangerous world. He wouldn't contact them or me until I turned twenty-one. Until I was old enough to reclaim my title and place in the mafia. Until I was old enough to marry and bear children. He hoped he could unearth the people responsible for all the attacks before then, but he never did. He never figured it out. He never came to get me."

"Until now," I say.

She nods. "All that time, River pretended to be me. He told her I was dead. Then he slowly trained her and hypnotized her to make her think she was actually me. Father only told one other person—Kek. He turned her into me. He took her out of foster care, although I don't think he ever technically adopted her. He got her out of that bad situation, gave her a future, but it was a future that was never truly hers."

She looks at me with tears in her eyes. "Father knew she was stronger than me. He knew she could survive when I couldn't in this world. He chose her, and she agreed."

Tears fall now, and I can't stand to not hold her. I move closer slowly, so slowly it's almost painful, waiting for any sign of her pushing me away, but I find none.

I hold my arm out to her, waiting to see if she wants to be held. She falls into my shoulder, and I wrap my arm around her, letting her cry.

"I'm a horrible person. I let River risk her life, her entire fucking life, for me," she wails.

"No, you're not horrible. Your father made that choice, not you. You were just a kid. And River was happy to take on the role. She played the role well."

Too well.

"She should have stayed Rialta and let me go live elsewhere. I shouldn't have come back," she says.

"Why? What do you mean?"

"The wedding. One of the guards handed me a glass of wine before the wedding, and I drank it without question. That's why I passed out. That's why my heart stopped. That's why they pumped my stomach. I was poisoned."

"That's not your fault," I say.

"In the years I've been gone, River has successfully avoided being poisoned, or shot, or kidnapped."

"Well, that's just not true. All of those things have happened to her too. She survived them, same as you."

"She's stronger. She should be Rialta Corsi."

I frown. "She's only stronger because she's been trained her whole life to be. No one can be Rialta Corsi better than you. You know why?" I put my finger under her chin, lifting it. "Because you are the only Rialta Corsi. And she's the only River Corsi. You are both strong ass women who can defeat anyone. You are stronger than this. You both are."

She leans into my chest. "I don't feel that way. I feel weak."

"That's because you're still recovering. You're still figuring out who you are after pretending to be someone else for so long. But I'll be by your side, and so will River. Together we will figure out how to survive this and accomplish whatever goals you set. We will figure out how to get your strength back."

She nods into my shoulder.

I hold her for a long time, so long that the sun begins to set and a chill creeps over us. We both needed the time to process everything she said.

Where has she been this whole time? What was her life like? Did she have a good life before she was brought here? I have a million questions, but she's spilled so many secrets today that I can't possibly ask anything just to satisfy my own curiosity.

We need to get back to the house soon, so we don't freeze to death and keep worrying River. I can't wait any longer to ask the most necessary question, though.

"So why marry me? You came back to reclaim who you are. Why marry a man you barely know, someone your father orders you to marry?" I ask.

"For one, the mafia won't accept a female as their leader. My father won't live forever, and he needs an heir."

"So find someone on your own, someone you could love. Find

your match in every way. You're a beautiful, intelligent, strong woman. You'll be able to find a man easily."

"You're someone I could love," she says in almost a whisper.

I suck in a breath. I don't know how I can respond to that. She's someone I could love too if it wasn't for my heart already belonging to another. But it's not going to be helpful to tell her that.

"Besides, I don't just need a good husband. I need a man who is strong and brave and fearless. I need a man who is fair but also a bit ruthless. A man who can take over the mafia, not a fairytale prince who can fall in love with me."

She's right. I still think she could find that man on her own, but I don't say anything.

"War is breaking out everywhere, or so I've been told. Order is needed. The Corsi mafia needs to regain power. They need to be feared once again. Our marriage could end so much death," she says.

"I don't see how us getting married solves anything."

She grins. "That's because you've never held real power before. You've never had the power of the mafia behind you. My father has done a lot of things right, but recently, he's made a lot of mistakes. He doesn't have the full support of the mafia. They're looking for new leadership—fresh, young blood willing to change things while also keeping with their traditions. They want to see that my father has arranged a marriage for me and married me off. That is the mafia way, after all."

"I'm not mafia, though. I'm not sure they'll accept me."

"They will. They've seen you fight in the games. They've seen how fearless you are. You're the brother of Enzo Black. They fear that and respect you because of it."

I nod, understanding. There is no way out of this. I'm going to have to marry her to save my family, to end the war, to protect Rialta.

I just hope I can find a way to free River in the process. It's not fair to her to stay our main protection. River has given enough, and

I know she still loves me. I have to stop trying to get her to admit it. I need her to let me go, so I can let her go. I need to break her heart completely once and for all so she'll leave and restart her own life.

"We also have to get married for her," she says.

I snap my head to Rialta, not understanding.

"River has given everything for this. She's literally given up her childhood through young adulthood. She risked her life. Everything she's been through, she went through to protect me. To protect my future. To give me a life once I came back. To ensure I was well protected by my husband. We have to get married—only then can she be free," Rialta says.

I stare at her, the truth of her words sinking in. We have to get married.

Rialta pulls back to look completely at me but remains close. My initial reaction is to want to back away because she's too deep in my personal space, but I only unwrap my arm around her shoulders.

She leans in and presses her lips ever so softly against mine. Her lips just barely graze mine. Her bottom lip trembles a little against mine as she kisses me. She's scared to death.

I put my hand over her heart and can feel how wildly it's beating.

"I won't hurt you. You don't need to be afraid of me. You don't need to rush anything you aren't ready for, even after we get married. We'll take everything slowly. And even after we're married, if you want out, I'll find you a way out," I say, wishing I could find one for me too.

She presses her lips harder against mine, deepening the kiss without opening her mouth. I'm thankful for her hesitance because I'm not ready to push anything further than this either. I have no idea how I'm going to be a good husband to her. I can protect her, I can be her hero, but her husband? I don't know how I'm supposed to want her, love her, fuck her.

"I know you won't hurt me, but I can't make the same promise to you," she says.

I stare at her, unsure of what she means. All I know is that I won't put anything past a Corsi, even a woman I've been looking at as meek and timid. I won't underestimate her. If she says she might hurt me, then I'll be ready for it.

I TRACKED THEM. I couldn't resist. I have a tracker on the car, but I should have put a damn tracker on Rialta. The girl is going to be the death of me. If she wants me to protect her, then she has to stop leaving without me.

I watch on my phone, trying to figure out how I'm going to get to them. I need a car. Arranging a rental car out here is going to be a pain in the ass, but I'll do what I have to.

The dot stopped about a mile from here. *Did they run into car trouble?*

If they did, I'm sure Beckett can handle it. Or they can walk back easily. But I can't stand to just sit here inside all day. I need to find out if they're okay. The other possibility is that they've been attacked.

I grab my gun and running shoes, and then I'm out the door. My legs cramp up immediately. I've already run today, and my legs don't want to do it again, but I force them forward.

I run through the empty fields, and then suddenly, I spot them. The car isn't broken down. They haven't been attacked. They just decided to have a damn picnic without telling me that's what they were doing.

I'm going to kill Rialta for doing this to me. Beckett too.

I stop at the bottom of a hill and watch them for a while. They smile at each other. They laugh. And then things turn serious. She's telling him about her past. I'm sure one of them will propose. They'll agree to get married for real this time.

I can't watch that part, so I turn around and run back to the house.

I find a tub of cookie dough ice cream in the freezer and bring it to the couch. I eat my feelings while watching action movies, sparing my heart from any rom-coms right now.

After two movies and an entire pint of ice cream, they still aren't back. I stare at my phone and see they haven't moved from the spot. There's no reason to go looking for them, so I curl up on the couch and wait for them to return.

And wait and wait and wait.

I wish I could sleep. I wish I could run away from this life. I don't know what I'd do, this is the only life I've ever known, but I'd do something different. Become a doctor or lawyer—they both protect people without sacrificing themselves.

Suddenly, the door opens.

I close my eyes tight, not wanting to deal with them tonight. It's late, and I don't want to hear the news. I'm sure I'll be able to face reality with just one more night of sleep.

"Shhh, she's asleep," Rialta says, giggling.

I'm not sure if Beckett believes that or not. He could always see through me.

I squeeze my eyes tighter and slow my breathing, so it appears I'm asleep. But then I hear a sound—the sound of saliva being exchanged.

I should keep my eyes closed. I really shouldn't look, but I like to punish myself. I open my eyes just a sliver, and that's when I see them—kissing.

Both of their eyes are closed, their heads are tilted to deepen the kiss, her tongue pushes deep into his mouth, and his hand rests on her hip.

My heart should be used to breaking by now, but once again, it shatters. There is no denying their feelings are growing, no denying they are falling in love.

Rialta opens her eyes just the slightest as her tongue dips deeper inside his mouth.

I snap my eyes closed, hoping she didn't see me peeking. I don't want her to know that I have feelings for him. He's going to be her husband, not mine. She doesn't need to know I'm madly in love with him. I don't want her to feel any guilt for loving him.

They slowly, painfully, make their way to her bedroom and close the door. Once again, they share the bedroom. I have my headphones ready, so I can ignore what happens once they enter the bedroom.

And once again, I don't sleep.

———

"You look like hell," Beckett says, standing over me and offering me a cup of coffee.

I sit up and take the coffee. "Thanks."

"Did you sleep at all?"

I avoid answering by sipping my coffee.

"Did you?" I reply.

He grins. "I got excellent sleep, thank you."

"What has you in such a chipper mood this morning?"

"It's time to leave," he says.

I frown. "What does that mean?"

"Lennox texted me early this morning. Corsi found my brother and his family and ensured their safety."

"Oh." I take another sip of my coffee as I process his words. "So that was the deal with Vincent? He protected your family and you..."

"And I marry his daughter," he finishes my heartbreaking sentence.

I nod, my stomach in knots. There was a tiny part of me that hoped the deal he concocted with Vincent had something to do with me, but now I know for sure it didn't. I'm not his family. I'm not the one he loves, not anymore. The bad thing about a man who can fall in love easily is that he can just as easily fall out of love.

I stare at Beckett, and he stares back. There is so much to say between us, so many feelings needing to be taken back. As much as he and Rilata needed an afternoon just to talk, we too need to talk.

I open my mouth to suggest that, even just twenty minutes, when Rialta runs out of the bedroom with a huge smile on her face. Her grin is the kind of smile and dreamy look on her face that says I orgasmed a million times last night.

Kill me, just kill me and put me out of my misery.

"Who is ready for an elopement?!" she squeals, grabbing onto Beckett's arm. She grabs his face and kisses him.

His face is a little shocked at her brazen kiss, but he doesn't resist. He lets her kiss him. I can tell by the bobbing in his throat that he's enjoying it.

They both turn to me.

"Eloping, huh? Congratulations. Are we headed back to a church or—"

"No, we're headed to Las Vegas! That's where you go to get eloped. I never wanted a big church wedding. I always wanted something fun and spontaneous," Rialta says.

I narrow my eyes at her, completely confused. A church wedding with the big princess dress is exactly what she's always wanted. I asked her before we arranged the first wedding. And it's what the mafia would expect of her. It's what Vincent would expect.

I don't know what's changed her mind or if Vincent knows, but I'm guessing he won't care too much as long as they're married.

"Let's go to Vegas then," I say.

AS RIVER DRIVES and Rialta sleeps against my chest in the backseat, it feels like River is our own personal chauffeur instead of someone special to both of us.

River doesn't seem to mind, though. In fact, I think she'd prefer to keep as much distance between us as possible. If there was a partition in this car, I'm sure she would have happily raised it. As it is, I don't think she's looked in the rearview mirror once. She's definitely avoiding us.

But I'm selfish, and I want her gaze. I want her eyes on me one last time before I get married again. I want all of her. I should be focused on breaking her heart, ripping it to shreds so she can finally start to heal, though.

My own heart is throbbing at the idea. It's wondering how it's supposed to survive when I long ago gave it to River. If I destroy her heart, I'm destroying my own. My heart isn't meant to survive anyway.

I want nothing but a black hole left in my chest when I'm done. I want River to move on, to forget about me and Rialta and the Corsi mafia. I want her to go find a new life. I want her to find something that makes her happy because there is nothing left here for her.

Returning my thoughts to my phone, I resume staring at the photo Lennox sent me that shows Enzo, Kai, Langston, Liesel, Zeke, and Siren glaring at the camera. They're clearly not happy, but they're safe on a private jet, ready to take them anywhere in the world. I don't know where they're headed, and I don't want to know; I just want them to be safe, and away from the war my ex-wife started.

We drive all day—River ignoring us, Rialta asleep on my shoulder, and me staring at my family.

We finally pull up to a private airfield. The plan is for us to take a private jet to Vegas. I'm guessing Corsi knows, or we wouldn't have been able to get a plane, and that makes me nervous as hell. It means I can't back out, or he'll put a bullet in my or my family's head.

I'm not sure if Rialta has figured that part out yet.

River stops the car in front of one of the planes she seems to recognize. Finally, she looks in the rearview mirror. Rialta still hasn't woken up. River doesn't say a word, but her eyes tell me everything I need to know. If I don't want to do this, let her know now, and she'll get us out of this, no questions asked.

I think of the photo I've been staring at all day. I think about River. I can't fail either of them; I can't risk any of their lives.

I give a quick shake of my head and lean down toward Rialta to give her a gentle kiss on the forehead, still meeting River's gaze. She gets out of the car and slams the door shut, waking Rialta immediately.

"We're here. You ready for this?" I ask.

Rialta stretches and looks around. "Where's River?"

"She's on the plane already, probably checking it out to make sure it's safe and ready for us."

"Hmmm." I expect Rialta to lean in and kiss me like she has done now about a half dozen times. Each kiss is startling. I have to remind myself each time the kiss is appropriate. I have to remember each kiss is just the beginning of my future. Each kiss is better than kissing Odette, but it's nothing like kissing River.

I brace myself for another kiss I'm going to have to pretend is pleasant, but Rialta opens the door and steps out.

Huh?

I get out after her and retrieve the one packed bag between the three of us from the trunk. We're going to need to get new clothes in Vegas.

I chase Rialta up the jet's stairs. And when I turn into the main cabin, I suddenly wish I could be anywhere else.

While I was expecting that Corsi might make an appearance, I wasn't expecting him, several of his men, and Lennox, Hayes, and Gage.

"We have quite a crowd," I say.

Corsi just looks at me sternly. He doesn't have to speak; I already see the threat in his eyes. If I don't marry Rialta this time, I'm a dead man. Or at least, someone I care about will die.

I nod as I push past him. It's not like it was my fault I didn't get married last time. Rialta was the one who passed out, not me. And I didn't have anything to do with poisoning her.

Lennox has an empty seat next to him, with Gage and Hayes sitting directly behind him. Rialta and River sit together, so I leave my bag with one of the attendants and slump into the chair next to Lennox, happy to not have to play the doting fiancé for a few hours.

"Do you know what you're doing?" Lennox leans over and asks me.

"Not a clue."

I tilt my head back and close my eyes, knowing I'm not going to figure it out here with everyone watching us so closely. It's looking more and more like I'm going to marry Rialta. I'm going to break River's heart. I'm going to convince the guys to take her as far away as possible. That's the only way to keep her safe.

The flight is mostly uneventful. Everyone sticks to their groups —Corsi with his men, me with mine, and the girls at the back.

When we land, Corsi and his men disappear without a word. "That was strange," Lennox whispers.

I nod. *What is Corsi up to?*

I don't know why he would agree to fly us all to Vegas when we could have just as easily gotten married in Chicago. Maybe his daughter has him wrapped around her finger more than I thought.

When we walk off the plane, a large SUV and a driver are waiting to take us to our hotel. The guys and I climb in the back first while we wait for the attendants to load our luggage and the girls to get on.

"What are you guys doing here?" I ask.

"We figured you would need us for whatever the plan is," Hayes says, patting my shoulder from the row behind me.

"I needed you to protect my family," I say.

"They're safe," Lennox says.

"How do you know that if you aren't with them?"

"We have them on surveillance. They're safe. Corsi has some of his best men protecting them," Gage says.

"You mean holding them hostage," I growl.

The guys are silent until Gage pipes up a moment later. "Corsi will keep his word; you know that. And the second you marry Rialta, you'll have power. You will be able to have some pull with the men. Corsi won't threaten that by hurting them in any way."

"I know, but..."

"But what if you don't marry Rialta?" Lennox asks.

I don't answer. I can't consider that option—it would ruin too many lives. I have to marry her.

Lennox looks to the other two, and they all hold their tongues. No one has any answers for me.

River and Rialta climb into the SUV. River doesn't make eye contact with any of them, but Rialta turns around in the front seat and looks at all of us.

"I'm Rialta Corsi. I don't think we've ever been formally introduced."

"I'm Lennox."

"Gage."

"Hayes."

She waves cutely at them all. "Are we ready for one hell of a wedding weekend?"

None of the guys respond.

She laughs. "Don't worry; I'll get you guys excited soon enough."

"That sounds ominous," Lennox leans over and says.

"You have no idea," I say back.

Rialta insists that the radio be turned on full blast as we drive to our hotel on the strip. She dances around in her seat and even gets River to smile and go along with her at one point. I can't keep my eyes off River—especially when she smiles. All I want is to see her smile, to see her genuinely happy.

Upon arriving at the hotel, I realize I have no idea what the room breakdown is going to be or what tonight or tomorrow holds. The night is still early; the sun has just set. How many hours do I have left before I'm a married man again?

I'm pretty sure I hate the idea of marriage at this point. I'd be happy to never get married again.

River's eye catches mine as she climbs out of the car, and I know it's not true—I'd marry her in a heartbeat. I'd marry her day after day after day if that's what she wanted.

I turn to the guys before I get out. "Be ready for anything."

Hayes snickers. "You are so going to get us all killed, aren't you?"

"I honestly don't know what I'm going to do."

"You've got it so bad, dude," Lennox laughs. "I hope when the rest of us find love, it doesn't start a war along with it."

I sigh.

"I don't want to think about any of you falling in love right now. We can only take one lovesick idiot at a time," Gage says.

We head into the flashy hotel full of people, and we all go into protective mode. In a busy crowd like this, it would be easy for anyone to hurt or kidnap Rialta. I have no idea why Corsi agreed to this unless he thinks our enemies are far behind us, possibly still in Chicago.

Rialta holds up a key, running over to us. "Daddy sprung for the penthouse suite. Come on, everyone! You're crashing in our room tonight."

I raise my eyebrows as she throws herself in my embrace.

"Are you sure about that? Don't you want to have a nice, peaceful, quiet night alone?" I ask. It doesn't surprise me that Corsi sprung for the most expensive room in this place, but I'm not sure I can handle being so close to River.

"Nope, tonight is about celebrating, having fun, and getting drunk. Let's party, people!" Rialta yells.

Hayes chuckles. "And I thought I was the most obnoxious one. Seems like I've been outdone."

I turn and look at the guys as I walk Rialta to the elevators while the others follow. I give them a look of desperation, but they just chuckle and shrug.

I sigh as I step onto the elevator with Rialta. She holds the door until everyone else gets on.

Hayes wraps his arm casually over River's shoulder as she steps on and whispers something into her ear that earns him a genuine smile.

Fuck, I have to stop staring at her.

I turn my attention to Rialta. "So the plan for tonight is to get drunk in the room?"

"Yep!" She almost jumps up and down at the thought.

"Happen to know where your father is?"

She shrugs. "Setting up surveillance on this place, I'm sure."

I nod.

"Stop pouting; this is supposed to be a fun night. You only get married once, and this is your last night of freedom," she says.

I cock my head. "Actually—"

She laughs. "Oops, I guess it's not your first rodeo. But it's mine, so let's have some fun for once and stop thinking about all the people who want us dead."

Suddenly, she plants a kiss on my lips. I gasp as she does because I'm not ready. I'm never ready for her kisses. And I'm definitely not prepared when my lips part, and she shoves tongue halfway down my throat. Or when her soft moan vibrates through my mouth. Or when her hand grabs onto my ass and squeezes.

She's definitely gotten more brazen since that first timid kiss.

A throat clears, and we stop kissing.

"Come on, you two lovebirds, don't keep hogging the elevators," Hayes says with River still under his arm as he keeps the elevator door open for us.

Rialta grabs my hand and drags me off.

I force myself not to look at River. The best plan is still my original plan. By the end of our time here, River should hate me. She should despise me. She should want to throw me over the balcony of this hotel. If I can do that, then we can both move on.

Rialta pulls me through the double doors to our penthouse suite. Instantly, I can see why she wants to share it with everyone— it's huge. I can't even see the end of the hallway from where we stand. Door after door lines one side, which I assume lead to bedrooms and bathrooms. The other side of the hallway opens to spacious, expensive-looking rooms.

Rialta heads in the direction of the bar.

"Make me something, fiancé," Rialta demands.

I'm not sure it's a great idea considering the meds she's been on lately, but there will be no arguing with her tonight. I've never seen her drink. I have no idea how she'll be or how high of a tolerance she has, but I'm guessing she should start with something easy.

I walk behind the bar while she pulls up a seat. She motions for the others to sit at the other barstools while I play bartender.

I pull out a bottle of champagne to start. It's too sweet for my tastes and probably most of the guys's, but they'll tolerate it if I don't offer anything else. They'll also realize it's so Rialta isn't encouraged to drink harder stuff too early in the night.

I pull out six champagne glasses and start pouring the bottle into them.

"My lady," I say, handing Rialta the first glass of champagne as I bow.

She laughs and takes the drink.

I start passing the rest out to the others, but when I get to River she shakes her head.

"No, thanks," River says.

Rialta frowns. "You have to drink; it's our joint bachelor and bachelorette party."

"Someone should be sober in case we're attacked," River says.

"Nope, that's Dad's job. Tonight, we're all drinking."

I set the glass down in front of River, letting her decide if she wants to deal with disappointing Rialta or not. I'm not going to deal with Rialta's wrath for not handing River her drink.

I take my own glass, and then Rialta lifts her glass up. "To happily ever afters."

"To happily ever afters," everyone says, clinking our glasses together and taking sips. Well, everyone takes a sip except River. She pretends to drink but doesn't actually drink anything. Rialta doesn't notice, but I wish River would drink—it would make the sting hurt less.

Rialta downs her champagne and then runs up to me, dragging me out from behind the bar.

"Someone turn on some music!" she shouts.

"On it," Gage says, getting up. A few seconds later, music is playing throughout the suite.

There is a large outdoor balcony that extends around the entire suite. She pulls me out there where the music can still be heard.

"Dance with me," she commands.

I yank her close against my body, knowing I should lean into this. She has the right attitude—have some fun with this and forget everything else. Forget all the pain and heartbreak. Remember the good that our marriage will do. Try to enjoy each other.

I'm going to need more alcohol.

Hayes pulls River out, and the two of them start dancing next to us.

Don't look at her. Don't look at her. Don't look at her.

I repeat my mantra while I dance with Rialta, but it's impossible to keep up when Lennox and Gage join in, dancing around River like she's the center of their universe. I know they're just trying to distract her and cheer her up as she watches me and Rialta dance, but it still burns just the same.

Rialta looks up at me with heavy eyes. "Kiss me like you love me."

"Rialta, I—"

"I know you don't, and that's okay. I'm not asking you to love me. I'm asking you to kiss me like you do."

I frown, and my grip on her hip slackens.

"Please," she whispers in such a sincere voice.

I don't know why she wants it. Maybe she wants to know what our future could hold someday if I did ever fall in love with her. Maybe she's not as excited about this marriage as I think. Maybe this is just as hard for her, but how she handles it is by partying and getting drunk.

I can give her this. I can try, at least.

I yank her tight to my body until we are pressed as close together as we can be. My hand slips down to her ass, squeezing tightly, and then I dip her back just a little as my lips come down hungrily against hers, devouring her.

My eyes are closed tight as my tongue sweeps across hers, and a demanding growl leaves my throat, claiming her. I let my hand run up her body, twisting her hair in a fist and yanking her back as my teeth come down on her bottom lip.

She whimpers against me as her eyes flutter open and her cheeks flush.

"Was that enough for you?" I ask.

Her eyes cut away for a second and then back to me. "That was perfect."

I smirk, knowing she's all hot and bothered because of that kiss. Her face is flushed, and she runs her tongue across her lip. She takes a deep breath and then says, "Are you ready?"

I blink, not understanding what she means. "Ready for what?"

"Ready to get married tonight?"

My heart skips a beat, my breath catches in my throat, and a knot forms in my stomach. I don't want to get married to her. I don't want to get married to her ever. But it might be best to rip the bandaid off before I do something stupid that will get someone I love killed.

"I thought you wanted to get married tomorrow? You don't have a dress. I don't have a tux. We don't have rings or—"

She puts a finger over my lips, shutting me up.

"We need to do it spontaneously. There is less of a chance of someone interrupting it, of things getting ruined."

I know she's right, but the dread in my stomach is overwhelming. I'm never going to feel right ever again. I'm never going to know real love. I'm always going to be separated from the one I love.

But River will be alive. She'll be safe. And she'll have a chance at happiness someday.

"Okay," I say.

I'm going to need a stronger drink to get me down the aisle.

I'VE NEVER SEEN someone find a chapel so fast. Or rush half a dozen people out of a hotel suite that fast. I don't know what the rush is or if she arranged this all with Vincent without me, but the transition was whiplashing. Within minutes we go from dancing on the roof, drinking champagne, and trying to keep my eyes anywhere but on Rialta and Beckett making out to jumping into a waiting limo.

Yea, Rialta definitely planned this.

She's all over Beckett in the limo as Hayes starts pouring everyone more champagne.

"Wait! No one can drink anything else!" Rialta says.

Hayes stops mid-pour. "Why not?"

"Last time I drank something before my wedding, I got poisoned."

Hayes looks at the bottle and then sighs, putting it back down. "I don't know how we are supposed to get through tonight on one glass of champagne," he mumbles to me.

I smile tightly. "Once we get to the chapel, I'm getting drunk. I don't care what she says. I tried it sober, and it damn near killed me.

You guys are going to need to be on your best behavior to keep everyone safe."

Hayes grumbles some more but agrees and passes on the message to the other two, who nod at me. They've got my back; they always do.

The limo stops outside of a chapel, and I feel like vomiting. How can this be happening so quickly? Last time I was prepared. I hadn't seen them together yet. I told myself it was for the best. But now, actually seeing them together, it feels like I'm about to attend my own funeral, not a wedding.

The second Rialta is out, I lean over to Hayes. "Hand me that bottle."

He happily hands it to me, and I gulp down several swigs before getting out of the limo. The second I'm outside and I see her holding his hand and kissing him again, I realize no amount of alcohol is going to help. I feel stone-cold sober.

"Fuck," I curse.

Hayes, Lennox, and Gage surround me, putting their arms on or around me.

"Don't lose faith. Even if they get married, it doesn't mean that's the end for you and him," Lennox says.

I nod, but he's wrong. If Beckett marries her, that will be it. There will be no going back. The mafia won't allow it.

We head into the chapel, where Rialta is talking giddily to the receptionist.

"We have thirty minutes until our time slot. Guys, head into that room and find something to put on. River, come with me," Rialta says, skipping into a room that says, 'For Brides.'

Hayes smiles at me encouragingly. Lennox matches my expression, looking like he's about to be sick. And Gage pulls up his phone, letting me know he's got the security part covered.

I can't look at Beckett. I'm not sure if I'll ever be able to look at him again. I just walk into the room that Rialta just disappeared into.

"Wow," I say when I see a heaping cart of wedding dresses in the corner.

"The receptionist said we can rent any of the dresses for the wedding. Help me pick one out," Rialta orders.

I walk over to the cart and start combing through them. They are very much what one would expect a chapel in Vegas to have. A lot of very short, skimpy dresses. A couple of boring A-line styles with no shape, so they'll fit practically anyone. And then a couple of big, poofy princess dresses. I hold up a couple of those out to show her.

"These are perfect!" Rialta squeals. She looks them both over and picks the one most likely to fit.

"What about you?" she asks as she starts removing her shirt.

"What about me? There aren't any bridesmaid dresses, and this isn't a typical wedding anyway. It's just about the two of you."

Rialta frowns. "No, you have to wear a dress. I'm over your all-black outfits like you're in mourning or something."

I am in mourning, I think, but can't say out loud.

Rialta walks back over to the cart and starts going through the dresses again.

I sigh and look around, walking over to the veils hoping to find something that will match Rialta's dress. There is no way she's going to share the spotlight with me, and those dresses are starch white. She should be the only one wearing white today.

"Found it!" Rialta carries a dress over to me.

I turn toward her and freeze.

"It's—" I'm speechless. It's perfect.

"It's perfect for you," Rialta says.

I smile and take the dress. It's a strapless ballgown with a black lace overlay on the bodice and a tulle skirt.

"Are you sure? It still has a lot of white, and I don't want to take away any attention on your wedding day."

"I'm positive. It's perfect for you. Please wear it."

I nod.

She grins, and we both get changed into our dresses. I comb my hand through my hair, and Rialta does the same, resulting in similar long waves.

I wish I would have thought to put a little makeup on.

"Makeup!" Rialta says, holding up her purse.

"You really did think of everything," I laugh.

"I did," she says coyly.

She sits in the makeup chair in front of the mirror and starts applying her makeup.

"So, how long have you had this planned?" I ask.

She shrugs. "A girl has to have some mysteries."

I shake my head. "If you want me to protect you, you really should let me in on what you're thinking sometimes."

"Maybe I don't want you to protect me anymore," she says.

I frown. "What do you mean?"

The door opens suddenly, and Vincent is standing there dumbfounded. I guess he didn't know about this.

"Really, River? You let her plan a wedding and didn't tell me or my men? How am I supposed to protect—wait, why are you wearing a wedding dress, River?"

"It's a decoy. If someone is trying to attack me, they won't know which of us to attack," Rialta answers before I can open my mouth.

"Good thinking," Vincent takes a step forward.

He walks over to Rialta. "You really do look beautiful."

"Thank you," she beams.

"You both do," he says to me.

I raise my eyebrows, shocked that he gave me a compliment. He almost never does.

"Are you almost ready?" he asks Rialta.

"Almost, but I don't want you or your men in the chapel," Rialta says.

"Why not?"

"Well, for one, that didn't work last time. And two, the chapel is tiny, and we don't want to draw any attention. You're better guards if you are outside, keeping an eye out for intruders," Rialta says.

Vincent frowns.

"Plus, you'll cry, and everyone will know you aren't the tough mafia leader everyone thinks you are. You can't ruin your reputation now," Rialta says.

"Fine, you're probably right. I'm just happy for you, Rialta. I've been planning this for a long time. I wasn't sure we'd ever make it this far. I wasn't sure if I could keep you alive long enough to get married. Your life is still going to be hard going forward, but we will do everything we can to protect you." Vincent pulls her into a hug.

"I know you will." Rialta looks directly at me with defiance. Rialta releases him. "Now get out of here; we have to finish getting ready."

Vincent leaves, and then Rialta turns to me. "Your turn. Let's get some makeup on your pretty face."

I sit in the makeup seat while she applies some eye shadow.

"What did you mean before when you said you don't want me to protect you anymore? Are you rethinking your plan of just having me as your main protection outside of Beckett? I'm sure his guys—Gage, Hayes, and Lennox—would be happy to help protect you. You can trust the three of them as much as you can trust me and Beckett. Or—"

"I don't want to talk about it right now. I just want to think about the wedding. Afterward, we'll talk. I'm sure of it."

She applies some lipstick and blush and then steps back. "Beautiful."

I turn to look at myself in the mirror, studying my dark eyeshadow and red lips. I love how I look. I don't know how she came through with the dresses and makeup, but she did.

We each find some heels in a pile in the corner. Neither of them fit very well, but no one will be looking at our feet.

"Veil?" I ask her, holding up two I think will work with her dress.

She looks between the two of them just as there is a knock at the door.

"It's time," Hayes says, poking his head in.

Rialta snatches a veil from my hand. "Let's go."

Suddenly my stomach is in knots, and huge butterflies are swarming again. This is my last chance to tell her how I feel about Beckett. My last chance to tell him how I feel. My last chance to stop this wedding.

Rialta heads to the door and then realizes I haven't moved. "You coming?"

I nod and follow her.

Hayes is still waiting at the door.

"Tell the guys to head in, and we'll be right there," Rialta says.

Hayes nods and then leaves.

Rialta pokes her head out the door a second. We wait a moment, and then she says, "Come on."

I can see some of Vincent's men standing guard outside the chapel door as Rialta hurries us across the lobby to the doors of the chapel.

"You ready for this?" I ask, plastering an overt smile on my face. I can be happy for her. I can.

She smirks. "Definitely. The question is, are you?"

She throws the veil on my head.

I frown. "What are you doing?"

"Protecting you for once."

She throws the doors open before I realize what's happening.

MY LEGS TREMBLE as I stand at the end of the aisle, even though it's a little different this time compared to last. For one, the aisle is about ten feet long, and I don't have the end of a sniper gun aimed at me. This time I don't really need the physical dot on my chest to keep me standing here, not after Corsi came to the groom's room and once again threatened River's life if I don't marry his daughter.

But I can't help my uncontrollable nerves as the wedding march comes over the sound system. I glance over to Lennox, Gage, and Hayes, who are all standing by my side once again. They all nod at me reassuringly. I'm doing the right thing—the only thing I can do to save River right now.

The doors at the back of the chapel open, and I take a deep breath, preparing myself for whatever dress Rialta will be wearing. She steps forward first, and the ballgown she's wearing is as big and fluffy as the one from our first wedding. This one probably cost about a tenth of the other dress and is at least one size too big, but somehow she pulls it off.

I force a smile onto my lips as she walks toward me, but damn, is my smile fake, just like everything about my life is about to be.

Rialta gets to the end, and I hold my arm out to her, preparing myself for what comes next.

"You didn't drink any poisoned wine this time, did you?" I joke. Although, a part of me wishes she did so we could delay this once again. I'm not ready. I'll never be ready.

"Of course not. But the question is, are you ready to finally get your happily ever after?"

My teeth rake over my bottom lip, unsure of how to answer. I don't want to hurt her feelings, not today, but I can't tell her that marrying her is how I get my happily ever after.

Rialta winks at me.

I narrow my eyes, puzzled as she doesn't take my arm. Instead, she steps to the side, mirroring the position of my men on her side of the aisle.

I stare at Rialta, who just motions with her head for me to turn and face the aisle once again. My heart skips several beats because I hope—damn do I hope—when I shouldn't. But I can't stop myself from wishing.

I turn, and the strongest, fiercest, bravest, most beautiful, incredible woman in the entire world is walking toward me. The dress fits her like it was handmade for her—a mix of black and white lace covers the bodice until the dress flares out with tulle at the bottom. Her raven-colored hair is long and wavy, covering her bare shoulders with a veil tucked in the back, her red lipstick popping against the shades of white and black.

She's my dream, my perfect match, and the woman who will push me to be the best version of myself just to keep up with her. But she's walking far too slow for my taste. I need to be married to this woman now.

I run to meet her, holding my arm out to her.

She stares at it like she can't believe it. "I—I don't understand."

I don't have words. I'm still in shock myself, but I know she needs to hear them.

"Rialta isn't the woman for me. She knows that. She saw how in love we are, and she refuses to be a wedge between us. You've protected her for almost your entire life; now it's her turn to protect you."

"I know, and I'm grateful, but I can't—Vincent will kill you." She tries to pull away, but I link my fingers through hers, stopping her.

I grin widely. "I never promised I'd marry Rialta."

"What? Of course, you did."

"No, I promised I'd marry his daughter. And you are as much his daughter as Rialta is."

Her lips part, but she doesn't say anything. She won't argue with me, which tells me she wants this as much as I do.

I closely stand in front of her to narrow her field of vision to just me. I grip her hand and stare deeply into her eyes.

"Do you love me?" I ask.

She swallows hard against the lump in her throat. "Yes, I love you. I've always loved you. I never stopped loving you."

"Same. I love you, River. I've always loved you, even when I shouldn't. And I never stopped loving you even when you tried to push me away."

She bites her bottom lip.

"Do you want to marry me?" I ask.

Her eyes drop, and look away.

"River Corsi, do you want to marry me? Don't think of anything else. Don't think about the consequences or the fear or anything; just answer the question. Do you want to marry me?"

Her chest rises and falls deeply, and then her face lifts, and she looks at me with a smirk. "You call that a proposal? I'm pretty sure you can do better than that," she teases.

I laugh, wrapping my arm around her tightly and spinning her around.

She laughs too before I set her feet back on the ground. "I'll marry you," she says in a whisper against my ear.

"Then let's go get married," I say with a now permanent grin.

With our fingers intertwined, we walk the rest of the short distance down the aisle. The wedding march is still playing, and it stops playing the second we reach the end of the aisle.

"I'm scared," River whispers next to me.

"You face a room full of dangerous men without breaking a sweat, but getting married to me is what makes you scared?" I tease, trying to calm her nerves, but I'm just as terrified.

I'm not afraid of marrying her—it's not a mistake, unlike my previous weddings. No, I'm terrified that I'm dreaming—I'll wake up, and this won't be real, or someone will try and take her away from me.

Her eyes are big as she looks at me. "I'm terrified of losing you, but this—this isn't a mistake. This is the best decision either of us has ever made."

A woman steps forward in a tux and starts the ceremony. I barely look at the officiant, just enough to know where we are in the ceremony; mostly I just stare at River.

"Would you like to say traditional vows or your own?" the officiant asks.

"Our own," both River and I say at the same time.

"Ladies first," I say.

River faces me, gripping my hand with both of hers, doing anything to prevent this from disappearing.

"I, River Corsi, have nothing. I'm no mafia princess. I have no inheritance. No title, no empire or kingdom. I have very little money and very few skills outside of being a good shot."

"With a great right hook," Hayes jokes.

River smiles. "What I do have are a lot of enemies. I have a father who will want to kill us both for this. A future with me is bleak. But I can offer you one thing, Beckett—I promise that I will never stop loving you.

"I loved you when I found out you were married. I loved you when you lied to me. When you tried to break me. When you pretended to love another woman. I loved you despite all the heartache. You're the other piece of me. I love you when we fight and bicker. I love you when you're being sweet and romantic. But most of all, I love you for saving me from myself. I love you, Hero."

I blink, and a tear rolls down my cheek. I didn't realize how much of a romantic I am until I met her.

"I, Beckett, am a monster. I've done horrible things. I've stolen, beaten, and killed. I've risked the lives of my family and friends. I'm no prince. While I have plenty of money, I have no kingdom. No title, no group that I belong to—not anymore. I have little more to offer you than being skilled with a gun, although my right hook is nowhere near as good as yours."

She blushes and laughs at that.

"But I can offer you my love—all of my heart. It's always belonged to you. I've fought it so many times. I've tried to stop loving you—it would have been easier for everyone if I had succeeded, but there is no way for me to stop loving you, ever. You're a drug to me, and I'm addicted to you.

"You think you have nothing to offer—no title, no money, no kingdom, but you're everything to me. You make me a better person. To me, you're my queen. And you've saved me more times than I can count. I could vow all the normal things—to be loyal and faithful and honest with you until death do us part, but I'm not going to. In our world, we do what we must to survive. I'll only make one vow—the same vow you made to me. I promise I'll love you forever, Queen."

We stare at each other without blinking, without breathing. I'm pretty sure our hearts have stopped, likely so we can rip them out and give them to the other.

"Do you have rings you'd like to exchange?" the officiant asks us.

"No—" I start to reply.

"Yes," Rialta and Lennox say at the same time.

My eyes shift from Rialta to Lennox, completely confused with how they both have rings. Were these rings made for me and Rialta? Or did they plan this switcheroo?

I take the ring from Lennox, and River takes the ring from Rialta. We each hold them in front of us to look at them. It's clear that Rialta, and it seems Lennox, each got rings for the two of us. The rings each have words etched into them.

River's smile lights up the room as she takes my hand and pushes the ring onto my finger, reading the etching as she does.

"I'll love you forever, Hero."

I can barely contain myself as the ring slides onto my finger.

I take her ring, which is thinner but otherwise as black and plain as mine. She's not really a diamonds girl anyway. It's exactly what I would have picked for her. I take her hand and slide the ring onto her finger.

"I promise forever, Queen."

Her eyes widen when I say 'queen,' and she looks down to see those words etched into the ring.

"How?" she looks from me to Lennox.

"We figured 'princess' was our word for you, and Beckett has always thought of you as more, so we took a wild guess with Queen." Lennox pats my shoulder. "But it was a stroke of genius on our parts since he included it in his vows."

"Lucky guess, not genius," I say, pushing Lennox back.

I look to the officiant, in desperate need of the next part, because I'm dying to kiss her.

The officiant smiles knowingly. "You are officially married. I can now pronounce you husband and wife. You may kiss your bride."

Before she finishes, my lips are on River's, and someone is going to have to pry me away to get me to stop.

IT'S ALL A DREAM—IT has to be. Any minute now, I'm going to wake up and realize this too is just a figment of my imagination, just like every dirty dream I've had about him these last few days.

But when he presses his lips against mine, reality hits me full force. His kiss is better than anything I've been dreaming about.

I fall into the kiss, and everything else drifts away. All the fear, the worry, the danger, everyone else—it all vanishes.

My entire world is the two of us kissing.

His lips feel like heaven against mine, and when he dips his tongue into my mouth, it's with a promise of walking through hell for me. I'm not a passive participant in the kiss either. My tongue battles his back.

I don't know what our future holds or if our marriage is to only last days, maybe even hours, before our lives are threatened. But what I do know, as his tongue whips through my mouth, is that we are in this together. We are putting each other first.

We are done pretending that we don't love each other. We are done pretending we are okay being with other people to protect each other. We will protect what we have together.

"Alright, you two lovebirds. We need to get out of here before Father figures out what happened," Rialta says.

Beckett and I break our kiss, revealing goofy grins on our faces. Neither of us is going to be able to stop smiling. I don't care if a hundred men enter the room with guns right now it won't wipe the smiles from our faces or get us to stop staring at each other.

"The limo is waiting in the back; let's go," Rialta says. She motions past us to the guys, knowing she's going to need their help to get us to do anything.

Lennox starts pushing Beckett from behind as Rialta pulls on my arm, and we walk through the back of the chapel. As we get to the back door, Rialta turns and looks at me.

"I need to borrow this." She snatches my veil from atop my head and puts it on her own. "And I need to borrow your husband for just a second."

I glare at her with a deep frown.

Everyone laughs, but I don't find it particularly funny.

Rialta rolls her eyes. "I'll give him right back, I promise."

She hooks her arm through Beckett's, yanking him forward before he can protest. The second we step outside, I see why she stole my veil and husband—some of Vincent's men are back here waiting for us.

She smiles and waves at them as she drags Beckett into the limo. The rest of us quickly climb in.

"We're ready to go," Rialta says to the driver through an intercom system, and we're off. She turns to me. "You can have him back now."

She motions for us to switch seats, and I quickly climb to the back next to Beckett. She takes a spot between Lennox and Hayes.

Beckett wastes no time, grabbing my neck and turning me toward him to get another kiss in. I get lost in the kiss—memorizing every touch of his hand, press of his lips, lap of his tongue, and scrape of his teeth. It's automatic after everything we've been through. Every time we've kissed or fucked, it felt like a goodbye. For once, this feels like the first of many.

"To Mr. and Mrs. Beckett and River Corsi," Rialta hoops and hollers at us.

We stop kissing, but we can't stop smiling.

"Corsi, huh? You going to take my last name?" I ask.

"Beckett was technically my last name. My first name is Eli, but everyone calls me Beckett. When I married Odette, they changed my first name to Beckett and made me take her last name of Monroe. I don't care what my name is; I just want it to be tied to you. So, Beckett Corsi it is."

I grin. "I like it. River and Beckett Corsi."

We both turn our attention to the others. "I'm going to kill you for putting me through that, Rialta," I say.

She smirks at me. "You got your prince charming, so I'd say it was worth it."

"Why, though? Why not just tell me your plan? Why make out with him constantly and dry hump him in front of me?"

"I had to be sure of your feelings. You would never voluntarily put yourself ahead of me, so I had to play detective. The easiest way to figure out how you felt was to see if I could make you jealous. If I could, then I'd know you loved him."

"And if I didn't get jealous? If it didn't appear I loved him?"

Rialta shrugs, drinking a sip of her champagne. "Then I would have married him. He's plenty good-looking, and he's an excellent kisser."

I glare at her, and the entire limo laughs.

"Hey, look at me," Beckett says, turning my attention back to him. "You got me. Don't think about all the times she kissed me; think about what I'm going to do to you when we get to the hotel."

"Why do we have to wait until we get to the hotel?" I breathe against his ear. If this life has taught me anything, it's that if I want something, I should never wait. Anything and everything can be taken from me in a split second, and right now, I want my husband.

Beckett doesn't hesitate either. He pulls me onto his lap as my lips land back on his. I can hear the others conversing, but it's merely background noise. All that matters right now is him. I need him right now.

I grab either side of his jaw as I plant a hot and heavy kiss on him. I can't hold back, and it makes him instantly hard beneath me.

He bucks once against me, letting me feel the full length of him as we kiss. I grind on top of him, needing him so desperately that I'll burst if I don't have him soon.

"Hurry," I whisper against his ear while his hand dives under my dress and rips my panties in half.

I need his touch. I need his cock. I need all of him—all of him that I never thought I'd get again.

He kisses down my neck, sucking hard and not bothering to be gentle while his fingers push between my folds, finding my sensitive clit and stroking it.

"Fuck," I moan against his shoulder at the simple touch. I know we have an audience, and I should be quiet, but I don't care. Everyone in this limo has seen me naked. Everyone has seen me struggle with loving him but not being allowed to have him. I don't care if everyone sees me come on my husband's dick for the first time.

"You're such a naughty, dirty girl, Ri," he whispers in my ear.

I run my tongue over his ear. "I don't care. I want you, and I won't wait another second."

I yank on his pants then, undoing the belt, button, and zipper. His fingers continue to work over my clit until I can barely contain my arousal. It makes it difficult to concentrate on what I'm doing, but I eventually free him from his pants.

I waste no time climbing on top of him. I need him more than I've ever needed anything, and it's clear from the hunger in his eyes that he needs me too.

His hand on my hip helps guide me down at the same time he

thrusts up. I gasp as he fills me in a way no other man has—all the way to my heart.

The growl he releases is loud and ferocious. He doesn't hold back. He doesn't care about the others in the limo, so neither do I.

I cry out as I move my hips over his cock. It's a feeling I never thought I'd get to experience again. I can feel literal tears in my eyes as I feel him move inside me.

I grab his neck again and kiss him hard. My forcefulness is going to leave us both bruised and bloodied, but I don't care. I don't care if our teeth clash or one of us bites down on the other too hard. It's just raw passion and hunger driving our kisses.

He pulls me back when my wet tears drip down my cheeks onto his face. He kisses every single one, taking away all of my pain as he continues to thrust inside me.

"This is real. I'm yours, and you're mine," he whispers. His voice cracks, and I can hear his pain. He, too, thought this would never happen again.

"This is real," I pant back as I kiss every inch of his skin I can access. I want his clothes off so I can kiss him fucking everywhere, but I can't fucking stop to strip him.

He drives harder into me, and I can barely hang on as I meet his thrusts, grinding my hips harder over his body.

"I love you," I pant, feeling free to say the words for the first time in a long time.

He grins. "Say it again."

"I love you. I love you. I love you," I chant over and over as my orgasm builds.

And then I'm exploding—my climax erupting through my body. I scream. I cry out. I gasp. I moan and groan. So many sounds leave my body as a lifetime of agony is released as well.

Beckett pumps into me one more time before filling me with his warm cum.

My head falls forward against his, and my eyes close. I don't need him to say anything; I can feel everything he's feeling.

"I love you too, my queen. I love you, Princess. I love you, Ri. I love you, River. I love you, my wife," he pants.

I grin each time he speaks words my heart has been aching to hear. Even if he felt them, I never thought those words would ever be spoken out loud. He had agreed to marry Rialta.

Rialta!

I still as Beckett's cock still rests inside me, the reality of what we just did overcoming me and my cheeks beginning to flush. I try to look out of the corner of my eye to see our friends' reactions, but I can't see without moving my head.

Beckett opens his eyes with a sly smirk on his face.

"What?" I ask.

"I love that you have no problem fucking me in front of others, but the second we're done, you turn redder than an apple. I don't think I've ever seen your cheeks so red," he chuckles.

I take a deep breath. "Well, I've fucked every guy in this limo." I lower my voice. "But it's strange to fuck you in front of Rialta. Twenty minutes ago, she was the one who you were supposed to marry."

Beckett's face darkens. "Would you change anything? Would you take it all back and not be married to me to spare your sister's feelings?"

I look deep into Beckett's eyes. "I wouldn't change anything. I didn't need to be married to you. Marriage is just a legal piece of paper our society has decided means something, but I am thankful for it.

"It means we belong to each other. It makes it harder for others to steal you away from me. You're mine. I would marry you again in a heartbeat, and I wouldn't take back that fuck for anything in the world."

He grins.

"But I'm sorry for Rialta," I say, still facing Beckett.

He laughs.

"What?" I ask.

"Turn around."

I don't know what will be behind me when I turn around, but what I see shocks me—a completely empty limo.

I turn back around, ready to lay into Beckett.

He's dying with laughter at my reaction. "They left the second you climbed on top of me."

I frown and jab him playfully on the shoulder.

"Fuck," Beckett curses, but it doesn't stop him from laughing, so I hit him a second time.

I climb off of him.

"You should have told me," I scold.

"Why? I wanted to see how much you wanted me. I needed to see it. I almost married Rialta because I didn't think you loved me. That was the only way I could ever agree to marry someone else, by the way. Even if marrying her was the best way to protect you and everyone else I care about, I could never have done it if I wasn't convinced, on some level, that you didn't love me."

"You thought I didn't love you?" I ask.

He shrugs. "I could make arguments for either. I thought several women loved me in the past, and I was always wrong. I don't trust my judgment."

I take his hand and put it against my heart. "And now?"

He smirks. "Now, I'm more sure than ever that I've found a woman who not only loves me but will fuck me in front of an audience to show me her love."

"I hate you," I lie with a grin.

"I hate you, too," he lies back with a gleam in his eye.

"Now what?" I ask.

He looks down at his watch. "Tomorrow, we face reality. We have to figure out a plan on how to face it, but not tonight."

"Are we going back to the suite with everyone? I'm not sure I'm ready to face them. Tonight, I just want you all to myself," I beg.

"I couldn't agree more," he says mischievously. He's up to something, something I'm probably going to like way too much.

FUCKING HER WAS HEAVEN. I have no idea how I was able to hold on so long. It was so incredible I thought I was going to come like a teenager within a minute of fucking her.

Through the intercom, I tell our driver to drop us off at the hotel next to our original hotel. If they need us, they can find us quickly, but I'm hoping we can get some alone time.

I text Lennox to tell Rialta and the others to stay hidden in the suite until morning. We need tonight alone, without anyone knowing we got married. Tomorrow we will face reality. Tomorrow we will figure out what to do about Corsi and everything else.

I turn my phone off. No matter what happens, I don't want to know about it until the morning. I made that clear to Lennox—I'm leaving him in charge, and I'm not to be bothered until morning, no matter what.

Ri and I need tonight. If we are going to figure out how to survive this world, we need tonight.

The limo stops in front of the hotel, and I take Ri's hand, leading her through the lobby. There's a line at the front desk, but I'll be dammed if I'm going to wait in it. I walk straight up to the front desk.

"I need a room, any room," I say.

"Sir, the line starts—"

The glare I give him shuts him up. I toss my credit card and ID at him impatiently, while River tries to hide her smile at my impatience. She doesn't seem bothered that we just cut half a dozen people in line.

We may be married, and I may have gotten to fuck her already, but that's nowhere near enough to satisfy me. And with our luck, the few hours left in the night might be all we have. I'm not wasting a single second of it.

The man behind the counter grins. "All we have left are our presidential suites."

He probably thinks I can't afford an expensive suite, what with us not booking a hotel room in advance, and my tux and her dress screaming trashy Vegas wedding. But money isn't the problem.

"Great. I'll pay double if you hand me the key in the next five seconds."

The key magically finds its way into my hand, but I think it takes more like ten seconds instead of five. I grab River's hand again, and we race to the elevator. Thankfully, the elevator opens the second she presses the button, and I pull her on.

We're practically panting, but all I allow myself is to hold her hand as the elevator slowly rises to the top floor.

"After all of that, you aren't even going to kiss me?" River asks.

I stare at the numbers as we ascend. "If I do more than this, we'll never leave this elevator. I'll fuck you against the wall. The cops will be called, and we'll spend tonight in jail."

She laughs. "You can't carry me down the hall like in the movies?"

"I have no control when it comes to you."

The doors open, but before I can tug on her hand, she starts running, and I give chase.

"What are you doing?" I shout after her.

"Putting us both out of our misery as fast as possible," she smiles back.

She stops in front of the suite door, and I almost slam into her. I take the key out of my pocket but hesitate a second.

"God, it's good to see your genuine smile. I thought I'd never see it again. I thought I'd get glaring, growling, sulking Ri for the rest of my life," I say.

"Open that door, and you can get moaning, screaming, coming Ri." She wiggles her eyebrows, and I capture her mouth with mine. I purposefully keep the kiss soft and light because I really want to double-check the security of the room before I fuck her. I want one incredible night without worry, and I need a clear brain to check the room.

When I pull back, her eyes are glossy, and her lips are swollen. "I thought you couldn't control yourself around me?"

"I can't."

I push the door open and brush past her, pulling my gun out as I search the room. I see her out of the corner of her eye, pulling a gun out from her outer thigh.

"You were made for me; you know that?" I say.

She rakes her teeth over her bottom lip. "And you were made for me. Now let's do a quick scan and barricade the door."

I nod, and we both go to work searching the multiple bedrooms, bathrooms, and living spaces. The suite is massive and over the top, similar to the penthouse Rialta has in the hotel next door. I want to curse the man behind the front desk for giving us this room, not because of how expensive or extravagant it is, but because of how fucking long it takes us to secure it.

When I make my way back to the front door, River already has it locked up with a chair wedged under the door handle. She really isn't taking any chances of being interrupted.

We're both still gripping our guns when our gazes meet. We've both been through so much, but this moment feels bigger than anything we've ever done. We might be married on paper, but we've lied and betrayed and hurt each other all for the sake of love. There's a lot of healing that needs to happen between the two of us. It starts with opening our chests and baring our hearts to each other, wounds and all.

Ri starts to walk toward me. Her tongue runs across her bottom lip, her eyes dilate with need, and her hands tremble. With each step, I see her knees almost buckle.

My own body mirrors hers—filled with lust and yet terrified.

She stops a foot away from me.

We both take a breath, unsure of where to start. *With words? With making out? With fucking? What will heal us? What will bind us together?*

Ri decides, taking charge before I can make up my mind. She jumps onto me, throwing her legs and arms around my body and crashing her lips down on mine.

Her lips on mine feel like the best place to start. That is until I feel her kick my gun out of my hand and aim hers at my heart.

"No more lies. No more betrayals. No more hiding things from me in the name of trying to save me. You said you'd never be my hero."

"And yet, you call me Hero," I say.

I eye the gun aimed at my chest. It's meant to threaten me, to make me vulnerable. She doesn't need the gun to do that, and I know she won't shoot me. It's just how we work.

"I call you Hero because that's what you are. It's why we've gotten into this mess. It's why you keep staying married to or almost marrying other people. I'm more than capable of taking care of myself."

I snatch the gun out of her hand and slam her back into the wall. "Are you?"

She narrows her eyes and bares her teeth at me. "You know I am."

I drop the gun and grab her jaw to kiss her hard, taking her breath away.

She melts against me and then does exactly what I would expect from her—she kicks me in the balls to free herself and send me crumpling to the ground. She stands over me, her legs on either side of my head, and the view makes me forget about the bruising pain in my balls.

I wrap my hand around her ankle and yank hard, forcing her to her knees on top of me. Her pussy lands on my face, and I lick up the length of her. Her legs shiver over me. I hold her tight, getting a better taste of her. She's already wet, her lips swollen for me, ready for me to take her, and we've barely even started.

But we need this. We need this fight to get our emotions out. We need a fresh start.

She doesn't let me lick her for long, even though she loves what I do to her body. She needs answers, just like I do.

She reaches for something nearby. I don't see what it is until I feel sharp glass at my throat as she straddles me.

"No more playing the hero role," she demands.

I shake my head. "I can't promise that any more than you can."

She growls. "I don't need you to save me. Promise me, or this is over. We are over. I need to be your partner, not your damsel in distress."

I grab her arm and roll us over until I'm straddling her and the piece of glass is pushed against her neck. "Promise me you will never risk your life to protect mine."

Her lips part, but no words come out. She can't do it either.

We should give up right here and now. This is the one promise neither of us can give. And it's the one promise we both need for this relationship to work. It's not worth risking everything our marriage will cause if we can't figure this out.

She sees the defeat in my eyes, but she's far more stubborn than I am. Thank god for her.

She shoves me off of her. I scramble to my feet quickly, expecting another assault. She won't stop attacking until I've made the vow she needs to hear. And if I don't, we'll be locked in this circle of lust and pain and desire forever.

She runs at me and grabs a chandelier at the last second, lifting herself up and wrapping her legs around my head. Her thighs become a vice grip around my head that could easily suffocate me, but all I can think about is tasting her again if I can lift her dress up.

I stumble back against a wall, a picture frame digging into my back. I jerk forward enough for it to fall to the floor. With my teeth, I grab onto the hem of her dress, and with my hand, I rip straight up. The material is cheap and thin, so I'm able to rip her dress all the way up in two.

River tightens her thighs around my head.

"Please," she says.

I don't know if her word is a cry for my vow or for my tongue on her wetness. I go with option two.

I bury my face between her legs. She squeezes her legs fiercely, but the second my tongue licks up her slit, she melts a little. Her thighs unclench and her hands grip my head, keeping me in place.

"Fuck, you taste delicious," I moan.

"Don't stop."

It's a trap. Everything is always a trap with her, but I don't care. I feast on her.

She grabs for my tie as I feel her close to coming.

I grin against her lips as my tongue dips inside her sweetness.

She gasps, unprepared for the orgasm I've just demanded from her. Then she's screaming my name.

I can't keep my balance, and I stumble away from the wall. She has no control either but holds onto my tie, pulling it so hard I can't breathe.

I stumble through the hotel room with her atop me, grabbing for walls and ending up knocking more decor to the floor. She hangs onto me for dear life.

I fall—we're going down hard. I don't know where we're landing, but I suspect it's going to fucking hurt. Instead, I'm met with the softness of a bed.

Thank fuck.

I roll on top of her, pinning her hands over her head. "We can't make these demands of each other. We can't, baby."

She struggles against my hold, hating to be constrained. I'm strong enough to hold her with one hand, but I'm not naive enough to think she isn't capable of getting out of my hold.

"Don't call me baby."

I smirk. "That's what you have a problem with? You don't want me to let you go?"

She rolls her eyes. "Why would I care about that when I can do this?" In an instant, she has me facedown with my arm pulled behind my back.

"Have I told you how much I love you lately, *baby?*" I chuckle.

Her teeth are at my ear, about to bite it off as she pulls my arm further, nearly popping it out of my shoulder.

"That's not my name," she growls.

"You can understand why I'd be confused about what to call you. Princess? Ri? Rialta? River? Fighter? Queen? What should I call you?"

She growls.

I laugh as she starts removing my clothes, ripping them from my body piece by piece. I don't fight it. I'm ready to get this tux off and feel her on my skin.

The second all of my clothes are off, I flip over, and she's straddling me.

I expect to see the fierce fighter in her eyes, but I'm confused by the pure agony present as well.

I narrow my eyes as I try to figure out what she's looking at. I follow her gaze and find that she's staring at my tattoo—the one Rialta inked herself.

She jumps off of me and heads to the bathroom.

"Ri!" I chase her, but the bathroom door slams in my face. My fist slams against it.

"Ri, open the door."

She doesn't.

"It's not what it looks like, just—" I try again.

I sigh and start picking the lock on the door, knowing she's not going to let me in.

When I finally get the door open, she's simply standing there, facing the mirror, completely naked.

I want to scoop her up in my arm, but that's not what she wants. She needs to deal with this—the feelings that I was about to marry another woman. She watched Odette and me together, I've caused her immense pain, and there is very little I can do except apologize for my part.

I can't take away the pain. I just hope that being with me is worth the heartbreak she felt before. She wasn't alone in feeling tortured; I felt it too.

But no more.

"I'm sorry," I say, barely over a whisper. That seems like the place to start.

"I'm sorry for marrying Odette. I'm sorry for agreeing to marry Rialta. I'm sorry for protecting you and hurting you. I'm sorry."

She doesn't look at me, but her shoulders slump a little, and her breathing slows. She heard me and accepts my apology.

"On the bed," she says in an annoyingly calm voice.

I take a deep breath but don't argue. I walk to the bed and lie down, waiting for her—to extract more revenge, to fuck, to forgive me? I don't know, but she can take whatever she needs from my body.

A second later, she's hovering over me with a lit candle she must have found in the bathroom.

I look at her suspiciously. "What's that for?"

"For burning that tattoo off your skin," she says slowly.

She tilts the candle, and hot wax drips onto my chest.

"And if this won't work, I'll cut it off," she says, her voice dripping in heartbreak.

She tilts the candle again, but I grab her wrist before it drips. For one, the candle definitely won't burn the tattoo off. For two, she needs to face it.

"Stop."

"No." Tears race down her cheeks.

"Look at the tattoo."

She looks away.

"Look at it, goddammit!" I yell.

She still doesn't.

"Please, for me. Please," I say as soothingly as I can. I need to control myself around her.

I take her hand and place it over my tattoo. Then I wait and wait and wait.

More tears stream before she finally decides to look.

I carefully trace her hand over the tattoos. We trace over the original tattoo the Retribution Kings gave me and then over the new crown—the one Rialta did.

"There's a reason the guys wrote 'queen' on your ring. They knew I thought of you as my queen. They knew this tattoo Rialta gave me was for you, not her. Look."

I trace her fingers over the word 'Ri.'

She stares at it intently as I try to explain.

"Rialta wrote 'Ri.' Even then, she knew there was a chance I wouldn't marry her. She gave me a choice. I chose you as much as you chose me. It's always been you."

"No," River says.

"No?"

She sobs and tilts her head down, her hair covering her face.

"No, she knew who you'd choose; that's why she wrote Ri. She hates nicknames like that. No one ever calls her Ri. That's my name, not hers."

She lifts her head, revealing dried eyes and a beautiful smile.

I exhale a deep breath and wrap my arm around her, pulling her into my chest.

"I love you so much. I'm so sorry, so sorry for all the pain I've caused you," I say.

Her lips fall on mine, kissing me like she's never kissed me before. I can taste her salty, painful tears but also her intense hope in the kiss.

Neither of us has had hope in a long time. We've been too focused on the reality of our situation. But now, we can have hope again.

"I need you. We still have a lot to figure out. A lot of pain to work through. A lot of promises about the future, but I need you—now," she says.

I grin and slide her hips down until my cock is straining at her entrance. I ease her down onto me, our lips and eyes never leaving each other.

"We really have a fucked up sense of foreplay, don't we?" I whisper.

She laughs. "I like our foreplay." Her eyes twinkle.

"Oh yeah?"

"Yeah."

I flip us over, settling her beneath me, and grab the still-lit candle she left on the nightstand.

Her lust-filled eyes widen as I hover the candle over her body, almost tilting it, but not quite. Then I pour wax over her full tits, ready for my attention.

She bites her lip as the hot wax rolls on her skin in sync with my thrusts.

"More," she moans.

I grin, loving how much we can push each other. Our sex life is going to be anything but normal—that I know.

I let the wax drip again across her chest, aiming for her left nipple.

When the wax hits the sensitive peak, she arches her back, grabs onto my hand, and digs her nails into me.

"You're so beautiful covered in wax, but now I want you covered in my cum."

"Bury it inside me first, then mark my skin," she says.

"Fuck yes," I groan.

I start pounding her harder, slamming into her depths as her hands rub the wax all over her breasts.

My mouth runs dry at the sight. *How did I ever marry anyone else? How could I have thought there was anyone else for me?*

We are both getting close to exploding when our eyes meet again. We haven't figured everything out, but it doesn't matter in this moment. This moment is about hope—and we both have a lot of it.

"Come with me," I pant.

And we do. We come together, her pussy clenching down, milking me for everything I have.

I fall on top of her, the wax sticking between our bodies. As I stroke her hair, our eyes are serious. We need to have more deep conversations, which will lead to more conflict, which means more destruction of this penthouse suite.

"Did you like that?" I ask.

"Yea..." She scrunches her nose and bites her lip. "But how do you feel about a foursome? I kind of miss the attention of four men at once."

My face goes white, and she bursts out in laughter underneath me.

I tickle her, not letting her go until she takes it all back.

"I'm kidding! I'm kidding! You're more than enough for me. I don't want other guys or multiple guys. I just want you, only you. Forever you," she says.

WE FUCK ALL NIGHT. We don't dare sleep. I'm not sure we'll ever sleep again anyway. We're too afraid of what will happen if we sleep. *What moments together will we miss? Will this will all be taken from us in a flash?*

It could—it really could.

We haven't talked about tomorrow specifically. We haven't talked about much since we started fucking like our time is running out.

It doesn't matter that we're married; nothing's changed. Every time we're together, it feels like we're about to lose each other all over again. That's what makes this so emotional.

The sun is starting to rise over the strip—another indication of our dwindling time before facing reality.

I'm lying on Beckett's shoulder in one of the many beds in this hotel room. His eyes are closed, but he's not asleep.

I nudge him with my head toward the window. He opens his eyes and sees the hint of yellow climbing over the mountains in the distance.

When he turns his attention back to me, it's with a deep scowl.

Tonight was supposed to heal us. It was supposed to mend our wounds and solidify what we mean to each other. It was supposed to be full of promises and plans.

And it was. It was so much more, but our lives are far too complicated to be solved in one night.

Beckett climbs out of bed. "Take a bath with me?"

I nod, and he takes my hand, helping me out of bed. Together we walk naked to the bathroom. Our skin is marked by each other—with cum, with candle wax, with nail scratches, with bruises from our thrusts.

Beckett starts the bathtub and sits on the edge, pulling me into his lap. He strokes my hair gently.

I open my mouth to speak, but he shakes his head. "Not yet."

I nod.

He's right. The most important part of the conversation can wait until the last minute. It won't ruin anything, but it's the most painful topic.

When the tub finishes filling up, Beckett climbs in and helps me sit in front of him.

I lean back against him, relishing feeling him in the warm water while he rubs a bar of soap all over my body.

"I love you," I say, trying not to break.

When we have the conversation, I have no idea what the conclusion will be. Even after the night we had, I'm not sure what he's thinking.

Will he want to end our marriage, end us, in order to save his family and me? Or now that we are together, will he fight with me by his side? Even if it means we, and most likely his family, will die?

I know what my answer is, but I never got him to vow not to play the hero role. And he never got me to promise not to risk my life to save him. We are both hopeless—hopelessly in love with each other to the point of sacrificing ourselves.

It's not healthy. It's not right, but it's love.

Love is messy. Love is complicated, and love requires sacrifice.

For most people, it means sacrificing a few hours on the weekend to watch a football game even though you hate football. Or go to brunch even though you'd rather sleep in.

But for us, our love requires more.

He pulls me tight against his chest. "I love you too, Queen."

He's called me that a lot lately, but I feel like the nickname is taunting me. I'm not a queen. If I was, we wouldn't be in this predicament. We'd have an army at our disposal to defend our love. Instead, the world is against us.

If I was a queen, I'd have money and power and the ability to control my own fate. Instead, loving him means we'll most likely die in a bloody war.

I sigh.

Beckett kisses the top of my head.

"Okay, it's time," he says, taking a deep, shaky breath.

"You sure?"

"Yes," he says somberly.

There's a pause. Neither of us speaks for a second, each hoping the other will go first.

"I can't live without you," we say at the same time.

I turn and look at Beckett.

"I can't live without you. I won't live without you, not again," he says.

"I can't live without you either, Hero. I won't. No matter the consequences, I'm tired of hiding. I'm tired of pretending. I'm tired of sacrificing our love to protect each other. We just end up hurt."

He nods even though it kills him to think about losing me. But this way, death will be the only way he'll lose me. He won't be doing it to himself by marrying someone else.

"So we're in this together, forever? No matter what?" he asks.

"I promise. We're in this together—forever."

We kiss—sealing the one promise we can keep to each other. This kiss isn't a battle; it's an orchestrated dance. Our promises slip back and forth to each other until we're content in our vow.

And then, we have to face the reality of our newly made promise far too soon. The second our lips separate, a knock pounds on the door.

We don't have to open it to know what faces us on the other side.

WE FRANTICALLY GET out of the tub, throw on robes, and grab our guns. We don't need to speak to know what we face. On the other side of that door is most likely a furious Corsi, and he's figured out that I married the wrong daughter.

A battle is about to explode. The Corsi mafia is pissed, the Retribution Kings are pissed, and we are their greatest enemies. *They will both come after us, but who came first?*

The mafia.

Corsi.

I look over at Ri as we walk closer to the door. Last night was incredible, and as much as we got what we needed out of it, it wasn't enough. Only a lifetime together could ever be enough.

We ruined the penthouse suite. Every room is in shatters with broken furniture, shattered glass, and artwork scattered around the floor.

But we started the process of healing ourselves in this room. *Are we about to be broken once again? Are we even going to survive what comes next?*

Ri holds my gaze, clearly thinking all the same things. My worry is mirrored in her face. We are hardly prepared for war—

mentally or physically. We're only wearing robes, for goodness sake. *How well can we actually fight in a fucking robe?*

"Together," she whispers, and I remember the promise we made to each other. We're in this together—forever. We will do whatever we have to do to survive and protect each other. Whatever actions we take, we are taking them with the goal of being together forever.

"Forever," I say back.

We both nod. Our love is about to face the ultimate test, but for once, I feel good about our chances.

We approach the door cautiously with our guns aimed at it.

The knock pounds again, angrier and more impatient than last time. I pull back the chair barricade under the door and look through the peephole.

Instantly, my pulse calms.

"It's Lennox," I exhale.

"Fuck," Ri says, her shoulders relaxing.

I quickly unlock and open the door. "What do you want?"

He glares at me as he steps inside with a bag in his hands. "Don't turn off your phone again."

He looks us up and down and shakes his head. "Were you really going to try to take on the mafia or Retribution Kings with a gun and a robe?"

I shrug with a lazy grin.

"You both really are mad."

I put my arm around Ri. "No, we're in love."

Lennox rolls his eyes.

"So, what's the emergency?" Ri asks him.

Lennox frowns, suddenly quiet. "Rialta ran away."

"What do you mean she ran away? She was staying in the same hotel room as the three of you!" Ri yells.

"Yes, and that hotel room is as big as this one. It's basically an entire floor. We didn't think she'd run. We worried about preventing people from coming in, not her escaping."

"How do you know she wasn't kidnapped? Jesus, what was I thinking?" Ri steps out from underneath my shoulder and starts pacing. "I have to find her. I'm supposed to protect her. Fuck, I shouldn't have left her alone."

I grab Ri's shoulder to stop her. "You didn't leave her. Last night was a lot of things, but it wasn't a mistake. Don't ever think that. Ever," I growl.

She nods, and I turn to Lennox, pissed at him for ruining my morning. "Why do you think Rialta snuck out and wasn't kidnapped?"

Lennox reaches into his jacket pocket and pulls out a napkin. He holds it out to us.

Ri grabs it and starts reading aloud.

"Tell River I'm fine, and I'm sorry. I just needed some space to think," Ri reads and sighs, balling up the napkin in her hand.

"We have to go find her," Ri snaps.

"Finding Rialta isn't your biggest problem at the moment. Corsi is furious that Rilata is missing, and he doesn't understand why he can't get ahold of you two," Lennox says.

"Fuck, what did you tell him?" I ask.

"I told him you both went off searching the second you realized she was gone and told us to stay back in case she came back. But I think he's suspicious," Lennox says.

"No, he's just disappointed in me. I've never let him down in almost twenty years, and now I did. He thought I was the perfect protector for her. He thought as long as I was protecting her, she'd be safe. Having a husband to protect her was just added protection," Ri says, running her hand through her hair in frustration.

"So what now?" I ask, looking at Lennox, knowing he already has a plan.

"I told Corsi we'd meet him at the airport to head back to Chicago in an hour."

"Why would we go back if we haven't found Rialta yet?" I ask.

"Because he thinks she went back," Ri says.

"Why would she go back?" I look at Ri.

"Well she wouldn't stay in Las Vegas. If she really ran, she wouldn't make it far. She doesn't have the skills. She doesn't have a fake passport or an endless supply of money. And she's not stupid enough to think she can evade us. She'll be back. There isn't much to do but wait for her, most likely in Chicago, and keep the news quiet," Ri says before glaring at Lennox some more. I want to do more than just glare at Lennox for fucking this up so royally.

Lennox tosses me the bag he's carrying, and I lift an eyebrow.

"Clothes," he explains. "And the plan is simple. You pretend you married Rialta last night. We all got blackout drunk partying and woke up to a missing Rialta. She just got cold feet after reality set in. We are going to meet Corsi on his plane, and the two of you are going to stay as far apart as possible. You don't touch, kiss, or give longing looks to each other. We keep your marriage hidden as long as possible, at least until we find Rialta. After that...well, I hope you two come up with a plan by then."

Ri and I head to one of the bedrooms to get dressed. The clothes Lennox brought are simple—jeans, T-shirts, and tennis shoes. We get dressed quickly, putting our guns in the back of our pants, and all the while, Ri doesn't even look at me. She's too focused on Rialta.

"Hey." I take her hand to get her to finally look at me. "Together."

"Forever," she says in return as if it's our mantra. Maybe if we repeat it enough, it'll be true.

I kiss her now one last time. After we leave this hotel, we can't steal kisses, we can't touch, we can't even look at each other. We have to pretend we hate each other if possible. We have to throw Corsi and his men completely off the scent of what happened last night.

I'm going to enjoy this kiss and take it with me for as long as I need it.

Ri seems to be in agreement as she wraps her arms around my

neck and tilts her head to deepen our connection. We cling to each other, pressing our lips together like the oxygen—we need this to survive.

The kiss is too long and too short, all at the same time. We know our time is up at the same time and let go. Our only chance of getting to kiss again is finding Rialta, ensuring my brother and his family's safety, and paying whatever price Corsi inflicts on us for betraying him.

Ri looks down at the wedding ring I put on her finger just last night. She takes it off without hesitation and stows it in her pocket. I hold my hand out to her, link our fingers together, and we head back out to an impatient Lennox.

He frowns when he sees our linked hands but doesn't say anything.

We follow him out into the hotel hallway, our hands dropping the second we leave the threshold of the suite door. It's painful but necessary. We don't look at each other—practice for what's about to come. But I can still see her out of the corner of my eye, and our promise still rings in my ear.

Together—forever.

Downstairs, a car is waiting for us. Gage and Hayes are already in the car. The second we climb in, the driver takes off toward the airport.

"I hope you guys had a good time last night because we all might die for it," Hayes says.

I know he means it as a joke. He's always the one to lighten the mood, but none of us can handle jokes right now. I'm sitting in the back with Lennox. Hayes and Ri sit in the middle, and Gage is sitting upfront with the driver.

Hayes reaches over, taking Ri's hand and giving it a squeeze. I'm jealous he can touch her while I can't. But when she leans her head over onto his shoulder, I realize my jealousy is pointless. I'd sacrifice my happiness for hers a million times over, and I'm thankful a friend can comfort her for a minute when I can't.

We make it to the airport in record time to find the private jet ready and waiting.

I keep my distance from Ri as we head up to the plane. She stops and talks to Corsi at the front of the plane while I head to the back.

Gage sits next to me on the plane with Hayes and Lennox behind me. Ri stays upfront with Corsi, and she doesn't look back. She gives me no indication of what their conversation is about, nothing to tell me if he believes our story or not.

That turmoil is what I endure the entire plane ride back until we land, and I get my answer far too soon.

The second we land, my arm is yanked behind me, and ropes come around my body and ankles. My gun is tossed before I even have a chance to reach for it, a piece of tape is placed over my mouth before I even get a word out.

What. The. Hell?

It happened so fast I didn't have time to react or fight back. I was surrounded by men I thought were my friends, men I considered practically family. And they were the ones who tied me up.

Gage, Hayes, and Lennox all surround me, each aiming a gun at me.

My eyes go to each of them, trying to understand why they did this. Why am I tied up? Why are they aiming a gun at me?

But then I hear the struggle at the front of the plane, and I suddenly no longer care about myself.

"Ri!" I yell, but the sound is muffled by tape.

I can tell by the scuffle of men and the sound of gunfire that Ri saw it coming and fought back. That's not necessarily a good thing —there's a chance she's hurt or dead.

"Ri!" I try again, struggling against the ropes they bound me with, but I can't get free. At least, I won't be able to get out of them fast enough to help Ri.

But it's too late—I see one of Corsi's men hold her up. She breaks the rule Lennox gave us, looking directly at me.

She's tied up in much the same way I am. Her arms are bound behind her, tape is across her mouth, and her ankles are bound together.

"Together," I say even though I know she can't hear me.

"*Forever*," she says back in my mind.

A single tear falls down my face as I watch her get yanked off the plane and realize how futile our promises are.

A moment after Ri is taken off the plane, Gage and Hayes grab my sides and help me stand before walking me down the aisle of the plane after her. I don't resist. I want to be wherever she is.

And then I spot two blacked-out SUVs, and my heart sinks—we won't be together. To keep our promise of together forever, we're going to have to fight our way back to each other. I have no idea if that will take a day, a week, a year, or a lifetime, but I do know it's a promise I intend to keep.

I'm shoved in the trunk of the second SUV, and I'm sure Ri is currently lying sideways in the back of the one in front of us. I don't know what's happening. I don't know why we are being separated. I don't know what Corsi plans on doing with us.

And I don't know why Lennox, Hayes, and Gage went along with this plan or if they had a choice. Even if they didn't have a choice, they had a chance to warn me.

The car starts moving, and I know I'm being driven away from Ri. I try to calm my breathing, knowing it's not helpful to get upset and worked up. I need to keep my cool to get out of these bindings. I need to solve one problem at a time to get back to her.

Lennox is sitting in the back, leaning behind his seat and looking at me. My eyes shoot daggers into him. When I get free, he'll be the first one I go after.

His face is blank and unreadable, but I swear I hear him say something—a whisper or maybe it's the wind, or maybe I want to believe that I haven't been betrayed by someone I thought cared about me again. The 'I'm sorry,' whether actually spoken or imagined, is too little too late. I would have accepted my fate if he had made sure Ri was safe. He didn't.

The one thing I have to be thankful for is that Corsi has Ri, not Odette. Corsi is pissed. He'll be angry with Ri—probably even punish her, but he won't kill her. Deep down, Corsi thinks of Ri as a daughter. He cares about her.

I just have to find my way back to her.

I HYPERVENTILATE in the back of an SUV as I watch Gage and Hayes lead Beckett out of the plane with Lennox holding a gun at his back. I thought they were his friends. I thought they would do anything to protect him. *What are they doing kidnapping him?*

I thought for a second we might be able to fight our way out of this. We were taken by surprise, but we had three allies at the back, ready to fight with us.

I was wrong.

They lead Beckett to an SUV behind mine. We're about to be driven in different directions, taken to different places for Vincent and his men to torture and punish us for what we did.

Separated—this was our nightmare. It's infinitely harder to fight together forever when we're apart. We'll find a way back to each other; we always do—even if we have to go through hell first.

And we will go through hell. Vincent is beyond pissed. I'm sure he figured out the truth by now. My only solace is that he won't kill Beckett. He still needs him to marry Rialta once he finds her.

Although, at the moment, I'm not sure I believe anything that Lennox said. Rialta may be safe and sound; she may have been kidnapped—I have no clue.

The car starts moving, and my heart rips in two—half of it stays with Beckett, while the other keeps me going long enough to get back to him. I'm lying on my right side and can feel the thin metal of my ring digging into my hip, a reminder of who I have to get back to.

I don't know how long we drive, but eventually, the car stops. No one talks in the car, so I don't get many clues about where we are or what Vincent plans on doing with me.

I'm yanked from the back, and my heart sinks. I realize where I am immediately, and everything I think we face is wrong. I'm carried into the building. I don't fight; there is no use. There are dozens of them and one of me. I'll have to wait to find a time to escape.

I'm carried down the stairs to the center of the arena—an arena I know all too well. The last time I was here, I was tied to a post, and a gun was aimed at my head.

It turns out the pole is still there, and that's where I'm taken. The ropes are loosened enough until one of the men can yank my arms over my head and strap me to the pole. My ankles are still tied, and I still have a piece of tape over my mouth.

I don't think about myself. All I hope for is that Beckett won't be joining me. I'm pretty sure Vincent can be persuaded to let Beckett live as long as he actually agrees to marrying Rialta and keeping her safe, but the Retribution Kings—they don't do forgiveness.

A loud cheer catches my attention, and I turn to see every seat in the building filled. I turn my head to the right, already knowing who I'll find walking on stage—Odette and Ryker. I wish I could say I have an ally in Ryker, but I don't—not anymore. The man who once helped me is gone.

They walk onto the stage, hand in hand, no longer hiding their relationship.

I turn my attention from them to the stairs, where I wait for

Beckett to be dragged down after me. But after a few minutes pass and he doesn't appear, I realize he isn't coming.

Where is Beckett? What did they do with him? Is he already dead?

My stomach heaves at that thought.

"Welcome everyone, and a very special welcome to our guest, Rialta Corsi," Odette says on the microphone.

I raise my eyebrows. *Really?* She's not even going to use my real name. *She's going to pretend I'm Rialta when she knows I'm not?*

The crowd cheers, but there is also uneasiness in the air. They aren't sure how they feel about their new leader being a woman and hanging out with the leader of another group. Ryker can never be the leader of the Retribution Kings without giving up his claim as leader of the Devil Crew, something I don't think he'll ever do.

"I've gathered you all here today to witness the retribution of Rialta Corsi. She and her family have done untold crimes against my family and me, which means they have committed crimes against all of us. Her family is responsible for my kidnapping, for my rape and torture. They are responsible for taking Beckett away from us—our leader, killed, because of her." A damn tear rolls down her cheek. She's going to play the heartbroken widow card.

Ryker wraps his arm around her and holds her tightly.

"I want to make it clear that Beckett Monroe did nothing wrong. He did what was needed to save and protect me. But this woman and her family—they are the ones in need of eliminating," Odette says.

The frenzied crowd cheers in agreement.

"So what should her retribution be? She's responsible for my kidnapping and torture, for Beckett's kidnapping and death."

I cringe every time she says Beckett is dead. He can't be dead; I'd feel it, right? My heart would know he's gone. If she has him, she stashed him somewhere. She wouldn't kill him so easily.

Me—I'm dead if I don't find a way to escape. I have no allies, no one coming to save me. I have to figure this out myself.

"Death!" the crowd chants over and over again.

Odette smiles, happy with the crowd's request. She and Ryker walk closer to me.

"Then death it shall be," Odette whispers into the microphone.

The crowd falls silent as Ryker hands Odette his gun with coldness in his eyes. Ryker looks at me and asks, "Any last words?"

He doesn't wait for permission from Odette or the crowd. He walks over to me and rips the tape off my mouth in one quick motion, leaving my skin raw and painful.

"Yes, I have some last words," I snap my head back, looking directly at Odette. "For one, I'm not Rialta Corsi."

There are gasps throughout the room.

I have to figure out how to play my cards just right to survive the night.

"My name is River. I'm an orphan that Vincent Corsi took and demanded I play the role of his daughter. He was trying to protect her. I've been their prisoner for most of my life. I've never hurt any of the Retribution Kings. In fact, I helped Beckett every chance I could."

The crowd is hanging onto my every word as I stare down Odette.

Your move.

She looks around, trying to figure out how to handle this. "You did hurt me when you took Beckett from me. You made him play your stupid games. He still died because of you!"

"I'm not loyal to Vincent Corsi. All I did, I did to survive, that was all." And I have to survive now. "Put my loyalty to the test. I can help the Retribution Kings get real retribution against the Corsi mafia. We can end them all once and for all. I know how to get to Vincent, and more importantly, I know how to get to his heir—Rialta Corsi."

The crowd murmurs and Odette's eyes are wild with frustration. She glares in Ryker's direction for a second since he's the one who started this. Her eyes tell me he'll pay for this later.

But then she looks back at me. "Fine. You want to prove yourself loyal to the Retribution Kings?"

I nod.

"You put Beckett through hell to win Rialta, only to kill him the second he won. We, Retribution Kings, are more honest. When we make a deal, we keep it," she says.

"Same," I reply.

She laughs at that.

"Fine, we'll give you a challenge soon. Show us how badly you want to be loyal to us. Show us how badly you are sorry for your part in Beckett's death. If you survive, then you will be one of us. Then we will see if the information you have is true," Odette says.

Odette turns off the mic and starts walking off the stage, Ryker trailing behind her.

I survived to live a little longer, but not much longer. Whatever task Odette creates will be sure to have one outcome—my death. All I've done is just prolong it a little longer.

But her words haunt me. Is Beckett alive or dead? She speaks with so much certainty about his death—she knows if he isn't already dead, he will be soon.

BECKETT

"YOU DIDN'T KEEP YOUR WORD," Vincent Corsi says as I come to.

I'm in a dark dungeon, my body still bound as I kneel in front of him like he's some sort of king.

"I did, actually," I grumble.

He frowns. "You're married to my daughter, Rialta Corsi?"

"No, but I never said I would marry Rialta Corsi. The agreement we shook on was that I would marry your daughter."

"Rialta is my only daughter," he snaps.

"Is she? I'm pretty sure you have an adopted daughter. And if you didn't legally adopt her, you can't deny that you care about her. River Corsi is just as much your daughter as Rialta Corsi."

Corsi doesn't answer me. He doesn't dispute my claim, confirming the truth. But I don't know what that means for Ri or me.

"Where is Ri?" I ask.

Corsi stares me down, and I assume he's going to answer me. But when he finally does, it's not much of an answer. "Being punished," he says.

I frown. "This isn't her fault! She did nothing wrong! She didn't plan it; Rialta did. And she would have done anything for her sister, anything for you."

"She failed to keep Rilata safe," he barks.

"Rialta's safe; she's just on the run. She needed space because she didn't want to be forced to marry someone she didn't choose," I say.

Corsi's jaw ticks, but he doesn't say anything. That single tick tells me a lot, though—there is definitely more to Rialta than I know.

I narrow my eyes at Corsi. It's almost like he's trying to tell me something but can't.

From the corner of my eye, I see who else is in the dungeon with me—Lennox, Hayes, and Gage.

"What now?" I ask Corsi, assuming I'm about to be tortured until I agree to marry Rialta. But I don't know what part the three behind me played in all of this.

"Now, you'll be punished," he says. Without warning, Corsi pulls his gun out and shoots me three times.

I fall to the floor, numb and most likely dying.

"You can tell Odette it's done. I'll send the video proof soon," Corsi says.

The room is going black, but my eyes are open enough to see three sets of feet walk past me.

Tell Odette it's done.

It hits me all at once—Ri is with Odette. And Corsi did this under Odette's orders to trade for his daughter's life. Corsi would never work with Odette and the Retribution Kings, but he would do anything to keep his daughter safe.

But which daughter is he protecting?

I gasp, the pain in my chest overtaking me, knowing I'll probably never figure it out.

I'M LEFT TIED to the pole for hours while Odette decides what challenge I'm going to endure before my death. I haven't accepted my fate—not yet, but it is a strong possibility that all of this ends in my death. However, that's something I'll gladly welcome if Beckett is indeed dead.

This isn't the first time I've worried about Beckett dying, but I've never been so close to getting everything I've ever wanted—so fucking close to getting my happily ever after.

All I've thought about the entire time I've been tied here is him. Trying to figure out if he's alive or dead. Trying to figure out if I still have a future with him. Trying to figure out what Odette would get from lying.

She probably told me to break me, but I'm not going to let her. I won't give in until I see Beckett's lifeless body with my own eyes. I refuse to believe he's dead, not after everything we've been through.

"Are you done crying yet?" Odette asks, walking back on stage in the empty arena with a dozen men behind her.

I stare her down. "You really think these men are going to stay loyal to you? They're called Retribution Kings. There is no room in their world for a queen to be in charge." I hate that it's true, but it is.

The men will soon rally around another man. They won't let Odette keep her power once she kills me, and they confirm Beckett is really dead. Her days are numbered.

She smirks. "Let's see how smart your mouth is after what I have in store for you." She snaps her fingers at the men behind her. Two of them glare at her; one rolls his eyes at her.

Yea, she's definitely losing them already. But they obey her, for now. Three men walk over to me and start untying me from the pole.

"Where's your boyfriend? Is he in timeout after he helped me?" I ask as the ropes come down from the pole, and my up-stretched shoulders finally get relief.

She glares at me, and I can practically see the steam shooting out her nostrils. If I'm going to die, it gives me satisfaction to get under her skin first.

"You have to survive everything you've put Beckett and me through. I doubt you'll survive the night; Beckett didn't," she says.

I pull on the ropes as the men jerk me into a standing position.

"What did you do to Beckett?" I ask.

She folds her arms across her chest and raises an eyebrow, realizing how to get under my skin—taunting me with news about Beckett.

"Survive tonight, and maybe I'll tell you." She licks her lips, looking at me like I'm her meal. "I should thank Ryker for sparing your life. Killing you quickly would have been too merciful. I'm going to enjoy torturing you."

She nods at the three men holding onto me, and they yank on the ropes around my wrists, pulling me off the stage and up the arena stairs. I don't look back at Odette to see what she's doing—I don't give her the satisfaction. I have to put all my focus on surviving what's next—at least until I find out if Beckett is alive or dead.

She better pray he's alive. If he's dead, she hasn't seen how dangerous I can be.

We walk to a hotel—the same hotel where I had to listen to Beckett and Odette fuck.

The three men drag me into the exact same room as that night. I know she's going to come. She can't resist watching.

"I thought this room would work the best. I have lots of happy memories in this suite," Odette says from the doorway, her hand running up and down the doorframe nostalgically.

I remember how I felt listening to them having sex, but I realize now that it wasn't fucking, it wasn't lovemaking—it was rape. She forced him to have sex with her.

"You raped him in here," I say.

One of the guys looks at me carefully, not sure he heard me right.

I pull against the ropes, trying to approach her, but the men hold me back. "You raped Beckett here. He wouldn't have ever touched you otherwise. He loves me, not you. You lied to him every step of the way. All you ever wanted was revenge."

"Revenge is who I am. It's who I was born to be. That's what the Retribution Kings care about—revenge," Odette says.

"Maybe, but do I deserve revenge for loving the man you manipulated? That's all I'm guilty of—loving him."

"You're guilty of a heck of a lot more," she snaps back.

I shrug. "I guess technically I did marry him."

Odette's mouth falls. "You bitch. Hold her down and remove her clothes." She slams the door behind her as she gives the order.

Two of the men act immediately, the third takes a second to snap to it, but eventually, all three men are yanking at my clothes and trying to get me onto the bed. I have no doubt what these men and Odette plan on doing to me, and it's something I won't allow.

My shirt is ripped down the middle, my pants are shimmied down my hips, and my bra is undone from the back. I want to fight back immediately. I want to stop them from even removing my clothes, but the best way to beat them is to wait, be patient, and work on the ropes.

While I let my outer facial expression appear frantic and terri-fied, I calmly lower my heart rate and breathing so I can focus on getting out of the ropes.

Unfortunately, the opportunity to escape doesn't come until the men have removed all of my clothes and slammed me down onto the bed with my arms pulled over my head once again. My ankles are thankfully still tied together.

Odette steps forward, towering over me with a sneer. "Not so tough and sassy now, are you?"

I let my bottom lip tremble a little, anything to make me look small and meek.

"A mafia princess—that's what you masqueraded as. You used tricks and deception to get Beckett to fall for you. You used your pretend mafia father to force him to marry you. You wanted to destroy the Retribution Kings and me; that was your assignment. You're nothing but a dirty, little slut. You're a princess of nothing. And my men are about to remind you of your place in the world."

Odette looks to the three men tying me down. "Do as you want with her. Touch her. Fuck her. Torture her. Make her wish she was never born."

She sits back in the chair in the corner, happy to enjoy the show.

She's going to get a show alright, but not the one she's expecting.

The men hesitate for a second. Removing my clothes is one thing; actually raping me is a whole other.

Soon I feel a hand squeeze my boob, then another hand. Once they get started, their confidence will build, and they'll have no problem raping me by the end.

Another hand grabs for my neck, and that's when I whisper, "Please."

His hand squeezes harder, most likely bruising my neck, while the other hands mark my boobs.

I cry out, and the sound I make isn't fake; the pain is real. I can barely breathe as the hand tightens on my neck. And the man squeezing my nipple has about pulled it off, while the third has dug his claws so deep into my flesh, I'll have permanent marks on my breast.

Because of their hesitation, I was going to let them live. But now they've shown me they're just as big of monsters as her, so they all get to die.

I have to endure more than I want. I have to endure their groping, sloppy kisses, and bites along my body. One touch between my legs is almost my undoing.

I'm patient, though. My time is coming. Soon they'll be dead on the floor for what they've done.

"Had enough yet?" Odette asks in a high-pitched voice from her corner chair. I almost forgot she's still here.

Another hand slides between my thighs. Tears burn my eyes, but I don't let them out. Nor do I let out the cry in the back of my throat. And I definitely don't let out the retort that would tell her I'm not broken—not even close.

"Spread her legs and let's see how long it takes to break her," Odette says.

I hold my breath, waiting for the moment the knife slices the ropes on my ankles free. It seems to take the man forever to saw slowly on the ropes, but I'm ready for the exact moment I'm free. I won't let them hold me or touch me a second longer.

The second the rope breaks in two, I make my move. My hands slip through the ropes at my wrists that I've been loosening. The guy strangling my throat gets a quick punch to the eye from me while I kick the guy who just cut me free in the eyeball.

The third reaches for his gun—excellent. He shoots, but too late —I'm already rolling into him. I knock the gun free and shoot him in the chest before he has time to react. Two more shots, and the other two men are down.

I aim the gun at the corner chair, but Odette's long gone.

I frown, pulling the rest of the rope off my wrists and ankles before climbing out of bed.

I'm still naked, but I don't give a damn about modesty. I have to get out of here before Odette sends more men to stop me.

I run to the door, throw it open, and am faced with a gun pointed at my head.

"I got her," Lennox says.

"Where's Beckett?" I ask immediately. He was the one who took him. He's half the reason I'm here.

He doesn't answer. Although his throat bobs up and down and his mouth opens as if he wants to speak but can't.

I'm pissed at him. He deserves to die for what he did. I still have a gun in my hand, and I know I could take him. But even if he deserves to die, I'm not sure I can do it, not yet. But I have no problem bringing him close to death.

I duck and charge at him.

He simply steps out of the way, and I run straight into Hayes's and Gage's arms. The gun is knocked from my hand, and sharp metal handcuffs are clasped on my wrists as my arms are yanked behind my body.

They push me back into the bedroom while Lennox keeps his gun on me.

"You're all going to die for this!" I scream.

"Don't worry. Unlike the others, we won't underestimate how dangerous you are, Princess," Hayes says.

Odette steps back into the room. "Clean this up and make sure she's thoroughly broken by morning time," she orders.

And then she leaves, too much of a coward to stay. She's too afraid I'll get free again and kill her like I did the others.

I look from one man to the next, hating them all. "Don't you dare touch me."

None of them speak as they approach me, and I squirm against my restraints. I may have let them fuck me before, but there is no way I'm letting these guys touch me now. The only problem is the guys that tried before weren't prepared—these guys are. I'm not sure I can get out of here unscathed.

Lennox is still holding his gun on me. Hayes is moving closer with a smirk on his face and an eagerness in his eyes. But it's Gage who catches me off guard when I feel the sharpness of a needle plunged into my neck before blackness consumes me.

24

RI

"WAKE UP, PRINCESS," Odette's voice rings in my head. A crowd laughs nearby, and I know I'm back in that damn arena again. Once again, I'm tied to the pole, but this time I'm sore, so fucking sore.

My head throbs with the power of a migraine. But it's not just my head and the drugs inflicting pain—I hurt everywhere. I look down at my body and realize I'm still naked. What bothers me are the bruises and cuts that weren't there before. The most I remember is having some rope burn around my wrists—but this happened after the drugs knocked me out.

I feel violated. I have no idea if I was raped or assaulted, but I was tortured. You don't get bruises like these without being tortured —and I know the three guys responsible.

I look up and find all three of them standing behind Odette like they've been loyal to her this entire time.

Fuck, Beckett and I really screwed up who we trusted. I won't be making that mistake again.

Ryker is on the stage too but isn't next to Odette. Instead, he has a gun aimed at a hooded man bound to a chair.

Beckett?

My heart thumps loudly, hoping it's him. But quickly, I realize it's not Beckett. This man has two arms, and my heart doesn't recognize his presence like it does Beckett.

"There you are. We thought you were going to sleep forever," Odette says with a laugh.

My brain is spinning with what to do, but this is a difficult situation to get out of without help. There are too many people for me to take down on my own. And I don't know if anyone is coming to my aid.

Together—forever.

Our promise to each other rings in my head. I'm not going to let this be the end. I'm going to find a way to keep my promise. It's the only promise I made to Beckett, and he made to me. He has to be alive. Wherever he is, he's fighting to get back to me, and that's what I'll do too. I'll fight until the very end.

"Have you had enough yet? Do you surrender? If so, I'll show mercy and put you out of your misery," Odette says, stepping right in front of me, waiting for me to answer.

"You haven't broken me. You think some bruises broke me?" I laugh. "You don't know who I am. I'm River Corsi. I was raised by Vincent Corsi and taught how to kill by Kek. I was brought up as a princess but also as a warrior. I wear a pretty dress and still kick all of your asses at the same time. You don't get to break me. I won't let you."

Odette narrows her eyes, crouching down to my eye level. "You may have been taught to withstand torture, but I can promise you from experience that someday that pain will catch up to you if you live long enough for the nightmares to start. In the meantime, let's try a different kind of torture, one to elicit a very different effect on you."

She turns and looks at the three men I thought were my allies but were actually my biggest enemies. They all walk over to me. Lennox starts undoing my ropes. He doesn't just untie me from the pole, but he unties my wrists completely. Gage unties the ropes at my ankles too.

"Going to drug me again so you can rape me?" I snap.

None of them answer. They don't even look at me.

Lennox grabs my wrists and yanks me to my feet. I don't have to look behind me to know Hayes has a gun pointed at me. They walk me over to within ten feet of the seated, hooded man.

I know—I know what they are going to ask me to do.

Ryker walks over to me. He empties his gun, leaving only one bullet, and then hands it to me with a solemn look. He walks back to Odette's side while the three Retribution Kings all aim their guns at me, ensuring I can't turn the gun on any of them.

"So you want to be a Retribution King?" Odette asks. "Then we have one initiation task for you. Can you seek retribution yourself?" The room quiets, waiting to see what I'm going to do.

"This man in front of you deserves to die for what he did. You have a single shot in that gun. Kill him, and you will be one of us," she finishes.

It's not that simple. Even if I did kill this man, she would never let me be one of them. She'd never just let me walk free.

"Who is he?" I ask.

"Does it matter? You want to be one of us; then you kill him. You'll be getting retribution for me; that's all you need to know," she snaps.

You'll be getting retribution for me.

I stare at the man. He hasn't moved, he hasn't squirmed, he hasn't fought to get free at all. He's been drugged. He probably isn't even awake. It might be a more merciful way to die, but this man doesn't deserve death.

I know who this man is based on her words—Beckett's brother, Enzo Black.

I don't know how the Retribution Kings got him. I thought Vincent had him and his family tucked safely away, but it proves the Retribution Kings are more powerful than I thought.

"And if I don't kill him?" I ask.

"Then they'll kill you," Odette says.

I figured as much.

"Where is Beckett?" I ask, looking at Odette.

"Kill him, and I'll tell you," she says.

"No. I'm done playing games. Tell me where Beckett is," I demand.

Odette sighs, looking bored. "I already told you, he's dead."

"I don't believe you."

"That's not really my problem. All you can do is save yourself."

"You want me to kill this man? You want me to crumble and break and become yours, then give me proof that Beckett is dead."

Odette stares at me for a second, considering my words. Then she turns to Hayes and gives him a nod.

Hayes frowns and walks forward hesitantly. For some reason, he doesn't want to show me the proof. Each step he takes toward me, my heart beats faster.

This can't be happening.

But I don't know why Hayes would be walking toward me if he didn't have proof.

He pulls out his phone.

No.

No, no, no!

He turns the screen toward me, and then he presses play.

Vincent is standing in front of a kneeling Beckett. The next second, three shots are fired. I've seen Vincent kill so many men like that, but never someone I loved.

One second the shots are fired; the next, Beckett is collapsed on the floor.

I tear my eyes away almost immediately.

It can't be true. It could be a fake video.

I look up at Hayes. I look into his eyes—all I see is heartbreak. Whoever they are loyal to and why, I don't know, but Hayes at least cared about Beckett.

And Hayes believes Beckett is dead.

"I'm sorry. I was there. He's dead," Hayes says in a whisper only I can hear.

The grief is instant, but I don't break down like I thought I would. I don't collapse and fall to my knees, giving up. That's not how I'm hardwired. All the training and hypnosis of my childhood take over, and all I can think about is revenge.

Maybe I'd be a better Retribution King than anyone thinks. Instantly, I know what I have to do.

Together—forever.

I'll be joining Beckett soon enough, but first...

I turn toward the man seated in the chair.

"Save yourself and kill your lover's brother or join the man you love in death, which will it be?" Odette says in hushed tones. Only those on stage heard her.

I raise the gun with a shaky hand and aim it at Enzo.

I fire.

The crowd gasps, all eyes on Enzo.

"I missed. I want to try again," I say.

I can feel Odette smirking behind me. "Hayes, give her your gun," she says.

Hayes hands it to me instantly, and now I'm the one smirking. I spin and start firing at Odette. I'm not going to survive long in a crowd of people that want me dead, but I just have to survive long enough to kill one asshole.

25

RI

I REALIZE the second I shoot why Odette wasn't afraid to let me hold a loaded gun. Ryker dives in front of her, taking the bullet meant for her.

I cringe, wishing he wouldn't have done that, but people do crazy things when they're in love. Odette knew Ryker loved her—he'd do anything for her.

I understand the emotion. Even though Beckett's gone, I'd still do anything for him, including fighting a war I can't win.

Odette made one very important mistake, though. When she ordered Hayes to hand me a gun, she didn't think to have him remove all but one bullet first. So even though Ryker protected her, she has no protection against the next bullet I send her way or the one after that.

I don't let her have any last words. I don't play my revenge slow and sweet. I just kill her with a bullet to the head and watch her corpse fall to the floor.

I turn around to find the stage being swarmed with men all aiming their guns at me. I don't know how many bullets I have left, but I'll kill as many of them as I can.

I start firing.

I should run, but I'm not sure I can survive the heartbreak. I should live for Rialta. I should live to protect her, wherever she is, but I can't. I can't live for other people, not anymore.

I've always thought I'd die fighting for someone I loved. I thought that person would be Rialta, but it turns out it's Beckett.

I shoot over and over again as bullets fly past me. Thankfully, their aim is horrible, but I quickly run out of bullets. Still, I don't run—not even when a man runs directly at me.

I punch him hard in the gut, but it's not enough. He wraps his arms around me and lifts me off my feet before jumping off the stage.

"Let me go!" I yell, but the man doesn't stop running, his grip on me unyielding. He just keeps running, and damn, is he fast. His scent is also familiar, but I can't place it.

He runs outside and across streets until we are deep in the nearby forest. Only then does he put me down. The second he lets go, I throw him a punch and a kick, knocking him to the ground. I jump on top of him, reaching for his gun and aiming it at his head.

He puts his hands up.

"Whoa, I'm thankful you missed before, but I know you won't miss from this close. I might want you to shoot me, though, if what they said is true. Is Beckett dead?" the man asks.

My shoulders slump, and I lower the gun. "Enzo?"

He nods. "Is he dead?"

"Yes," I whisper.

I collapse, and Enzo catches me, keeping me from falling onto the ground. We sit, facing each other.

I take a moment to study his features. He's similar to Beckett in a lot of ways, but also so different. They share the same dark hair, eyes, build, and even smell.

But Enzo has an easiness around him. He's a man who has found his purpose, his love, his life. He's a man who has lived a full life and still has people to live for.

"I'm sorry. I should have protected him. I shouldn't have married him. I shouldn't have—"

Enzo wraps his arms around me. "Just as I should have protected him. He's my brother, and I failed."

"He's my husband, and I failed."

The tears start on both of us. "Fuck!" I yell.

"Fuck!" Enzo yells.

The release isn't enough for either of us, but we can't stay here, not with so many people after us. I couldn't protect Beckett, but I can at least keep his brother safe. That's what Beckett cared about most.

I jump up, wipe my tears on the back of my arm, and hold out my hand to him. He takes it and removes his shirt, handing it to me.

I slip it on, grateful for its length covering my ass.

"We need to get you out of here. Beckett wanted to know you're safe," I say.

"He wanted to know you're safe, too," Enzo says.

"I'm not sure I can leave."

"I understand, but I'm not leaving you here. You can come with me, or I can take you anywhere you want to go, but I won't leave you here."

I nod. "I want to go home."

I need to know if Rialta is safe, and I still have revenge I need to finish for Beckett. Plus, I can't be with this man that smells so much like Beckett—I'll break completely.

We run through the woods until we reach a car. Enzo jumps it and drives; I'm too shaken up to even consider driving. He doesn't ask me for directions, somehow knowing how to get to Vincent's headquarters.

I'm thankful. I'm not in the mood to talk or think or anything.

Once we get close, Enzo decides it's time to talk. "I know you aren't ready, and you may never be ready to meet us—Beckett's family—but if and when you are, we're here. We would love to get to know the woman Beckett loved so fiercely. He risked everything for you."

I shake my head. "You don't want to meet the woman responsible for his death and for almost getting you and your family killed."

Enzo takes my hand and gives it a squeeze. "You aren't responsible for his death. You're responsible for his life—for him finding something worth fighting for. I've only just met you, but I know exactly why you're the woman for him. Unlike the other women Beckett fell for—you're the real deal." He stops the car and lets go of my hand. "And I owe you; you saved my life. I'd be dead too if it wasn't for you."

"I'm so sorry," I say.

"Me too."

He reaches over and hugs me.

I hug him back, but it's painful. It leaves me needing more, but no hug in the world is enough right now.

He eventually lets go.

"I'm not leaving town until I know you're okay. But go be with your family right now. I'll find you before I leave," he says.

I nod and climb out of the car, heading into the warehouse building Vincent uses as mafia headquarters.

Enzo thinks I'm here to be with family, to heal. Really, I'm here to take down Vincent for killing the man I love. And once I do that, the mafia won't let me survive.

I march into the spacious room filled with Vincent's men.

"Where is he?" I ask, to no one in particular.

One of the men points toward the front of the room.

I'm laser-focused as I walk toward Vincent. All I see is him.

I don't have a weapon. I'm only wearing a T-shirt. I should have thought my plan through more, but it doesn't matter—Vincent Corsi is a dead man.

"Thank god!"

That voice.

I turn and see Rialta running toward me. She tackles me with a hug, wrapping her arms around me.

"I was so terrified, but I should have known that River Corsi always survives," she says.

She tightens her grip on me, and finally, I hug her back.

It's good to know she's okay before I kill Vincent. I'll die knowing she's alive. I don't know who will be left to protect her. Unfortunately, the mafia will choose someone for her to marry that will continue Vincent's horrible legacy, but that was always her fate as long as she stayed.

I hug her tighter before my eyes turn back to Vincent. But then I see the men sitting at his table talking to him—Retribution Kings.

Gage, Hayes, and Lennox.

I take a deep breath as I let go of Rialta, my plan changing. I'll kill them all with my bare hands.

I start running toward them with that intention when nearby doors open suddenly. My breath catches in my throat as Beckett is pushed out into the room.

"THEY WERE JUST BAGS; it can't hurt that bad," Corsi says.

I blink, my entire torso throbbing. But I look down and realize I'm free of restraints and there is no blood, just my badly bruised body.

"It still hurts like a motherfucker," I say.

"I'm sure. But if you're going to stay married to my daughter, you'll have to get used to a little pain."

I raise my eyebrows as I pull myself back into a sitting position. "You're going to let me stay married to Ri?"

"I don't have a choice. It seems she's chosen you. And as you said, I've come to think of her like a daughter too, as much as I tried to keep it a strictly business relationship. I tried for years to be the ruthless mafia leader everyone feared, including her. But she was never afraid of me, even when she was hypnotized and didn't remember everything. Why? I loved her and was never as cruel as I needed to be to her," Corsi says.

"You were pretty cruel. You made her play a horrible game where she thought she was going to have to marry a monster at the end of it."

"Well, I could have been worse."

I lift my shirt, looking down at the bruises on my chest. Even though it hurts, he somehow missed hitting every vital organ. If the bags did penetrate my skin, I wouldn't have died from any of the shots.

"Good shooting," I say, surprised.

"Who do you think taught Ri how to shoot?"

I grin. "So what now?"

Vincent turns serious. "Now, hopefully, your men have rescued both of my daughters."

"My men?"

"The Retribution Kings."

"You mean Lennox, Gage, and Hayes?"

He nods.

"I thought—"

"They're still loyal to you, although probably currently devastated that you died."

"If they are on my side, then why did you let them think I died?"

"They aren't very good actors, and I need the rest of them to think you're dead."

"Why?" I ask, annoyed.

"Those were the terms to get Rialta back."

"The Retribution Kings have Rialta?"

"She'll be free soon when they show Odette the video of your death, and she sees how heartbroken your men are."

"And Ri?" I ask.

Vincent gets quiet.

I jump up. "What the hell happened to Ri?"

"Odette has her but have a little faith. Ri is the strongest person we both know; she'll survive. She always does."

"And if not?"

"I have a team ready to go in and get her as soon as Rialta is secured."

"So you're putting Rialta's life above Ri's once again?"

"No, I'm giving both of my daughters the best chance of survival."

"I'll go. Let me lead the team."

"Actually, you need to do something else first."

"What?" I ask. I'm really getting annoyed pulling teeth with this jackass.

"While you've earned my forgiveness, you need to earn the rest of the mafia's if you want to live."

"They still want me as your replacement?"

"No, Rialta is my heir. They won't recognize Ri as my heir, even if I see her as my daughter. They see what you did to Rialta as a betrayal. It leaves us all in the same situation as before—no husband or future heir to step into my shoes."

"Why don't you just choose someone in the mafia?"

"For one, there aren't many men anywhere near Rialta's age. And two, it just causes infighting. It's better to marry outside the family."

"It's not going to be me," I snap.

"I know that."

"So, what do I have to do?"

———

Hours pass, but finally, Corsi's men come to get me. They don't tie me up, but they roughly drag my bruised body out of the dungeon and up to the main floor. They shove me hard into a room filled with mafia men.

But my eyes only care about one person—Ri.

We run to each other, and she jumps at me uncontrollably, knocking me to the floor.

"You're alive!" she says.

"So are you," I say, in awe of her as always.

"Together," she whispers.

"Forever."

And then she kisses me—a hard, fast kiss. "I thought you were dead."

"Never."

The room is silent as they watch us, and I know what I have to do. Slowly, we stand up. No guns are pointed at us, but there might as well be.

"So what now?" Ri asks, intertwining our fingers. "Do we kill Lennox and the others?"

I stare at her, realizing she doesn't know the truth. "No, they were just trying to save Rialta and keep us safe."

She turns to me. "Are you sure?"

I nod.

"Thank god, I really didn't want to kill them."

I laugh at that. "No, you really didn't want to think your judgment in people was that off."

We get up off the floor, and I turn to the crowd.

"Now, I need to apologize to all of you. I need to apologize because I fought for the right to marry your princess and become your leader. I thought that's what I wanted, but I was wrong." I look to Ri.

"I fell in love with this woman you all know: a strong, fierce woman—my equal in every way. I fell in love even when I shouldn't have. I fell in love with her again and again and again." I squeeze her hand.

"I know I agreed to marry Rialta Corsi and become the new heir, but I can't. I'm in love with River. You deserve to have a leader who is devoted to you, not in love with someone else."

"You can have a whore on the side and still marry Rialta. A lot of us do!" someone shouts from the crowd. Many of the men chuckle their response.

Ri scrunches her nose at that thought, and I'm sure Rialta thinks much the same.

"I'm sorry, but I can't be the heir."

The crowd breaks out into a cacophony of objections.

"You won! That was the deal!"

"You don't get to back out! If you do, you die; it's the mafia way."

"Kill him; he knows too much!"

Ri tries to step in front of me, but I won't let her. "Together," I whisper, holding her at my side. If they are going to kill us, then they can kill us side by side. I refuse to let her save me, and I know she won't let me save her.

"Forever," she smiles back.

We will fight them together until our last breaths. If that is to be our retribution for falling in love, then so be it. We would both fall in love with each other again and again, even if it only meant brief moments of happiness together.

"Wait!" Corsi says, suddenly, stepping in front of us. "Don't kill them!"

The men lower their guns.

"They are both the best fighters any of us have ever seen. Beckett's talents would be wasted as the leader. He's a much better soldier. And you've all seen River's skills. They need to be protecting, not leading," he says.

I don't disagree with that. Although, I'm not sure I want to spend my life protecting Rialta and whatever bastard she ends up marrying. But that's a battle for another day. As long as I get to be with River, that's all that matters to me.

There's some mumbling, but the crowd seems to agree with Vincent's assessment.

"But who will marry Rialta then? Who will be your heir? She's twenty-one. It's time to find the next heir," someone says from the crowd.

"It just so happens I got an offer I think would make a perfect husband to Rialta and a great mob boss. But, of course, we need to put him to the test first," Vincent says.

The crowd seems to agree with Vincent, but before we can hear who it is, Ri pulls me out of the room and back into the hallway, away from any man who decides to take matters into their own hands and shoot us as traitors.

She touches me all over my chest. "You're alive."

I grin. "You seem surprised?"

"I just expected to be the one to rescue you; I am your hero after all," she says with a sly smile.

"That you are." I kiss her, dipping her back. "You're also my wife, my forever, the love of my life."

She giggles.

"But I'd really like you to put some pants on. I'm tired of everyone seeing your legs."

"Is that so? I was thinking pants won't be necessary for what I have planned next." Her eyes twinkle with sultry sin.

I bite down on my bottom lip, growling. "I want to do just that, but first, I need to know we're okay. Are you okay with what Vincent proposed?"

"I will always protect Rialta, just like you will always protect your family."

I nod, looking her over. "Did Odette hurt you?"

The door opens again, and the Retribution Kings join us in the hallway.

"Technically, that was us. Sorry," Hayes says. "We knocked you out so you'd feel less of the pain. And I promise, we didn't touch you anywhere inappropriate," Hayes says.

"You did this to her?" I fume.

Hayes nods.

I punch him. Then Gage. Then Lennox.

"Thank you for doing what you could to protect her and Rialta," I say.

"Thank you for not being dead," Hayes says.

"And thank you for killing Odette," Gage says to Ri.

"You killed Odette?" I ask her.

She nods.

"Badass." I kiss her firmly. "Thank god."

She smiles somberly. Killing someone never feels good, even someone that deserves to die.

"You need to call your brother!" she says suddenly. "He thinks you're dead."

"Already called him. He's on his way over right now," Rialta says with a sad smile as she steps into the hallway.

I don't know why she's upset. I don't know who her father is going to make her marry, and I don't care. Right now, all I care about is Ri.

I grab Ri, lifting her up until her legs are wrapped around me. "I need you, now."

I start carrying her down the hallway, happy to fuck her in the first room I can find. Apparently, it's a bathroom. I flick the door locked behind us as my mouth descends on hers, remembering our bathroom encounter after her group fucking with the guys.

"Together," I whisper into her mouth.

"And forever," she bites back against my lip.

I grin. Our forever is going to last a long time.

BECKETT GRABS my hand and leads me out of the galley where Kai, my sister-in-law, and Enzo, my brother-in-law, are busy cooking dinner for everyone. I love spending time on their yacht with them.

I've loved getting to know his family, but we never get much time together alone when we're here. At least, not enough time for us. Just fucking in our bedroom at night isn't enough, so I'm glad Beckett leads me away from people onto the main deck and then up more stairs.

I raise an eyebrow. "Shouldn't we be sneaking off to our room?"

"This is way more fun," Beckett says as he yanks me to him and kisses me like it's our first and last kiss. It's the way he always kisses me.

I smile against his lips. I've been doing a lot of grinning the last few weeks.

Grinning because I have him, and the personal threats against us are gone.

Grinning because Vincent finally told me he loves me and considers me a daughter.

Grinning because of how great Beckett's family is.

Grinning because the Retribution Kings are no longer a threat to us while they decide their next leader.

Grinning because keeping Rialta safe keeps us occupied and gives us a purpose greater than ourselves.

Grinning because being able to fuck Beckett whenever I want is the greatest thing I've ever experienced.

His hand slides up my thigh under my dress. "Have I told you how much I love it when you wear a dress?"

I laugh as he palms my bare ass. "It's the only reason I wear dresses."

He grins against my lips as his hand slides around my thigh, finding my knife. He grabs it and flings it away, sticking it into the railing.

I laugh. "What? You don't like it when I hold a knife against your throat while I fuck you?"

"As much as I love it when you mark my body, I much prefer marking yours more." His teeth come down on my bare shoulder, and I moan as he pretends to suck my blood like a vampire.

"I'm sure you do." I reach into his pants and pull out his cock, wrapping my hand around it and pumping him.

He groans at my touch, letting his head fall back.

I smirk, knowing I have control now.

I slide down his body until I'm on my knees in front of him and put his cock in my mouth.

His hand immediately fists my hair, trying to dictate my movements. But as I take him down my throat, he has no control, no power—it's all me.

Before I can make him come, he yanks on my hair so hard his cock pops out of my throat. That's when the battle begins.

Somehow my dress gets ripped in two.

His shirt gets thrown overboard.

We break the couch we didn't notice at first.

We're both bleeding, sweaty, and covered in each other's cum by the time we're done.

"Will you two stop breaking all our furniture and fucking where everyone can see you?" Enzo says.

I laugh against Beckett's chest as we sit curled up on the floor of the top deck.

"I'll pay you back for the furniture, but I told you we needed a longer honeymoon," Beckett replies.

"We let you borrow a yacht for a month. You'd think that would be long enough," Enzo shouts back.

"Forever won't be long enough," Beckett pants.

"Just get back down here—with some clothes on. Dinner's finished, and the kids have been traumatized enough," Enzo says.

"If you don't want us naked, you're going to have to toss some clothes up," Beckett says.

Immediately some clothes hit us each in the face. I grin—apparently, Enzo was prepared for this situation.

"Speaking of babies," I say, wiggling my eyebrows.

"Are you finally ready to take a pregnancy test?" Beckett asks.

"No." I stare down at my stomach. "But I'm close."

I haven't had a period in weeks. I have no idea if I'm pregnant or not. Honestly, I'm not sure how I feel. *Do I want kids? Can kids even be a part of our lives if we are constantly going to be protecting, always putting ourselves into harm's way?*

I don't know.

And if we are pregnant, would Rialta understand if we can't be her main protectors anymore?

I don't know.

"Whether I am or not, we'll figure it out together," I say.

He kisses my forehead. "That we will."

There are unlimited dangers out there still. The most important task is trying to figure out who has wanted Rialta dead all these years. It's someone on the inside, someone that knows too much.

They succeeded in killing every member of Vincent Corsi's family except her, and they'll keep trying. Until we figure it out, we'll do our best to keep her safe. Just like we keep each other safe, and just like our families protect us.

We get dressed and head downstairs for dinner. We all barely fit around the table. Enzo and Kai, Zeke and Siren, Langston and Liesel, and all of their kids are here—all members of Beckett's family. Hayes, Gage, and Lennox are here too. They've become family to both of us.

Lastly, Rialta beams at me from her place at the table.

I sit down with Beckett to my left and Rialta on my right, who is seated next to Lennox.

"He's insufferable," Rialta says, not caring if he overhears her.

"I thought you liked him?" I ask.

"Father is crazy if he thinks I'll marry him."

I look from her to Lennox, who doesn't seem the least bit phased as he drinks his wine. If he hears her, he doesn't care she's sitting next to him and whining about him.

"He did save your life, you know."

"That doesn't mean I have to marry him."

I reach to grab my own wine glass, but Beckett knocks my hand away. I may or may not be pregnant, so I shouldn't drink until I know. I need to take the test tonight. I need to know what my future holds.

I look at Rialta—my sister, in every way that matters. Lennox was the one who proposed marriage to Rialta. Vincent approved. After all, Lennox was the one who saved her, and ultimately, that's what Vincent cares about.

"If you don't want to marry Lennox, then you better find someone worthy of marriage in Vincent's eyes, or I don't see what choice you have," I say.

Rialta shoots daggers in his direction. "Don't worry, I will," she says.

I sigh and turn to Beckett. "We are going to have our hands full with Rialta for a while, I think."

He laughs. "Our lives would be boring without her."

"I'm boring, huh?" I raise my eyebrows, sliding my hand under the table to grab for his crotch.

"You, my queen, are anything but boring," he whispers.

But I'm not done with him. He doesn't get to make a comment like that without some punishment. I grab his cock, and he bites back a moan.

"Oh my god! Can you guys not at the table? Wasn't your show on the top deck enough?" Rialta asks.

Everyone rolls their eyes and groans when they realize what Rialta is insinuating.

Beckett and I laugh as I remove my hand.

"We never have enough," we say at the same time and look into each other's eyes, silently sending lust-filled promises of more broken furniture after this dinner. We are going to owe Kai and Enzo a fortune by the time we leave, but it'll be worth it.

For once, we can kiss and fuck like we have forever together, *but what's the fun in that?* Our impatient need to be together drives our lovemaking like time is running out, like we don't have forever and ever to love each other.

Although, forever is exactly what we have.

———

Thank you for reading Ri & Beckett's story! I hope you enjoyed it! Lennox's story is next!

One-click LENNOX Here

Rialta Corsi is the last woman I want to marry.
She's a prim princess, who doesn't belong in my world.
But I made a deal.
And I don't back out of my promises.
Even if the woman I agreed to marry drives me crazy,
I'll marry her.

But she's not ready to enter the world of Retribution Kings.

JOIN ELLA'S NEWSLETTER & NEVER MISS A SALE OR NEW RELEASE → ellamiles.com/freebooks

Love swag boxes & signed books?
SHOP MY STORE → store.ellamiles.com

TRUTH OR LIES:

Taken by Lies #1

Betrayed by Truths #2

Trapped by Lies #3

Stolen by Truths #4

Possessed by Lies #5

Consumed by Truths #6

SINFUL TRUTHS:

Sinful Truth #1

Twisted Vow #2

Reckless Fall #3

Tangled Promise #4

Fallen Love #5

Broken Anchor #6

LIES SERIES:

Lies We Share: A Prologue #0.5

Vicious Lies #1

Desperate Lies #2

Fated Lies #3

Cruel Lies #4

Dangerous Lies #5

Endless Lies #6

RETRIBUTION GAMES SERIES:

Mistaken Hero #1

Forbidden Princess #2

Tempted Hero #3

Fatal Princess #4

Tortured Hero #5

Dangerous Princess #6

RETRIBUTION KINGS SERIES:

Lennox #1

PRETEND SERIES:

Pretend I'm Yours

Pretend We're Over

Pretend: The Complete Series

DIRTY SERIES:

Dirty Obsession

Dirty Addiction

Dirty Revenge

Dirty: The Complete Series

ALIGNED SERIES:

Aligned: Volume 1

Aligned: Volume 2

Aligned: Volume 3

Aligned: Volume 4

Aligned: The Complete Series Boxset

UNFORGIVABLE SERIES:

Heart of a Thief

Heart of a Liar

Heart of a Prick

Unforgivable: The Complete Series Boxset

MAYBE, DEFINITELY SERIES:

Maybe Yes

Maybe Never

Maybe Always

Maybe: The Complete Series

Definitely Yes

Definitely No

Definitely Forever

Definitely: The Complete Series

STANDALONES:

Finding Perfect

Savage Love

Too Much

Not Sorry

Hate Me or Love Me: An Enemies to Lovers Romance Collection

ABOUT THE AUTHOR

Ella Miles writes steamy romance, including everything from dark suspense romance that will leave you on the edge of your seat to contemporary romance that will leave you laughing out loud or crying. Most importantly, she wants you to feel everything her characters feel as you read.

Ella is currently living her own happily ever after near the Rocky Mountains with her high school sweetheart husband. Her heart is also taken by her goofy five year old black lab who is scared of everything, including her own shadow.

Ella is a USA Today Bestselling Author & Top 50 Bestselling Author.

Stalk Ella at:
www.ellamiles.com
ella@ellamiles.com